"I need to talk to you about Fawn, but first I have something I need to take care of."

"What?"

"Scarlett was real antsy around that fallen tree trunk," Lacey said. "I want to go take a look at what she was reacting so strongly to."

Creed nodded. "I'll go out there with you."

She studied him for a moment, then gave a short dip of her head. "Can you keep Regina and the others here until we finish checking out that tree trunk?" she asked.

He narrowed his eyes. "Why? Don't tell me Scarlett is trained in cadaver search, as well."

Lacey shook her head. "She started out that way but hated it. She apparently just really did not like the smell and would be very skittish when she got close to a dead body."

"Can't say I blame her," he muttered.

"And she would sneeze. She was acting that way out by the tree."

Creed froze. "I see. And you think there's a dead body out there?"

"I don't *think* so. I'm...*afraid* so."

USA TODAY Bestselling Authors

Lynette Eason

and

Christy Barritt

Desperate Search

2 Thrilling Stories

Following the Trail and *Dangerous Mountain Rescue*

LOVE INSPIRED
INSPIRATIONAL ROMANCE

LOVE INSPIRED®
INSPIRATIONAL ROMANCE

ISBN-13: 978-1-335-47600-5

Desperate Search

Copyright © 2023 by Harlequin Enterprises ULC

Following the Trail
First published in 2022. This edition published in 2023.
Copyright © 2022 by Lynette Eason

Dangerous Mountain Rescue
First published in 2022. This edition published in 2023.
Copyright © 2022 by Christy Barritt

Recycling programs
for this product may
not exist in your area.

This is a work of fiction. Names, characters, places and incidents are either the product of the author's imagination or are used fictitiously. Any resemblance to actual persons, living or dead, businesses, companies, events or locales is entirely coincidental.

For questions and comments about the quality of this book, please contact us at CustomerService@Harlequin.com.

Love Inspired
22 Adelaide St. West, 41st Floor
Toronto, Ontario M5H 4E3, Canada
www.LoveInspired.com

Printed in U.S.A.

CONTENTS

Lynette Eason is a bestselling, award-winning author who makes her home in South Carolina with her husband and two teenage children. She enjoys traveling, spending time with her family and teaching at various writing conferences around the country. She is a member of Romance Writers of America and American Christian Fiction Writers. Lynette can often be found online interacting with her readers. You can find her at Facebook.com/lynette.eason and on Twitter, @lynetteeason.

Books by Lynette Eason

Love Inspired Suspense

Rocky Mountain K-9 Unit

True Blue K-9 Unit

Wrangler's Corner

Visit the Author Profile page at LoveInspired.com for more titles.

FOLLOWING THE TRAIL

Lynette Eason

For I know the thoughts that I think toward you, saith the Lord, thoughts of peace, and not of evil, to give you an expected end. Then shall ye call upon me, and ye shall go and pray unto me, and I will hearken unto you. And ye shall seek me, and find me, when ye shall search for me with all your heart.

—*Jeremiah* 29:11–13

Dedicated to Jack Eason, my husband
and my everyday hero. I love you so much.

ONE

Lacey Lee Jefferson was worried. In fact, she was borderline terrified. Her sister, Fawn, had been silent for the past five days, not answering texts, emails or phone calls.

And Lacey'd had enough. She'd been avoiding calling Fawn's work because of her sister's strong stance about not receiving personal calls while on duty, but desperate times called for desperate measures. So, she'd called and learned Fawn, a doctor at the hospital, had taken a three-month absence, only to return to work for two days before dropping off the radar once more.

This morning, Lacey had made the three-hour journey out to her childhood home, where Fawn still lived, and had found it empty, with no indication where her sister might be.

Which was why Lacey now stood outside the sheriff's department in Timber Creek, North Carolina. Only her missing sister could have enticed her back to this town for the first time in six years. She pushed through the glass doors and made her way to the receptionist's desk, bracing herself for any animosity that might flare when the woman realized who stood in front of her. "Hi, Sherry."

Sherry Olson looked up from her computer screen and

her eyes widened. "Well, as I live and breathe, if it isn't Lacey Lee."

"Just Lacey these days, thanks." Sherry and Lacey had graduated high school together. And as far as she could tell, there was nothing but surprise in Sherry's eyes. Relief nearly sent Lacey puddling to the floor.

"It's good to see you," Sherry said. "It's been a long time." Not long enough, as far as Lacey was concerned, but... "What can I do for you?"

"Have you seen Fawn lately?"

Sherry frowned. "No, not that I can think of, but we don't exactly run in the same circles. She's still working at the hospital, right?"

"Right. She was at work last week for two days, then never came back for her next shift. Before that, she'd taken a three-month leave of absence, but it's been a week now since anyone's heard from her."

"What? That doesn't sound like Fawn."

"No kidding. That's why I'm here. I want to talk to someone about doing a missing person report. Fawn's not answering her phone at all—or returning calls or texts. Everything goes straight to voice mail and I'm really getting worried." Understatement of the century.

"Oh my. That doesn't sound good." Sherry picked up the phone. "Creed, someone's out here to see you."

Creed? Creed Payne? Well, of course it would be Creed. He was the sheriff, after all. The sheriff with the smoky gray eyes and wavy dark hair, broad shoulders she'd cried on more than once as a teen. Creed... It disturbed her that her heart still sighed at his name.

Sherry hung up. "He said to send you on back to his office. Go down the hall and it's the last door on the left."

"Thanks."

Lacey knew exactly where Creed's office was. He'd

brought her to this building when she was seventeen years old, shown her the corner office that the sheriff used and said, "That's going to be mine one day."

She'd thought it terribly shortsighted of him and told him he was meant for bigger things, that he was selling himself short.

"Thanks a lot, Lacey. Glad you think so much of my dreams." He'd shoved his hands into his pockets and stalked away.

Lacey had been crushed. Desperate to talk to him before she left for college, she'd gone home, packed up her car and called him again. His mother had answered the phone and said she didn't know where he was. Lacey had tried to find him, searched the whole town, but hadn't been able to locate him before she'd had to leave. And now she was going to talk to him for the first time in six years.

She raised her fist to knock when the door opened, and there he stood, larger-than-life. He was just as she remembered—and so much more. He'd filled out and become a man.

Their eyes met.

His widened.

Her heart thundered.

His lips parted, formed her name—

"Creed! Creed!"

He jerked his head at Sherry's shriek. "What is it?"

Sherry stood just in the hallway, her face pale, fist clutched around the phone. "Little Hank's missing. This is Joe, saying he and Denise can't find him. They've been searching for over half an hour."

Denise Banks and Joe Gilstrap from high school? They'd married? Fawn hadn't mentioned that.

"Where'd they last see him?" Creed asked. Sherry held

the phone out to him and he snatched it. "Joe? When did you last see Hank?… Uh-huh… Okay… I'm heading that way. Keep looking and I'll be there soon." He hung up and gave the phone back to Sherry. "Tell Ben."

She hurried back down the hall. Creed sighed and grabbed his Stetson from his desk. "Hank's five years old. Poor kid has wandered off and is probably scared to death. We need to find him before it gets dark."

"Want some help?" Lacey asked.

He narrowed his eyes. "Sure. We can use all the volunteers we can get."

"What about a search-and-rescue dog?"

"That's on the wish list. Unfortunately, we haven't raised the funds for it yet."

"No, I mean I have one. Scarlett's in the car."

He blinked at her for a good three seconds before he huffed a short laugh. "I really hope you're not kidding."

"Not kidding at all. She's a redbone coonhound with one of the best tracking noses in the country. I'm a contract K-9 handler for the Mecklenburg police department in Charlotte. When I'm not doing Search and Rescue operations, I have my own training facility with several volunteers and one part-time paid employee."

His jaw dropped. "How long have you been doing that?"

"For about three years."

"That's…incredible. Like an answer to prayer." He nodded. "Okay, then, let's get Scarlett and go find Hank."

"I'll just need something of Hank's to let her get the scent."

"I'll arrange it on the way."

"I'll follow you."

He strode out of the office and down the hall, his long legs eating up the distance. "Ben! Mac!"

"Coming!" Ben Land stepped out of his office. He spotted Lacey and his eyes widened. "Hey there, Lacey Lee. How are you?"

"It's just Lacey now, Ben. I'm doing fine." Mostly.

"Let's catch up after we find this kid."

"I'd love to." He'd always been kind to her in high school. More so than most after her father went to prison.

He looked at Creed. "Mac's not here, but he'll meet us there."

"Great."

Lacey hurried to her truck and waited for Creed and Ben to pull out of the parking lot. She fell in behind them, and Scarlett let out a yip from her spot in the back.

"You ready to go to work, girl?"

Two more barks answered her, and Lacey smiled before focusing her concentration on following the men up the mountain. About halfway to the top, Creed pulled into a long driveway that ended at a two-story log cabin home. The wooded area behind the house appeared to go on for infinity, but Lacey knew exactly what was on the other side of those woods.

Her sister's house.

Technically, it was half hers, too, but she'd not laid any claim to it. However, Fawn loved their childhood home and had been happy to stay there while working at the hospital fifteen minutes away. Lacey hated it. All it did for her was symbolize loss and remind her of days she'd rather forget.

Goose bumps pebbled her skin, but she did her best to ignore them while she opened the door to Scarlett's customized back seat and snapped the lead to her collar.

The dog hopped down, her droopy ears flopping around her head while her tongue hung from the side of her mouth. Her dark eyes watched Lacey with expectation. "Hang on, girl."

More cars pulled up, and soon the front yard was full of townspeople ready to help search for little Hank.

"Lacey? Is that you?"

She turned to see Isabelle McGee headed toward her, followed by Katherine Gilroy—no, O'Ryan now, according to Fawn—one of the doctors in town. Lacey tensed, then allowed herself to relax slightly when she saw no condemnation in either pair of eyes. Interesting. She'd thought after what her father had done, the grudge would have been held infinitely. Had she been wrong? "Hey, how are you guys?"

"Good," Isabelle said. "What brings you back to town?"

"I'm looking for Fawn. Have either of you seen her lately?"

Isabelle shook her head and Katherine frowned. "I saw her last week at the hospital. I had to go in to see a patient and we passed in the hall. We didn't get a chance to chat, but I wanted to ask her if she was all right."

"Why?"

"She looked rough. Like she'd had too many sleepless nights or was getting over an illness. But we've been so busy that I haven't had a chance to catch up with her." And while Katherine and Fawn were both doctors and often in the hospital at the same time, they weren't close friends, so it wasn't likely Katherine would have thought any more about it.

"Okay, thanks."

"Isabelle?" A man about her age, dressed in the local deputy uniform, hurried toward them.

"That's Mac," Katherine said, her voice low.

"Isabelle's husband."

"Yes."

"Lacey, are you and Scarlett ready?" Creed hollered at her from the tree line.

"Ready!" She shot the two ladies a tight smile. "Do you mind asking some of the people here if they've seen or heard from Fawn? I'm getting desperately worried about her."

"Of course," Isabelle said. "I think I even still have your number in my phone, if it hasn't changed."

"It hasn't." She'd kept the same number for many reasons. One of those reasons stood waiting for her.

"I'll get it from Isabelle," Katherine said. "Go find Hank, please. I'll be looking, too, in case he needs medical attention."

With a wave, Lacey darted toward Creed and the terrified parents. When she reached them, they all eyed Scarlett with flares of hope. "Thank you for doing this, Lacey." Denise's dark brows furrowed further. She had a small sleeping baby strapped to her chest. "When Creed called and said you were here with a search-and-rescue dog... Well, you're an answer to our prayers." She clasped her hands under the baby's rump. "You can really do this?"

"Scarlett and I can. I need something of Hank's that has his scent on it."

"Um, yeah," Joe said. "Creed told us what to get. Here." He passed her a bag. "It's the pajama shirt he wore last night."

"Perfect. Where did you last see him?"

"On the screened-in porch." Denise swiped the tears on her cheeks even as more fell. She patted the baby's back. "I needed to change the little man here, but hadn't brought a diaper out with me." She ran a shaking hand over the infant's head. "I'm just getting used to this whole two-children thing, and sometimes I forget..."

"It's okay, honey," Joe said. "This isn't on you."

Denise drew in a shuddering breath. "Anyway, I ran to get one and some wipes. When I came back, there was a hole in the screen and Hank was gone." A sob shook her, and Joe slid an arm around her shoulders.

Lacey's heart ached for the couple. "Could someone have taken him?" If he'd been put in a car...

"No," Joe said. "We have security cameras, and the footage showed him kicking the screen out and walking away. He's a curious kid..."

Well, that was better than being snatched. "All right. So, what I'm going to do is give Scarlett a whiff of this, then kind of walk her around until she picks up the trail."

Denise nodded, and while Joe looked a little skeptical, his expression held a desperate hope.

The long lead attached to Scarlett's harness would allow the dog the freedom to run at a pretty good pace while Lacey followed. Lacey tapped her pocket and Scarlett fairly danced with excitement. She knew as soon as she did her job, she'd get to play with her favorite toy. A tennis ball.

Lacey opened the bag with Hank's shirt and held it for the animal. "Scarlett, seek."

Scarlett stuck her snout in the opening and got her whiff.

"Scarlett, seek. Find Hank."

Scarlett's tail wagged, and she lifted her head, black

nose quivering, ears waving in the wind. With a short bark, she started pacing, alternating nose in the air and near the ground. Soon, she gave another bark and took off like a shot for the woods.

"Here we go," Lacey said. She followed Scarlett at a fast jog, her hand wrapped around the end of the lead. Footsteps fell into place behind her. She shot a quick glance back and noted Creed's expression.

He was coming along whether she wanted him to or not.

Too bad he hadn't felt that way six years ago.

Creed couldn't help that his heart beat faster. Not just because he was jogging after Lacey and Scarlett, and not just because a child was in danger. But because Lacey Lee—Lacey now, he reminded himself—was back in town.

Lacey. He'd thought he'd moved on from the heart-break she'd caused him, but all it had taken to bring it back was to find her standing outside his office door.

Sherry's timely interruption had kept him from blurt-ing out something he might've later regretted. He hon-estly had no idea what he'd been about to say, and now he'd probably never know. He was okay with that. But when she hadn't hesitated to offer her help to find Hank, he'd found himself admiring her all over again.

No. He had no intention of getting involved with Lacey this time. Not that she'd offered him the oppor-tunity. He didn't even know how long she'd been in town before she'd stopped in to the station. And he had no idea why she was there. He ordered his heart to chill, forbade it from yearning for something that was so far in the past he shouldn't even remember the slightest detail.

But he did.

He watched her lithe form dodge trees and undergrowth while she kept a steady pace. She'd done this many times before and seemed to excel at it. That could only work in Hank's favor. *Please, God, protect that little boy. Please let us find him alive and just fine.*

They had to. He refused to think of the alternative. Lacey pulled to a stop while Scarlett walked in circles. "What is it?" he asked.

"She's not sure which way to go."

"We're almost to your property line."

"I know."

The dog walked to a fallen tree trunk, sniffed and shook herself. Barked and backed up, whining, then sneezed twice. Lacey's frown took on a deeper, more intense look. Then Scarlett walked back to Lacey and looked up at her, sad eyes pleading for help. She really wanted to find the person attached to the scent. Lacey opened the bag with the pajama tôp and let Scarlett get another sniff.

"She okay?"

"Yes. I think so." Her gaze lingered on the tree trunk, a stormy look in her eyes.

"Lacey?"

She blinked and nodded. "Yes. She still has his scent." As though she understood, the dog spun off in the direction toward Lacey's old home. "This way," Lacey said.

"I'm right behind you."

He stayed with her and Scarlett, with the dog weaving back and forth, nose in the air. Then she stopped. Barked once and made a beeline for the old shed at the back of Lacey's property.

"Think he went in there?" Creed asked, starting to feel

slightly winded at the fast pace. Lacey looked like she could go another few miles.

"I don't know. Dad always kept it locked, but Fawn may not have." They reached the shed while Scarlett nosed the walls. "She definitely wants to go in."

Creed followed Lacey around to the door. "Weird. The lock is still on there," she said. "I don't know why she'd want in if Hank's not in there."

He passed her, his gaze scanning the structure. "Hank? Can you hear me? If you can, answer. I want to take you home to your mama and daddy. They're waiting on you."

Silence.

"Hank?" Lacey called. Scarlett continued her attempts to find an entrance to the building.

Creed stopped. A little blue blanket lay on the ground next to one of the boards. He pressed on the plank and the bottom of it swung inward. "Lacey? Over here." She hurried to him.

He nodded to the blanket. "It's possible Hank crawled through and couldn't get back out."

Scarlett ducked down and scrambled through the hole.

"Hold the board, will you?" Lacey asked.

He did and she crawled after Scarlett. Creed knelt and peered inside. There was no way he'd fit. "Lacey? You see him?"

"Yeah! He's here. Pull the board off. I'm going to pass him through to you."

"Is he okay?" Creed jerked the board off and the two beside it. When he looked inside, he could see Lacey with the child in her arms. Hank's head rested on her shoulder.

"Hey, little man," she said, her voice low and soft. Comforting. "You sure have a lot of people looking for you."

"I want my mama," the boy said. A tear tracked down

his filthy cheek and Lacey brushed it away. Hank lifted
his head and rubbed his eyes. "I got lost-ed."

"I know, sweetie. We're going to take you to see your
mama right now, okay?"

"'Kay. I like the doggy. He *lick-ted* me."

"*He's* a *she*," Lacey said. "Her name's Scarlett, and
she's been looking for you."

Hank yawned, and Scarlett stood on her hind legs to
nudge him, pulling a giggle from the little guy.

Lacey looked up and her eye caught Creed's. "He's
cold and a little pale, but he found a spot at the back of
the shed and crawled under a tarp. He's got a few scrapes,
but nothing major. I'm sure he's hungry, but overall, I'd
say he's none the worse for wear for this adventure."

Creed unzipped his jacket and shrugged out of it. The
wind bit at him, but he'd survive. Lacey picked her way
through the old tools and passed him the little boy. Creed
set him on his feet for a brief moment while he wrapped
the big coat around him like a blanket, then lifted him
into his arms. *Thank You, Jesus.* The prayer whispered
from his lips and his heart lightened exponentially. "I'm
sure glad to see you, kid."

"Hi, Mr. Sheriff. Can I go home now?" Creed knew
Hank from church, and the little guy had dubbed him
Mr. Sheriff from the moment they'd met. He had no idea
why, but he was fine with the title.

"Yeah, that sounds like a really good idea."

Hank snuggled down against him. "I'm tired and hungry. I want some pizza and apple juice and a big bag of
naminal cookies."

At Lacey's raised brow, Creed translated. "Animal
cookies."

"Oh, right. Of course." She patted Hank's back. "I'm

pretty sure your mom and dad are going to give you just about whatever you want right now."

Hank didn't answer and Creed smiled. "He's asleep."

"Wow. That was fast."

"Kids."

She shuddered. "There are a lot of things in that shed that he could have hurt himself on. I'm so glad he's okay."

"Me, too. Why don't we let his parents know?" Creed pulled his phone out of his pocket and used one hand to dial Joe's number. "We found him," he said in lieu of a greeting. "And he's just fine. Sleeping on my shoulder. Jump in your car and meet us at Lacey and Fawn's place. We'll be waiting on you inside."

Lacey started to lead the way when a sharp crack echoed around them and the dirty window of the shed exploded.

TWO

Lacey let out a short cry and dropped to the ground. Creed hit his knees as well while he hunched over the child in his arms. "Get behind the building!" The second shot hit the wooden side of the structure. "Go!"

He grabbed her arm, and Lacey shoved to her feet and bolted around the corner of the shed. Scarlett followed. "Scarlett, down." The dog dropped and watched Lacey with intent eyes. "Stay." Creed huddled next to her while trying to dial one-handed. "Give me Hank," she said.

Without waiting for him to answer, she pulled the boy into her arms, and he looked up with a frown. "Am I home?"

"No, baby. Go back to sleep." Hank gave a disgruntled sigh but dropped his head to her shoulder. She eyed Creed, who had his weapon in his hand and was peering around the corner with the phone pressed to his ear. "Was someone shooting at us?" She hiss-whispered the words.

"Definitely. Thankfully, they appear to be a bad shot."

"But…why?" She could hear the phone ringing.

"I have no id— Ben, we've got a shooter out at the Jefferson place. You and Mac get out here with some backup, will you?… Yeah… Tell Joe and Denise to hang back until we make sure the shooter's gone, but reassure them that Hank's fine. And we plan on keeping him that way."

He hung up and silence greeted them. No more gunshots. No movement that she could discern. "Could have been a hunter, maybe?"

"This is private property," Creed said. "Not that some people care about that…"

Sirens sounded. She tucked little Hank closer and checked on Scarlett. She was still and quiet as she'd been ordered to do, although when Scarlett caught her watching, she crawled forward and nudged Lacey as though asking if everything was all right. Lacey scratched the dog's ears. "Stay."

Because they were huddled behind the building at the back of the house, she couldn't see the cruiser pull in, but the blue lights flashed their arrival.

Footsteps pounded toward them and Hank roused once more. "I wanna see my mama. You said you were taking me to my mama. Where is she?"

"She's here, Hank. Just hold on a few more minutes. Please?"

"Why?"

"Because we have to make sure it's safe."

His eyes widened slightly and a shiver ran through him, but she wasn't going to lie to him. He was old enough to understand what it meant for an adult to want to make sure the situation was safe for him.

"Mama! I want my mama now!" His top-of-his-lungs scream pierced her eardrums. So, he might be old enough to understand, but that didn't mean he had to like it, of course. He struggled to get out of her hold and she had to squeeze him tighter than she would have liked.

He screeched again and Creed spun to take him from her. "Hank, stop it."

Hank froze midscream. Creed didn't raise his voice, but the firm tone reached through to the little boy. Then tears filled his eyes and spilled over his dirty cheeks. Lacey's heart nearly broke for the child. All he wanted was his mother.

"Creed!" Ben's shout reached them.

"Be careful, Ben. I don't know where the shooter is."

"Regina and Mac are out there looking but need some direction. Where'd the bullets come from?"

"One took out the window on the other side of the building. The second hit the wall. So I'd say east." He glanced around the corner and Lacey figured he was trying to discern exactly where to send the other deputies. "There's a pocket of trees just past the little horse pasture. It's in direct line with the building."

"Stay there until I give you the all clear."

"Copy that." Creed looked at Lacey. "You okay?"

"Yeah." She nodded to Hank. "Looks like he is, too."

He'd fallen back to sleep on Creed's shoulder.

"Creed?" Ben's voice came over the radio.

"Yeah?"

"We're here at the clearing," Regina said. "There are signs that someone was definitely here. The underbrush is stirred up pretty good, and there's an indentation in the ground like someone knelt here. But there are no discernible footprints or anything like that. On the first pass, there's no real evidence to collect. Whoever pulled the trigger picked up any casings."

"All right," Creed said, "nothing we can do about it now." He paused. "Hang out up there for the next few minutes. Just until we get this little one delivered back to his family."

"Sure thing."

Creed caught Lacey's eye. "Let's get Hank into his mama's arms."

"Works for me." Lacey stepped around the building, called for Scarlett to heel and headed for the house.

Creed fell into step beside her. "That was some pretty impressive work you and Scarlett did out there."

"Thanks. It's what we've trained for."

"I know. I guess I'm trying to figure out how to ask you something."

"What's that?"

"Do you want a job?"

Creed shut his mouth so fast, he nearly bit his tongue. Had he really just offered employment to the woman who'd broken his heart? There was no way he wanted to be stuck working with her day in and day out, a constant reminder of how she'd chosen the big city over him—over them. Then again, she could accuse him of doing the same thing to her.

But that was different. This was his home.

And hers, too, whether she wanted to admit it or not.

She laughed, her green eyes crinkling at the corners. "Um…no, but thanks."

"Seriously," he found himself saying, "it would be full-time with benefits and everything."

"As what, Creed?"

"A deputy. And leader of the K-9 unit."

"You don't have a K-9 unit."

"We would if you started one."

She gaped at him.

"Hank!" The frantic cry stopped any reply she might have been forming.

"Mama!" The little boy jerked up and around, nearly tumbling out of Creed's grasp. Only his quick reflexes kept him from dropping the kid. Instead, he lowered him to the ground and the child shrugged the heavy coat off and closed the gap to throw himself into his mother's arms. Joe was right there holding his wife and child close, tears streaming down his cheeks.

Creed's heart clenched as he was reminded once more why he stayed in this small town. Because he was good at his job and these people needed him to be here.

Regina, Ben and Mac joined them, their matching frowns telling him more about what they'd found—or rather, hadn't found—up on the mountain.

They approached while Lacey pulled out a tennis ball and gave it a toss toward an empty space in her massive yard. Scarlett took off like a shot, her sheer joy in the reward bringing a smile to his face. He looked back at Regina and Ben, his lips turning down. "Nothing?"

"No." Regina shook her head. "Sorry."

Ben shrugged. "Maybe it was a hunter who ran when he realized what he'd done."

"Or she," Regina said.

Ben dipped his head. "Right. Or she. And I'll just say that the location the person picked was pretty much perfect. He—or she—had a good line of sight for the shed. And a lot of the area around it, including the house and the driveway."

"So," Creed said, "probably a hunter waiting for a buck to put in an appearance." What else could it be? "All right, let's get back to the station and get the paperwork all done."

He turned to Lacey. "I guess we need to chat."

Lacey raised a brow at him. "Chat?"

"You were coming to see me for a reason. And the reason got interrupted by our hunt for Hank."

Her expression darkened. "Yes, I need to talk to you about Fawn, but first, I have something I need to take care of."

"What?"

"Scarlett was real antsy around that fallen tree trunk," she said. "I want to go take a look at what she was reacting so strongly to."

Creed nodded. "I'll go out there with you, and we can talk on the way."

Lacey studied him for a moment, then gave a short dip of her head. "Can you keep Regina and the others here until we finish checking out that tree trunk?" she asked.

He narrowed his eyes. "Why? Don't tell me Scarlett is trained in cadaver search, as well."

Lacey shook her head. "She started out that way but hated it and was terrible at it. She apparently just really did not like the smell and would be very skittish when she got close to a dead body."

"Can't say I blame her," he muttered.

"And she would sneeze. She was acting that way out by the tree."

Creed froze. "I see. And you think there's a dead body out there?"

"I don't *think* so. I'm…*afraid* so."

THREE

And she was afraid to think who it might be. But the feeling in her gut told her to prepare herself. Lacey snapped the leash onto Scarlett's harness and started off toward the woods. She didn't have anything for Scarlett to sniff, so she simply acted like they were going for a walk. Scarlett was completely fine with that.

"Tell me about Fawn," Creed said, shortening his long stride to match hers. "What's going on with her?"

"She's missing, as far as I can tell. We text just about every day, even if it's just a short 'Hey, hope you have a good day' kind of text. We miss a day here and there, especially since Fawn's work at the hospital has her on some erratic hours and she has to sleep during some of my awake hours, but when the third day went by with no word from her, I got concerned. It's been five days, and I've gone past concerned straight into scared to death for her." Especially considering how Scarlett had been acting around that one particular area this close to home.

"What about your mom? Has she heard anything?"

"No—and she was one of the first people I asked, but she and Fawn don't really talk. Fawn didn't agree with this new marriage and was giving Mom the silent treatment. I think the last time they communicated was on

Fawn's birthday six months ago. I'm not keeping Mom in the loop on this. Not until I know something definite."

"Ouch."

"Yes, but Mom marches to her own drummer." She glanced at him. "Fawn's a lot like our mother in that sense. The things that bother her don't bother me. And vice versa."

Before he could respond, Scarlett stopped and bayed. Then raced back to Lacey, shaking her head and sneezing, tugging on the leash to get away from the area. "That's her 'alert' that there's a dead body, and I just don't know if I can…look."

"You're afraid it's Fawn."

"Yes." *Please don't be, please don't be. Please, God, don't let it be my sister.*

He nodded. "Stand back and let me see what I can see."

Lacey hesitated, then held back, leading Scarlett away from the area. She was more than happy to follow Lacey, who tied her lead to a limb, then walked back over to join Creed, who was scouting the tree. He looked up. "Okay, looks like this trunk is covering something up. I'm trying to figure out a way to move the trunk without disturbing anything that might be underneath. Why don't you go stay with Scarlett?"

She curled her fingers into fists. "I can help."

He eyed her. "You sure?"

"We're trained in this kind of thing. Let's do it right. If my sister is the one—" She pulled in a steadying breath. "Or even if it's not her and it's someone else, they deserve respect and justice."

"And there's no way it could be an animal?"

Lacey raised a brow. "You know better than that."

"Yeah, I do, but you can't blame a guy for hoping."

"Dogs know the difference. They can track the scent of a decomposing human while ignoring the dead squirrel in their path. It's truly amazing." She met his eyes. He knew all that, but talking was helping keep her heartbeat from flying out of her chest. "No, there's a dead person down there. The freezing temps are just keeping us from smelling it."

He nodded. "I believe you."

She motioned to the wood. "I'll get this end if you'll grab that one."

He gripped the trunk with his gloved hands. Lacey did the same on her side, and together they shifted the heavy wood away and set it to the side.

When she looked down into the shallow grave, her breath caught. The body was face down, rolled to her side, but she had long auburn hair and was dressed in a lab coat. The blue-and-white bracelet encircling her right wrist sealed it for Lacey.

She pressed her lips together and met Creed's eyes. "It's her." *Hold it together. Don't cry. Don't*— Tears leaked, splashing over her lashes and onto her cheeks. "Aw, Creed, it's Fawn. I g-gave her that bracelet for her b-birthday."

His arms came around her just as her knees gave out. He lowered her to the ground and pulled her close, burying her face against his chest. "I'm sorry, Lacey. I'm so sorry."

A sob ripped from her. She fisted the material of his coat and bit off the other cries that wanted to escape. She pulled herself together, even while wondering if her heart would ever feel whole again.

Creed let his heart break with hers. He'd known Fawn all her life, and while they hadn't been close in the past few years, he'd considered her a friend.

Lacey pulled back, scrubbing the tears from her eyes. "I'm sorry."

"Lacey, please." He cupped her chin. "You don't have anything to be sorry for. I… I don't even know what to say. This is beyond awful…" He let her go, and Scarlett whined from her spot, tugging at her lead.

Lacey walked over to the dog, dropped to her knees and buried her face in the sleek brown coat. When she drew in a shuddering breath and pulled back, Scarlett swiped her tongue over Lacey's cheek. Creed waited, giving her another moment, then said, "I'm going to have to call the medical examiner and a crime scene unit."

"I know." She stood and met his gaze. The agony there nearly killed him.

He took her hand. "Cry if you need to."

"I'll cry later," she said, her voice hoarse. "For now, we need to take care of Fawn."

He gave a slow nod. "All right. Come on."

She and Scarlett followed him back to the edge of the woods. He'd have to guide the others to the body. Fawn. She wasn't just a body. She'd been a person, a sister, a daughter, a friend, a respected member of the medical community, and more. His throat tightened and he cleared it. "I know it's painful, Lacey, but did Fawn have any enemies you can think of?"

"No, not offhand." She paused and swiped a stray tear. "I don't know how she died, Creed, but her death wasn't an accident. She didn't crawl in that little wooded area and pull that trunk over the hiding place. This has all the signs that someone killed her and didn't want her found."

"I agree."

"I thought you did when you asked if she had any enemies. Sorry. I don't know why I felt compelled to point it out."

He squeezed her shoulder. "It's fine, Lacey."

While they waited for the crime scene unit, Regina, Ben and Mac hurried over to meet them. Creed gave them the rundown of what they'd found and the deputies paled.

"Wait a minute," Ben said. "I saw Fawn at the hospital a couple of days ago. She looked worn-out and I commented that she needed a vacation. She said she'd just had one and was glad to be back at work."

"What day was that?" Creed asked.

"Um… Tuesday, I think."

"That's the last day I heard from her," Lacey said, her features pinched. "She never let on that anything was wrong—if anything *was* at that point."

Creed guided Lacey out of the way of the gurney. The medical examiner nodded, his eyes shadowed. "Lacey. Heard you were back."

"Hi, Zeb. Yeah, I'm back. For now," she said. "Word travels fast in Timber Creek. I guess some things never change." Lacey knew everyone in town, just like Creed.

Because most people who grew up in Timber Creek only left for a short time before finding their way back. Or they never left at all.

Except Lacey. She'd left and would be leaving again.

He shook the thoughts from his head. Dwelling on the past and dreading the future weren't going to accomplish anything helpful in the present. While they waited, Zeb examined the area of the body he could see, collected anything that he thought might be evidence and then directed Regina and Ben on how to extract the body.

Once Fawn was in the body bag and on the gurney, Zeb directed Ben and Mac to help put her in the back of the coroner's van, then walked over to join Creed and Lacey.

"I'm really sorry, Lacey."

She nodded and absently scratched Scarlett's ears. The thump, thump, thump of helicopter blades caught her attention, and she looked up to see a news chopper hovering overhead. Far enough not to disturb the area, but their cameras were good. "Creed?"

"I see them." He pulled his phone from his pocket and barked orders about getting rid of the bird while Lacey's gaze stayed on the van until the doors were shut.

Creed stomped back over, his face twisted in a scowl. The helicopter banked off and he shook his head. "Vultures."

The chopper forgotten, Lacey turned her eyes to Zeb. "How did she die?"

Zeb hesitated, then met Creed's eyes. Creed gave a fraction of a nod and Zeb sighed. "It looks like she was hit in the head with a blunt object."

At Lacey's sharp gasp, Creed squeezed her fingers. "Thanks, Zeb," she said, her voice so low he barely heard it. "Take care of her."

"The best." He looked at Creed. "I'll be in touch." He paused. "I'll let you know now that I'm the only ME at the moment and I'm backed up on cases. The other doc took a job in Arizona and left without notice. It may take me a while to get to her. I'm not talking weeks, but possibly a couple of days. I'll do a preliminary scan and see if I can locate anything that can be run through the systems, like DNA or hair or fibers or whatever, but the actual autopsy will have to wait a while."

Creed nodded. "Understood."

He left and Lacey didn't move until the van was out of sight. Then she clicked to Scarlett and started walking.

"Where are you going?" Creed asked.

"To get my SUV and bring it back to the house."

"Okay. Anything I can do to help?" He wasn't ready to let her out of his sight yet. She'd just had a major tragedy, and he wasn't sure she was thinking clearly.

"Help? I don't know, Creed." She drew in a shuddering breath. "All I know right now is that I came home to find her, and I have. Now I need to find her killer, and I'm not leaving here until I do."

"That's my job, Lacey. My department's job."

"That offer of a job still stand?"

He had a feeling he knew where this was going. "Yes."

"Then let's try things this way. I'll take a leave of absence from my current position and work with you on a contract basis until we find Fawn's killer—and see what we can do about starting a K-9 unit." She paused. "As long as my boss is willing, I'll stay until you have at least one handler on board. After that, well, we'll just have to see where we are at that point. If you're agreeable."

"I'm agreeable. Welcome to the Timber Creek Sheriff's Office."

FOUR

"But?" she asked.

"But you know as well as I do—you can't investigate your sister's death," he said, his voice soft, falling into step beside her.

"Not officially, anyway. I know." She stopped walking and he turned to face her. "But if I'm part of the department," she said, "I can be privy to information you wouldn't tell me otherwise."

He studied her for a moment, his eyes shadowed, unreadable, but he finally nodded. "All right. We'll get the paperwork all drawn up and finalized. I really do want to start a K-9 program. That can be your job while you're here. Not investigating Fawn's murder."

"I get it, I promise." She started walking again. Her head pounded with the thought of everything she was going to have to deal with in the coming weeks. "I need to call my boss and let him know what's going on and ask for some time off."

"Of course."

Lacey made the call, his heart breaking all over again as he listened to her explain the situation. When she hung up, she bit her lip. "What could she have done for someone to do this to her?"

He shook his head. "If you don't know, I sure don't. You said you were texting with her right up until a few days ago."

"Right."

"And she never let on that there was anything wrong?"

"No." She paused. "Not verbally, anyway."

"What does that mean?"

"It means that she never said anything was wrong, but I sensed something. I asked her about it a couple of times. She said everything was fine. I thought she sounded weird, but then it would pass. I figured she'd fill me in when she was ready. If there was anything to fill me in on. I really just thought she was tired from work." Tears threatened and she only managed to keep them at bay through sheer willpower. "*Now* I keep asking myself if what I thought I was sensing has to do with her death." She shook her head. "Why didn't I press her for answers?"

"You think she would have told you if you had?"

"I don't know. And, honestly, at the time, a part of me was relieved that she didn't give me another problem to deal with." She bit her lip and looked away. She'd never forgive herself for not getting in the car and making the trip to confront Fawn about whatever it was she was hiding.

"Come on, Lace—"

"No, I'm serious. I've been under so much stress at work and I just couldn't…deal with anything else. I told myself that once I was out from all the pressure at work, I'd figure out what was going on with Fawn. So, that's on me."

"You worked a lot?"

"All the time. Literally. I ate on the run and slept when

I could. The demand for well-trained dogs is high and I was training left and right. I was also working shifts with Scarlett with the department and it seemed like I was getting at least one call every day." Lacey raked a hand over her ponytail and pulled it tighter. "But Fawn knew she could tell me anything. And if she needed me, all she had to do was say the word, and stress or no stress, work or no work, I would have dropped everything to be here for her. She *knew* that." Lacey paused. "At least, I thought she did."

They'd reached her SUV, and Scarlett raced to her door to sit and wait.

"She's an amazing animal," Creed said.

"Thanks. We've spent many hours working and training." And just maybe that training would be something she could use to her advantage when it came to finding Fawn's killer.

"You did a great job with her."

"I appreciate that." Lacey opened the door and Scarlett hopped up to settle in her spot. The dog sighed and placed her nose between her paws while her dark brown eyes bounced between Lacey and Creed.

"I'm impressed," Creed said, "although I guess I shouldn't be. You've always loved dogs and planned to go into law enforcement." His gaze touched lightly over her features. "You're probably way overqualified for this little town. I'm not sure it can afford you."

"Well, right now, you don't have to worry about it. I'm here until we find Fawn's killer and set up your K-9 unit."

"Good. I'll follow you home—er... I mean, to Fawn's house." He sighed and paused. "I assume you're staying there?"

She pressed her fingers to her eyes. "I hadn't thought

that far ahead, but yes, I guess I am. Doesn't make sense that I would pay for a hotel when the house is now mine." Just saying the words out loud made her nauseous.

"See you there."

Five minutes later, she walked back into her childhood home, and Creed was right behind her. She stopped just inside the foyer and took in the details. The dining room was to her left and had been redone to the point that she didn't recognize it. And yet she did. In front of her, the wall that had separated the den and kitchen had been removed to create one big open space.

Just a few hours earlier, she'd stopped in only long enough to verify that Fawn wasn't there before she'd dashed off to the sheriff's office. In those brief moments she'd been inside, she'd noted the differences Fawn had made in her efforts to restore the old farmhouse, but now Lacey paused and took in the details while she fought the grief clawing at her. "The windows still need the blinds put up. They're stacked over there next to the fireplace. I guess that was her next project."

"At least she has sheets over the windows for now."

"Yes." Lacey fell silent for a moment, then shook her head. "She always loved this old place."

"But you didn't."

"I did at first. But then came to hate it, as you well know."

"Lacey," he said, his husky voice a soothing balm to her battered spirit, "your father's actions shouldn't—"

She whirled. "I don't talk about him." At his flinch, she sucked in a breath. "Sorry, I didn't mean to snap, but please, don't bring him up again."

He frowned but nodded and cleared his throat. "Fawn was really making some good progress here, wasn't she?"

Lacey's shoulders relaxed a fraction. "She always said if medicine hadn't been her calling, she would have loved her own design show." Again, her throat tightened, and she fought to keep her feelings from showing. For years, she'd learned how to bury her emotions. She didn't need them getting in the way now. "Last week, when I talked to her, she said she was almost finished with the kitchen." Lacey walked through into the den and noted the kitchen area to her left. Granite countertops had replaced the peeling laminate. The wood floors had been redone, and stainless steel appliances now graced the spaces where the old yellow sixties ones had been. "She sure was enjoying that gas stove," Lacey said. "She hated the old electric range with the uneven burners."

"She was doing all this herself?"

"She and a few friends who were helping her out."

"What friends?"

"Danny Main was doing the electrical for her, and Nancy Stone was in charge of the plumbing."

He pointed to cans of paint next to the wall. "They're labeled. She picked different colors for each room?"

Lacey looked at the cans.

"She did. She told me each room was going to be a different color, even though there was only a very subtle difference in shade. I pointed out that she was going to have to change her rollers and clean everything in between." She gave a small laugh that she had to bite off before it turned into a sob. She cleared her throat. "But that was Fawn. She didn't care about minor inconveniences like that. She had more patience than I'll ever have."

Lacey walked down the hall toward the master bedroom. Creed and Scarlett followed, letting her set the pace. "Fawn did everything necessary to make the house livable before doing the blinds and paint. That was smart. As for help, I think Carol Malone was going to help her paint, but yeah, Fawn was doing the majority of it." She drew in a shaky breath. "I don't understand her need to stay here, but she was a lot like you. She wasn't leaving."

"People needed her here—or she thought they did."

"Yeah, I didn't get that either. After the way we were treated—after my father—" Ugh. She'd just snapped his head off for bringing the man up, and now she was doing it. "It was hard." She paused and let her gaze roam the room again. "The only reason this house wasn't taken to pay off my father's debts when he went to prison was because it was in my mom's name." She shot him a sad smile. "Did you know that?"

"Yeah. Mom mentioned it. Said she was glad that y'all still had a roof over your heads."

She fell silent while she led the way to the second floor. To the right had been her old room. She went to the door and pushed it open and flipped the light switch on. All of the furniture had been removed, except for a desk situated in the middle of the room, facing the window. "When he went to prison," she finally said, "I just..." She stopped and shuddered. "He betrayed everyone in this town, and people seemed to think the rest of us were just like him, waiting to steal whatever they had left."

He frowned. "Wait a minute, now. Come on, Lacey. You don't really believe that."

She laughed, then winced at the pain the sound held. "Yes, I do. And you know it's true."

"I'm sorry," he said. "Deeply sorry."

"For what?"

"For...not noticing that. You obviously believe it's true about the town thinking ill of you, but I never... I just..."

"Didn't see it."

"Yeah."

"Because everyone loved you and your family. You had no reason to see it."

His frown deepened and he tilted his head. "I don't know if I agree with that, Lacey."

"It's okay. You don't have to." She shot him a small smile and gave a slight shrug. "I also think Fawn thought she owed it to the people in town to stay." Lacey covered a yawn, exhaustion mingling with her grief. "Sorry. I'm a bit wiped."

"Understandable." He started to say something, then stopped.

"What?" Lacey asked.

"Did Fawn say that? That she owed it to the towns-people to stay? Because that's—" he sighed "—wrong. Look, you said not to talk about your father, but—"

"I brought him up, so I guess I can't complain."

"Right. Look, he did a really rotten thing—"

"He stole from people who trusted him. That's a bit more than a rotten thing." Her father had been a well-respected financial adviser. Until he'd been caught fleecing his clients—most of whom had been friends. Some who had children the same ages as Lacey and Fawn.

"Well, you were right about one thing. Some things really don't ever change," he said, his tone wry.

She blinked. "What?" It hit her. She'd just interrupted him twice. "Oh. Sorry."

He shot her a smile. One tinged with sadness, regret and…longing? He blinked and the look was gone, leaving her to wonder if she'd imagined it. He walked to the window and pushed it open. With a glance back at her, he climbed out.

"What are you doing?" she asked.

"Sitting. Remembering the good times we had out here."

Remembering the conversations that lasted for hours? The talking about their futures? The sweet kisses that always ended too soon? She walked over and looked out. "You're right. Those weren't just good times. Those were the best." She laughed. "I interrupted you an awful lot out here." She climbed out to sit beside him.

"I never minded your interruptions, Lacey."

The tenderness in his voice nearly took her breath away. "Well, it's a lousy habit that I thought I'd broken, but five seconds back in Timber Creek and I'm right back where I started. Unbelievable."

"Like I said, I never minded. Still don't."

"Well, I do." She scrubbed her burning eyes with her palms. "Fawn used to get so mad at me for that." A sob caught in her throat, then escaped. "Oh, Creed, what am I going to do without her?"

His arms came around her as the next cry slipped out.

Like a lot of men, Creed had never been comfortable with a crying woman, but this was Lacey, and she'd cried on his shoulder more than once as a teen. He'd even cried on hers a time or two. Right in this very spot. So, now, while he let the grief flow, he let his long-held anger and hurt slide to the back burner.

He pulled her close and let her sob out her grief, wishing he had the words to help. But he didn't. Lacey finally sniffed and swiped a hand over her face before he could offer the hem of his shirt.

Scarlett walked to the window and poked her head out, her eyes never leaving her mistress's face. "She's okay, girl," Creed said, his voice soft. He scratched the dog behind her ears, and while she seemed to appreciate the reassurance, he wasn't sure she was convinced. Scarlett hopped out onto the roof and placed a paw on Lacey's knee.

Lacey choked on another sob and then lowered her forehead to the dog's. Finally, her heart-wrenching cries faded and she stilled. Then sniffed. Creed held his arm out. "Wanna use my sleeve?"

She choked on a half laugh, half sob and shook her head. Instead, she used her own shirt and he gave her some time to get herself together.

"I'm sorry, Lacey. I feel kind of helpless here. Tell me what to do."

She shook her head. "You did it. You let me cry without feeling self-conscious about it." She stood, slipped back into the room, trailed by Scarlett, and simply stood there. "Let's check the rest of the house. I don't think she did any structural changes up here. Not like downstairs."

He followed her to the other two bedrooms and bathrooms, then back down to the master. "There," she said. "I noticed that, but it didn't hit me how weird it was."

"What?"

"The dresser drawer. It's open." She walked over to it and pulled the drawer fully out. "And that's even more weird."

"Can you explain?"

"You know Fawn was a neat freak. She'd never leave a drawer cracked and she always kept her clothes just so. But these T-shirts are unfolded and…well, it looks like she just dumped them in here."

"Maybe she was in a hurry or something."

"No." She opened the drawer beneath it. "This is the same way."

"You think someone searched them?"

"Maybe. I don't know. Nothing else in the house looked off, so…" She shrugged.

His phone buzzed. "I hate to do this, but I've got to go. Regina, Ben and Mac are still out at the scene and I want to go have a look before it gets dark. Do you have anyone you can call to stay with you tonight?"

She looked up from the drawer. "I could call Jessica Hill, I guess."

"You still talk to her?"

"Not often, but we keep up. Exchange Christmas cards and such. I agreed to be in her wedding because it wasn't here." Jessica and Lacey had been best friends in high school. "She's one of the few people in this town who didn't make me feel like a pariah after Dad went to prison. But…she just had a baby not too long ago, so she might not be the best person either."

"What about Miranda Glenn?" Creed asked.

"Think she just had a baby, too, didn't she? She was closer to Fawn, anyway, but…" She dragged the word out. "She'd be a good one to talk to and see if Fawn said anything to her about any issues she may have been having—and hiding from me." Hurt flashed in those eyes he'd once thought he'd spend a lifetime staring into, and just like when they were teens, he wanted to be the one to take the pain away. To be her hero. But she'd rejected him back then, made it clear that he wasn't the priority in her life.

He cleared his throat. "I really need to go. I'll check on you after I finish at the scene."

"And let me know what you find?"

"If there's anything found, we'll talk."

"Thank you, Creed." She rubbed her eyes. "I guess I'll look around the house and see if there's anything that will give me a clue as to what was going on with her and where she was the last three months before I call Jessica. Even if I don't stay with her, it would be good to check in with her and see if she'd seen Fawn."

"Good idea. Let me know if you find anything."

"Of course." She nodded and he headed for the door. Once he was in his SUV, he sat there for a moment, reading text updates from Regina. He'd admit texting had its benefits, but he'd much rather talk on the phone. He dialed her number.

"Creed," she answered midring. "I assume you got my messages."

"I did. I'm on the way."

"See you when you get here."

It didn't take him long to reach the area. In fact, if Lacey looked out of her kitchen window, she'd be able to see the law enforcement vehicles still on her property. The crime scene unit had finally arrived, and he recognized Garrett Smith, the lead investigator. Garrett waved him over and Creed joined him at the spot Regina, Ben and Mac had found earlier.

He pulled little blue bootees on over his shoes and signed the log. Being careful where he stepped, Creed walked over to stand close to where the shooter had been and looked out, through the trees, straight at the shed in Lacey's backyard. And if he turned just enough, he could see the area where Fawn had been buried. "If you were going to kill someone," he said, "why bury her on her own property?"

Garrett shrugged. "I don't know. I wouldn't."

Creed looked at Regina. "Give me some scenarios that would make you do that. I have a few that I can come up with, but—" he shrugged "—humor me."

"The only thing I can think of is if the killer did the deed, then panicked. Buried the body and hoped no one would come looking this far from the house."

"But with a dog, she was easy to find."

Regina frowned. "But the department doesn't have a dog. Maybe the killer knows that."

"Or wasn't thinking straight," Garrett said. "That fits with panicked. I'd say that might be more likely."

"Maybe the killer didn't think Fawn would be missed," Regina said.

"I have a hard time with that one," Creed said. "Everyone in town knows Fawn and Lacey are tight. And Fawn has a ton of friends at the hospital."

"So, maybe it was someone who stumbled on the place and decided to help themselves. Only Fawn caught him, and he killed her."

"That would fit with the panic burial," Creed said, "but the house was untouched." At least, it had appeared to be. He called Lacey. "Hey," he said, when she answered. "Can you check and see if you notice anything missing, like jewelry or silver or—I don't know—whatever?"

"You think Fawn was killed by an intruder—she caught him, he killed her and hid her body?"

"That's a theory."

"The only thing that I've noticed out of the ordinary was the messy clothing in the drawers. Let me look around and I'll shoot you a text if I find anything else that looks off."

"Thanks."

He hung up and turned back to the scene. "You know, from here, you have a really good view of the house, too. The back of it, anyway. With some binoculars, you could even see inside, if there weren't sheets over the windows."

"You think someone's been watching the place?" Ben asked.

"No idea. Just making an observation." But the thought made him uneasy.

"But why shoot at you?"

"At first, I thought it was a hunter who needed some extra target practice, but now…" He pursed his lips. "I don't know. Even I can see the shed with no trouble. Whoever was shooting had to see there were people there."

"Then why shoot?"

"Maybe to get us away from the shed? Keep us from getting too close to Fawn's body?"

Regina nodded. "Could be either…or neither. Let's check out the shed just to be thorough."

FIVE

Lacey lay on Fawn's bed and stared at the ceiling. She'd done a cursory walk through the house and hadn't noticed a thing missing. The silver was all there, Fawn's jewelry box was untouched and the smart TV still sat on its stand in the corner of the den. She'd let Creed know, then collapsed onto the bed.

She never did get around to calling Jessica. Instead, she'd dialed her mother's number and had just gotten off the phone with her. Her mother had still been crying when they'd hung up. Lacey's tears had been retriggered, of course, and now the box of tissues was empty on the floor. She needed to get up, but her sinuses were clogged, her head pounded and moving required effort.

She definitely needed to move, but numbness nailed her to the mattress. Scarlett lay at her feet, lifting her head every so often as though checking on her.

Lacey slid her gaze to the dresser. The disarray of the drawers still bothered her. Fawn would never leave her clothes like that. So, why were they *like that*?

Her phone rang. Creed again. Answering his call was the only thing that could inspire her to move at the moment. She snagged the device from the end table. "Hi."

"Do we have permission to search this outbuilding? The shed where we found Hank?"

"Of course." She sat up, her lethargy fleeing. "Why?"

"We're speculating, that's all. Wondering if the shooter was trying to distract us away from the shed. And while we have no proof of that, we're trying to cover all bases."

"I understand. You can search it. Just break the lock. Whatever you need to do."

"Thanks. Be thinking about people who know Fawn. We're going to need to talk to them."

"I've already made a mental list, but I'll write them down."

"I should have figured. Stay strong, Lacey," he said, his voice low. "We're going to find out who did this."

Her heart lightened a fraction. She loved that he included her in that statement. "I know. It won't bring Fawn back, but she deserves justice." She paused. "I *need* her to have justice."

"One step at a time. I'll let you know if we find anything."

"Thanks, Creed."

She hung up and swung her feet to the floor. Scarlett watched from her spot on the bed. "You can stay here," Lacey said. "I'm just going to start a more thorough search of the house."

Lacey went to Fawn's closet and opened the door. She closed her eyes and breathed in the scent of her sister. A subtle hint of her musk perfume and strawberry shampoo. Tears wanted to flow once more. "Stop it," she whispered. "Focus."

For the next two hours, she went through the closet, working her way through all of the pockets. And there were a lot. Fawn loved clothes and had a good eye for style. One would never guess she frequented thrift stores and yard sales to dress herself.

In the end, the search produced two tubes of lip balm and almost six dollars in change. And a note scribbled on hospital letterhead to call Miranda Glenn. Below the reminder were several names. Derrik Jones, Robert Owen, Selena Hernandez. She sent a picture of the paper to Creed via text, then tapped the message: Found this in one of Fawn's pockets. I have no idea who these people are, but maybe you can figure it out.

Good job. Worth investigating.

Her eyes landed on the old childhood photo albums stacked against the back wall of the closet, and she sank to the floor to grab the top one. She flipped through it, the memories flooding her. As much as her father had hurt their family by his actions, they'd had some good times before it all came crashing down, she had to admit. Times that had been buried in the tiniest corner of her mind and mostly forgotten.

Now they surged to the surface, bringing her to tears once more. Beach trips, mountain camping adventures with just the four of them, theme parks and more. She slammed the book closed and shut her burning eyes. "God, I don't know if I can do this," she said out loud. "I need Your strength because mine is about gone." She checked her phone to find she'd missed a text from Creed. He'd sent it thirty minutes ago.

Nothing in the shed. Heading to the morgue to speak with Zeb. No need for you to come, even though I know that's going to be your first thought. He hasn't done the autopsy yet, of course, but I thought if I showed up, he might stop and fill me in on anything he might have found in his initial examination. I'll be in touch.

With another prayer for answers, she slipped out of the closet to find the house pitch-dark. The only light came from the closet. She turned it off, not needing it. She knew this house like the back of her hand—minus the changes in the kitchen. Scarlett waited at the bedroom door, ears cocked. Lacey went to the dog and placed a hand on her head. "What is it, girl?"

Scarlett spared her a quick glance before she walked out of the bedroom and down the hall to the kitchen. Goose bumps pebbled Lacey's arms and she shivered. Scarlett went to the door and barked once. Her signal that she needed out. After Lacey stopped at the thermostat to bump it up a degree, she flipped on the small table lamp next to the back door.

As soon as Lacey opened the door, Scarlett darted straight to the bushes along the side of the house. The fence would keep her from wandering too far.

Lacey scanned the property, hunching her shoulders against the chill. She'd forgotten how dark it was here in the middle of nowhere, and she didn't like it any more now than she had as a kid. Scarlett barked, ears pricked, hackles raised, and Lacey's chills multiplied. "Scarlett! Come."

The dog backed up, ears twitching, reluctant to obey, but trained well enough that she would anyway. "Scarlett, come."

Scarlett whirled and raced to Lacey. Once they were both inside, Lacey shut and locked the door, her mind racing. Was someone out there? Like the person who'd shot at them? She grabbed her phone and called Creed.

He answered on the first ring. "Hey, I can't talk right now. Can I call you back in a few?"

"Um…yeah. That's fine."

A pause. "Everything okay?"

"I'm not sure." She checked her weapon. "Scarlett was acting weird. I think someone may be snooping around outside."

"Okay, stay put. I'm on the way."

"No, do what you have to do. I'm going to take Scarlett and kind of scout around the area." Having part of the yard fenced didn't mean someone couldn't have slipped through the gate.

"Look, I know you're a cop and very capable, but even cops need help sometimes. So just don't take any chances."

She heard the words he didn't say. *Don't do anything stupid.* He was right. She didn't like it, but… "Okay. Fine. Will you send someone?"

"Already on it."

"Let them know I'll have my gun, please."

"Of course."

She hung up and went to each window in the house, finding them all locked and secure. While the house still needed to be better insulated, one of the first things Fawn had done was replace the old drafty windows. Too bad she hadn't installed an alarm system.

Scarlett pushed her nose into Lacey's hand. "It's all right, girl. I may just be a little paranoid." Which was understandable, of course.

For the next few minutes, she paced from one end of the dark house to the other, peering out the window and beginning to regret her call to Creed. Keeping the lights off inside should have given her a bit of an advantage to see if anyone was lurking outside, but nothing set her internal alarms off. She looked at Scarlett. "If all of this stress is over a rabbit, we're going to have a serious chat."

Scarlett yawned and settled on her bed, lowering her snout between her paws.

Which made Lacey feel a lot better—and a little like the boy who cried wolf. She made her way to the front door and looked out just in time to see a police cruiser pulled to the top of the U-shaped drive. Regina climbed out, hand on her weapon. Lacey opened the door and stepped out onto the front porch. "Sorry. I think I'm overreacting."

"Overreacting how?"

"I thought someone was lurking around the house. In the bushes. Scarlett was acting weird, and after getting shot at today—" She shrugged. "Now I'm feeling kind of silly."

"Nothing to feel silly about. Getting shot at is kind of terrifying."

"No kidding." Another cruiser turned into her drive and Lacey bit off a groan. After all, she was the one who'd made the call. "Creed, too? Thought he was headed to the morgue."

"He called me and said to get over here and that he was headed here, too. Said the morgue could wait."

Creed parked behind Regina and stepped out of his car. "Lacey? You okay?"

"I'm fine. I was telling Regina I think I overreacted." Heat climbed into her cheeks, and she was thankful she was in the shadows of the porch light. If he thought she was incompetent, he might rethink his offer to join the force. Which shouldn't matter since she couldn't investigate Fawn's case.

And she was leaving as soon as they found Fawn's murderer and set up the K-9 unit for Creed. For some reason, she had to remind herself of that.

He flipped on a flashlight he held in his left hand. "Why don't we find out? Want to help clear the area?"

At least he hadn't told her to go back inside but was treating her as a fellow officer. "Gladly."

"Then lead the way."

She pulled her weapon—just in case she wasn't over-reacting—and started for the bushes Scarlett had been so interested in.

Creed followed Lacey while Regina went in the op-posite direction, stating she'd radio if she found some-thing. In the meantime, he lit the way for Lacey. She approached, caution in her stance. "This is stupid," she muttered. "If someone *was* here, he's not anymore."

But he noticed she didn't lower her guard. Every inch the professional, she cleared the bush, then the next and the next, until she finally lowered her weapon and turned to him. "Nothing."

Something on the ground caught his eye. "Maybe not nothing."

"What do you mean?"

Creed knelt and shone the light. "It's a pen with the hospital's logo on it."

"Well, Fawn worked there, so that's not so odd. The fact that it's out here kind of is, though."

He shook his head. "Fawn's probably been dead for a few days. This pen is clean, for the most part. A little dirt to brush off, but definitely not one that's been out here long." He stood and clicked the radio on his shoul-der. "Regina? You find anything?"

"Found some trash in one area that's pretty well hidden on the other side of the fence, but is up the hill far enough that it has a clear view of the house. Food wrappers, water bottles and beer cans, that kind of thing. Everything was in a plastic grocery bag and tied off. Looks to me like it was something teenagers might have done, not a shooter."

"Well, bag it all and we'll send it to the lab. Who knows what we'll get?"

"Copy that."

"And can you bring me an evidence bag?"

"You found something?"

"Maybe."

Seconds later, Regina handed him the bag and a pair of gloves. Once he had the gloves on, he snagged the pen and slipped it into the bag. Regina sealed and labeled it. "Thanks," he told her.

"Sure thing. One other thing of note that makes me think Scarlett may have heard someone. The fence was unlatched. And since you can only lock or unlock it from the inside..."

Lacey sucked in an audible breath. "Right. Good to know. I'll buy a lock for it ASAP."

"Good idea." She waved the evidence bag. "If y'all are okay, I'm going to get this back and stored until we can get it sent off first thing in the morning."

"I think we'll be fine. If you'll take care of that, I'll hang out with Lacey a bit longer."

Regina nodded and headed for her cruiser while Lacey stood glaring at the bush, hands on her hips. Then she sighed and turned to face him. "You want to come in for a few minutes? I need something to drink. I'm sure you could use something, too."

"Sounds good."

"Coffee, water or tea?"

"Coffee."

While she popped the pod in the Keurig, he found the cream and sugar. Scarlett watched them from her spot on the floor. "She likes to be around people, doesn't she?"

Lacey shot the dog a fond smile. "Yeah, she definitely doesn't like being left alone too long."

The Keurig gurgled its "I'm finished" noise, and Lacey handed him his steaming mug half-full. He caught her eye. She remembered. Before the eye contact got awkward, he added enough milk to turn the java a light brown and topped it off with a tablespoon of sugar. "Why don't you just drink the milk?" she asked.

He grinned. "You never did understand a good cup of coffee."

"Coffee-flavored milk." She rolled her eyes, and his heart cramped at the banter. He'd been a frequent Saturday morning visitor and coffee consumer in this very room. Shoving the memories aside, he waited while she made her cup of coffee—and left it black. He shuddered and followed her to take a seat at the kitchen table.

"You know, this is a perfect property to raise dogs on."

She narrowed her eyes at him, and he wondered if he'd overstepped. Before he could apologize, she nodded. "It really is, but I have a place."

"Who's taking care of your dogs while you're here?"

"There are only three dogs at the moment, and they'll all be going to their new homes in less than a month. For now, a couple of volunteers and my part-time person are stopping by several times a day to check on them, feed them and so on. They're good people." She sipped her coffee. "Interestingly enough, one of my volunteers is the owner of the property I've been renting for the past few years."

"Renting? You didn't buy something?"

"No."

"Why not?"

She shrugged. "I don't know. I meant to, of course, once I got to know the area, but I just never got around to it. I stayed so busy with the department and business was booming…" Another small lift of her shoulders. "Before I knew it, the years had passed and the place was…comfortable."

But she didn't say *home*. Now, *that* was interesting.

She glanced at the window again. "You think there really was someone out there?" she asked. "And that someone dropped the pen?"

He let her change the subject. "It's impossible to know for sure, but I think we need to err on the side of caution. Especially after today. Until we know who or what that shooter was aiming at, it's best to watch your back."

"They were shooting at us. I'm not buying the errant-bullets idea."

After a pause, he said, "Yeah, I think so, too." He shook his head. "But most people who own weapons around here are proficient with them. Meaning, they hit what they aim at. If the shooter wanted to hit one of us, I think he would have."

"Maybe. You think it was a warning?"

"I'm hoping it was." He shook his head again. "The only person who knows for sure is the one who pulled the trigger." She covered a yawn and Creed frowned. "Why don't you go get some rest? I'll stay here and keep an eye on things."

She hesitated, like she was debating whether or not to take him up on it, then nodded. "I'll sleep better knowing you're here." More hesitation. "What's the plan for in the morning?"

"I talk to people who knew Fawn. Try to get a picture of her last couple of days and who saw her last. That kind of thing."

"I spoke to Katherine O'Ryan right before we started looking for Hank. She said she saw Fawn at the hospital last week—probably right before she was killed—and said she looked rough, like she'd been sick or something."

"But she wasn't sick?"

"Not that I know of. She never said."

"I'll talk to Katherine again."

"I want to help."

"You can't."

"Not officially, I know. We've already covered that. But I want to talk to people, too. Unofficially. Surely, there's no law against a sister talking to her murdered sister's friends."

"No, there's no law." He massaged his temples. "Let's discuss it in the morning. Why don't you try to get some rest?"

"Okay." She paused. "Thanks, Creed."

Her whisper reached him and touched something deep in his heart. Something he'd thought he'd managed to purge after she'd walked away from him. He let his gaze linger on her face, then cleared his throat. "Of course. Good night."

She clicked to Scarlett and the two of them disappeared down the hall.

Creed lowered his coffee cup to the coaster, refusing to acknowledge that he could possibly still be attracted to the woman who'd stomped all over his heart. He focused on the events of earlier and admitted she was right.

Someone *had* shot at them. That fact continued to rattle around in his tired brain. One shot might have been an accident, but two? When they were standing there in plain sight? He was going to have to go on the assumption that someone had been aiming at them with the intention of killing—and the fact that the shooter hadn't cared that a child might get caught in the cross fire.

So, who did he know in this town that he'd grown up in with the ability to commit cold-blooded murder?

SIX

Lacey had tossed and turned enough to send the comforter to the floor and Scarlett leaping down after it to escape her restless mistress. But, Lacey realized with some shock, she'd slept a few hours.

Low voices from the kitchen reached her and she quickly showered and dressed. She rubbed Scarlett's ears. "Come on, girl. Time for you to go out and for me to get a status update on Fawn's case." If there was one.

When she stepped into the kitchen, Regina and Creed had a newspaper and several pictures spread out on the table in front of them, empty mugs pushed to the side. They looked up at her entrance. "Good morning," Lacey said.

"Good morning to you, too," Creed drawled. "You get some sleep?"

"A bit." She let Scarlett out into the backyard, then looked at Regina. "What brings you here?"

"Creed and I have been taking turns sleeping and keeping watch."

"That's over and above. Thank you."

"Happy to do it."

"What are you looking at?"

Creed passed her the newspaper. A picture of her and

Scarlett was on the front page. The headline read K-9 Finds Body of Missing Doctor.

Lacey shuddered and shoved the paper away. "Ugh."

Creed covered her hand with his. "I'm sorry. I thought about hiding it, but—"

"There's no point in that."

"I know."

He set the paper aside and Regina pointed to the other pictures laid out. "They're photos of your property taken by a drone. We believe that the shooter wanted to keep us away from something."

"Like what?"

"Finding Fawn's body is the first thought that comes to mind," Creed said, "but we thought looking at the property from a different angle might give us some new information, reveal something on the property that sparked a reason for the shooting."

"And does it?"

"Not really."

"Oh."

"Yeah. Sorry. We just keep circling back to the shooter not wanting us near Fawn's body." He sighed. "It was a good idea." He pulled one of the pictures toward him. "And actually—" he pointed "—here is where the shooter picked for his hiding spot. We knew it was a good one, but looking at it from above, it's downright genius."

"I see what you mean," Lacey said, her voice low. "He's got a view of the house—even the fenced-in spot, the area where we found Fawn, the shed…everything. And there—" She pointed. "A path straight back to here that leads to the road. There's a fence there, but it wouldn't be any trouble to go over it."

"And have a car waiting right there for a quick get-away."

"But what were they doing up there?" Lacey asked. "And with a long-range rifle? No one would know we were going to be searching there."

"Or they were *afraid* the search might extend that far and went to wait and see."

Lacey nodded. "Of course. But how did they get away so easily? Officers were all over that area." Whenever anyone went missing, law enforcement sent officers to neighboring towns to help search. "Why didn't they see a vehicle or something?"

"They may have," Creed said, "and simply mistaken it for a volunteer's."

True. She sighed. Scarlett barked at the door. Lacey let her in, and she went to the bowls at the end of the cabinet. "I guess you're ready to eat, huh?"

Regina stood. "I need to go give my sister a break. She's been with Mom all night." Fawn had told her that Regina's mother was in the late stages of dementia.

"I'm so sorry about your mom."

"Thanks." She walked toward the door. "I'll be back on shift later this evening. If I learn anything before then, I'll let you know."

"Thanks, Reg," Creed said.

She left, and Lacey filled the bowls with food and water, then scratched Scarlett's floppy ears. The dog sighed her contentment. "Why don't we go into town and start asking questions?" Lacey said. "I'll be ready when Scarlett's finished eating."

He nodded. "I'll drive, if that's all right with you."

"Fine with me. Do you mind if Scarlett comes? She'll be fine in the back seat. I have a seat-belt harness for her."

"Don't mind at all. Who do you want to start with?"

"Miranda Glenn. She and Fawn were close friends. If anyone knows what was going on with Fawn, it's her."

He nodded. "She has a new baby, so I feel like she's probably at home, but I'll call her on the way to make sure."

After Scarlett finished her last bite of food, Lacey snagged her lead and they followed Creed out to his cruiser. Lacey hooked Scarlett into the harness, then climbed into the passenger seat to fasten her own seat belt. Her stomach twisted at the thought of the upcoming questions she was going to have to ask people who'd known her all her life. The people who'd turned their noses up at her when her father went to prison. And one man in particular who'd screamed at her in the cafeteria of her high school.

Tucker Glenn, one of the lawyers of the only law firm in town. Miranda's husband had not been happy when he'd learned who was responsible for his father's sudden financial crisis. He'd gone ballistic, and she and Fawn had been his targets. She closed her eyes on the image and swallowed the nausea that rose each time she thought of that day he—

"You okay?"

Creed's question pulled her from the past. She sighed. "No, but I know, in time, I will be."

Creed cranked the SUV and backed out of her drive. Miranda and Tucker Glenn lived in a sprawling home just outside of town. Close enough for convenience, but with the illusion that they were in the middle of nowhere. Fawn had mentioned Tucker and Miranda had purchased the place three years ago. Lacey had never been inside the home she'd admired from afar as a youth, but Fawn had been a regular visitor after Miranda and Tucker became the new owners.

Creed called Miranda and got permission to stop by, but Lacey noticed he hadn't mentioned she was with him. They rode in not-quite-comfortable silence for a few minutes. Then he said, "I owe you an apology."

She blinked. "Why?"

"For refusing to tell you goodbye when you left."

She fell silent. "That really hurt," she finally said.

"I know."

"But I know I hurt you, too."

"You did." He sighed. "We hurt each other. We were young and stupid and immature. It's probably a good thing we went our separate ways. Not the way we did it, of course, but…" He shrugged. "It gave us some time to grow up."

She twisted her hands together in her lap. "Yes. I agree with that."

"For a long time after you left, I was angry. Seething. Hurting. And then something happened."

"What?"

He shot her a small smile. "I started to heal."

"Oh."

"And I…forgave." He lowered his eyes, then lifted them to meet hers, the softness there making her heart hitch. "After about a year," he said, "I was tired of carrying that load of anger around and decided the only way to move on was to let it go."

She swallowed. "I'm glad." But he still hadn't tried to get in touch with her. To clear the air.

"I know what you're thinking," he said. "Once I'd let go of the hurt, I had a burning need for closure, to make things right, but I was—"

"Afraid?" She clamped her lips together. Would she never stop interrupting the man?

He cleared his throat. "*Unsure* of my reception should I reach out to you." He paused. "Okay, yes, *afraid* is probably accurate."

Most likely, she would have hung up on him or slammed the door in his face. After his massive rejection, the initial pain had morphed into a raging anger that she'd been unable to let go of for a long time. A fact she was definitely not proud of. "At that point in time," she said, "you were wise to keep your distance."

He nodded. "I'd talked to Fawn—"

"You did? She never said." She grimaced. She'd interrupted him. Again. "Sorry."

"I finally convinced her to listen to me." He rubbed a hand over his mouth and sighed. "I asked her how you were doing and if you still hated me."

"I never hated you." Much.

"Fawn talked about you a lot. She showed me pictures with your dogs and how happy you were." He shook his head and kept his gaze on the road. "I couldn't call you after seeing that. My need for closure was just that— *mine*. Fawn made it clear that you'd moved on and contact with me would be an unwelcome disruption."

Lacey's jaw dropped. Literally. When she could speak, she snapped her mouth shut while she struggled for words. "She never said," she finally croaked out. "She never said a word to me about that."

He nodded. "I asked her not to." His gaze met hers once more. "But I want to know something."

"What?"

He pulled to the curb in front of the Glenns' home. When he cut the engine, he didn't move to get out, but looked at her. "Are you still holding on to the past anger and hurt?"

"No." She wasn't, was she? "But don't ask me for a specific moment in time when I made the conscious decision to move on. I buried myself in work, stayed busy day and night. I'd fall into bed on the few hours I took off and sleep like the dead. At some point, the pain faded, but my work habits didn't." She shot him a rueful smile. "I became known as the one who'd take the extra shift or train 'just one more' dog. The only time I took off work was when Fawn came to visit."

"But you never once came to visit her."

"No."

"Why?"

She gave a silent mental groan but refused to lie to him. "There were a lot of reasons, but mostly because I didn't want to run into you."

The words shouldn't have carried as much punch as they did, but they struck a raw nerve and Creed flinched.

"So," she said, "maybe I wasn't quite as over everything as I liked to think." Her words were low, almost a whisper.

Okay, that helped ease the pain a bit.

"Throughout the first couple of years," she said, "I picked up the phone many times to call you, but then stopped. I told myself the ball was in your court. I'd apologized, asked you to talk, and you'd opted not to. The fact that I never heard from you seemed to indicate you hadn't changed your mind, so I think I just...gave up. Convinced myself you'd never forgive me."

"I'm sorry, Lacey." His husky voice vibrated between them. "I really am."

She gazed at him, her eyes shiny with unshed tears, but she nodded. "I am, too."

"So…" He held out a hand. "Friends?"

"Yeah." She clasped his fingers and her soft touch sent shivers through him. Just like old times. He smiled and she squeezed. "Friends."

He let go of her hand and immediately wanted to grab it back, rewind and tell her he still wanted more than friendship, but for now, they had work to do. And then she'd go home. So…friends it would have to be. For now—and probably forever.

Lacey unhooked Scarlett from her harness and the dog jumped down to shake herself. Then she looked at Lacey as though asking, "What now?"

Creed laughed. "She's got some expressions, doesn't she?"

"It's funny, isn't it," Lacey said. "I can usually figure out what she's thinking."

"Yeah, you were always good at being able to read anything that breathed," he said. Especially him. He remembered the times they communicated with a simple look, then cleared his throat and let Lacey and Scarlett lead the way up the steps to the door. He stayed close behind her, protecting her from anyone who might decide to take another shot at her. Then again, if the shooter had simply been trying to distract them from finding Fawn's body, the reason to shoot at them no longer existed.

But…no need to take any chances.

Lacey knocked. A firm rap that would get someone's attention inside, but hopefully soft enough not to startle a sleeping newborn.

Footsteps sounded from inside and then the door opened. Miranda held her baby in the crook of her left arm. When her gaze landed on him, she frowned. When she saw his companion, she gasped. "Lacey Lee Jefferson? Are you kidding me?"

"Hi, Miranda. Just Lacey, please."

She eyed Creed. "You didn't say anything about bringing Lacey."

"Sorry. Is it okay?" He'd simply told her he needed to talk to her about a few things, but had been intentionally vague.

"Of course. But what's going on?"

"I wanted to ask you some questions about Fawn," Lacey said.

"Fawn?" Miranda shifted the sleeping infant to her shoulder and backed up. "Um…okay, but can you leave the dog outside? I'm not a fan."

Lacey raised a brow, then glanced at Creed. "I'll just go put her back in the car."

"I'm sorry," Miranda said, "but I don't want the dog around the baby and…dogs make me nervous."

"Of course."

"While you do that, I'm going to go answer my phone. I can hear it ringing."

She walked away and Creed unlocked the car. Lacey ordered Scarlett back into her seat, then scratched the dog's ears. "Stay here, girl. You'll be fine for a few minutes."

The dog heaved a sigh and lay down across the seat to settle her nose between her paws.

Lacey rejoined Creed on the porch.

"She doesn't seem happy about being left behind," he said.

"She's not, but she'll be okay." She glanced at him. "And don't think I make a habit of leaving her in a vehicle—I'm only doing so because the weather is cold and we're only going to be a few minutes. If it was summer, I'd never do it."

"It never crossed my mind that you would."

Miranda appeared and opened the storm door once more. "Come on in." She kept her voice soft, almost a whisper.

Lacey and Creed stepped into her foyer.

"Let me just put TJ down." Miranda walked to the bassinet located next to the recliner, lowered the baby into it, then gestured for them to have a seat on the couch. "He's a good baby. Sleeps through just about everything—except at night, of course."

"TJ?" Lacey asked when she was settled.

"Tucker Junior." Miranda smiled. Beamed, actually. "Tucker's always wanted a son named after him. Now he has one."

"Congratulations," Creed said.

"Thank you." She continued to smile as though the baby had turned on a light inside of her. "We have a lot of plans for this little one. Tucker can't wait for TJ to be old enough to start grooming him for a successful law career. He's already designed the logo for the office. Glenn and Glenn, Attorneys at Law."

Creed blinked. "What if TJ doesn't want to be a lawyer?"

Miranda laughed and flashed a tight smile. "Of course he will. Why wouldn't he?"

Creed had nothing to say that wouldn't sound harsh, so he just bit his tongue and nodded.

"You look amazing," Lacey said, breaking into the awkward moment. "Clean hair, makeup and dressed. You're a superwoman."

Miranda chuckled. "For the first time in over a week.

When my mother was here helping, it was fairly easy. She never wanted to let go of him. But this morning, I told Tucker he wasn't going to work—and definitely not meeting up with his hunting buddies—until I had a shower and felt human again." She sat in the recliner and folded her hands in her lap. "What did you want to ask me about in regard to Fawn?"

"Have you seen her lately?"

Miranda frowned. "No, but that's not unusual. She stays so busy with the hospital these days that we can go several days without talking and weeks without getting together. We do text often, though."

"When's the last time you talked to her in person?" Creed asked.

Miranda tapped her lips. "Two weeks ago? No, that's not right. Last week? Monday, maybe?" She sighed. "I'm sorry. Days are blending together right now. She came by to see TJ shortly after he was born and then said she was going to be busy playing catch-up at work—she was involved in some kind of research project—and it might be a while before she could get back. I told her I had six weeks—then I was meeting her at the gym as soon as I was cleared. She laughed and told me to take advantage of my 'enforced exercise downtime.'" The woman shrugged. "That was on the day she came to see TJ, which was the day after he was born, so, yes, about two weeks ago. I'm sorry. I haven't really thought about it, to be honest. Having a newborn is a lot more work than I ever imagined, and I don't have time to think, much less process time." She shot a loving look at the baby. "But I wouldn't change a thing."

"So, you saw her during the three months she took off work?"

Miranda frowned. "No, I didn't. I just saw her after TJ was born. We texted quite a bit while she was on her sabbatical—wherever that was—but I didn't see her. I don't think anyone did."

"Did she say where she was?"

"No." She pursed her lips. "And I could tell she didn't want to talk about it, so I didn't press her. I figured she'd tell me in her own time."

"I'm sure." Creed leaned forward. "Do you know if Fawn was having any trouble with anyone in town or at work?"

"Trouble?" Miranda raised a brow. "Not that I can think of right off. Why?"

Lacey met Creed's gaze, then flicked back to Miranda. "You haven't heard?" Lacey asked.

Miranda's expression changed. She frowned again, worry flickering in her eyes. "No. Heard what? Why are you asking all these questions about Fawn?"

SEVEN

"Fawn's dead, Miranda," Creed said softly.

Miranda blinked at him. "What? No, she's not."

"I just assumed you saw the paper."

"I don't do anything but take care of a baby and try to sleep when he does, so no, I haven't seen the paper. Please, what are you talking about? How can she be dead?"

"We found her...body—" Lacey could barely say the word without choking "—yesterday. I'd been trying to get in touch with her, and when I couldn't—and I couldn't get you on the phone or a straight answer from her work—I came to find her."

Miranda's hand lifted as though in slow motion to cover her mouth while her eyes filled with tears. "What? No. That's not possible. I just...saw her. Talked to her. Didn't I?"

"Like you said, you've probably lost all sense of time." Lacey paused. "Why didn't you call me back? I left you a couple of messages."

"I... I didn't get any messages." She pushed her hands into her hair, then smoothed it down and shook her head. "I'm just not on my phone much these days. Half the time I can't even find it. Did you try to get Tucker?"

"No. I didn't…have his number."

Creed shot her a quick look, and she avoided his eyes. She could have gotten the number. She'd just wanted to try every other avenue first. Fawn hadn't really cared for Tucker ever since he'd yelled at her and Lacey about their father stealing his family's money. And she'd thought Miranda deserved better. Lacey agreed. But, for the sake of keeping the peace and seeing her friend, Fawn and Tucker had learned to tolerate each other—although Fawn said he would throw in a snide comment about their father whenever he got the chance. Fawn ignored him.

By the time Lacey had been ready to break down and call Tucker about Fawn's lack of communication, she'd already known she was going to have to come back to Timber Creek to find Fawn herself.

The baby stirred and let out a soft cry. Miranda jumped to her feet and picked him up. "I need to feed him."

Creed stood. "We'll get out of your way, then. Do you mind calling if you think of anything else?"

"Of course I will."

"Thanks, Miranda," Lacey said. "One more question. What gym did you and Fawn go to? I never heard her mention a specific one, just that she was trying to be good about working out on a regular basis in order to keep her stress levels under control."

"It's Mike's Gym on South Main Street."

"Thanks." Lacey noted the woman's tenderness in holding the baby, and a pang of longing shot through her. She'd always wanted children—and had thought she and Creed would be raising them together. When they went their separate ways, that dream had withered and died. She forced a smile. "It was good to see you." Strangely, she meant the words.

"You, too, Lacey."

Once they were back in Creed's cruiser—and Scarlett had an appropriate belly rub that earned her forgiveness for being left behind—he looked at her. "Bit of a controlling person, isn't she? Miranda, not Scarlett."

"Ha. You think? I wonder what she'll do if TJ decides to be an artist instead of a lawyer."

"I'm not sure I want to be around to see that reaction." He paused. "You okay?"

She shot him a small smile. "You don't have to keep asking me that, you know."

"Okay, sorry."

"And you don't have to apologize for asking either. But thanks for being concerned." A sigh slipped from her. "I'm okay at the moment. Being proactive in searching for Fawn's killer—albeit unofficially—helps." She paused. "I was worried how Miranda would feel seeing me on her doorstep."

"She seemed a little hesitant at first, but warmed up pretty quickly."

"I guess Tucker's dislike of me doesn't extend to Miranda."

Creed had been there for part of Tucker's verbal tirade in the lunchroom at the high school her senior year. Fawn had come to eat lunch with her, and Tucker had walked in and let them have it. Fawn had yelled back and told him off, but Lacey had sat there, feeling the wound of each word Tucker hurled.

Creed had arrived late to lunch and walked in on the tail end of everything. Lacey had managed to hold on to her tears until the school resource officer hauled Tucker away from the area. She'd even managed to convince Fawn she was fine until her sister left. Then Creed had ushered Lacey out to his car and held her while she'd wept.

His hand covered hers, pulling her out of the memory, and she could tell he'd been remembering that shared moment from their past, as well. "You were always there for me, Creed," she said. "You always had my back." Until he hadn't. She cleared her throat. "All right, what's next?"

"The hospital."

"I've talked to everyone Fawn ever mentioned from her work."

"What about her supervisor?"

"Yes, him, too. He was less than helpful, just sounded like he had more on his plate than he knew what to do with."

"Okay, I've done the paperwork for the subpoena on her credit cards, her bank stuff and her phone records. I'm just waiting on that to come back."

Lacey pressed her palms to her eyes. "If I knew where to find that stuff, I'd just give it to you. Then again, she may have paid all of her bills and stuff online, and I'm not sure I can figure out the passwords."

"It's okay. It shouldn't be much longer."

Lacey paused. "Come to think of it, I don't remember seeing her laptop anywhere. I'll go through her desk when I get home. In the meantime, why don't we head to the gym before we go to the hospital? It's only about a mile from here."

"And not too far from the café," he said. "Want to grab a bite to eat afterward?"

"Sure."

When Creed pulled into the parking lot of the gym, Lacey swallowed a surge of emotion. Fawn had always been big into working out and staying in shape, but once she'd started at the hospital, she'd gotten out of the habit of going. About a year ago, she'd told Lacey about her renewed efforts in the gym. "You should come home and join me."

"I don't need a gym. I have the dogs."

"You just don't want to come home."

"Timber Creek's not my home anymore."

"I know," Fawn had said, "but a sister can hope, can't she?"

"Lacey? Hello? You there?"

Creed waved a hand in front of her eyes and she blinked. Heat crept into her cheeks. "I'm sorry. I was just thinking that Fawn wanted me to come home. Move home for good. I balked, of course. Wouldn't even consider it." She frowned. "Maybe if I hadn't been so… selfish…she'd still be alive."

"What do you mean? Give up the job you love and move back to a town you hate because your sister asked you to?"

She huffed a short laugh. "Well, when you put it like that…" She paused. "Sounds kind of silly, doesn't it?"

"A little."

"And, I have to admit, coming home hasn't been nearly as traumatic as I thought it would be—discounting Fawn's death." That was about as traumatic as one could get. "I'm just talking about the townspeople. Everyone has been so…nice." Of course, she hadn't run into a whole lot of people yet.

"Welcoming?"

"Yes. Fawn said…"

"Said what?"

"…said I should give the town a second chance, that I'd built it up so much in my head as a horrid place with no one good here." Tears wanted to flow once more. "I wish I'd listened to her," she finally said on a whisper.

"No one blames you or Fawn for what your father did. He's the one who stole money and blamed it on bad investments, not you." She shot him a sideways glance of disbelief and he sighed. "Okay, there may be a few individuals with misplaced anger, but the majority don't."

She nodded. "I think I'm starting to see that." She turned to Scarlett. "Sorry, girl. You have to stay here this time, too."

Scarlett hesitated as though she couldn't believe Lacey was doing this to her again. "You'll be fine. Rest while you can. We could get a call at any time."

The dog tilted her head, realized she wasn't going and dropped onto the seat with a huff. When she turned her head away from Lacey, Lacey bit her lip on a smile and looked at Creed. "Guess she gets an extra-long belly rub when we get back."

He shook his head. "She's not a happy girl."

"She'll be fine."

He followed her into the gym and Lacey made her way to the desk. A young man in his late twenties shot her a dimpled smile. "Hi. Welcome to Mike's. Sheriff Payne, good to see you." He returned his attention to Lacey. "I don't think I've seen you around. What can I do for you?"

Lacey ignored his flirty smile. "Hi, Mike. I'm Lacey Jefferson. Do you know my sister, Fawn?"

"Of course. She's a regular. Or was. I haven't seen her in forever."

"When was the last time she was here?"

"Let me just check the computer." He shook the mouse, clicked a few keys, then looked up. "She was here a little over three months ago."

Lacey shot a look at Creed. "There's that three-month time frame once more."

"Something wrong?" Mike asked.

"She's dead," Creed said. "Someone…murdered her."

"*Murdered* her?" Mike's eyes had gone wide and his jaw swung open. He finally snapped it shut. "But…how? Why?"

Keeping her emotions under control, she gave him the short version. "Now we're working on figuring out the why. And the who. Can you tell us anyone she might have had an issue with?"

"Not an issue bad enough to kill her over." He frowned and shook his head. "No, no one comes to mind. Everyone loved Fawn." He rubbed a hand down his face, then paused. "She has a locker here. Do you want to take a look?"

Lacey raised a brow. "Yes. Absolutely."

"I don't know the combination to her lock."

"I've got bolt cutters in the SUV," Creed said. "Hang tight while I grab them." He left and returned in under a minute. "Where's the locker?"

Mike nodded toward the hallway. "Down there. Women's on the right, men's on the left." He consulted the computer once more. "She paid via a monthly draft for locker number six." He drew in a breath. "Hey, wait a minute. I just thought of someone you might want to talk to."

Creed raised a brow. "Who?"

"Gracie Martin. She's a trainer here. She and Fawn often worked out together. Gracie also works in the membership office. Maybe Fawn talked to her?"

"Is Gracie here now?"

"Yeah. She's in the office. Two doors before you get to the women's locker room."

Lacey hesitated, then held out a hand for the bolt cutters. "I'll take the locker. You take Gracie Martin. Is that all right?"

"Sure." Creed handed her the cutters. "That'll keep us from having to clear out the ladies' locker room so I can be in there."

"Take notes," Lacey told him. "I'm going to want a word-for-word replay. Please?"

"You got it." He followed her down the hall and stopped at the membership office door. Lacey waited until he stepped inside and introduced himself to the young woman at the desk before she pushed into the locker room. Straight ahead were the toilets. To the right were several rows of lockers. Behind the lockers were the showers and the sauna. The place smelled of hair spray, shampoo and sweat.

One of the showers was running, and another woman Lacey had never seen before stood in front of the mirror, drying her hair.

Lacey bypassed her, searched for locker number six and cut the bolt off just as the hair-drying woman finished up. She turned to watch, her eyes wide. "What are you doing?"

"It's okay," Lacey said. "I'm a cop." She pulled her jacket away from the badge she'd clipped on her belt.

"Oh. Okay. For a minute there—"

"Yeah. It's all good."

The woman tossed her brush into her bag, snagged it and headed for the door.

Lacey opened the locker door. Her sister's scent—a mixture of her strawberry shampoo and her light perfume—wafted out to bring the tears to the surface once more. A picture of the two of them was taped to the inside of the door. They stood at the edge of the lake, arms across each other's shoulders, beaming at the camera.

Lacey remembered that day like it was yesterday. Her father had been in good spirits and whisked them away to the lake for a fun afternoon of tubing and swimming. She had no idea where her mother had been, but the good memory of her father was there before she could cut it off.

"Aw, Fawn, that's so you." A picture to remind her of the good times so she wouldn't dwell on the bad. "I wish I was more like you, sis."

The door to the room opened and the woman from the shower exited, but Lacey barely registered that as she forced herself from memory lane to pull the gym bag—the only other item in the locker—from the opening.

She carried it to the bench and unzipped it to reveal the contents. A clean change of clothing consisting of a long-sleeved T-shirt, leggings, socks and a pair of tennis shoes. She also found shampoo, a towel, hair dryer—and a set of keys. Lacey frowned. That was odd. Why the keys? Seemed like Fawn would have kept them with her. Unless they were a spare set that she wanted to keep in a safe place?

The squeak of a shoe on the tile near the showers caught her attention, and she looked up just as the lights went out.

Lacey stilled, her hand tightening around the material of the bag. "Hello? Someone's in here." Silence. "Can you turn the lights back on, please?"

Nothing.

Then her ears picked up the sound of soft breathing. She curled her fingers around the keys and threaded them through her knuckles. The only light in the area came from the hair dryers mounted on the wall. The built-in "night-light" cut through the shadows in that area while Lacey was in pitch-black darkness.

She grabbed Fawn's bag and headed away from the door she'd entered and aimed herself for the emergency exit. The door that would sound an alarm as soon as she pushed through it.

Just as she reached for the handle, something slammed into her back. The bag dropped from her hand and she let out a sharp cry. Pain raced into her shoulders, and she found herself shoved against the wall, cheek pressed tightly against the unforgiving surface. She couldn't even move the hand that held the keys. "Stop!"

"Go back where you came from or you're going to find yourself as dead as your sister. This is the last warning you'll get."

"Did you shoot at me?" She gasped the question.

"Yeah, and next time I won't miss." He flung her to the ground and pushed out the door.

When the alarm sounded, Creed stood. So did Gracie, the woman who'd promised she had no idea who might have it in for Fawn. "Where's that coming from?" he asked.

"The women's locker room. Someone went out the emergency exit."

"Lacey!" He bolted out of the office and hit the door to the locker room, only to pull up short when he realized the lights were off. "Lacey!"

His shout echoed through the empty area and he bee-lined toward the exit. He reached the door and raced through it into the back alley. The fading roar of a motorcycle reached him and the alarm abruptly cut off.

"Lacey!"

"I'm here." She rounded the corner at the back of the building, weapon in hand.

"Are you okay?"

"I'm fine, but he got away."

"Who got away?"

"The guy who attacked me in the locker room."

Creed's heart dropped. "*Attacked* you? I need details, please."

"The lights went out. I heard him near the bathroom and bolted for the emergency exit. He caught me and slammed me into the wall." She touched her cheek and he noted the red area.

"Then what?"

"He ran out of the emergency door. I chased him and he jumped on a motorcycle and took off." She pointed to the camera mounted above the door. "We need the footage from that camera."

He nodded. "I'll request it."

He also put a BOLO out on the motorcycle, then turned back to her. "Did you have time to look in Fawn's locker?"

"Yes, but I don't think it's going to tell us much." She paused. "Although, there was a bag with a set of keys in it." She lifted her hand as though surprised to see she still clutched the keys. "I dropped the bag."

"Let's get it and see if you missed anything." Her color was returning and her breathing had evened out. "Feeling better?"

"A lot. He said for me to go back where I came from and that this was the *last* warning I'd get." She met his gaze. "I asked him if he was the shooter. He said he was and next time he wouldn't miss."

"Whoa."

"I know."

"And you didn't get a look at him at all?"

"No." She paused and gave him the once-over. "But he's probably an inch or two taller than you. He was solid. He pressed me up against the wall—" a shudder rippled through her and Creed wanted to get his hands on the guy "—and he didn't have an ounce of fat on him," she said. "He was strong. Very strong." She rubbed her sore arm. "He threw me around like I was a rag doll, and I'm not exactly tiny."

No, she was five feet seven inches and probably in the range of a hundred and forty or fifty pounds. Not exactly rag-doll status.

"But," she said, "I guess that answers one question."

"What?"

"Sounds like Fawn wasn't the victim of some random intruder who killed her and moved on. There's something else going on here."

"I agree." Creed rubbed a hand down his cheek. "All right, we need to regroup." He thought for a moment. "We're doing the right thing in talking to people here in town, but you need to keep searching the house."

"I know."

He nodded to the keys in her hand. "And I want to know what those go to."

"There are only four. It shouldn't be too hard to figure out what they fit." She held them up. "This one looks like an extra house key." She moved to the next one. "This looks like a key to her mailbox, maybe? I noticed she had a new one with a lock, and this key looks fairly new." She held up the third key. "No idea what this one could be, but this last one is similar to the one that might be a mailbox key."

"Does she have a home office? A desk drawer or a file cabinet?"

"Yes, I saw a desk in her guest room. I'll check and see if there's a lock when I go back. I'll also be looking for any current bank records or credit card statements." She touched her cheek and worked her jaw.

"You need to get checked out at the hospital?"

"Nope. I'm fine. Just sore. Did Gracie tell you anything?"

"Not much. She did say Fawn seemed to have something on her mind. When Gracie asked her about it, she said she had a big decision to make and wasn't sure what to do about it."

"But no details?"

"No. Gracie said she asked, but Fawn brushed her off."

"A big decision," Lacey said slowly. "I have no idea what that could be."

"We'll find out."

"Yes," she said, drawing in a deep breath. "Yes, we will. In the meantime, I know one thing for sure."

He raised a brow. "What's that?"

"From now on, wherever I go, Scarlett does, too."

"I think that's probably wise."

EIGHT

Lacey's phone rang and she snatched it to look at the screen. "It's Katherine."

"Go ahead and take the call while I take care of getting the footage," Creed said.

She nodded and swiped the screen while she followed him back into the gym. "Hello?"

"Hi, Lacey. I'm sorry to bother you, but I heard about Fawn and I'm so sorry."

"Thank you, Katherine. I appreciate it."

"I remembered something and I wasn't sure whether I should repeat it or not, but in light of Fawn's death, I'm going to do something I try never to do."

"What is it?"

"It's a rumor floating around the hospital about Fawn being involved with another doctor."

"Involved? Define *involved*."

"I'm not sure exactly *how* involved, but the rumor implied they were seeing each other. Like dating."

"Fawn never mentioned that to me. Who is he?"

"I don't know. I don't even remember where I heard it from. I don't like gossip and try not to listen to it. However, I have a friend who admired Fawn from a distance.

He wanted me to find out if she was dating anyone while he worked up the nerve to ask her out."

"Who?"

"His name is Kevin Garrison. Anyway, I spotted Fawn at the hospital about a year ago and asked her if she was interested in being set up on a blind date. She said no because she was seeing someone. But said to ask her again in a couple of months because she wasn't sure her current relationship was going anywhere."

"But she was definitely seeing someone."

"Yes. She said it was complicated and she was still trying to figure things out."

Complicated. Awesome.

"Did she say what she meant by *complicated*?"

"No," Katherine said, "and I didn't press her for details because we didn't have that kind of friendship. I did offer to listen if she ever wanted to talk about it, but we never spoke of it again after that conversation."

"Okay, thank you. I appreciate you calling."

A hospital page in the background came through the line. "I've got to go."

"I heard. Thank you again." Katherine hung up and Lacey tucked her phone into the back pocket of her pants.

"What was that all about?" Creed asked.

She told him. "Feel like a visit to the hospital to see if we can figure out who this doctor might be?"

He nodded to her cheek. "If you'll let someone check you out."

"I don't need to be checked out, Creed. I'm fine."

"This time."

She sighed. "Right. Well, he achieved his goal. He scared me to death and issued his warning. I guess he'll be watching to see if I leave town or not."

"Which you're not."

She shot him a tight smile. "You know me so well." His eyes darkened, and a flash of longing made her want to reach out to him. To say they could figure out their differences and try again. Instead, she curled her fingers into a hard fist. He looked away and cleared his throat and the moment was gone.

"Also," he said, "you know those three names you found written on the paper from Fawn's pocket?"

"Yes?"

"I just got a text from Regina. She was running them down for me, and they all work at the same hospital in Charlotte, but they're heads of different departments."

She frowned. "Okay. Why would she have their names?"

"I don't know, but I'm going to hazard a guess that Fawn was interviewing for jobs."

"What? No. Fawn loved her job in the ER here. I can't imagine her wanting to leave."

He narrowed his eyes at her. "I hate to say this, Lacey, but it sounds like Fawn was living a very different life than the one she led you to believe."

Lacey scoffed, then fell silent. "But why?" she finally asked.

"That, I can't answer."

She bit her lip and frowned at him. "You think the job was the big decision she had to make? The one she mentioned to Gracie?"

"I'd say that's a real possibility."

Once they were all back in his vehicle, he aimed it toward the hospital. He glanced at her. "Who did you talk to when you called to ask about Fawn?"

"Her supervisor."

"Anyone else?"

"One of Fawn's coworkers, Dr. Jill Holloway, but she said she hadn't seen Fawn since she'd taken her sabbatical. She said she was off the two days Fawn worked before she disappeared." She frowned. "She was also going to check with someone else who was close to Fawn, but by the time I left home to come here, we hadn't connected again. She was one of the first people I'd planned to talk to after you and Miranda, but…well…you know how things played out."

"I do." He pulled into the parking spot reserved for law enforcement and they climbed out of his cruiser. Lacey released Scarlett from the back, buckled her "uniform" around her identifying her as a working dog, and they pushed through the revolving door.

Lacey and Creed walked to the information desk, where Pauline Coulson, a woman in her midsixties who'd taught Lacey's fifth-grade Sunday school class, spoke into a headset. "Transferring you now." When she hung up, she smiled. "Creed, so good to see you." Her gaze slid to Lacey and her smile into an expression of deep sorrow—and not a hint of condemnation. "Lacey Lee Jefferson? Oh, my dear, I'm so sorry to hear about Fawn."

"Thank you." Word had spread. Lacey refused to allow the tears to surface once more. "I'm heartbroken, as you can imagine."

"Indeed. Everyone who knew Fawn has just been shattered by her death. What can I do for you?"

"We're here to speak to Dr. Jill Holloway. She worked with Fawn. Is she here today?" He glanced at Lacey. "Guess we should have checked on that before coming out here."

Mrs. Coulson turned to her computer, and after a few clicks, she looked up. "She is. She's in the emergency department." Her frown deepened the creases in her forehead. "Is there anything I can do?"

"When was the last time you talked to Fawn?" Lacey asked.

"Her first day back from her leave. I was hoping she'd enjoyed her sabbatical, but it didn't look like she had a very good time."

"Why?"

She shrugged. "She was wan and pale. And she seemed sad."

"So not sick?"

"No, she didn't seem sick, just not her usual bubbly self."

"Do you know what she was possibly sad about?"

"I have no idea. She always said hello and we chatted occasionally, but we weren't close."

"Okay, thank you." Lacey noticed the cafeteria to her right and the three lab-coated figures walking into it. "Mrs. Coulson, you have a pretty good view of the cafeteria. Did you notice anyone Fawn ate her meals with? Anyone who stood out to you?" Like a male doctor she could have been involved with? Lacey kept that last thought to herself.

Mrs. Coulson rubbed her chin. "No, can't say I ever thought about it. She'd go in there with a lot of different people from various departments. Sometimes with nurses, other times doctors. Most of the time with Dr. Holloway." She shook her head. "But no one specific person who made an impression on me."

"Thank you, Mrs. Coulson," Creed said. "Appreciate your help."

The woman came around the counter to hug Lacey. "Please let me know if there's anything I can do for you."

Lacey smiled and patted her shoulder. "Thank you." She clicked to Scarlett and headed for the ER before she completely broke down. She didn't have time for tears. Fawn needed her to get her justice.

Creed stepped up beside her on the other side of Scarlett. "Do you know Dr. Holloway?"

"No. Fawn said she was new to town. She's only been here about a year, I think."

They walked to the doors of the ER and Lacey prepared herself to see people she hadn't talked to since she'd left town. "Why don't you see if Jill can talk to us anytime soon?"

Creed nodded. "Sure." He went to the desk and chatted with a man who looked familiar, but Lacey couldn't place him. When Creed nodded to her, she and Scarlett followed him and the worker through the electronic doors and into the back.

"Come this way," the man said. "You can wait in the conference room. I'll let Dr. Holloway know you're here." His eyes met Lacey's for a brief second, and she blinked at the expression in them. Judgment and disdain.

So, there it was.

Lacey took a seat at the table and Scarlett lay down next to her. "Who was that?" Lacey asked Creed once he was seated across from her.

"Tucker Glenn's brother, James."

"That was *James*? I didn't recognize him, but that explains the look."

"I noticed that, too. I was hoping it went past you."

She raised a brow at him. "If I wasn't looking for it in every person I come across, then maybe I wouldn't have seen it, but…" She shrugged.

"You look for it."

She pulled in a deep breath and nodded. "I do." She glanced back at him. "It was bad in high school, Creed."

"I knew it was at first," he said, "after your father was arrested. But as time went by, it seemed to get better."

She sighed. "If it did, I couldn't tell. Everywhere I went, I felt like people were watching. Judging. Waiting for me to lift something from their shops, snatch their purse at church or…whatever. I told you about it."

He studied her and then pursed his lips. "Yes. And I apologize again that I didn't take it as seriously as I should have." He leaned forward and clasped her hands. "I really am sorry."

For a brief moment, Lacey allowed herself to enjoy the warmth of his touch, to remember walking hand in hand on the path around the lake, those stolen summer moments that she cherished but couldn't think about too often without the pain of her loss overwhelming her. Before she could answer, the door opened and a woman about Fawn's age stepped into the room. Her eyes were red-rimmed as though she'd been crying and had just managed to get her tears under control. "Hi, I'm Jill Holloway. James said you needed to talk to me."

"Do you have a moment to sit down?" Creed asked.

"A brief one." She slid into the chair at the end of the table and looked at Scarlett. "Beautiful dog. Fawn told me a lot about your K-9 job. She was very proud of you."

"Thank you," Lacey said, ignoring the way her throat wanted to close and the tears threatened to fall. "You and I talked a bit on the phone, but then you were called away to an emergency."

"I remember, but I told you everything I know." She swiped a tissue under her eyes. "Sorry. I'd just heard about her death before James found me. Our supervisor called a quick meeting to let us know. I'm so sorry."

"Thank you. It's been a shock for sure." *Focus, Lacey. Get her justice. Then you can grieve.* "How well did you know her?"

"Really well. We told each other everything." She frowned. "At least, almost everything."

"Then you know where she was those three months that she seems to have dropped off the earth?"

"No. That's what I meant by *almost*." She sniffed. "She said she was taking a leave of absence, but wouldn't tell me where she was going. She texted every so often to let me know she was okay, but other than that, I don't have a clue what she was doing."

"That doesn't sound like Fawn," Lacey said. But then, a lot of things weren't sounding like her sister. At this point, she was starting to wonder if she even knew her. "Another friend of Fawn's said she was seeing someone. A doctor. Do you know who that might have been?"

Jill's eyes widened a fraction. "Um, no. Sorry. I don't know who he is."

"But you knew she was seeing someone." Lacey leaned in. "Come on, Dr. Holloway… Jill… Fawn's dead and someone killed her. When you and I talked on the phone a couple of days ago, she was only missing. But now things are real, and I want to know who killed her. If you know whom she was dating, then, please, tell me. I'm not going to accuse him of anything, but I—" She glanced at Creed. "*We* would like to talk to him."

The woman sighed and looked at her watch. "I don't know who it was. I promise. But yes, it was someone here at the hospital, I think. When we were working the same shift, I'd cover for her every so often so she could meet him."

"Meet him where?"

"I don't know. I asked her once and she said it was better if I didn't know."

Well, that didn't sound good. "Was he married?"

"Honestly, I don't know, but...that was my first thought, too. I even asked her, and she just said she wasn't ready to talk about it yet."

"Did you know she planned on leaving the hospital?" Creed asked. "That she was interviewing with a hospital in Charlotte?"

Jill frowned. "What? No, she wasn't. What makes you say that?"

He held up his phone. "My deputy Regina just texted and said she'd talked to two of the men. They've confirmed Fawn had interviews with each of them. They were done online."

"When?"

"One was two months ago, and one was three weeks ago."

Jill sat back in her chair and stared at Creed. "She didn't tell me."

"She didn't tell me either," Lacey said. "On the phone, you said there was someone else who could possibly tell me more."

"Dr. Charles Rhodes," she said. "I don't know what he can tell you, but he and Fawn were working together on a new project. I'm not sure of all the details, but part of it was a trial drug to help Alzheimer patients."

"Thank you."

Jill stood. "If I think of anything else, I'll let you know." Tears rose to the surface once more. "I'm so sorry about Fawn."

"Thank you."

And then she was gone, leaving Lacey and Creed looking at each other.

"Dr. Rhodes?" Creed asked.

Lacey rose and gathered Scarlett's leash. "Let's go."

Creed had let Lacey carry that conversation without interrupting because she'd spoken to the doctor already. And he'd wanted to watch Jill's facial expressions and body language. All of which had come across as open and honest, with nothing to hide. None of which was very helpful, except to rule her out in his mind as being a suspect.

On the way down the hall, Creed placed a hand on Lacey's arm and she stopped to look at him. "I need you to back off at this point."

"But, Creed—"

"I'm serious, Lacey. Up to this point, I can explain your presence in the investigation. Fawn and Miranda were friends and it's natural that you would talk to her about Fawn. While the locker at the gym might be a tad harder to justify, it's not impossible. Even talking to Dr. Holloway, Jill, was slightly okay since you'd already spoken with her. But this is a different situation."

She visibly struggled with his words, then finally nodded. "All right. I'll keep my mouth shut and let you do this. Just don't make me sit outside. Please."

He sighed and nodded. "Only if you promise not to interfere in the questioning."

"I promise."

Dr. Rhodes was in a meeting when they arrived at his office, but the administrative assistant told them she thought he would be finished soon and they could wait if they wanted.

They wanted.

Seated on the couch, Creed looked around. "Well, this is nice," he murmured, glancing at the decor.

"He's got an administrative assistant and everything," Lacey said just as softly. "I take it he's not a regular doc."

"No, looks like he's at the top of the food chain."

Scarlett nudged Lacey's hand and she scratched the dog's ears. "Are you bored, girl?"

Creed smiled. "She's been very patient."

"She has a really good temperament. I found her in a local shelter, just sitting behind the fence, staring at me with those big dark eyes. She was one of those rare finds where you know she's just the one you've been looking for."

"Yeah, I know about those kinds of finds." His eyes held hers, and when her cheeks instantly turned pink, he knew she'd gotten the message behind his words.

"You can go in now." The woman behind the desk spoke and Lacey shot to her feet. Creed and Scarlett rose and followed her into Dr. Rhodes's office.

The man had entered through a different door and was already seated behind the mammoth-sized desk. He stood and shook their hands while Creed introduced them. He settled in his chair once more, then gestured for them to have a seat on the couch that faced him. "What can I do for you?"

"I'm sure you've heard about Fawn Jefferson by now. That she was found murdered."

The man swallowed. "Yes. I'd heard."

"I believe you knew her?" Creed asked.

The man paused a fraction, then folded his hands on top of the desk and nodded. "I knew Fawn very well. In a professional capacity, of course, but the more I worked with her, the more I came to appreciate her as a person. As a friend and colleague. She was a brilliant woman. But…why are you asking me about her?"

"Your name was given to me during a routine questioning of one of her friends."

"I see."

"So, do you know of someone she was seeing?" Creed asked. "Dating? Rumor has it that she was involved with another doctor here at the hospital, but she was keeping the relationship secret for whatever reason."

He frowned. "I can't imagine why she'd keep it a secret, unless it would have been a conflict of interest or something. There's no policy that says doctors can't date. There *is* a policy that says you have to sign a statement that you're in a romantic relationship with someone you work with, but I'm not sure how many people actually do it."

"Well, if she was wanting to keep the relationship a secret, she wouldn't fill out a form announcing it," Creed said. "Did she confide in you as to why she was taking off for three months?"

"She didn't. She just said she had some personal issues she needed to take care of, and she'd be in touch. During the three months, she did field some questions about the research she and I were doing in the trial with Alzheimer patients, but other than that, I never heard from her." He blew out a low breath and rubbed his forehead. "I can't believe she's dead."

"That makes two of us," Lacey muttered. Creed wished he could ease the pain so clearly written on her face.

Creed let his gaze roam the office. The man had a plethora of pictures behind him on the credenza. "You have a large family. Looks like you all are very close."

Dr. Rhodes turned a fond eye on the collection. "Yes. We are. My daughter just had her third child a couple of weeks ago." He smiled. "The more the merrier."

"How many children do you have?"

"Three. Ages sixteen, eighteen and twenty-four. I also have three grandchildren. A boy aged four, a girl aged two and the newborn." He nodded to the pictures. "They're my life. I don't know what I'd do if I lost even one of them."

Lacey flinched and Creed covered her hand and squeezed. But one picture in particular caught his eye. "Is that Fawn in one of them?" Creed asked.

The doctor nodded. "Once we started working together, I introduced her to my family and we all fell in love with her. Everyone's going to miss her." He blinked and swiped a hand over his eyes.

"Looks like y'all went hunting together?" Creed pointed to the picture of Fawn holding a rifle. She was flanked by two other women.

"That was a onetime thing for Fawn, but I'm part of a regular group who hunt when we get the chance. My wife and daughter-in-law go occasionally. We invited Fawn along the last time we went." His lips curved upward. "She hated it. Said it was a one and done for her."

"No, she could never kill anything," Lacey murmured. "She was a good shot and knew how to handle a weapon, but she wouldn't kill for sport."

Lacey looked away, her throat working.

"Um, how did you know Fawn?" Dr. Rhodes asked.

"We were very close," Lacey said. Which was completely true. She met the doctor's gaze and smiled.

"I see." He still looked confused as to the relationship, but Creed let it go.

"Thank you for your time. If you think of anything else, will you call?"

"Of course."

Creed stood and Lacey did the same. Only she staggered slightly. Creed snagged her upper arm and lowered her back into the chair. "Whoa. What's going on?" He knelt to look in her eyes, noting her suddenly pale face. A sheen of sweat had broken out across her forehead.

"Nothing," she said, waving him off. "Sorry. I just felt a little dizzy when I stood."

Dr. Rhodes rounded the desk and knelt in front of her. "Let me just check you out here."

Lacey held up a hand. "It's really not necessary. I think it's just that I haven't eaten much in the last few days."

"That could be it," the doc said, "but I'd feel better if you'd let me have a listen and check your blood pressure and pulse. In spite of my fancy title as Research Director and pretty office, I really am licensed to practice medicine."

After a moment of hesitation, Lacey gave a short nod. "Fine. Thank you."

Dr. Rhodes checked her out, then stood and walked to the front of his desk. "Blood pressure is fine, heart sounds good. We can figure out if it's your blood sugar fairly easily." He opened a drawer and pulled out a pack of crackers. "Any allergies? Peanuts? Gluten?"

"No, nothing."

He handed her the crackers. "Eat these. If it's low blood sugar, those should help."

Instead of arguing, Lacey ate the crackers, and to Creed's relief, within a few minutes, color started to return to her cheeks. "You should go home and get some rest," Dr. Rhodes said. "And eat a good meal of mostly protein and healthy carbs."

Lacey nodded. "I'll do that. Thank you."

The doctor glanced at his watch. "I'm sorry. I'm late for another meeting."

"Of course," Creed said. "Sorry to keep you, but thank you for talking to us."

The doctor smiled, but it was tinged with real sadness and grief. "I hate the reason for it. I'm going to miss Fawn. We all will." His eyes misted and he shook his head. "But," he said to Lacey, "thank you for letting me use this." He tapped the stethoscope he'd placed back around his neck. "These days, it sometimes feels like it's all for show. Mere decoration so I look the part. Take care of yourself, and I really hope you find Fawn's killer soon."

"Thank you. I do, too." He left through his back door, and Lacey, Scarlett and Creed went out the main one to find the administrative assistant on the phone. She waved and they continued their trek to the elevator.

"Ready to get something to eat?"

"I think that's probably a good idea."

"Want to head across the street to the diner for a burger or a salad?"

"A burger sounds great."

Creed let Lacey lead the way, then got in front of her to hold the door for her and Scarlett.

His phone rang and he stopped to glance at the screen. "I need to take this."

"I'll get us a table."

He nodded and watched her step into the crosswalk, Scarlett at her side. The roar of an engine caught his attention. The sleek black Mustang in the lane raced down the street.

Straight toward Lacey and Scarlett.

NINE

"Lacey! Stop! Watch the car!"

Creed's frantic shout froze her. The engine of the approaching car reached her. She stopped. Then realized the vehicle had changed course, driving on the wrong side of the road, to aim right at her and Scarlett.

Lacey pulled on the leash. "Heel!"

She spun to run back toward the hospital sidewalk with Scarlett close at her side. Spectators screamed and ran, desperate to get out of the car's reckless path.

Lacey bolted behind a cement column, pulling Scarlett with her. Tires squealed, and when the Mustang hit the column, the impact sent vibrations through her body while pieces of cement rained down over her. But the column held.

"Lacey!" She heard Creed calling her name, sounding like he was far away. But then his hands were wrapped around her upper arms and his petrified gaze met hers. "Are you okay?"

"Yeah, yes, I'm fine." At least, she thought so. "Scarlett!"

The dog rose up on her hind legs and planted her paws on Lacey's chest. She hugged the dog, then gathered her wits. "Who is it?" she asked. "Who's in the car?"

But Creed was already moving toward it. Sirens sounded.

"There he goes!" The shout pulled her attention to the figure running from the scene. The spectator pointed. "Someone stop him!"

Creed put on a burst of speed and Lacey hurried to the car. The seat would have to do as an article for Scarlett. "Scarlett, scent." She pointed to the seat. "Get the scent, girl."

Scarlett went to work, pushing her nose at the leather. Then she backed up and Lacey let the lead out to let her go. Scarlett took off like a shot, heading in the same direction as Creed. Lacey dodged people and other vehicles, trying to keep up with the dog while making sure Creed stayed in her line of sight.

The man who'd nearly run her and Scarlett over disappeared around the side of a building and Creed ran after him. By the time Lacey caught up with him, he was breathing hard and looking frustrated. "You lost him?"

"Yeah. He just vanished."

Scarlett had her nose in the air and darted to the back door of one of the businesses, then looked back at Lacey.

"She wants to go in."

Creed tried the handle. "It's locked."

"Well, he didn't float through the door."

"He didn't have time to pull out a key. My guess is it was propped open, and he went through it, then locked it behind him."

"Then he would have gone straight through and out, right?"

"Probably."

Lacey took off once more, this time leading Scarlett to

the business's front door. "I'll check inside just in case," Lacey said.

"I'll hang out here and see if I spot him."

She nodded and led Scarlett inside, ignoring the looks of the patrons. "Anyone see a guy come running through here and out the door?"

"I did." A little girl about eight stuck her sucker back in her mouth.

"And he went out the door?" Lacey asked.

"Yep. He was running fast, too. Almost knocked me down." She scowled. "That was mean."

"It sure was." She paused. "Did he still have on a mask or could you see his face?"

"He had on a mask. It was kinda scary, but he was in a hurry."

Lacey rushed to the door and looked out. Creed stood on the sidewalk, hands on his hips, scowl on his face. He spotted her and shook his head.

"Can I pet your dog? What's his name?" The little girl had come up behind her and stood patiently waiting for Lacey's answer.

"This is Scarlett. She's working right now. Maybe when she's off duty. Okay?"

"Okay. I know all about special dogs like her."

"Tabitha? Tabitha? Where are you?"

"That's my mom."

"I figured."

"Lacey Lee?"

The voice came from behind her, and she turned to see her friend from high school with a newborn strapped to her chest and clutching the hand of a toddler. "Jessica?"

"Yes." The dark-eyed, dark-haired woman blinked at her. "You're back?"

"Yes. I came looking for Fawn because she wasn't answering her phone—and found her."

"I just heard about an hour ago. I'm so very sorry."

"Thank you." Lacey backed toward the door. "I'm kind of in a hurry, but call me and let's catch up sometime." Jessica nodded and Lacey looked at the little girl. "Thank you for your help."

"Anytime."

Lacey smiled at the grown-up response, then pushed through the door and out into the sunshine to find Creed waiting for her. They walked to his cruiser, keeping an eye on the traffic. When they stopped at the wreckage, Regina stepped forward. "Hey. You two okay?"

Creed hung up and nodded. "We're fine. The guy got away. He obviously wasn't hurt bad enough to slow him down any."

"Well, the car's stolen and the owner reported it about five minutes after it happened. He wasn't happy."

"He's not going to be any happier when he sees the condition."

"Yeah, I didn't mention that part."

"Okay," Creed said, "I'm going to let you, Ben and Mac finish up here while I take Lacey home. I'll get her statement and do mine as well, and I'll email it to you later tonight."

"We've got this."

"Thanks."

Lacey watched Creed work and realized that, in spite of the pain she blamed on him, she admired him greatly. He was a professional through and through and hadn't let their past hurts influence that professionalism. Whereas she'd arrived in town expecting someone to try and knock the chip off her shoulder.

The little spiritual tap on her conscience made her grimace. *Sorry, God. Forgive me, please.*

She waited for Creed to finish, and they walked together to his cruiser, where she buckled in Scarlett, then climbed into the passenger seat once more.

Creed aimed the vehicle toward Fawn's home—she was having trouble calling it *her* home—and Lacey rubbed a hand down her face. "All right. I need to think."

"Which means—"

"I talk."

"That's what I was going to say."

She wrinkled her nose at him. "Sorry. So…"

"So…"

"So, something happened, and Fawn decided she needed to take a three-month leave of absence from the hospital."

"But we don't know what happened."

"No, that's the key. When we know what caused her to do that, I have a feeling the trail will lead straight to her killer. But we don't know that yet. So, let's focus on what we do know."

"She went back to work for two days and then disappeared again. She had to have been killed after her shift on her second day back and before her next shift the third morning."

Lacey steeled herself against the grief and forced herself to view this as a case, not a loss. "But during the two days back at work, she looked tired, sad, worn down, troubled. Right?"

He nodded. "So, why go back to work if she was feeling bad?"

"Well…she wouldn't if she was contagious. But if

she'd just had a bad night or something was bothering her emotionally…"

"She'd force herself to go because she'd already been gone for three months and didn't want to miss any more days?"

"Exactly. That would be like Fawn. She's always had a very strong work ethic—which is why her taking off for three months—and hiding it from me and everyone else—just doesn't make sense unless something was very, very wrong."

"Maybe she and the doctor broke up and she was trying to get past the worst of the hurt."

She shook her head. "Now, that I don't see." She pursed her lips. "But then, I wouldn't have seen a lot of this, so whatever it was, it was something she couldn't talk to me about." And that only added to her heart-shattering grief.

Creed pulled into Lacey's drive and shut the engine off. "You're coming in?" she asked.

"Do you mind? I want to check out your house."

She tilted her head and narrowed her eyes. "You don't think I'm capable?"

"More than, but I think we've discussed that it doesn't hurt to have backup occasionally. And after the attack at the gym and—"

"Almost being roadkill?"

"I would have put it a little differently than that, but yes."

She nodded. "Of course. You're right. I'd appreciate that."

They climbed out of the car, and he pointed to the open area across from the shed where they'd found Hank. "That'd be the perfect spot for a kennel."

She raised a brow at him. "So you've said."

"I know." He quirked a smile. "Just making sure you're paying attention." He let his gaze roam the land. "Lots of level land. What more do you need?"

"That's cute, Creed. You know as well as I do I'd need a lot more than just the land."

"But it'd be a start, right?"

Lacey backed toward the door, her gaze thoughtful.

"Let's go inside," he said. "We've been so busy dodging bullets and cars that we haven't had a chance to talk a little about your position with the department."

"My position?" She led the way into the house, and once again, the new-home smell hit him. Wood, stain and paint. Plus a hint of whatever shampoo Lacey used. She'd been back fewer than two days and already she'd left her mark on the place.

Scarlett found a spot in front of the fireplace and settled her nose between her paws. Before Creed took his seat on the couch, light snores from the dog reached him. "I guess she's tired."

"She's been busy lately." Lacey dropped into the wingback chair next to the bookcase and lowered her face into her hands.

"Lacey?"

She looked up. "Sorry, I'm just thinking."

"About?"

"That I need to be a big girl and admit I was wrong about the people in this town." She blew out a low breath. "I let fear keep me away. Fear of what I thought I remembered about this place. Fear of facing what my father had done. Fear of facing the people he'd done it *to*. Fear of—" she looked away from him "—a lot of things."

Fear of running into him—which she'd already mentioned. "And now?"

She met his gaze. "I like my life in Charlotte, Creed. It's a good life. If Fawn hadn't…wasn't…*dead*… I wouldn't be here and be so…"

"So what?"

"Confused!" The word burst from her, and she groaned, then dropped her head against the back of the chair. "I'm confused."

"Because?"

"Because I don't hate it here as much as I thought I would."

Creed's heart leaped in his chest and he immediately squashed the surge of hope. She might not hate it here, but she'd just told him how much she loved her life in Charlotte. "I'm glad," he said softly.

"Yeah, me, too. People have been really nice. That's probably due to Fawn staying and being her irresistible self. And now that she's dead, I guess no one wants to add to the pain by reminding me of the past. Maybe. I don't know." She shrugged and cleared her throat. "But that's not what you wanted to talk about." She clasped her hands and leaned forward. Then stood. "Oh. Before we talk about that position, I want to check Fawn's desk." She grabbed the keys from Fawn's gym bag.

"Good idea." He followed her into the guest room. All of the furniture had been put in storage while the floors were being done, but a small desk with a drawer and file cabinet stood in the center of the room, facing the window.

"Guess I'll have to look into getting her stuff out of storage."

"Well, it won't be hard to figure out where she had it. There's only one storage facility in Timber Creek."

"At least you have one."

She walked to the desk and tried the drawer. It slid open. "Well, it's not locked, but let's see if one of the keys works." The third one fit the desk. "Good to know. All right, she's got pens, pencils, a notepad, a bag of M&M's, stapler and paper clips. That's about it."

"I would think she'd keep all of her paper stuff in files."

"She would." Lacey tugged on the top drawer of the built-in two-drawer file cabinet. It slid open. "Okay, not locked either."

"Most people don't keep their file cabinets locked at home."

"I do."

"Well, you're in law enforcement."

She shot him a tight smile, pulled out a stack of hanging folders and passed them to him. She took a handful, and together, they made their way to the kitchen, where they went through each folder. She finally came to a piece of paper that stopped her. "It's a list of usernames and passwords. Oh, thank you, thank you, Fawn. We can get into her phone records and anything else we need."

"Perfect."

"Since I have no idea where Fawn's laptop is, I'm going to get mine. Be right back."

When she returned, he pulled the chair around beside her and they went through Fawn's cell phone records first. "Would you have any reason to know any of these numbers?" he asked her.

"No, but that's a hospital extension." She called it and Creed waited. "Oh, sorry. Wrong number." She hung up. "That was Dr. Charles Rhodes. Hopefully, he won't bother calling me back, thanks to the different area code on my number."

"She called him a lot and vice versa."

"Well, they were working on that project together."

"Yeah, but at ten o'clock at night?"

She frowned. "That is kind of suspicious." A sigh slipped from her. "You think he was the one she was involved with?"

"Hard to say, but not out of the realm of possibility."

"I just can't see her involved with a married man. That's so not Fawn."

"Several calls to this number." He rattled it off and she nodded.

"That's Miranda's number." She pointed. "And that's mine. And that's Jill Holloway's." She sighed. "What if I print this off and you have someone go through each number? This could take forever and I want to look at her credit card statements."

"Sounds good."

She set the printer in motion and moved on to the next website. "She only had two credit cards. One to the home improvement store, and the other looks like it was used for groceries and other odds and ends. Nothing weird on there and she paid it off when she got the bill. I hate to say it, but I don't think her phone records or credit cards are going to tell us anything."

"Print those out, too, for the last three months. I'll have Ben or Regina go through them when they have time."

"Sure."

When he had the printout tucked into his back pocket, she rested her chin on a fist and looked at him. "So, about that position…"

"I've been rethinking the offer."

She blinked. "Oh. Okay, then."

"Not as in I don't want you here. I do. But since you've made it obvious you're heading back to Charlotte, why don't we start interviewing people for the lead position? Help me find dogs without breaking the budget. You know, that kind of thing? Be my consultant."

"Sure, we can do that."

"Perfect. I'll put an ad in the online law enforcement journal and see if we get some bites." He paused. "Um, no pun intended."

This time her laugh was genuine, and it wrapped around him like a warm blanket. "I've missed that," he said. "I've missed *you*, Lacey." He missed her laughter, her goofy sense of humor, her listening ear. He missed kissing her. A lot.

She sighed and a sad longing flickered in her eyes. "I've missed you, too, Creed, but it makes no sense to revisit old feelings when it will just lead to heartbreak when it's time for me to leave again."

He studied her, turning her words over in his mind. "Yeah, you're probably right." He still wanted to kiss her, though. But more than that, he wanted to convince her to stay and give them another chance.

"Change of subject?" she asked.

"Okay."

"When do you think the ME will have the autopsy done?"

Her voice cracked, and it was all he could do not to get up and go to her, pull her into his arms—

"I don't know," he said, keeping himself firmly planted in his seat. "Shouldn't be too much longer. You heard

Zeb. He has a backlog of cases, but I imagine we'll hear something tomorrow. If not, I'll call him."

Lacey nodded. "Not that there's a hurry, I guess, other than to have Fawn's funeral." Her jaw tightened and she looked away. "I can't believe I'm talking about burying my sister."

"Aw, Lacey, I wish I could do something to—"

"Catch her killer, Creed." Her shimmering eyes met his and the pain there took his breath away. "That's all I need."

He couldn't stand it. He stood, crossed the room and pulled her into his arms. She buried her face against his chest and let out a sigh that sounded like she'd finally come home. With one finger, he lifted her chin and searched her eyes, hoping she'd read the question in his. "Oh, Creed," she whispered. "I've missed you so much."

He couldn't do it. Kissing her right now when she was grieving and vulnerable would be taking advantage, and he considered himself way far above something like that. Instead, he pressed his lips to her forehead. "I know, Lacey, but we just agreed now isn't the time to revisit our old feelings."

"Is it wrong to want to?" she asked, her voice soft and barely there.

"No. I feel the same way, but you're leaving and I'm staying and that's that. Neither one of us believes in having a fling, so let's not open ourselves up for another world of hurt by thinking anything we might have now won't crash and burn with your exit."

She didn't answer but didn't protest either. Clearing his throat, he stepped back. He wouldn't survive losing her a second time, so it was better to let her go now. "Okay, so here's the plan. I'm going to fix you another meal full of protein and healthy carbs, and you're going to rest. Deal?"

"But—"

"Don't argue. Those crackers were good enough to tide you over for a while, but you need real food. Let me do this for you, okay?"

She nodded. "Okay."

TEN

Lacey's phone woke her early the next morning, the insistent alarm finally dragging her out of her heavy sleep. With a pounding head and a mouth full of cotton, Lacey struggled to remember why she felt so horrible.

Scarlett nudged her, then swiped a tongue over Lacey's cheek. "Thanks, girl. I know you need to go out. Hang on a sec." She rolled out of bed and into the bathroom while Scarlett waited with her usual patience.

In the middle of brushing her teeth, last night finally came back to Lacey in flashes. Creed had insisted she eat a protein-filled meal that he'd fixed for her with the contents of Fawn's fully stocked refrigerator. And then she'd taken a sleep aid and fallen into bed while he promised to keep watch on the house. After her three-month sabbatical—or whatever one wanted to call Fawn's absence—she'd grocery shopped and filled up her fridge and freezer like nothing was wrong. Like she'd never been gone.

Lacey rinsed her mouth and stared at her reflection. "Where were you for those three months, Fawn?" Because it wasn't here. Was it? Had Fawn been here for the whole three months, hiding away like a hermit while she dealt with whatever it was she needed to deal with?

And what about her mail?

Lacey finished up her morning routine, then made her way into the den, where she found Creed sitting up on the couch, his phone pressed to his ear. "Yeah. Got it. I'll ask her." He looked up and his gaze met hers. "Give me five minutes to get everything set up." He hung up.

"You need Scarlett?"

"And you." He rubbed a hand down his cheek. "Ben's outside keeping an eye on things so I could grab some sleep. He just let me know that his aunt called him. She works at the assisted-living home next door to the hospital and one of their residents was found missing this morning."

She let Scarlett out and nodded to Creed. "I'll get ready. Will you let Scarlett back in when you hear her bark?"

"Sure."

Within ten minutes, Lacey was ready and she, Creed and Scarlett were in Creed's cruiser and heading toward the facility. "I just thought of something this morning," she said. "Will you check with the post office and see if Fawn stopped her mail service for those three months?"

He cut her a sideways glance. "Good thought. Yeah, I can do that." He activated the Bluetooth and called Mac, asking him to look into Fawn's mail service.

"Got it. I'll text you what I find out in case you can't talk."

"Perfect."

When they arrived, a woman in her late forties was waiting for them at the entrance to the large brick-and-cream-siding building. Six white columns lined the front porch, with steps leading to the massive double oak doors. Creed parked. "That's Ben's aunt, Rianne Matthews."

"I think I remember her from church."

They climbed out. Lacey released Scarlett from her safety restraint and snapped the lead onto her harness.

Rianne rushed down the steps. She held a paper bag and thrust it toward Lacey. "Thank you so much for coming so fast. Our missing resident is named Ethan Mays. This is the shirt he wore yesterday. I figured you'd need it."

"Yes, ma'am," Lacey said. She took the bag. "Do you know which way he headed?"

"Not exactly. We have security cameras, of course, but we didn't see how he got out. However, I have my suspicions. In the basement, where they do the laundry, the workers sometimes leave the door open because it gets so hot in there from the dryers." She closed her eyes. When she opened them, tears shimmered. "The cameras show an orderly checking on him, and then five minutes later, Ethan walks out of his room and down the hallway to the exit. When he comes out at the bottom of the stairwell, he's on the first floor, but then he goes to the basement stairs and disappears. If the door at the bottom wasn't properly closed and locked, then I'd say that's how he managed to get out of the building."

Lacey nodded to the fence. "Can he get off the property?"

"I wouldn't think so. Not unless he managed to climb the fence. But it's a huge area. We have seventy acres, a lot of it wooded. And…" She gulped. "There's a large pond that some of the residents use for fishing and supervised swimming when the weather permits. It's on the other side of the back fence, but there's a gate and there are areas that need repairs. The repairs are on the schedule for this week, but since it's been so cold, and we haven't been using it…" She waved a hand. "Never mind all that. What's important is finding Ethan as quickly as possible."

She swiped a tear from her cheek and Lacey patted the woman's shoulder. "We'll do our best." Lacey opened the bag and held it out for Scarlett to get a whiff. "Scarlett, find Ethan. Find." Lacey tapped her pocket with the tennis ball.

Scarlett danced in a circle, her ears flying around her head, then shoved her nose at the bag once more. When she pulled back, she lifted her snout and sniffed one way, then another. She walked to the porch, then trotted around the side of the building and stopped. "I'd like to take her down to the exit," Lacey said, "where you think Ethan might have left. I think she'd have a better chance of getting the scent from there."

"Follow me."

The woman led the way and Scarlett trotted next to Lacey, through a maze of hallways, then down a set of stairs that led to the basement. Lacey let Scarlett have another sniff and the dog went straight to the exit. Lacey looked at Rianne. "Looks like your suspicions are right on target."

Rianne pushed the door open and Scarlett darted out with Lacey right behind. Lacey let the lead slacken and Scarlett raced toward the bench in the little garden about twenty yards away. The whole area was beautifully landscaped and the spring flowers were starting to bloom, but this early in the morning, there was a chill in the air that put the temperature in the low forties.

Creed kept pace with her. "This feels familiar."

"Hank?"

"Yeah."

She shot him a glance. "Let's pray the ending is just as happy."

"Exactly."

Scarlett loped toward the back of the property, where the wrought iron fence stretched long and far. She stopped and looked to her left, ears lifting, attention focused.

"What does that mean?" Creed asked.

"I don't know. Something distracted her."

"Scarlett, seek." Lacey waved the bag at the dog and Scarlett focused once more. She trotted to the fence, then started looking for a way through it. "He must have climbed over," Lacey said. She glanced the length of the fence within her sight range. "I don't see any area that needs repair here." Scarlett rose on her hind legs and placed her paws on the wrought iron. "She definitely wants to get to the other side."

"Then I guess that's what we'll have to do." He looked at her, then Scarlett. She knew exactly what he was thinking.

"It'll work," she said.

"What?"

"I'll go over first and you pick Scarlett up and over the fence and I'll help her down."

He blinked. "That's kind of scary that you can still read me so well, but yeah, that's exactly what I was thinking."

Just like the old days. She'd almost always known what he was thinking. *Almost.* She'd even known he had plans to be the sheriff of Timber Creek one day. She'd thought he would either wise up to his potential or she could change his mind and convince him he was better than a small-town sheriff. Her selfishness hit her square between the eyes and she almost lost her grip on the bars.

Stop it! Focus on finding Ethan.

Lacey cleared the wrought iron fence, grateful the top was a flat black piece and not spikes that could have been dangerous to navigate. She dropped to the ground and turned to find Creed lifting Scarlett over. She wrapped her arms around the solid animal and lowered her to the ground. Scarlett took off at a run and Lacey fell into step behind her, clutching the lead. Creed's footsteps pounded behind her and they slipped into the wooded area.

"There's a path," she said. "Scarlett's right on it. I feel sure Ethan came this way."

Scarlett led them through the woods, following the dirt path. "She's taking us to the pond," Creed said.

They broke through the tree line and into a small clearing. Lacey paused and Scarlett kept her nose in the air. "That's a pond?" Lacey asked. "Looks like a small lake to me. The water actually looks clean."

"Yeah, there's a little beach next to the dock. And two canoes."

"I'm sure the residents love it, but..."

"Yeah. This could be a problem if Ethan came this way."

Scarlett tugged at the lead and Lacey let her go. She led the way to the dock, and the bad feeling in Lacey's chest grew with each step.

She spotted something on the wood and walked out on the dock. "Hey, Creed? I found something. A rubber worm. I think he was here." She leaned over to pick up the item and something whipped over her head.

"Lacey!"

She turned at his running footsteps. He dived at her, wrapped his arms around her and yanked her into the cold water.

* * *

It was April and it wasn't exactly warm above the water, but pond water in the spring was cold enough to steal his breath. The chill soaked through his skin into the depths of his bones. Creed kicked, aiming for the surface. He'd surprised Lacey with his dive and he worried she hadn't had time to suck in a breath.

He broke through and gasped while Lacey did the same, coughing and sputtering. "Wha—" She wheezed in more air and coughed again.

He shook the water from his eyes, and before she could lambaste him, he grabbed her hand and pulled her toward the shelter of the dock. When his feet touched the bottom, he led her to one of the thick red cedar posts. And registered Scarlett's frantic barking. Then a splash. "Scarlett, come!" He didn't know if the dog would obey his voice or not, but Lacey was still trying to breathe and he needed the dog with him, not a target for whoever had sent that bolt whipping over Lacey's head.

The dog swam toward him and he hooked a free arm around her to pull her to him. She rested on his forearm, trusting him to keep her afloat.

"C-Creed?" Lacey said. He still had his other arm wrapped around her waist. "Wh-what are you doing?" she asked. Her teeth were already chattering. From the shock of his move as much as the cold, no doubt.

"Someone shot at you."

Her eyes widened. "Again?"

"Again."

She frowned and swiped the water from her face. "I didn't hear a gunshot."

"It wasn't a rifle. It was a crossbow bolt. I think. Some kind of arrow, anyway. Stay here with Scarlett." He ignored her croaked protest and slogged his way to the edge of the dock. He peered around the last post. Nothing on the beach area caught his attention. But behind the trees...

He stepped out for a better look at the movement, only to feel himself yanked backward the very moment he saw the flash of something headed toward him, then felt the sting of fire against his side. He yelped and slapped a hand over the burn. He spun to find Lacey narrow-eyed and furious. "Someone is shooting at us once more and you think you're invincible?"

Scarlett could touch bottom and was swinging her brown head back and forth between them, confused at the interruption of her search.

"No, I just—"

"Almost took a crossbow bolt through your gut." She moved toward him. "Let me see." Blood mingled with the water, but not so much that he was worried.

"I think it's just a graze, but thanks for pulling me back in time."

She shuddered and pushed his hand away, then peeled his shirt from the area. He hissed. "I need to call for backup."

"Is your phone working, by any chance?" she asked.

"Probably not."

She popped hers out of the clip on her belt and handed it to him. "The case is waterproof." At his raised brow, she shrugged. "I never know where Scarlett's going to take me. Or when I'm going to be dunked." She examined his wound and the touch of her cold fingers on his skin raised goose bumps all over. "It's more of a groove than a graze. You need stitches."

"Nah, it'll be all right."

He thought he heard her mutter "Stubborn" before she glanced at him. "Why don't you call whoever you need to while I keep watch on the woods?" She waded to the nearest post and peered around while he dialed 911 and waited for Dispatch to pick up.

"Nine-one-one. What's your emergency?"

"Nancy, this is Creed. I need backup out at the assisted-living pond. Someone's shooting a crossbow at us. Get everyone available out here. Who's the closest?"

"What?" Even as she asked the question, he could hear her fingers flying over the keys. "Are y'all okay? Um... Mac's on the way. In fact, he's less than a mile from your location. You should be hearing his siren soon."

"Good. Send Ben, too. And yes, we're fine." Discounting the fact that his side burned. But not as bad as he would have expected. The cold water was probably having a numbing effect.

"On it," the woman said. "I can get Regina out there, too, but she just took off on a personal errand, so it might be a while before she can get turned around."

"No, don't call her. By the time she could get here, I'm hoping we'll have this under control."

"Ten-four." More clicking. "Ben is on his way, as well."

"Thank you." He hung up and kept his gaze on the tree line.

Scarlett barked and headed toward the shore. Lacey grabbed her lead and pulled her up. "Scarlett, stay." The dog stopped, but her focus was on the wooded area just visible from their position under the dock.

"She hears someone," Lacey said. "Or smells someone."

"So, they're still out there."

"I'd say yes."

Creed itched to go after the shooter, but he'd be too exposed between the dock and the trees to risk it. "Come on, Mac," he muttered.

No sooner had the words escaped his lips than he picked up the sound of a siren. Scarlett barked again and Creed noticed the movement behind the trees just ahead. He spotted the fleeing figure and darted after it.

"Creed!"

Her cry was one of frustration with him, not a warning of trouble or a need for help. He ignored her and kept going. She and Scarlett followed, but as soon as he reached the tree line, a motorcycle roared away in the distance. He used Lacey's phone to call Mac.

The deputy answered halfway through the first ring. "McGee here."

"The shooter got away on a motorcycle." He assumed it was the shooter. No one else would have had a bike waiting. "Put a BOLO out on it. It had some red trim. I didn't get a plate. Ben is coming this way. See if he spots it."

"Ten-four. You okay?"

"Yeah. Fine. Just want this person caught."

"I'm on it."

Lacey caught up with him. Shudders racked her every so often, reminding him that he was freezing. And they still had a man to find. "We need to get some dry clothes and warm up."

"I'm not leaving until we find Ethan. Movement will keep me warm enough."

"Liar."

"Okay, well, I might be cold and uncomfortable, but I won't freeze to death. I'm heading back to the dock to get the rubber fishing worm I saw before you tackled me.

And the bag for Scarlett. I dropped it when you shoved me into the water."

He nodded. "All right. I'm right behind you. Mac and Ben are chasing down the shooter." He pressed a hand to his throbbing side and found it had started bleeding once more. If it had ever stopped.

"We need to get you to the hospital," Lacey said, frowning at him. "You definitely need stitches."

He grimaced. The last place he wanted to go was the hospital. "After we find Ethan and only if Katherine is available to meet me there."

"Agreed."

Once Lacey retrieved the bag with Ethan's scent and Scarlett had gotten another good whiff, the dog raced toward the trees with Lacey right behind her.

ELEVEN

Lacey followed Scarlett, dodging limbs and the undergrowth. Scarlett continued to plow down the path. When she rounded the next tree, she slowed, her head moving, nose twitching. Straight ahead, Lacey spotted a bare foot at the same time Scarlett beelined for it.

"We found him, Creed. Call it in, will you?" He had the only working phone.

Lacey raced to the foot and touched it. Cold. But not deathly cold. She moved to Ethan's head and placed her fingers against his neck. "He's got a pulse!" He groaned and opened his eyes. When they landed on Lacey, he gasped and struggled to sit up. She helped him lean against the tree trunk. "Hi, Ethan. Don't be afraid. I'm here to help."

For a moment, when his eyes met hers, they sharpened. "What happened?"

"You wandered away from home, Mr. Mays—Ethan. Scarlett and I came to take you back."

He shivered and crossed his arms, his arthritic hands clasping his biceps. "Cold."

"I know. The paramedics are coming, and they'll have a nice warm blanket for you."

He frowned. "You're the one who needs the blanket. You're all wet."

She let out a laugh but couldn't help the tremor that shook her. "I f-fell in the pond."

"I wanted to go fishing."

"I saw the worm on the dock." The rubber worm that had saved her life. "Did you drop it?"

He rubbed his head. "I don't know."

"It's okay." She patted his hand. "Why don't we get you warmed up?"

He drew back. "No. I have to wait here."

"Why?"

"In case he comes back. He said he would get me a fishing rod."

Lacey caught Creed's eye, then looked back at Ethan. "Who said that?"

"The man."

"Did you know him?"

"I… I'm not sure. Seems like I might have known him, but I can't think of—" He slapped his head. "Ah! I can't remember!"

Lacey grabbed his hands before he could hit himself again. "It's okay, Ethan. Really, it's okay."

His eyes had clouded once more. "Who are you?"

"My name's Lacey."

Scarlett moved in front of Ethan and placed a paw on his knee. The man lifted a hand to run it over the dog's soggy head. "Nice dog."

"She is. Her name is Scarlett."

He rose to his feet. "I had a dog."

"Hold on. The paramedics are coming to make sure you're all right and then take you to the hospital."

"No. I don't want doctors." He pulled away from her and stumbled. Creed caught him and held him while

Ethan muttered, "No doctors. Don't like doctors." While he spoke, his hands sought out Scarlett's soggy ears. He rubbed and the dog moved closer, her eyes intent, seeming to understand the man's fragile state.

"Ethan," Creed said, "it's all right. Scarlett will stay with you."

Ethan looked down. "Good dog."

He started to walk, his hand on Scarlett's back, and Creed moved to stop him. Lacey snagged Creed's fingers. "Let him walk. He doesn't appear to have any serious injuries. He's awake, he's talking and he's going in the right direction. Scarlett's helping him keep his balance. The faster we go, the faster he gets any help he might need."

Creed stayed close to the man's side, ready to catch him should he need to. He looked back at her. "I want to know who told him he'd take him fishing."

She nodded. "Once we get him turned over to the paramedics, you need to go back and collect that worm. It's evidence. Someone gave it to him and enticed him down to the dock."

"Yeah." He nodded, his face thoughtful, tense. "And... I think whoever that person was knew I'd ask you and Scarlett to come hunt for him."

Lacey let her brain wrap around the thoughts coming at her. "Well, after the story in the paper about our role in Hank's rescue and Fawn's death, it wouldn't take a rocket scientist to figure out if an elderly Alzheimer patient went missing..."

"I'd call you," Creed finished. "Yeah."

"This was a setup, wasn't it?"

"I can't say for sure, obviously, but... I'm leaning toward that conclusion. Especially since we were sitting ducks out here near the pond." He shivered and narrowed his eyes. "I'm freezing. Come on. I want to see security footage at the facility and find out everyone Ethan came into contact with."

"A shower and some dry clothes would be nice, too."

"And that."

Lacey heard the paramedics before she saw them. They stepped out of the tree line, and she recognized the two paramedics hurrying toward them. Annie Kitts and Hannah Ligon. "Hi, Lacey," Annie said. "Glad to have you back."

Hannah stared at Lacey, her eyes guarded and cold. Hannah's parents had been victims of her father's crimes. Annie's had not.

"Hi," Lacey said. "This is Ethan Mays. He's cold, but doesn't appear to be hurt. We found him asleep, but not unconscious."

Annie and Hannah went to work. Lacey stepped up to Ethan and placed a hand on his shoulder. "I'm glad you're okay."

His eyes met hers, clear again for the moment. "Thank you." He patted Scarlett's head.

"Ethan?"

"Yes?"

"Who gave you the worm?"

"The man. Said to come to the dock to go fishing."

"What was his name?" She had to try, now that he seemed to be "back."

"I don't know. He looked familiar, but I don't know why." Ethan closed his eyes. When he opened them, desperation flashed at her. "I have trouble with my memory a lot. I'm sorry."

"It's okay."

Hannah sighed. "Can you move? We have a job to do, you know."

Lacey frowned at the woman's rudeness, but decided not to address it. "Yeah, sure."

She stepped back and met Annie's gaze. "Could you check Creed's side? He got grazed by a crossbow bolt."

"What?"

"Lacey, I'm fine."

Creed and Annie spoke at the same time.

Lacey crossed her arms and stared at him until he sighed. "Fine." He pulled up his torn shirt and Annie leaned in for a look.

"Ouch," Lacey said. "That looks even more painful than my first glimpse in the water."

"A bit."

"It's still bleeding, too," Lacey pointed out.

Creed narrowed his eyes at her. "It'll stop."

"You need stitches," Annie said, "and possibly an antibiotic. No telling what's in that water. You should probably head to the hospital."

Lacey nodded. "Okay, we'll go there now."

"Hold on a second—"

"What if it was me, Creed? What would you make me do?" He sighed and muttered something she missed. "I'm sorry—could you repeat that?"

"I said fine, I'll go to the hospital and get checked out."

"That's what I thought you said."

"Let's go."

Hannah's gaze hadn't left Lacey. "You shouldn't have come back here," the woman blurted. "We're all still trying to forget the devastation your father left behind. You showing up just brings back a bunch of bad memories."

"Hey now, Hannah. That's not nec—" Creed started to protest.

"Well, if someone hadn't killed my sister," Lacey interrupted, "I wouldn't be here. But don't worry. As soon as her killer is found, I'm out of here."

Hannah flinched. "Yeah. Sorry about Fawn," she muttered.

"I am, too." Lacey walked away and Creed fell into step beside her, his hand searching for hers. He squeezed and Lacey drew in a shaky breath even as she took comfort in his touch. "I don't know why I still let people get to me. I thought I had developed a thicker skin."

"Hurtful words still hurt."

True enough. "I guess Fawn didn't remind her of our father and his crimes, but I do. Wow." Lacey did her best to shrug off the pain and focused on the fact that she really liked holding Creed's hand.

Which was why she pulled away.

She was leaving. Falling in love with Creed again would only cause her—and him—more damage than what a few barbed comments did. The kind of pain that there were no words for. She'd been there and done that and wasn't interested in a repeat performance. They'd settled this last night, so why was she revisiting it?

"Here," Annie said, walking up to them. She held two blankets. "Use these and get them back to me at some point, will you?"

"Thanks." Lacey ignored Creed's narrow-eyed scrutiny and took one of the blankets. Creed did the same, and side by side, with Scarlett's lead clutched in her right hand, they walked to his cruiser. "I think I should probably drive. I'm not the one that's been bleeding everywhere."

"I can't let you drive. Official vehicle rules and all that."

"I would think you could make an exception here?"

"Nope."

"And if you pass out at the wheel?"

He slid her a glance that held a mixture of amusement and pain. "I promise I wouldn't drive if I thought I was going to pass out." He paused. "If at any point I start feeling woozy, I'll pull over and call for Regina or Ben to come get us."

She sighed. "Fine, but I'm going to be watching you very closely."

"I wouldn't expect anything different."

Once they were all buckled in, he cranked the engine, flipped the heat on high, then pulled into the street.

"Hospital," Lacey said.

"Yeah, yeah. But I'm calling Katherine to ask her to meet me there—assuming she's not already there."

"Works for me."

He activated the Bluetooth and managed to track down their doctor friend, who promised to meet them at the emergency room.

Now, if they could just get there without anything else happening, Lacey might be able to catch her breath.

Creed pulled into the police-reserved hospital parking spot and shut off the engine. Lacey had been true to her word and watched him like a hawk all the way. He really would have made other arrangements had he felt woozy or like he was struggling to drive, but he still felt energized from the adrenaline rush. He figured he had another few minutes before it would crash and leave him shaking.

"Creed? You okay?" Lacey asked from the open passenger door. Scarlett was already out of the vehicle and waiting patiently at her side. He nodded and she shut the door.

Creed climbed out, stifling a gasp at the pain the movement caused. Lacey wrapped a hand around his biceps as though to hold him up. "If I fall, just get out of the way, okay? I'd squash you like a bug."

She laughed and the sound washed over him like a wave of warmth. His heart clenched, and once again, the pain of losing her flashed through his mind in vivid detail and saturated with heartache.

"Good to be compared to a bug."

"What? No, I'd never—"

"I'm teasing. Let's find Katherine."

Yeah, they needed to do that before he made a complete fool of himself. "I'm going to call my mother and ask her to bring us some dry clothes."

"That would be lovely."

"What size do you wear?"

She told him. "A brush would be nice, too. My hair needs some TLC in a very desperate way."

He paused. "May I use your phone?"

"Of course."

He took it and passed the information on to his mother, who demanded to know if he was all right. "Yes, I promise, I'm fine. And so is Lacey."

"Creed, be honest. I know you think you're protecting me by not giving me all the details, but I'll tell you right now, that just makes things worse."

"Mom—"

"Because my imagination can come up with all kinds of scenarios, as you know."

Boy, did he.

"Do I need to come stay with you? Take care of you? Bring you some food?"

"Just the clothes, please."

"Fine, but if I think you're hurt worse than you're letting on, I'm not going to be happy and neither will your father."

"I know. Thank you."

"I'll be on my way shortly. Give Lacey a hug for me."

"Will do. Thank you."

"I love you, Creed."

"I love you, too, Mom." He hung up and let out a slow breath, then a short laugh. His mother could be a force to be reckoned with and he loved her dearly.

"She doesn't hate me, does she?" Lacey asked.

"Hate you?" Creed eyed her. "Not at all. She told me to give you a hug. She's missed you."

"I've missed her, too. There were days she was more of a mother to me than my own mom."

He gave her a side hug and kissed the edge of her temple. "I know."

Lacey went still and Creed mentally slapped himself for initiating the intimate moment, then dropped his arm. "That was from Mom."

"Of course."

Katherine stepped into the waiting room, dissipating the awkward moment. She raised a brow. "What happened to you two? You look like drowned rats." Katherine's youthful features kept one guessing her true age. The only reason Creed knew how old she was and how well qualified she was in her profession was that he'd known her since they were kids.

"Long story," Creed said.

"Well, follow me. You can tell me while I'm doctoring whatever it is I'm doctoring."

Lacey nodded at him. "Scarlett and I'll just wait here."

"Oh no you don't," Creed said. "If I have to be checked out, so do you." He wasn't letting her out of his sight. Someone had just tried to kill her. Leaving her alone in the waiting room wasn't an option.

"What?" She gave a huff of laughter. "I'm not the one who got shot."

"Shot?" Katherine's eyes went wide and bounced between him and Lacey. "No one mentioned anything about bullets."

"It wasn't a bullet." Creed scowled. "It was a bolt from a crossbow."

"Oh well, then. Of course that's *so* much better." Katherine rolled her eyes and Creed noticed Lacey struggling to keep a straight face.

He lifted his jaw and narrowed his eyes at Lacey. "I'm not going unless you go, too."

"How old are you? Ten?" He kept his gaze steady, and Lacey threw up her hands in surrender. "Fine. I'm coming, too. Come on, Scarlett. Let's keep the baby company."

Creed snorted, Katherine laughed, and they all made their way through the double doors of the ER.

Katherine stopped in front of a room. "Um. Do you need separate rooms? Because it's kind of busy here and I'm not sure we have another one to spare."

"I don't need a room at all," Lacey said with a pointed look at Creed.

He grabbed her hand. "She can share mine." He pulled her through the door and pointed to a chair in the corner. "You take that." He looked at Katherine. "I imagine I need to lie down for this?"

"Probably best."

A nurse bustled into the room pushing an IV pole. "Which arm you want this in?"

"I don't need that."

"It's fluids and antibiotics," Katherine said. "You need it. It won't take long to go through the bag. Now, let me help you get your shirt off and this gown on."

Creed groaned, but let her have her way. Soon, he was stretched out on the gurney even while he shot a scowl at the nurse. "You get one try."

"Grumpy today, are we?"

"Sorry," Creed muttered.

"But—" she flashed him a tight smile that said he didn't intimidate her in the least "—the good thing is, I only need one stick. Trust me."

Lacey sat in the chair, a bemused expression on her face while the nurse aimed the needle at the inside of his left elbow. He flinched, but sat still until the woman looked up. "Good job," she said.

He blew out a breath. "I hate needles."

"Do you mind if I take a look now?" Katherine asked.

"Go for it."

She did, then leaned over and sucked in a breath. "Whoa."

"Whoa? Did you learn that diagnosis in med school?"

She gave his shoulder a light punch. "Cute." She stepped back and turned to Lacey, who pulled the blanket tighter around her shoulders. "Did you get shot, too?"

"No. Thanks to Creed, I'm fine. Just cold and wet and in need of a hot shower and dry clothes."

"All righty, then," Katherine said to Creed, "I'm going to get this cleaned up, numbed up and stitched up."

"That's a lot of *ups*," Creed said. "Like two too many. You really think numbing and stitching are necessary?"

She met his gaze. "Absolutely. That bolt dug a nice groove in your side."

He sighed. "Fine."

"Told you so," Lacey said with a slight smirk.

He gave her a rueful smile and grimaced.

Katherine patted his hand. "You want anything for pain?"

"Nothing that will knock me out."

"All right. I've got something that'll take the edge off. It might make you a tad sleepy, but it definitely won't knock you out. Be back in a few." She whipped out the door and silence fell.

Creed shifted and winced. Lacey moved to sit on the bed beside him. "Thank you for saving my life," she said. "I have no doubt that bolt would have wound up hitting me if you hadn't acted."

He covered her cold hand with his and squeezed. "I'm just glad I saw it coming." He hadn't known what it was heading their way, just that the flash of whatever he'd seen probably wasn't good, and he'd reacted. "I hope Regina or someone managed to retrieve the bolts. We might be able to trace them back to where they were purchased from."

"And the worm."

"Maybe. It's possible they all came from the same place."

"I'm just mad that this person is dragging innocent people into whatever he's doing. Ethan Mays could have been seriously hurt—or worse."

"I know." He ignored the throbbing in his side and focused on one important fact. "I need a new phone."

"Can Ben or Regina grab one for you?"

"Yeah. Do you mind if I use yours to call and ask?"

She handed him the device for the third time and he worked out the details. He'd just hung up when the door opened once more and Katherine entered, holding a syringe in her right hand. "All righty, got something here that will have you feeling better in a few minutes. No new allergies, right?"

"Nope."

She dispensed the medicine into the IV port, then went to work cleaning the wound. When she sat back, she grabbed a suture kit. "All of the nurses are with other patients, so I'll just take care of this myself."

"I can't believe I'm letting you stick needles in me."

"Ha. That's funny. I used to beg you to be my patient and now I finally get to doctor you." Katherine had had a volatile childhood and had wound up living with Creed and his family for a while during her teen years. She was the sister he'd never had.

Fifteen minutes later, she was finished and he sported twelve new stitches and a white bandage. "Keep it clean and you'll be fine. I can take the stitches out in a couple of weeks."

"Thanks." He caught her hand. "I appreciate you taking the time to meet me here."

"I had patients to check on anyway, but even if I didn't, you know I don't mind. In fact, I would have been mad if you *hadn't* called."

"That's why I did."

"I'll look in on you in a bit." She looked at Lacey. Her phone buzzed and she glanced at it. "Creed's mom is here. I'm going to let her come see for herself that Creed and you are alive and kicking, but I'm going to encourage her not to stay long."

"Thank you," Lacey said. "Getting dry would be awesome."

She opened the door, and Creed's mother walked in, set a large bag on the floor and went straight for Creed. She stopped short of grabbing him but looked into his eyes. "You're all right?"

"Yes, Mom, I promise."

She turned her attention to Lacey. "And you're okay?"

"Yes, ma'am."

"Okay, then. I've been instructed not to linger, so I just need hugs and then I'm out of here until you tell me what else I can do to help. Your father sends his love. He stayed at the store, but said he'd close it and come if you needed him." His dad had owned the Timber Creek General Store since before Creed was born and took pride in serving the residents of Timber Creek. His mom gave him the once-over yet again. "He'll be relieved to know you're okay. I'll call him as soon as I get back in the car. Now, hugs, please."

Creed obliged. Then she went to Lacey and pulled her tight. "I've missed you, Lacey Lee."

"I've missed you, too, Mama Payne."

Creed's heart swelled along with the lump in his throat. It was good to see them together again.

"I can't tell you how sorry I am about Fawn," his mother said, her voice low, but he caught the words.

"Thank you."

"Come see me when you can."

"Yes, ma'am. I will."

Creed smiled as the door closed behind her and he looked at Lacey. "Told you she didn't hate you."

"Yeah," she whispered.

Creed's lids grew heavy. The pain meds were working—and while he didn't feel like he *had* to sleep, they were relaxing him enough that the idea was appealing. He yawned. Lacey scooted forward and passed him some clothes. "I'm going to find another bathroom while you change. I'll also let someone know you need some new sheets. Then I'll be back."

He frowned. "Be careful."

"I will. I'm not going far. Then you can sleep for a while. You have until the IV bag empties. You might as well recharge."

It sounded like a pretty good idea to him. "Is there a guard on the door?"

Lacey nodded and snagged the bag with the rest of the things his mother had brought, then clicked to Scarlett. "Jimmy from Security is here. He's going to stay until we walk out of here."

Or trouble walked in.

TWELVE

She'd never take dry clothes for granted again. *Grateful* didn't come close to expressing her appreciation of the effort.

While Scarlett waited patiently next to the door, Lacey had managed a sponge bath in the bathroom, then washed her hair in the sink and toweled it dry before pulling it up into her usual ponytail. Then she cleaned the pond water and muck from Scarlett, much to the dog's mortification, but Lacey insisted and Scarlett had endured. "Well, you smell better," Lacey had muttered. "We'll do a better job later."

Scarlett had ignored her, still obviously miffed.

Once Lacey was dressed and clean, she'd emptied her weapon and dried it as best she could. She reloaded it and replaced it in the shoulder holster and decided she felt halfway normal. Even though her mind wouldn't shut off.

While Creed slept, Lacey scratched Scarlett's ears and mulled over a thought that had been niggling at the back of her mind ever since they'd walked into the hospital. Dr. Rhodes was a hunter. He'd been friends with Fawn. What if they'd been more than friends? What if he was the doctor she'd been seeing?

The very thought of her sister sneaking around with a married man made her stomach turn. It wasn't something she could even envision Fawn doing, but…she couldn't quite dismiss the possibility without a little investigation.

And then there was the crossbow. A hunter's weapon. She needed to talk to Dr. Rhodes.

Creed looked like he might sleep for a while longer, so she rose and slipped out the door to walk to the nurses' station. "Could I have a pen and paper?"

The nearest nurse handed her the items, and Lacey returned to Creed's room, where she wrote him a short note about what she was going to do. He probably wouldn't be happy if he woke up and found her gone, but she wasn't going far and she'd be safe enough in a busy hospital.

And she'd have Scarlett with her, as well. Scarlett was a mild-mannered animal most of the time, but she was very protective of Lacey should the need arise.

Lacey left the note on the magnetic board that faced Creed's bed. As soon as he opened his eyes, he'd see it.

She gathered Scarlett's lead and left the room once more to make her way to the elevator that would take her to Dr. Rhodes's office.

When she arrived, she found the administrative assistant's desk empty, so she walked through to the doctor's office. The door was cracked. She knocked. "Dr. Rhodes?"

No answer.

Lacey gave the door a slight push and it swung inward to reveal the inner office empty, as well. "Okay," she muttered. "What do you think, Scarlett? Should we see if we can find out the answer to one of the questions burning in my mind?"

Scarlett looked up and tilted her head as though trying to figure out what Lacey was saying. "Come on, girl." With Scarlett beside her, Lacey slipped into the doctor's office, shut the door behind her and walked to the credenza behind his desk to get a closer look at the display of pictures.

She already knew the man was a hunter, but most hunters used more than one weapon. She stepped closer, examining them one by one. And there it was.

A crossbow.

Rhodes stood with several other men she didn't know, but Tucker Glenn was there with his arm around Rhodes. Next to Tucker was Keith Webb, another high school friend who'd gone into law. He, Tucker and another partner had opened the only law firm in Timber Creek. Each man held a crossbow. That was what had been niggling at the back of her mind. She'd noticed the picture from her and Creed's visit.

Then again, there were probably quite a few people in Timber Creek who hunted with crossbows. Just because the doctor did didn't mean he was the one trying to kill her.

But someone was and this seemed the right place to start asking questions. She turned and her eyes fell on the doctor's desk. A pen like the one found on Fawn's property lay on top of a closed manila folder. Two more were in a mug next to his laptop. Not that the pens meant anything. Everyone in the hospital probably carried them.

She turned and caught her breath. She knew that shirt hanging on the hook. Fawn had bought it on her last visit with Lacey. They'd spent the weekend laughing and shopping, and Fawn had fallen in love with the top.

A door shut in the outer office and Lacey jumped. She really didn't want anyone to know she was here, so she headed for the other exit next to the credenza.

"I'm telling you," a man's voice said just outside the closed door. "I can't find it."

"And I'm telling *you*. We don't have a choice. You need to keep looking or we're all going to be in trouble." Dr. Rhodes sounded mighty upset about something.

Lacey ushered Scarlett out the door and quickly followed. She pulled the door almost shut behind her, leaving a thin crack to look through. Dr. Rhodes stepped into his office and looked back over his shoulder. "I don't have time to discuss this." He took his white lab coat from the hook behind the door and shrugged into it. "Just find the book and everything will be fine."

"I've got to go before I'm missed. I'll keep looking on my end. You keep looking on yours."

"Of course."

The other man's footsteps faded, and Lacey regretted she hadn't gotten a look at him. Security footage should help her figure out who he was. The conversation between the two men had been curious, but nothing incriminating. She didn't care about a lost book. She wanted to know who'd thought it'd be a good idea to lure a sick man out to the dock and then shoot to kill when she and Creed arrived.

She shut the door, careful to hold the handle so it made as little sound as possible, then turned to lead Scarlett down the three steps and into the hallway of the hospital.

Her phone buzzed and she didn't recognize the number. "Hello?"

"Where are you? Are you okay?"

"I'm fine, Creed." He must have used the landline next to his bed to call her. "I'm on the way back to your room right now."

"When I woke up and you weren't here—"

"Didn't you get my note?"

"Yeah, but anyone could have forced you to write that."

Ouch. He wasn't wrong. "I'm fine. Sorry I scared you."

"I'm ready to get out of here. As soon as you get here, we can leave."

"Ten-four." She picked up the pace and made her way back to his room in record time. She knocked.

The door opened and Creed stepped out, fully dressed in a clean long-sleeved T-shirt and jeans. Lacey's heart hammered. He'd changed a lot in the six years she'd been gone. From boy-man to full-grown man. She'd loved the boy-man, but now she almost couldn't pull her gaze from him. It wasn't even his looks, although he was certainly easy on the eyes, but it was more his attitude, his heart for the hurting, his desire to help the underdog. And when he looked at her the way he was doing now—

She cleared her throat. "Ready?"

"Yeah." He pressed a hand to his side.

"How are you feeling?"

"Not bad, but Ben and Regina are coming to pick up my cruiser and take you home. Katherine told me I couldn't drive, thanks to the drugs she fed me." He scowled. "I didn't think about that when I consented to take them."

"Most of the bedroom furniture is in storage, but you can come back to Fawn's house and crash on the couch for a while. I can fix you dinner and we can talk. I have some things I need to fill you in on." Like her impromptu office visit. "I'll take you home when you're ready."

He hesitated, then nodded. "Sounds good."

Ten minutes later, they were in a department-issued cruiser with Regina at the wheel, Creed in the front seat, and Lacey and Scarlett in the back. Creed programmed his new phone as he rode, and Lacey watched the mirrors, half expecting someone to ram them, shoot at them or even try to blow them up. She wanted to tell him about the picture and the pens in the doctor's office, but he was preoccupied at the moment and she didn't want to be distracted from watching their tail. However, she could tell he was still alert and aware of their surroundings since he looked up every few seconds.

They arrived at Fawn's house without incident and Regina pulled into the drive and cut the engine. "I'll just wait here until y'all give me the all clear to head out."

Lacey studied Fawn's front door. "I don't think that's going to happen anytime soon. Someone's either in Fawn's house right now, or they've been here and gone. Because I didn't leave that door cracked."

Creed pulled his weapon. "I'll go in first."

"Scarlett, stay." The dog settled back onto the seat. Lacey snagged her gun from her shoulder holster and aimed it at the door. "I'm right behind you."

"I'll go around the back," Regina said. She hurried off and Creed used his elbow to nudge the door open.

He stepped inside and sucked in a breath. "Uh-oh."

"What do you mean, uh-oh?" Lacey entered and moved to the side. "Well, that's just great."

"Yeah." Someone had trashed the place. Furniture

upended, cushions slashed, lamps broken on the floor and bookshelves tossed.

She nodded to the hallway. "Let's clear the place. Then I'll have a look around."

Together, they walked through the house and returned to the living area. Creed holstered his weapon and notified Regina the house was clear. Lacey retrieved Scarlett from the vehicle. The dog stepped inside, her nose twitching. "Wish I could use her to find whoever did this," Lacey said.

"That would be ideal."

Scarlett hesitated, obviously confused by the chaos. Lacey pulled her bed out from under a couch cushion, cleaned the area in front of the fireplace and laid the bed in the spot. "Come here, girl. Scarlett, bed."

Scarlett bolted to her bed and settled on it, her eyes bouncing between Lacey and Creed.

Creed touched Lacey's arm. "I'll help you clean this up."

"You don't need to be cleaning. You need to be resting." She sighed and rubbed her eyes. "Why don't you let Regina take you home and I'll take care of this mess?"

"No way. I'm not leaving you here alone."

"Okay, fine." She went to the recliner and righted it. "At least they spared the upholstery on this. Make yourself comfortable here and I'll see if I can put the couch back together."

"The cushions are slashed."

"I'm aware, thanks." She picked one up. "But only on one side. I can sew the fabric back together and simply put the repaired side down."

"You can do that? Sew, I mean?"

She planted her hands on her hips and lifted her chin.

"I'm not completely helpless in the domestic arena, you know."

He chuckled, then winced and pressed his side. He had to stop doing that for a while. "I didn't mean to imply that you were."

She pointed to the recliner. "Sit. Relax. Close your eyes. I'll go through the house and bag anything that might be considered evidence."

He lowered himself into the chair just as Regina stepped inside. Her eyes widened at the scene. "Wow. Someone's not happy with you, are they?"

Lacey grimaced. "Apparently not."

"I've gone around the property and found nothing to indicate anyone was here other than in the house." She glanced around. "I'll get the evidence collection kit from my cruiser."

"Thanks," Lacey said. Within seconds, she was back, and the pain in his side was such that Creed seriously wondered if he could rise from the chair should he need to.

"I've got this, Creed," Regina told him. "Lacey and I can work the scene. Stay put."

He hesitated, but with the eyes of both women lasering holes in him, he decided to cave. "All right."

"Good choice," Lacey muttered.

Creed's eyes may have closed. And he may have even slept, because the next thing he knew, he could hear Lacey walking back into the den. Funny how he knew it was her simply by the way she walked. What wasn't so funny was how very aware he was of her approach. She stopped next to him and he opened his eyes. The den was clean and the sofa looked like nothing had happened. She'd already sewn the fabric?

"How long was I out?" he asked.

"About three hours. Regina just left, but Ben said he was going to come by and keep an eye on the place. I'm going to work in the kitchen. While I'm there, I'll see if I can throw together a salad or something. I think there's a rotisserie chicken in there, too."

"Sounds good. I'll help."

"You will not," she snapped.

Her glare nearly singed him. "What? Why are you looking at me like that?"

"Because you're stubborn."

"Yes. I know."

"Rest, Creed, please? You need to heal."

A knock on the door startled both of them and Creed's hand went to his gun. She raised a brow at him. "I doubt the intruder is going to come back and knock."

"You never know," he muttered.

Lacey went to the window and glanced out. When she smiled, Creed's heart rate went down and he allowed his shoulders to relax a fraction.

Katherine stepped inside and shut the door behind her. "I came to check on my patient and make sure he's taking care of himself."

"He's obnoxious," Lacey said. "He wants to help me in the kitchen."

"That's a no, Creed." She gave him the same look Lacey had drilled him with. Did women practice that look? Whatever the case, it was very effective.

"Tattletale," Creed called out. He could easily see and hear them from his spot in the recliner.

She rolled her eyes at him and Katherine laughed. "Glad to see you two getting along so well." She held up three bags. "I brought dinner." In her other hand, she balanced three drinks.

Lacey's nose twitched, much like Scarlett's when she got the scent. "Oh yum, what?"

"Burgers, fries and shakes. Creed gets the peanut butter one. Lacey and I get the chocolate ones."

His stomach rumbled and he held out a hand. "You are the best sister a guy could ask for."

Katherine passed him the shake. Then she and Lacey each took an end on the couch and used the coffee table to hold the food. No one spoke for several minutes while they inhaled the burgers. Then Katherine took a sip of her shake and looked up. "How's the side?"

"Fine."

"Right." She pulled a small bag from her purse. "I brought some bandages in case you didn't have any. There's some antibiotic cream in there, too."

"Thanks."

"Where's Dominic?" Creed asked her.

"Debating whether or not to come home and help you find Fawn's killer."

Dominic O'Ryan was Katherine's husband of four months. He was also a US marshal and friend to Creed. "Who's he after now?"

"No one. He's guarding a judge who's been receiving death threats." She wiped her hands on a napkin. "He said to tell you he knows it's out of his jurisdiction, but he has some leave and he's willing to use it if you need some help guarding Lacey here." She eyed him. "Or if you need some guarding."

"That's generous of him, but I'm not ready to call in reinforcements just yet."

She nodded. "I'll tell him."

"And I need to tell you something that I discussed with Regina while you were sleeping," Lacey said.

"What's that?"

"I think Dr. Rhodes was the doctor Fawn was involved with."

THIRTEEN

Both Creed and Katherine looked at her like she'd grown another head, but the thought had been swirling around in her mind ever since she'd overheard Rhodes and the other man talking.

"You know Dr. Rhodes is highly respected at the hospital," Katherine said. "He's a family man and an all-around good guy. I don't see it."

"No one saw my father for what he was either," Lacey said, her tone sharper than she'd meant it to be.

Katherine grimaced. "Okay, I'll have to give you that one."

"I'm sorry. I'm not trying to be snippy. Just let me explain." She recounted her experience in Dr. Rhodes's office, explaining about Fawn's shirt being on the back of the door, then repeating the dialogue she'd heard. "And he's got a picture of him and some of the other men in town that he's friends with. They're all holding crossbows."

Creed frowned. "A lot of hunters use crossbows."

"I'm not saying he was the one who shot at us, but I think he might be connected to the person who did. Like maybe it was one of the men in the picture or maybe he's friends with someone who wasn't in the picture. I don't know." She shrugged. "Could be he just knows him and they're friends but doesn't have any idea his friend is a killer."

"But what reason would said friend have to come after you?" Katherine asked.

Her head started to pound. "I don't know. I really don't know. It's so very confusing." She rubbed her eyes. "But they were looking for something, and I think the guy that was giving Dr. Rhodes a hard time wanted Rhodes to find it."

"But he hadn't."

"No." She waved a hand. "Hence the break-in."

"Then we need to ask Dr. Rhodes who he was talking to."

She nodded. That would fall under his responsibility. "Any word on the autopsy?" she asked Creed. "I need to know when they'll release her—" she couldn't bring herself to say *body* "—so that I know when to schedule the funeral."

"Yeah, the ME promised to get it done tomorrow."

"Good." On the one hand, she wasn't in a hurry to say her final goodbyes to Fawn, and yet she was. The funeral would bring closure. Not like finding her killer would bring, but it would help.

Lacey's phone rang and she snatched it from her back pocket. "It's Miranda."

"See what she wants," he said. "I'm going to make some calls of my own while you talk to her."

"And I'm going to head home," Katherine said. "I'll let myself out."

Lacey nodded. "Thank you for the food and everything."

"Of course. We'll talk later."

Lacey swiped the screen just before the call would go to voice mail and lifted the device to her ear. "Hi, Miranda."

"Lacey, I'm glad I caught you. I just wanted to check in with you and see if you'd made any progress in finding Fawn's killer?"

"Some. Hold on a second." She paused and walked into the kitchen, where she pulled her AirPods from the charger and slipped them into her ears. Might as well be productive while she talked. "I'm glad you called. I have a quick question for you."

"Sure."

"Do you think it's possible Dr. Rhodes could be the man Fawn was involved with?" Silence from the other end of the line echoed back at her. "Miranda?"

"Oh, sorry. Where did you get his name?"

"From one of the other doctors we talked to at the hospital. She never said the two of them were romantically involved, but as close as they were, he seemed like a good candidate. When we went to see him at his office, he had a lot of family and friends pictures on the credenza behind his desk. Fawn was in several of them. Of course, it could all be completely innocent. I don't want to say anything without evidence to back it up."

"That's good. No need to stir that pot."

"Do you think you could ask Tucker if he knows anything about who she might have been seeing? I mean, he and the doctor run with a pretty tight-knit group. Maybe one of them knows something?"

"I don't really think anything will come of it, but, sure, I can ask Tucker."

"Thank you."

"I mean, I knew Fawn and Dr. Rhodes were friends, but I can't really see him cheating on his wife. Like you said, he and Tucker are friends, and Tucker's never said a word about any sign of infidelity."

And the truth was, if Tucker knew the doctor was cheating, he might keep his mouth shut about it and Miranda would never know. "Considering Tucker's past with our father, how did Tucker feel about Fawn and you being friends? I mean, Fawn said they got along because they both loved you, but deep down, she said he still harbored resentment toward her."

Silence once more. "You're not accusing Tucker of anything, are you?"

"What? No. Not at all. But you were there when he screamed at Fawn and me in front of the whole school cafeteria. Was he still angry with Fawn?" *And me?*

"Absolutely not. He's gotten past all of that. It took some time and counseling, but he came to realize that you and Fawn had nothing to do with your father's actions. He and I were Fawn's friends. We often had dinner together and Fawn would come spend holidays with us when she wasn't with you." A lengthy pause stretched until Miranda said, "You didn't know all that."

"No." Wow. Had she known Fawn at all? "I see. Well, thank you for filling me in."

"Is everything okay, Lacey? Besides the obvious, I mean."

Lacey told the woman about the trashing of Fawn's home.

"Oh no, Lacey, I'm so sorry. Can I do anything to help?"

"No, but thanks."

"Okay, well, keep me updated on the investigation, will you? I can't stand that someone did this to her."

"Of course."

Lacey hung up and went to work on cleaning the rest of the kitchen. She and Katherine had gotten the worst of it, but there were still areas that could use some scrubbing.

A noise behind her spun her around. Creed stood in the doorway. "You okay?" he asked.

"Yeah." She told him about her conversation with Miranda. "I think we should have another talk with the doctor and straight up ask him if he was having an affair with Fawn." She couldn't believe those words were coming out of her mouth. "I also want to know who he was talking to in his office, what they're looking for and if he trashed my—*Fawn's*—house."

"I'm going to try to get ahold of Dr. Rhodes. If I can't, I'll get Ben to go find him. He also brought me some things, so I'm going to grab those. I can keep an eye on the house while he and I talk."

"Anything I need to know about?"

"He brought the papers for you to sign, since we can't seem to get that done."

"Oh. Right."

"Second thoughts?"

"No. My boss knows I'm going to be gone for a while." She shot him a smile. "One of the perks of working all the time is that I have tons of leave built up, and he's a compassionate guy. He knows I need to take care of Fawn's arrangements and...stuff."

Creed nodded.

"All right. I'm just going to be right outside. Call or text me if you need anything."

"I'll be fine, but thanks. I think I'm going to do some

more searching and see what I can find. And probably some more cleaning."

"I can help you when I'm finished. Be right back. Lock the door behind me."

"Yes, sir." She saluted.

He rolled his eyes and stepped out onto the porch. "I'll be back."

"I'll probably be here."

With another eye roll, he shut the door behind him.

Scarlett nudged her hand. "I know, girl. Come on and I'll let you out the back and you can take care of business."

While Scarlett was outside in the fenced area, Lacey headed upstairs. The two bedrooms were almost finished but needed painting. Then she could get the furniture out of storage and—

What was she thinking? She didn't need the furniture that was in storage because she wasn't planning on staying here. She could sell the stuff and then the house once it was completed. She drew in a deep breath. "Okay, so that's the plan," she muttered. "Find Fawn's killer, have the funeral, finish fixing up the house and put it on the market."

The thought of burying her sister grieved her like nothing else. Not even her father's crimes or her breakup with Creed—although that came close. But what surprised her was the sadness that overwhelmed her when she thought about putting the house on the market.

"Why does that make me sad?" she whispered. "I'm so weird."

But it was definitely something to think about.

Creed slipped into the passenger seat next to Ben and leaned his head back. His side throbbed and he should probably take some more pain meds, but for now, he needed information Ben had. And the overnight bag. His mom had provided a change of clothes, but he needed a razor and a few other items. Ben handed him the bag. "What'd you find out?"

"Got the footage from the gym's camera. You wouldn't believe the fuss the owner put up."

"Probably afraid he's going to be sued or something. And?"

"Parking-lot camera shows him following you and Lacey into the parking lot."

Creed frowned. "How'd I miss that?"

"I don't know. He didn't get out of his car right away, and when he did, he never showed his face."

"Plates?"

"He parked so the plates weren't facing the camera."

"So, he knew where the cameras were."

"Absolutely. That's even more evident as the footage plays. The guy gets out of the car and already has his hoodie pulled up. He went around to the side of the gym and entered on the west end."

Creed raised a brow. "He has a key to the gym?"

"That was my first thought, too," Ben said, "but no, members can use their card to scan in and bypass the front desk."

"Then they should have a record of the entry."

"Yep."

"So, who was it?"

"Gillian Fields."

Creed scoffed. "That wasn't Gillian Fields who attacked Lacey. The guy was big, muscled and mean."

"I know. I know Gillian, and when I talked to her, she

said she lost her card and hasn't gotten a new one yet because she keeps thinking it's going to show up."

"When did she lose it?"

"The day Lacey was attacked."

Creed frowned. "Wait a minute. We had no idea that we would be visiting the gym. That was strictly a spur-of-the-moment thing. We went straight from Miranda's."

"Then someone knew you'd wind up there eventually?"

"No." He shook his head. "There's a connection to this Gillian Fields and whoever followed us to the gym."

"What kind of connection?"

"Someone with access to her purse keys."

He nodded. "All right. I'll talk to her again."

"And Miranda Glenn was the only one who knew we were going to the gym."

"I'll see if she said anything to anyone."

"Thanks, Ben. Now, what about Fawn's mail service? Did she stop it?"

"She didn't."

"So, she was coming here to get it or…?"

"No idea. We're still looking into that."

Creed looked around. The nearest neighbor in sight of Fawn's mailbox was about a quarter of a mile away. Properties in this area were spread out, but they were there. "Okay, the only way to get to this mailbox is to turn on Hillside Road. You'd pass six houses before getting back here to Fawn's. Let's see if anyone noticed a strange car—or maybe even a familiar one—driving this way over the past three months. It might not have been every day, maybe just a couple of times a week, but surely, someone saw something. Fawn's property is a dead end."

"Good point. I'll see if I can run that down."

"Good. I'm ready to find this person and put them away for good."

Creed's phone buzzed. His mother. He frowned and tapped the screen. "Hi, Mom."

"Someone broke into the store, Creed!" His mother's sob nearly tore him in two.

"Mom, stop. Tell me what happened."

"Your father had closed the store early and was doing the monthly inventory when someone kicked in the door. They punched him in the face, grabbed the cash on the counter and ran out the door."

Creed's stomach dipped. "I'll be on the way shortly, Mom. I just need to make sure Lacey's safe before I can leave. Is Dad okay?"

Ben looked at him. Creed muted the phone. "Call Mac and tell him to get out here. Then call Lacey and let her know to hunker down with her gun until Mac gets here. I need you to take me to the store—or the hospital. Not sure which just yet."

Ben grabbed his phone and punched the screen.

"The paramedics are here with him now," his mother was saying. "He…he has a b-broken nose and a frac-tured cheek, but they said he'll be fine. But he might need surgery."

His heart pounded. "Hang tight, Mom. I'll be there as fast as I can." He turned back to Ben. "Where's Mac?"

"On the way. He'll be here in ten minutes. Regina is on her way to the store. She said for you to stay with your parents."

"Lacey?"

"I'm guessing it won't take her that long to get out here."

He was right. The door to the house flew open and she ran to the car. Ben rolled the window down.

"Creed, are they okay?"

"Yes, but I need to get to them."

"Of course you do. Go."

"I'm not leaving you alone. Mac is on the way."

"I'll be fine. Now go."

"Get back in the house and lock the door. Then let me know when Mac gets here."

"I will. Give them my love."

He nodded and she darted back into the house. Creed glanced at his phone. A text from Zeb, the coroner. I managed to get to Fawn Jefferson's autopsy earlier than expected. I'll send you the report. Call me if you have questions.

Five more minutes and Mac would be there—and Lacey was armed. He nodded to Ben and they whipped out of Lacey's drive to head toward town.

FOURTEEN

Lacey's phone buzzed with a text. Mac had arrived and was parked on the curb. She walked to the window and waved at him. He waved back, and she turned, pressed fingers to her eyes, then dropped her hands and returned to the guest room.

This was where Fawn had planned to spend time working. She'd already painted two walls. The paint can sat to the left of the closet, and Lacey decided she might as well finish the other two. Maybe the mindless activity would help her gather her thoughts, go over the evidence in her head and figure out what she—and everyone else—was missing. And she could pray for Creed's father.

Scarlett joined her in the room and settled on the floor to watch her. "So, the paint is here, but where are the brushes?" The dog yawned and closed her eyes. "Well, you're a big help."

Lacey went to the guest room closet and opened the door. She'd glimpsed inside in her earlier search, but now started pulling things out. It wasn't a huge closet, but it had a lot of stuff. Well organized and neat, but packed. And she wanted to know what was in here. A few clothes hung on the bars and three cleaned paintbrushes sat on the shelf to her right, along with a drop cloth and several rags. Good to know. She'd come back to those.

Finally, she had everything out, including suitcases. Fawn had piled several blankets over something in the corner, a stack of pillows in front of them. And while Lacey had noticed this in her earlier search, she hadn't realized it was more than just a pile of blankets. Now she caught a glimpse of something behind the top pillow. She moved it and sucked in a breath. A two-drawer file cabinet.

Had her sister hidden it on purpose? Or was it just a convenient place to stack things when one had a lot of stuff to store? She pulled on the top drawer.

Locked.

Lacey spun, raced to grab the keys she'd found in the gym bag and hurried back. The second key slid home and she opened the drawer.

Files upon files.

She opened the bottom drawer. The same, only it was half-full. A large bag took up the other half of the drawer.

"Okay, then," she told Scarlett, "looks like our plans have changed. The painting is going to have to wait."

It took her four trips, but she pulled every file from the drawer and set everything in the corner of the room. She dropped the bag next to the nearest stack and settled herself on the floor in front of it. She started with the stack of files to her left. Car insurance, home warranty, various receipts from the renovation, a life insurance policy with Lacey as the beneficiary for almost half a million dollars.

Lacey nearly choked. "Oh, Fawn…" she whispered. The bag kept snagging her attention, so she opened it.

And found cash. A *lot* of cash. Lacey pulled it all out with shaking fingers and counted it. Twenty thousand dollars. "What in the world, Fawn?" Maybe it was simply some kind of emergency stash.

But…for what? She snapped pictures of it, then stuffed it all back in the bag and zipped it shut. She went back to the files, hoping she would find something that would give her a clue about the money. She found the bank statements and eagerly scanned them, looking for the large withdrawal.

But even going back a full year, there was nothing.

Could Fawn have another account she didn't know about? Probably not. She had a checking account and a savings account.

Time passed, and when she looked up, it was dark outside. She shot a text to Creed. How are your parents?

His reply came back shortly.

At the hospital with Dad. He's going to be okay. A broken nose, but no surgery required. His cheekbone is fractured, so he'll have to be careful not to do any more damage, but he'll be going home shortly and I'll head back to your place to relieve Mac.

Did you catch the guy who did it?

Not yet, but Dad has more cameras than the average store. Regina's already started going through the footage.

Can I help?

No, the best thing you can do is stay put and stay safe. Please, Lacey.

She grimaced. I'm staying put. Found some more files in the guest closet, so going through those.

Good. Let me know if you find anything.

I found something, but not sure how it relates. It's a bag of cash. I also found her bank statements, but nothing to indicate that she withdrew a large amount of cash in the last year. No idea where it came from. I found her life insurance policy and other pertinent documents.

She set her phone aside and sighed.

Scarlett had started pacing, her gaze swinging toward the door, then back to Lacey. "Need to go out, girl?"

Scarlett raced for the stairs. Lacey let her out, filled the dog's bowls, then returned to the room. The next file she found was labeled Medical.

Lacey went to the chair and opened the folder on the desk under the lamp. The first thing she saw was a medical bill for a gynecologist in South Carolina. But it was the copy of an ultrasound picture that sent shards of shock shivering through her. F. Miller. Then it had the date of the ultrasound and the fact that the woman was eight weeks pregnant.

The air left her lungs and she wilted even while her mind quickly did the math. The baby would be a couple of weeks old if she had carried it full term. Older if she'd delivered early.

Lacey quickly flipped through more pictures. Two months later, at sixteen weeks, there was another ultrasound. This one confirmed it was a boy. And this was another copy of the original. So where were the originals?

And the next five pictures, from a private imaging

company located five hours away—why so far?—showed the baby in full 3D at seven and a half months. Lacey gasped. He was beautiful. Perfect in every way. Who was he? Why did Fawn have pictures of another woman's ultrasound? She traced a finger over the little hand. All four fingers and his tiny thumb, spread like he was waving at her. Another picture showed him yawning. In the next, he was sucking his thumb.

Lacey swallowed hard and texted Creed. I found ultrasound pictures in Fawn's filing cabinet. The woman's name on them is F. Miller. Miller was their mother's maiden name.

Her phone rang and she snatched it up. "Creed?"

"Are you sitting down?"

"Just tell me."

"I just read the autopsy report. I was getting ready to call you when I got your text."

"Okay." She could barely breathe, scared of what he had to say and wanting to shake him for not saying it faster. "What?"

"Fawn recently either *had* a baby or lost one."

"What?" Lacey let out a laugh of disbelief. "No, she didn't."

"Autopsy says she did." He paused while Lacey's brain scrambled for words. "I think those pictures may be of Fawn's child," he finally said. "It makes sense."

"No. That's impossible."

"Lacey—"

"She would have told me." Her words sounded strained and desperate even to her own ears.

"She might not have, Lacey. If she was pregnant by a married man—"

"But why use a different name?" F. Miller. Fawn Miller?

"To make sure no one discovered whatever deception she was involved with. A nonprofit pregnancy center would do the ultrasounds for free. What's the name of the clinic?"

"Harrisburg Women's Clinic."

"Hold on." Seconds later, he said, "Yeah, it's a free clinic."

Could it be? "Miller is my mom's maiden name, Creed. I think you might be right." Her heart squeezed. "It's a boy," she said around a tight throat. "She had a son if she gave birth and he wasn't stillborn or anything."

"Look for adoption papers."

"I've been through almost all of the files. There aren't any adoption papers so far."

"Okay, one more thing and this is going to hurt."

"Tell me."

"Zeb said the first blow to Fawn's head didn't kill her." Lacey stifled a gasp. "Her hyoid bone was broken."

"She was *strangled*? Oh, Creed, no…" Tears overflowed to drip off her chin. She sniffed and wiped them away. "Finish telling me, please. All of it."

"Zeb said the bruises on her throat indicate that someone held an object there. Whoever did it didn't use his hands, so there's no prints. Most likely, it was a piece of wood or something."

A sob slipped from her.

"I'm so sorry, Lacey."

She drew in a steadying breath. She could cry and grieve later. Voices in the background reached her while her mind spun with the new information. Her sister had been strangled.

"Hang on a sec again," he said.

She held, fighting tears and a dark fury at the person who'd done this to her sister. *Strangled.* She was still trying to wrap her mind around it when he came back on the line. "I've got to go," he said, "but I won't be much longer. There's nothing I can do here. Dad's going to be okay, so I'll be heading back your way shortly."

"Okay. Thank you."

"I know this is a shock, Lacey. We'll process it together when I get back."

"Yeah."

"'Bye."

She hung up and pressed shaking fingers to her lips. "Oh, Fawn, I'm so sorry. Where's your baby?" Had she miscarried? Had he been stillborn and Fawn had needed time to heal and process? But the timeline didn't work. Fawn would have taken her three-month sabbatical around her sixth month of pregnancy. Meaning she planned to give birth, then go back to work.

After she gave the baby up for adoption?

She wasn't planning to keep him, as there was nothing in the house that even hinted there was a child coming. Then again, maybe she had put everything in storage? But that made absolutely no sense. Fawn wouldn't have been fixing up the house and not have had a nursery ready for her child if she'd planned on keeping him.

A noise from downstairs stiffened her spine until she remembered she'd let Scarlett out and the dog probably wanted back in. She ran down the steps and opened the door and Scarlett brushed past her. Lacey shut the door and hurried back up the stairs, only to stop and sniff. Gasoline?

Scarlett barked. Then barked a never-ending sound that said she wasn't happy.

Lacey's phone buzzed from the guest room and she raced to retrieve it. A text from Mac. Stay inside. Someone just tossed liquid onto your front porch. I'm going after him.

Fury stiffened her spine and she snagged her weapon from the floor near the stack of files. She dialed Mac's number, and it rang four times, then went to voice mail.

With a groan, she called Creed.

As soon as he picked up, she said, "Someone's here. Mac's not answering his phone and I smell—" A loud crash, the breaking of glass, and a whoosh came from the first floor, sending her scrambling down the stairs. Scarlett's barking took on a new edge of frantic.

"Scarlett!"

"Lacey!" Creed's shout shook her out of her panic even as she stared at the wall of flames lining the front of the house.

Another crash from the kitchen.

"Creed, the house is on fire!" She ran toward the sound and stopped as soon as she came to the entrance to the kitchen. Flames were already licking quickly in her direction. Two more booms from the den spun her. Scarlett bounded to her, barking and spinning. Lacey jammed her gun into her waistband and grabbed the dog's collar with her free hand, her heart pounding. "I'm trapped, Creed! Someone threw Molotov cocktails inside. At least three, maybe more!"

Smoke lodged in her lungs and she coughed.

She heard him giving Ben orders to call for help. "I'm on the way!"

"Check on Mac. He's not answering." She had to get

away from the smoke—and the paint cans before they exploded. Coughing, she and Scarlett bolted upstairs to the guest room. Already the smoke was swirling in the room and the smoke alarm blared. Lacey shut the door behind her, dragged in a lungful of clean air, then raced to the closet to snag two pillows. She stuffed them against the crack left between the door and the floor.

"Lacey! Talk to me!"

She just realized Creed was yelling at her on the phone. "I'm in my old room. I'm going to be in our spot and will need a ladder to get down!"

"Fire truck is on the way. Hold tight."

Like she had a choice.

Scarlett whined and backed away from the door. Smoke continued to fill the room in spite of her best efforts to stop it with the pillows. She went to the window and opened it. Cold air rushed in and smoke billowed out, but she was able to grab another gasp of pure night air.

She glanced back at the bedroom door. The pillows were burning. Lacey grabbed the bag of money and the medical file with the ultrasound pictures. She shoved them out the window and climbed after them, planting her feet securely on the roof. "Scarlett, come."

The dog hesitated. Then, with trust in her eyes, she followed Lacey out the window. Lacey kept a tight hold on the animal's collar with one hand and shut the window with the other. Grateful for a pocket of fresh air, she looked in the direction of town and could see the flashing red lights of the fire trucks and blue lights of the law enforcement vehicles.

But what about Mac? *Oh, please, God, let Mac be all right.* "I'm out on the roof, Creed. I have Scarlett with me."

"I'm just a few minutes away."

"Please check on Mac. I haven't seen or heard from him. I'm worried for him."

"We'll check on him. You just concentrate on staying alive."

As the flames licked closer, she wondered if the person after her would finally win.

Creed left his parents in the good and caring hands of some friends from their church and headed as fast as he dared toward Lacey's home. Ten minutes later, Ben was turning into her drive, and the sight that greeted him made him nauseous.

The fire trucks had arrived ahead of them and already had the hoses aimed at the burning home. Another truck was backing toward the window that used to be Lacey's old room. Creed couldn't see her, thanks to the thick smoke, but he pictured her and Scarlett on the roof, waiting for the ladder to reach the edge. *Please, God, get her down safe.*

Ben pulled to a stop next to Mac's car and threw the cruiser in Park. "You check on Mac," Creed said. "I'm going after Lacey."

Ben headed for Mac, and Creed sent up a silent prayer for the man while he aimed himself toward the back of the house.

"Lacey?" His shout turned several heads, but the truck was there and the ladder was almost in place. He looked up and Lacey's gaze locked on his.

"Creed?" Creed turned to see Parker Adams, the fire chief, coming toward him. "What are you doing here?"

"Lacey called me."

"We're trying to get her down. She refuses to come

down until the dog is safe, but apparently the dog is being skittish and my guy can't get close enough to grab her. And Lacey isn't strong enough to force her."

"Scarlett knows me. Let me try."

"Yeah, fine. Just hurry. The fire is burning hot and getting closer to her."

Creed ran to the ladder, grabbed the face mask someone held out to him, then hurried up the stairs to come face-to-face with a struggling Lacey. She coughed and her eyes and nose streamed from the smoke.

"Give me Scarlett!"

"Scarlett, go."

The dog hesitated.

"Come here, girl," Creed said. "Scarlett, come."

Another coughing fit shook Lacey. Scarlett barked and took a few steps closer to Creed. That was all he needed. He lunged forward and grabbed the dog's collar. Scarlett balked at first, but Creed was stronger and he soon had her in his arms. He turned and passed her to the firefighter behind him.

Smoke swirled, flames shot from the roof toward the sky and a loud crack echoed around them. The roof started to collapse, and Lacey screamed even as she catapulted toward him. Creed caught her with one arm. Fire of a different kind arched through his stitched side, but he held on to Lacey with his left arm and clung to the ladder with his right. She swung below him, legs pumping air. "Grab the ladder, Lacey!" He was going to drop her if she didn't do something. And fast.

She must have heard the desperation in his tone, because she launched herself toward the nearest rung and hooked her elbow around it. "I got it," she rasped.

"Hang on!"

"I can't."

"You can. I'll help you, but you've got to pull yourself around in front of me. We'll go down together."

"Creed…"

"Now, Lacey!"

She groaned, and he grabbed a handful of her T-shirt, and with his help, she maneuvered herself around to the right side of the ladder. Creed sucked in a breath and grimaced at the agony shooting in his side, but began the descent. One rung at a time.

When they reached the bottom, Scarlett barked, frantic to get to her. "Let her go," Lacey said. The firefighter did and Scarlett hurtled herself at Lacey. "Good girl. Sit."

Scarlett sat. Lacey looked up at Creed. "Got a rope? Her lead is toast."

"No, but we'll find one. Now come on. You need oxygen."

He led Lacey to the back of the ambulance, and Annie slapped a mask over her face. "Scarlett, down. Settle." At Lacey's hoarse command, Scarlett dropped on the floor beside the gurney, eyes watching everything, nose twitching, sides heaving with her pants.

Annie and Hannah were once again the paramedics on call. Annie placed a dog oxygen mask over Scarlett's snout and Creed was surprised the animal didn't try to shake it off.

Lacey looked at Creed and pulled the oxygen mask away. "Mac?"

"I'm going to go find out. Be right back."

Creed left her and jogged back to the car where he found Ben soaking wet and passing a bottle of water to an equally saturated Mac. Mac blinked up at them, his eyes foggy.

"What happened?" Creed asked.

"Found him on the ground around the side of the house," Ben said. "He was hidden by the bushes, but the hoses got us."

"I saw someone sneaking around," Mac said, "and went after them. Whoever it was got the drop on me." He pressed a hand to his bleeding head. "Man. That smarts." His eyes sharpened and homed in on Creed. "Lacey?"

"She's okay. Some smoke inhalation, but nothing she can't recover from."

Mac's face reflected his relief. "I'm sorry, man."

"Don't worry about it. You can ride in the ambulance with Lacey to the hospital."

"No, I'm okay."

"As your boss, I'm telling you to get checked out."

"Gotcha."

Creed and Ben helped Mac to the ambulance. "Got another rider for you."

"Mac," Lacey said. "You're okay." She blinked back tears when Mac climbed inside and sat on the floor. "I was so worried about you." Creed's heart tumbled over itself at the fact that she cared so much for the safety of his friend when she'd just lost her childhood home and barely escaped with her life.

"Yeah." Mac groaned and leaned his head back. "I'm so sorry, Lacey. I can't tell you how sorry I am."

"It's just a house, Mac. We're alive, and I'm grateful."

Mac squeezed her hand and Creed looked on. "I'm right behind you two. See you at the hospital."

He shut the door and turned to give orders to Ben. "Get a crime scene unit here and the arson unit from Asheville. This guy had to have left some kind of evidence behind, and I want it found before it's too late."

FIFTEEN

At the hospital, Lacey was diagnosed with mild smoke inhalation, but there'd be no permanent damage. Fortunately, she'd managed to get to clean air fast enough, and after medications and oxygen treatments, she was feeling much better. Katherine stopped in with orders to rest and the key to her former apartment located above the local medical clinic. "It's furnished, but because no one's lived there in a while, I've called in a cleaning crew. By the time you get there, it should be in order."

Lacey took the key with a tight throat—more from her emotions than the smoke—and nodded her thanks. Then frowned. "A cleaning crew? At this time of night?"

Katherine winked. "They're a special kind of crew. You're staying here for the night, but the apartment will be ready for you around ten in the morning."

"Thank you, Katherine," she whispered. Then cleared her throat, grateful that it was only a tad sore. "How's Mac?"

"Slight concussion but heading home to Isabelle to rest."

"He'll have the next few days off to heal," Creed said. He'd been sitting silently in the chair near the window.

Lacey turned to look at him, noting the pained creases in his forehead and his hand pressed to his side. "Did you get checked out?"

"I'm fine."

Lacey simply turned her eyes to Katherine, who raised a brow at Creed.

Creed sighed and pulled his shirt up to reveal he'd ripped his stitches loose. Katherine shook her head. "You two are going to have quite the story to tell your kids one day."

Lacey froze and Creed stilled.

Katherine flushed. "I mean, not *your* kids as in your kids together, but just *your* kids. If you have any with other— Okay, I'm going to stop now and go get a suture kit to fix that wound. Be right back."

She was out the door before Lacey could blink. Then she laughed. And coughed. And laughed some more. Creed looked at her with concern. "You okay?"

"Yes." She wiped her watering eyes. "Sorry. I guess it wasn't that funny. Maybe I just needed the release of laughter, which has been sorely missing from my life lately." She took another hit of oxygen and caught her breath. Thankful to be feeling better, she tried to ignore the fact she was so tired, she could barely keep her eyes open. Then she remembered the bag and sat up with a gasp. "Where's the stuff I threw down out of the window? The bag?"

"It's at the office with Ben."

She flopped back with a relieved sigh. "Good."

"No idea where she got the money?" he asked.

"No. Not a clue." She bit her lip. "And the autopsy showed she was pregnant. I can't even..."

"Yeah."

Lacey nodded. "I guess we can make an educated guess as to what she was doing those three months."

"She was hiding her pregnancy."

"From me and everyone else." She shook her head. "So, where's her baby?"

"From the way people have described her, it sounds like she could have lost him."

"Yes." She'd thought of that.

"Or," he said, "maybe she gave him up for adoption. Maybe she took the time to work through all that comes with that."

"Possibly." Lacey yawned and forced her eyes back open. She frowned. "No, wait. The dates from the ultrasound and her leave of absence would put her going back to work a week after she gave birth. Unless she had him early or something."

He ran his hand through his hair. "So, she finds out she's pregnant. The father is likely the mysterious doctor she'd been seeing—possibly Dr. Rhodes. Maybe she told him she was pregnant and he didn't want anything to do with that."

"Maybe the twenty grand was a payoff of some sort?" Lacey asked. "His altruistic gesture that says, 'I don't want the child, but I'm not a bad guy. Here's money to take care of you and the baby for a while.'"

He nodded. "And maybe Fawn felt like she couldn't raise the child on her own—or she just didn't want him."

"She'd want him." Lacey breathed deeply from the oxygen mask. The talking was hurting her throat, but she *had* to figure this out. "Or maybe she wouldn't." She threw her hands up. "I have no idea at this point. Mostly because I have to admit that I have no idea who Fawn was." The thought made her want to cry. She'd thought she and Fawn were close, but by Lacey keeping her distance, it had been a false closeness. Add in Fawn hiding secrets and keeping Lacey in the dark about her personal issues and troubles and...yeah.

"You knew her," Creed said. "You just didn't know all her secrets. The sister you knew and loved was still there. Just because she withheld this from you doesn't mean she was some stranger."

"Well, she feels like it."

He sighed. "I know. I'm sorry." He rose to kiss her forehead and Lacey's heart nearly jumped out of her chest. When he drew back, his gaze met hers and she couldn't decipher the look.

"Creed—"

"Get some rest, Lacey. There's a guard on the door. I'm going to check on my dad. Then I'll be back to stay in that surprisingly comfortable chair the rest of the night."

"Oh, Creed, you don't have to—"

"And then I'll take you home—well, to Katherine's old place—in the morning and we'll get a fresh start on looking into Fawn's pregnancy and who might have known about it, why she felt the need to keep it a secret, where the money came from, and so on. And I'm going to call Dr. Rhodes right now and ask him if the baby is his."

"I must be a bad influence," she murmured. "You just interrupted me twice."

He chuckled, and Lacey let her eyelids flutter shut. She was too tired to think straight, but because Creed was by her side, she'd be able to sleep.

On the way home from the hospital the next morning, Creed finally got ahold of Dr. Rhodes. He hesitated a moment, then put the phone on speaker so Lacey could hear. "Thank you for taking my call."

"I suppose this is about Fawn?"

"It is. I'm just going to come right out and ask you. Did you have an affair with her?"

A heavy sigh filtered through the line. "Yes. I did."

Lacey gave a small gasp, then pressed her fingers to her lips.

"Did you know she was pregnant?"

A long pause. Creed glanced at Lacey. "Dr. Rhodes?"

"Yes. I knew," he finally said.

"And did you give her twenty thousand dollars?"

"Well, you've really done your homework, haven't you?" His low voice filtered through the line, a combination of weariness and hesitancy...and maybe a fraction of relief mixed in. "I did. I told her whatever she decided about the child was her decision, but I could have no part in its life."

"What was her reaction to that?"

"She was hurt, but she understood. We never sugar-coated what we were doing and neither of us had blinders on. Fawn never asked me to leave my family for her and I never offered. But...it wasn't a fling. It wasn't a one-night stand. I loved Fawn."

"But you tried to pay her off to get rid of the baby."

"Yes." His sigh echoed through the line. "I did. I'm not proud of it, but I didn't kill her."

"Why didn't you just come clean when we asked you?"

"Because I was scared. Scared because, in your eyes, it would give me a motive to kill her. And I didn't, but I couldn't figure out if I had an alibi or not."

"I'm going to need one."

"I know. Give me the day and time you need one for and I'll find a way to provide it."

Creed told him and the man promised to get back to him. "One more question. Lacey overheard a conversation between you and someone in your office about you needing to find something or you would be in trouble. Who were you talking to?"

"She heard that?"

"She did."

"That was Dr. Fitzgerald. Some data on our project was misplaced and it could have ruined the entire thing. All that hard work down the drain. I was devastated. But we wound up finding it, so everything worked out."

"I see. You know I'll be talking to Dr. Fitzgerald."

"Of course. Talk to him. I have six other doctors who can back that up."

"Thank you, Dr. Rhodes." He hung up and Creed asked Ben to keep an eye on the man. "Watch him. If he tries to run, arrest him."

"On it."

He was going to have so much overtime to pay out this month.

Creed shot Lacey a glance. "Well, that answers a few questions. We're getting closer."

"Yeah." She wiped a stray tear and sniffed. Then straightened her shoulders and pulled in a deep breath.

Creed spun into the medical facility parking lot and parked. He climbed carefully out of the driver's seat with his hand pressed to his side. This time, he'd refused all drugs that might keep him from driving. Together, he, Scarlett and Lacey walked up the steps, and he pushed open the door, holding it for Lacey and Scarlett. As soon as they stepped inside, he followed and could smell someone had been doing some deep cleaning.

Lacey sniffed. "Wow."

Katherine came out of the kitchen, followed by Miranda, Jessica Hill, Annie, the paramedic, and two other ladies. "Surprise," Katherine said.

Lacey let out a low laugh. "The cleaning crew?"

Katherine nodded. "Just finished up."

Miranda walked over and hugged Lacey. "I'm so glad you're okay."

"Me, too," Jessica said.

Annie replaced Miranda and gave Lacey a quick squeeze. "We all are."

"You guys…" Lacey swallowed and a tear dripped down her cheek. "I don't even know what to say."

"Try 'thank you,'" Creed said.

She elbowed him in his good side. A light tap that would have had more force behind it if he hadn't been injured. "Thank you," Lacey said. "From the bottom of my heart, thank you." She walked into the den area. "Oh, look, a bed for Scarlett right there in front of the fireplace." She pressed her hands against her chest as though her emotions were too much. She turned back to the group watching, then looked at Scarlett and pointed. "Scarlett, bed."

Scarlett loped over and made herself comfortable on the oversize cushion. The ladies laughed and Jessica clapped. "She loves it."

"Of course."

"All right," Katherine said, "you have a couple of weeks' worth of clothing hanging in the master closet, a few towels, a change of sheets and all that you should need for a comfy stay. Creed, we got some more clothes from your mom so you can have something that doesn't smell like smoke. There's enough dog food and treats for Scarlett that I should be her new BFF. Oh, and a well-stocked fridge, including a couple of casseroles you can heat and eat. Easy enough, right?"

"Oh my." Lacey shook her head, and Creed thought his heart would burst at the love being shown to this woman who thought everyone in town hated her. Who thought she *deserved* to be hated because of her father's actions.

Katherine gave her one more hug. "We're going to get out of here so you can get some rest."

"But before we do that," Jessica said, "I wanted to invite you to my baby shower."

Lacey raised a brow. "But you just had a baby."

"Yes, but the shower was rescheduled because I had her early. Please say you'll come if you feel like it. It's a drop-in, so you don't have to stay long if you don't want to, but I'd love to have you there. And don't worry about a gift. Just come."

"When?"

"Day after tomorrow."

"Um…yes, sure, I'll try."

"Well, it's at my house," Miranda said, "so leave the dog at home, okay?" She laughed. "Sorry, that sounded kind of rude. I didn't mean it that way."

Lacey gave her a gentle smile. "I didn't take it that way. Of course. I'll leave her here." She'd noticed Miranda staying away from Scarlett. "Bad experience with dogs?"

"Something like that." She clapped her hands. "Then I guess we'll see you at the shower. Feel better."

"Thank you."

Miranda turned and left, followed by the others echoing her well-wishes.

Soon, it was just Creed and Lacey left in the place, and he motioned for her to sit. "Relax. I'll fix some food and arrange for some security on this place."

She nodded. The fact that she didn't argue or offer to help told him an awful lot about her state of mind.

Once he'd fixed both of them a plate of chicken casserole, he carried it to the den, handed her the food and made himself comfortable on the couch. "I don't know about you, but I think the fire thing was a pretty desperate act."

"I know." Her brow remained furrowed.

"What are you thinking?"

"Just trying to fill in the puzzle. Someone was watching the house even before I came back."

"Yes, looks that way."

"I'm also convinced someone went through all of Fawn's drawers before they decided to be bold and just trash the place. I also think," she said slowly, "they didn't find what they were looking for, so they simply burned the house down. I'm not sure they were actually trying to kill me, but were more interested in getting rid of whatever it is they were looking for. Although, maybe killing me in the process could be considered a bonus. Who knows?"

"You think the person knew about the money and the ultrasound pictures?"

She nodded, then looked up and met his gaze. "I don't know about that, but it makes sense. More than that, though, I think that there was more than one person."

That stilled him. "Why do you say that?"

"Because the little cocktails came in the back and the front almost simultaneously."

"Well, it would explain how someone was able to sneak up behind Mac. If his attention was on one attacker, the other could have knocked him out." He paused. "I think the break-in at my parents' store was a distraction."

She raised a brow. "Why?"

"Because they needed Ben and me gone in order to get to you. The way to make that happen was to make the attack personal."

Lacey swallowed hard and shook her head. "Okay, if that's the case, then they probably didn't plan on Mac getting here quite so fast and decided to just take care of him when he went looking for them."

"Maybe. Or they figured one person would be easier to deal with than two. They might have thought I'd take off, leaving Ben alone to guard you. Either way, their plan worked to a certain extent. They only had to deal with one person."

She ate three bites, then set it aside. "It's good, but I'm about to fall asleep where I'm sitting. I'll eat after I take a nap. But before I find my way to the bed, I need to know if there's anything else the autopsy report came back with."

Creed sighed. "Nothing I haven't already told you. Just that she'd been pregnant—either having given birth to a live child or had a late-term miscarriage."

"And she was hit in the head with something that knocked her out and then someone strangled her while she was unconscious?"

"That's what it looks like, according to Zeb. There's no pattern to the head wound, no shards of wood or glass, just dirt. The kind of dirt that matched where she was buried."

"So no speculation about what the weapon was?"

He shook his head. "Zeb said he wasn't willing to make any guesses, but the weapon was probably something grabbed on the spur of the moment, something found around the house—which brings us back to a 'fit of rage' impulse killing, not a planned, premeditated thing."

"Okay. Thanks."

She stood and sniffed, and he had a feeling she was trying to hide the fact that she was crying. "I need a shower and a change of clothes," she said, her voice husky. "I think I'm going to go do that."

He rose, walked to her and pulled her into a hug. She wrapped her arms around his waist and sighed. Then stepped back as though lingering was against the rules. And, he supposed, it kind of was, based on their previous conversation. "Lacey…"

Her gaze met his. Tears were there, but she blinked them away. "Yes?"

"I'm glad you came back."

A small, sad smile curved her lips. "I… I…think I am, too, but…"

He closed the distance between them. Lowered his head but hesitated a fraction of an inch from her lips. If she wanted to push him away or step back, she could. But she didn't. She gripped his biceps to pull him nearer, and he settled his lips over hers, kissing her, reliving the past and hoping for a future with her. A sigh slipped from her and she slid her arms around his neck to thread her fingers through his hair. He deepened the kiss, hoping every emotion he couldn't seem to find the words for came through loud and clear.

And then it was over. He stepped back, his throat tight with longing and more words he wanted to say.

Lacey opened her eyes, more tears glinting in them. Then she rose up on her tiptoes to kiss him on the cheek. Without another word, she walked around him and headed toward what would be her bedroom tonight.

Creed settled on the sofa to keep watch over the woman he'd fallen in love with again.

Or maybe he'd never actually stopped loving her.

Whatever the case, he steeled himself against the familiar pain her leaving was going to bring him once again.

SIXTEEN

He didn't want her to go, but he didn't care enough to come with her. Same old, same old.

So...stay.

The voice inside her head nudged her and she shrugged it away.

The reason for leaving no longer exists.

"Stop it," she whispered.

But that kiss...

She groaned and slapped a hand to her head. "Don't think about it."

But how could she not?

Scarlett whined from her spot at the foot of the bed. Lacey walked over to scratch the dog's ears, then turned to pace the room, reliving the moment they'd kissed. It was like she'd never left. Like they'd never argued. Like they were going to be together forever.

But they weren't.

They *had* argued.

And she *had* left.

And he'd let her go.

"Arghhh!" The growl hurt her throat and sent her into a coughing spasm. She sipped on the bottle of water she'd found in the bathroom and caught her breath.

She'd take a shower, swallow some more meds and then have a nap. She went through the closet and the bathroom and found everything she needed for a shower, some shampoo and a change of clothes. The toothbrush and toothpaste were a much-appreciated added bonus.

Twenty minutes later, she was under the covers, her mind spinning once more with something triggered by Creed's statement and kiss—and the stunning thought that she wanted to stay. She had friends here who'd taken time to come help her. Friends she hadn't really counted as friends.

She sat up, overwhelmed with one thought. "I shut everyone out," she murmured. "It's me." Every relationship she had was on her terms. Even the ones back in Charlotte. She was closer to her dogs than any of the people she would have called friends before this morning. Not that they weren't good people, but she'd never encouraged them to know her.

And, in spite of her "I have a great life in Charlotte" speech, it wouldn't bother her overly much to leave them all behind.

Why?

Because deep down in her subconscious she'd known she'd want to come home one day? That she'd been clinging to the hope that Creed would call her and tell her that they'd work it out no matter the distance between them?

"No," she said. Scarlett lifted her head and looked at her. "It couldn't be that, could it, girl?"

Scarlett yawned and closed her eyes, but Lacey's stayed wide-open, sleep having fled. Had she really lived the last six years of her life with the hope that Creed would come after her?

No way.

Maybe.

Quite possibly.

Since her breakup with Creed, she'd not accepted one single date offer from anyone. There'd been several men who'd asked her out, and she always had an excuse why she couldn't go.

She sucked in a breath at her self-analysis and set off a coughing spasm. When her lungs calmed down, she rolled over and closed her eyes. *Take a nap, Lacey. It'll help.*

Not really thinking she'd sleep, she was shocked when she rolled over to look at her phone and saw two hours had passed. She rose, dressed in sweats, heavy socks and a long-sleeved T-shirt that smelled like vanilla and roses. She smiled. Katherine had donated this one. "Come on, girl," Lacey said to Scarlett. "Let's go get some food. And then we'll call the insurance company." The thought of all she needed to deal with was overwhelming, but it couldn't be helped.

When she walked into the den, she found Creed on the phone, his laptop open on the coffee table. He looked up and met her gaze. "Yeah, thanks," he said into the phone. "Got it. Talk to you in a little bit." He hung up and Lacey raised a brow. "Dr. Rhodes has an airtight alibi for Fawn's death. He was hunting with two of his buddies, and they have time-stamped videos of him celebrating the buck he bagged."

"So, he didn't kill her."

"No. He's most likely the baby's father, but he didn't kill her."

His eyes narrowed and Lacey gulped. *Please, please, please don't bring up that kiss.*

He didn't. Instead, he said, "How do you feel?"

"I'm all right. A little sore throat, scratchy lungs and a bit of a headache, but I'm breathing fine. Everything should clear up in a day or so."

"I'm glad." He sighed. "I was scared for you."

"I was scared for me, too." She nodded to his laptop. "You mind if I use that to order a baby gift for Jessica?"

He pushed it toward her. "Help yourself. Password is LaceyLeeJ100."

She froze, met his gaze and then sighed. "We're a pair, Creed Payne."

"I'm hoping."

She ignored the two words, not wanting to give him hope by telling him what she was thinking. If she decided to stay in Timber Creek, she had to be 100 percent sure that was what she wanted.

But she knew one thing: she desperately wanted to find a way to be with Creed for the rest of their lives.

But first, she needed a baby gift for the shower. "If I'm going to that baby shower, we need to make sure everything is safe for me to be there. I can't put anyone at risk."

Creed pursed his lips and nodded. "I get it. I don't think you'll be putting anyone at risk. The only people who've been in danger are you and me."

"What about Hank? You were holding him."

"And the bullets were aimed more at you. The bullets never came close to him."

"And being almost run over in the middle of the street?"

"Only you. Granted, the car could have hurt someone if he hadn't run into the concrete barrier, but he didn't."

"And while Ethan Mays could have been hurt, he wasn't anywhere near when the bolts came our way. He—or they—want me to be alone," she said slowly.

"Although, they don't seem to mind you getting caught in the cross fire."

"But I put myself there. And they could have killed Mac but didn't."

"Why do you think?"

Creed drew in a breath. "Because whoever killed Fawn is the one after you. He needs you out of the way for a reason. He's not randomly killing people. As long as he—they—whoever—can't get to you, they'll wait and bide their time. But give them an opportunity and they're going to take it." He paused. "I'll go with you and watch the house. If I see anything that sets off my internal alarms, I'll let you know, and you can simply leave."

She nodded. "That works for me."

"For now, I have a couple of friends who are going to watch this place while we're here."

"Friends?"

"I don't have enough manpower. I won't leave you unprotected, but I've also got a town to keep up with. Regina and Ben are working overtime while Mac heals. I'd love two or three more deputies, but..." He shrugged. "Money." He kept his gaze on hers. "I need some help and I'm not too proud to ask for it. I have it in my budget for two more deputies. And one of those people has got to be the leader of the K-9 unit." And he wanted that person to be her.

She didn't look away. "I'm thinking about it. Seriously." Hope flared in his gaze and she snapped her lips shut. "But I'm not making any promises. There's a lot to consider, so I'm not in a rush to make a decision, okay?"

"I understand." He paused. "But just in case you decide not to take the job, I have a list of candidates for you to look over. I need to have someone in mind and be ready to act when…if…you say no. Do you mind?"

"Of course not." A flicker of…something…ignited in her gut. She wasn't sure she could put a name to the feeling, but was very aware she didn't want anyone else starting the K-9 program. She wanted to do it. But Creed expected her to refuse.

For the next few hours, she sifted through the names and résumés that had already come in and found several applicants who would be perfect for the job.

Except they weren't.

Because they weren't her.

Two days later, Creed was still mulling over the fact that Lacey was thinking about taking the job. His heart beat faster just knowing she wasn't turning him down cold. She wanted to stay. He could see it in her eyes.

But what if she chose not to?

He ran a hand over his head and down his cheek. He'd borrowed her shower once again but hadn't bothered to shave. For now, he was making plans to keep Lacey safe while she attended the baby shower.

Two of his buddies from the Asheville Police Department had agreed to guard the apartment for the last two days, and all had been quiet, but they'd left and now it was up to him, Ben and Regina to watch out for Lacey.

He'd also learned that the break-in at his parents' store very well could have been a distraction to get him away from Lacey's home so the person could make his move to burn her home to the ground.

Who else would know about the baby? The ultrasound pictures? The money? Who would willingly burn up twenty thousand dollars in cash?

Someone who didn't need it?

Someone who thought it could be traced back to them?

Someone who didn't know it was there and thought they were just going to kill Lacey for whatever reason?

The questions spun through his mind with no answers in sight.

Lacey walked into the den and his heart did that flip-flop thing it had done ever since he'd seen her in the middle school cafeteria. It had taken a while to work up the nerve to ask her out. When she'd said yes, he'd been over the moon.

And then she'd walked away six years into their relationship.

At least now he knew she'd looked back while doing so.

"You look great," he said.

"Thanks. I hope they don't mind casual. My wardrobe is pretty limited."

"I think they'll understand."

"Yes."

"One thing. When I talked to Dr. Rhodes about his alibi, he mentioned his wife was going to be at the shower. He asked me to ask you not to say anything about the affair with Fawn."

"I won't, but now that you've said she's going to be there, I wouldn't mind having the opportunity to talk to her and see how well she knew Fawn."

"That might be a good idea. Her body language should tell you a lot about how she felt about her." He scratched his nose. "One thing I keep coming back to. If she knew about the affair, she has motive to kill Fawn."

"True."

"Dr. Rhodes is adamant that she didn't know, but—"

"What if she did?"

He nodded.

Lacey shoved a strand of hair behind her ear. "Then I'll find that out while being as subtle as I possibly can."

"Perfect. You ready?"

"Yep." She grabbed the gift that had been delivered yesterday afternoon. She'd also ordered wrapping paper, tape and ribbon.

Creed had watched her take great care in wrapping the age-appropriate play gym before she'd bothered to eat breakfast. "She'll love it," he said.

Lacey shot him a half smile. "I'm nervous about going to a baby shower. How ridiculous is that?"

"Why?"

"Because I don't know who else will be there and what they may think or say about me being there. Dumb, huh?"

"I would never call your feelings dumb."

Scarlett padded over with her new lead in her mouth. Lacey had ordered that, too.

He looked at Lacey. "I think she plans on going with us."

"I'm fine with that, as long as you don't mind her staying in the car with you."

"Not at all." He led the way down the steps to his cruiser. "If you think of it as an assignment to get information, will that help settle your nerves?"

"Hmm. Maybe." She frowned. "Actually, yes."

"Then do that and let everything else roll off your back. Although, I think you'll find you're having a good time."

She buckled Scarlett into the back and then herself into the passenger seat. Her tight expression pulled Creed up short. "What is it?"

Lacey shot him a sideways glance. "If I have a good time, I'll feel guilty."

"Because of Fawn."

She sighed. "I know life goes on, Creed. I really do. But it just seems wrong to enjoy it."

"What would Fawn want?"

A sad smile curved her lips. "I know what she'd want, but like I said, it's going to be hard—especially if we wind up not finding her killer."

"Oh, we'll find him. One way or another, we'll find him."

"And yet I'm taking the time to go to a shower, taking the lead investigator—that would be you—away from the case."

Creed snagged her fingers with his right hand while he drove toward Miranda's. "You're not taking me away from the case," he said. "I have my laptop and my phone. I'll be working. And when you're finished with the shower, let me know, and we'll compare notes."

She nodded as they pulled up to Miranda's house.

SEVENTEEN

Lacey walked up the steps to Miranda's home and rapped her knuckles against the door. It swung open and Jessica greeted her with wide eyes and her baby strapped to her chest. "You came!"

"You invited me. And I wanted to come."

"I'm so glad." Jessica grabbed her hand and pulled her through the foyer and into the kitchen. "Grab a snack and come visit."

Annie turned from the counter, a carrot stick dripping with ranch dressing in her hand. "Hey, Lacey. Glad to see you made it."

With an escort and an agenda, but she'd made it. Lacey wove her way through the kitchen and into the den, where she took in the expensive decor. Leather furniture softened by knitted afghans and colorful pillows graced the center of the room. The built-ins on the far wall held a large smart TV, books and family pictures. When she and Creed had been here last time, they'd not made it to this more relaxed area.

Jessica followed her and took a seat in the wingback chair. She had a stack of gifts beside her and Lacey added hers to it. She made small talk for a few minutes before another newcomer claimed the woman's attention. Lacey halfway listened while she let her gaze roam the other occupants, looking for one in particular. She'd never met Joanna Rhodes before, but would know her from the pictures in her husband's office.

Lacey spotted her at the food table. The woman had her dark blond hair pulled up in a stylish bun, with a few wispy strands loose around her temples. Her makeup had been expertly applied and Lacey figured her lipstick wouldn't dare fade even when she ate the small plate of food in her left hand. Lacey walked over and smiled. "Hello, Mrs. Rhodes."

The woman turned. "Hello." She frowned and smiled at the same time, and Lacey knew she was trying to pull a name from her memory.

"I'm Lacey Jefferson, Fawn's sister."

"Oh!" Surprise flashed briefly, along with another emotion Lacey couldn't put her finger on. "I was terribly sorry to hear about her death. Are they making any progress on finding who killed her?"

"Some." Lacey picked up a plate and two cucumber sandwiches. She needed some food before her blood sugar tanked again. After two bites, she wiped her mouth. "Were you and Fawn close?"

"No, not very. And it's Joanna. I knew Fawn, of course. She worked with my husband at the hospital."

"I know. Your husband had pictures in his office of Fawn and your family. That's how I recognized you. I would have thought you'd have been very close."

"No. Like I said, my husband and Fawn had a business relationship. That's all."

The woman's denial and lack of eye contact made it clear that she knew more than she wanted to say.

"Were Fawn and your husband—"

"I'm sorry." Joanna pointed over Lacey's shoulder. "I see someone I need to speak with about setting up a photography session for my new grandbaby. Excuse me."

She bolted away faster than if Lacey had announced she had the plague.

Lacey almost went after her, but speaking of pictures...

She walked to the built-in bookcases that encased the television and noted pictures of newborn TJ. One in particular caught her eye. Tucker Glenn held the baby close, the adoration on his face exposed for all the world to see. Only a couple of weeks old and already little TJ dominated the home. She smiled. She might not care for Tucker, but it was obvious he loved his son.

From there, she walked to the other side and froze. A framed group of ultrasound pictures rested on the bottom shelf. The same pictures she'd found in her house just before someone burned it down. Granted, most ultrasound pictures looked similar, but these were from the 3D set. And that little hand sticking up and waving at her was exactly the same as the one in Fawn's home.

Sickness swirled in the pit of her stomach while unanswered questions battled it out in her mind.

"Lacey?"

She turned to see Miranda looking at her, a frown creasing her forehead. "Hi."

"Glad you could make it. I noticed you looking at the pictures. Everything okay?"

"Oh yes." She had no idea what to think of what she was seeing, but she had enough sense to not blurt out her questions. "I...ah...was just thinking what a cutie TJ is. Very photogenic."

"Thanks. He is." An adoring smile smoothed her features. "You know, Tucker and I tried for a long time to have a child and it just never happened. We thought about adoption, but then I wound up pregnant with TJ and we got our happy ending."

"I see." Lacey forced a smile. "I'm so glad it all worked out for you. Where's TJ now?"

"Tucker took him to see his parents. I didn't think I could handle him and being an attentive hostess all at the same time."

"Well, I'm sure Tucker is enjoying the time with TJ."

"Very much so."

"Miranda, how well do you know Joanna?"

"Very well. We're great friends."

"Was she great friends with Fawn, too?"

"Of course. The three of us were together as much as possible. At least, we were before TJ was born and Joanna's new grandbaby arrived. But yes, the three of us were very close." Clouds flickered through her eyes. "I don't know what we'll do without Fawn. It won't ever be the same again. If I didn't have TJ, I'd—"

"Miranda?"

The call from across the room pulled the woman's attention from Lacey. "I guess that's my cue."

"Of course."

She left and Lacey drew in a steadying breath, then turned to snap a picture of the ultrasound photos. She aimed herself in the direction of the hall bath with a glance over her shoulder. Jessica had just begun to open her gifts. The gift she'd brought was at the end of the line, so she figured she had a few minutes to look around. What she was looking for, she had no idea, but if those pictures were of Fawn's baby, then that meant Miranda was claiming TJ was her child when…he wasn't. And that meant Miranda was hiding something. And so was her bestie, Joanna. Frustration gnawed at her. She kept gathering bits and pieces of information and couldn't figure out how to put them together to make sense in Fawn's death. So, she'd keep searching for more pieces.

The house was a large ranch but laid out simply. The main living area was in the center of two wings. It only took her a few minutes to walk back through the kitchen and down the hall to her right to peer in the rooms. She found TJ's nursery elaborately decorated with trains and planes. With a tight throat, she backed out and shut the door, then went to the next room.

The master. More pictures of TJ.

Lacey made her way past the festivities once more and walked into the other hall. A guest bath to her right, and to her left was a large guest room complete with sitting room and an en suite bath. The door was open, but she noted the dead bolt that locked with a key. Weird. Why would someone have a dead bolt on a bedroom door? The only reason she could come up with sent that "something's not right" feeling curling in the pit of her stomach. She stepped into the room and noted a television was mounted on the wall opposite the couch and a small desk was under the window.

Lacey caught a whiff of strawberry that reminded her of Fawn and decided it smelled a lot like Fawn's closet. Had her sister used this room? Maybe for the three months she'd dropped off the radar?

But…why?

And…had she been *locked* in here? But she'd had access to her phone and internet, so if she'd been held against her will, why hadn't she simply told someone once she'd been released? Or escaped?

The bits and pieces were driving her crazy. She needed the full picture.

She shut the door behind her, noting that it felt heavier than a typical interior door, but slid that fact to the back of her mind since she had no idea what—if anything—it could mean. She had to focus and be quick before she was missed.

Hopefully, if anyone noticed her absence, they'd think she'd simply slipped out and gone home. Lacey moved to the bathroom and she discovered it had been meticulously cleaned, but a bar of soap, like the kind her sister used, sat in the dish near the faucet.

Heart in her throat, she pulled out her phone while she walked to the closet. She opened the door and sucked in a gasp. Hanging on a hanger toward the back was a pregnancy suit. In fact, there were several different sizes going from smaller to bigger.

The pieces started to fall into place. Miranda had faked her pregnancy and now had Fawn's baby. Lacey knew it; she just didn't know how to prove it. She exited the closet, walked to the desk and noted the Bible in the corner. She wondered if it was there for show, then pulled the middle drawer open. Empty.

As were all of the other drawers.

She checked the dresser and found linens and several items of stylish maternity clothes. Had Miranda worn those with her fake pregnancy body? Lacey pulled out her phone to take pictures of everything. She tapped Creed's number. When it didn't ring after several seconds, she checked the signal.

Nothing. "What?" How was that possible?

She walked to the door and turned the knob.

Locked.

Her heart dropped.

Someone had locked her in the room.

Creed had walked the perimeter of the Glenn home with Scarlett, letting the dog stretch her legs and run for a few minutes. It was a huge party, big enough to make Creed wonder if the entire town had shown up, and cars were parked in the drive as well as the grassy area to the side of the house. He and Scarlett dodged the vehicles, and a few newly arriving ladies, and made their way back to the cruiser.

As soon as he opened the door, planning to get Scarlett settled and to make some calls about Fawn's case, Regina called him.

"What's up?" he asked.

"I talked to the ultrasound office. It's a very swanky place that caters to the rich and famous. A well-to-do couple funded the place in the hopes that it would attract pregnant ladies who wouldn't otherwise go to that type of place. All that aside, one of the workers said she remembered Fawn, and that she was accompanied by another woman."

"Did she say who?"

"No. And she was cut off from saying more by another worker. And *that* person said they don't have security cameras."

Creed paused. "I'm not sure I believe that."

"I didn't either, especially since their biggest attraction to their clientele is their confidential and privacy assurances. Seems to me that they'd want cameras for the added security. Regardless, we're still looking into that.

After some digging, I found out they also work with some high-priced adoption lawyers. Everything is handled privately and quickly. But the security footage was my main focus. I called a friend of mine who's a cop about an hour away from there and asked if he could verify that. And if they do have cameras, then we needed the footage."

"They think they're protecting their clients by hiding anything that might reveal who's used their services."

"Yeah."

"Let me know what he finds out."

"Will do. And before I go, I've got some information on Gillian Fields. She works for a medical equipment supply company on Main Street. I talked to her about her gym card and she said she noticed it was missing after a visit to the hospital."

"Weird."

"Yes."

She hung up, and Creed noticed more people leaving the shower. Ladies had been coming and going ever since Lacey had gone inside, but it seemed like an exceptionally large number were climbing into their cars and heading out.

But no sign of Lacey.

He sent her a text, then scanned the two ladies exiting the front door. Both wore frowns and both glanced backward as though in concern. Lacey was still in there. She was probably talking to Miranda or something. When he spotted Carmen Houser, he climbed out of the car and walked toward her. "Hey, have you seen Lacey?" He and Carmen had graduated high school together. She worked as a teller at the local bank.

"I saw her come in but didn't get a chance to speak to her before she disappeared."

"I'm sorry—what?"

She laughed. "Not literally. I saw her talking to Joanna, then Miranda, and I got distracted when Jessica opened my present. By the time I went looking for her, she was already gone."

Gone? "Gone where?"

"No idea, Creed. I don't have her on my list of friends I track."

He wasn't even going to ask her if she was serious. "Thanks."

"Although, to be honest, she might still be in there. Miranda wasn't feeling well all of a sudden, so we decided to leave."

"Not feeling well? She okay?"

"Yes, I think so. She just got really light-headed and dizzy and said she had to lie down. Then Joanna said she wasn't feeling great, and at that point, I was afraid it might be something in the food."

"Uh-oh."

"Exactly. I hadn't eaten anything and wasn't about to at that point." She paused. "So, are you two a thing again?"

He shot her a tight smile. "Thanks for the information, Carmen. Good to see you."

She laughed and walked toward her car while Creed pondered whether or not he should go in. He sighed. Carmen hadn't seemed concerned about anything other than getting food poisoning, so he'd give Lacey a few more minutes, then go check on her.

EIGHTEEN

Lacey beat on the door until her hands hurt. She'd pounded and cried out for the past five minutes and no one had come. She finally decided the room was sound-proof. Which chilled her. Why would they need a sound-proof room?

The lock clicked and Lacey spun. Miranda stepped inside and shut the door behind her. In her right hand, she held a gun that she lifted and pointed at Lacey.

"Miranda?" she whispered. "You killed Fawn."

"It was an accident." Miranda's eyes filled with tears for a brief moment before they disappeared, and her gaze hardened.

"Then why cover it up?"

"Are you kidding me? I would have been arrested. Gone to jail. Possibly lost my son."

"You mean Fawn's son."

Miranda gasped and paled. "No. *My* son."

"You may call him your son, but Fawn gave birth to him."

"How do you know?"

"I found a copy of the ultrasound pictures in Fawn's guest room closet."

"That's not possible. She *never* left here. Not for the full three months. She gave birth in that bed right there."

"Well, I guess she managed to make copies some-how, because they were in her closet." Lacey's fingers clenched into fists. "*Why* did you kill her?"

Miranda shuddered and Lacey fingered her phone in her pocket, wishing she could somehow get out of the room and call for help. "I didn't mean to. She was say-ing stuff like she was making a horrible mistake, that she wanted him back and wanted to help figure out a plan to do that." A scoff slipped from her. "There was no way that was happening. I'd gone through the whole charade of being pregnant and having the child and—" She waved a hand. "There was no way. When I refused to discuss it, she said she was sorry, but that she had to do the right thing, the honest thing. That I needed to give TJ back to her and come clean. I was stunned. I couldn't believe she'd turn on me like that. We were at her house in the yard. She was planting flowers. The shovel was lean-ing against the side of the house and I grabbed it and…"

"Hit her," Lacey said, her voice dull. Almost mono-tone. She'd wanted to know what had happened and now she knew. "And then you strangled her to make sure she never woke up."

Miranda's eyes widened. "What? Strangle her? No!"

"The ME says you did."

She frowned. "I hit her, and she grabbed her head—there was so much blood that I was…shocked. I couldn't believe I'd done that. She screamed at me that I'd lost it. I still held the shovel and I guess she thought I was going to hit her again, so she ran toward the woods…" Her eyes darkened. "I called Tucker, hysterical. He came to the house and went to the woods looking for Fawn. He said he found her on the ground. That she'd fallen and bled out." Miranda shoved a hand against her mouth. "I never meant for her to get hurt, but I couldn't let her take my baby."

"Miranda, Fawn was strangled. The ME said the blow from the shovel wouldn't have killed her."

Miranda's brows pulled tighter across the bridge of her nose and confusion clouded her eyes. "But..." Realization and horror dawned. "Tucker," she whispered.

"Yeah, Tucker." Miranda's hand shook and her finger twitched on the trigger. "So, knowing that you're not a murderer, are you going to kill me and become one?"

"I... I don't know. I have to think." A tear slipped down her cheek. "Tucker said she was dead when he found her, that I'd killed her, and we had to hide her. He covered her up out in the woods where he said he found her, but said he was going to have to move her. He was pacing and talking and trying to come up with a story for her disappearance. I told him that we didn't need a story because we weren't going to know anything about where she went."

"So, he panic-buried her," Lacey murmured. They'd been right about that. "Why shoot at us? Was that you?"

"No..."

"Who?"

"That was James."

"Tucker's brother?" She remembered him from the hospital.

"Tucker hadn't had a chance to move her, and when he saw where the hunt for Hank was leading, he called James and told him to scare y'all away from the area. He said he shot at the shed, hoping to distract you."

"But Scarlett found her anyway."

"Stupid dog. If you hadn't brought her into the picture, Fawn would have just stayed missing."

"You had to know I'd come looking for her."

Miranda shrugged. "I figured you would, but I also thought that if I could just act normal, you'd eventually give up and go away."

"But I didn't, so you tried to run me over, shoot me with a crossbow and burn me in my home."

"Tucker was in a panic and James would do anything for Tucker. So, the two of them did all that."

"Who did you tell we were going to the gym?"

"James. I told him Tucker needed him to make you go away."

"So, he stole a key card and attacked me in the locker room." She rubbed a hand down her face. Well, she'd wanted all the pieces to the puzzle, but this wasn't quite the way she'd wanted to get them. "Who burned Fawn's house down?"

"That was James's idea. They were looking for Fawn's journal. She wrote in it constantly. When they couldn't find it in her house, he told Tucker they just needed to burn it down. With you in it."

Lacey shuddered at the coldness of it all. "Where's the journal?"

"I guess it was in the house. We searched all over the place here and couldn't find it. There's no telling what she wrote and we couldn't have it found in case—"

"She wrote the truth?"

"Yes," Miranda whispered.

Lacey gripped her temples and shook her head. "I can't believe this. I can't believe Fawn agreed to be locked in a room for three months." She couldn't believe any of it.

"She knew my need for control," Miranda admitted.

"I was petrified she'd change her mind. She agreed to the lock, the soundproofing, the cell signal blocker, everything. All to reassure me—and it worked. She even let me keep her laptop."

"But I talked to her on the phone. She answered my texts."

"I was there for every conversation and I monitored every text."

"And the ultrasounds?"

"A friend's clinic. No questions asked."

It was scary how well she'd worked to cover her tracks. "Creed's waiting outside as we speak," Lacey said. "In fact, he'll probably come looking for me shortly."

"Then I guess we'd better make sure he doesn't find you just yet until I figure out what to do."

She backed out of the room and shut the door faster than Lacey could move.

She walked to the twin bed and stared at it, picturing Fawn laboring to give birth. All alone, maybe a little afraid in spite of all her medical knowledge. The rage shuddered through her and she grabbed the comforter and pulled it off, letting out a harsh scream. She grabbed the pillows and, with another yell, tossed them across the room. One landed on the desk, knocking the lamp to the floor and shattering the Tiffany design. Next came the sheets. Then she hefted the top mattress and sent it crashing into the pictures on the wall. They tumbled to the floor. The sound of the breaking glass was incredibly satisfying.

She started for the box springs and froze, breathing hard, face wet with sweat and tears. A small journal with a cover like the one she'd given Fawn lay there as though waiting for Lacey to find it. She'd given Fawn the little book the same time she'd gifted her the bracelet.

This was what everyone had been so desperate to find and it was under their noses the whole time. Lacey snatched up the journal, took it to the desk and flopped into the chair. She had to think. To escape. But she'd been all over the room and attached bath and could find no way out. Maybe Fawn's words could help her. Once she caught her breath, she opened the cover and began to read.

Well, I might as well use this to pass the time. I have no idea why Lacey gave me a journal, but maybe it was for this moment, this...time in my life.

My life. Wow. I've really done a number on it— in addition to all the issues my father's actions have left me with. But maybe this is the way to fix it and make things right for at least one person whose life he ruined. Tucker Glenn. I never thought I'd call him friend, but over the last few weeks, he's been different. Kind. Less scary. Which is nice. I wish I'd had the strength to leave Timber Creek like Lacey, but, after Dad did his thing, I felt like I had to stay. To make amends. Which is stupid, but nevertheless, the feeling is real. I'm not the one who's the criminal—and yet, I guess I am. Seven months pregnant and I'm participating in an unbelievable scheme. I seriously can't believe I'm doing this. But...it's a situation of my own making. I freely admit that. I made a choice that I wish desperately I could take back. A choice with consequences I thought about but risked anyway. A choice that has led to the deception—and pain—of many people. So, I guess I'm not so different from my father after all. Lacey would be mortified. Ashamed and disappointed. Which is why I can't tell her. And why I'm really starting to hate myself.

Lacey stifled a sob and slammed the book shut. She rose and paced to the window. She tried to raise it yet again. And again, she was met with unmoving resistance. She grabbed the desk chair, hefted it and slammed it against the window. The chair bounced off the glass and fell to the floor.

"Argh!"

She went to the book once again, reading and pacing, absorbing Fawn's words in one part of her mind, while the other part worked furiously on an escape plan.

The truth is, I don't think I can actually go through with this. Then again, how can I not? I feel I have to at this point. After all, what am I going to do with a child? Charles doesn't want him, and I understand that. I don't hold that against him. And Miranda has gone through such a massive deception of pretending to be pregnant. The woman deserves an Oscar. Although, I had no idea until a few days ago what she was doing. I thought she was hiding out so she could claim the child as her own. I was partially right. She definitely wants to claim the baby as hers, but she's been parading around in a pregnancy suit! She's worn it 24/7 apparently. Unbelievable.

I've been reading the Bible again and feeling convinced that I'm doing a terrible thing. I don't want to do this. I want to find a way to keep my son—I've named him Hudson Christopher simply because I like the name—and give him the family that he deserves. I'm definitely not sure about Miranda as a mother. She's incredibly controlling, and I'm worried she'll control this baby right into a psychiatric ward.

Fawn went on to talk about how she'd agreed to stay in the room and basically be Miranda and Tucker's prisoner in order to appease Miranda's obsessive fear that someone would find out Fawn was pregnant.

I've about had enough, Fawn wrote.

Lacey flipped the page. Fawn had been studying the Bible and growing closer to God.

One thing about being confined in this room is it's certainly given me some downtime. Time to read and to pray and to reflect. I'm so thankful God still loves me even when I'm not lovable. I should have told Lacey about the baby. She would have offered to help, but that's the problem. I don't want to disrupt her life when she's finally found some peace. And if I tell her about the baby, I'll have to tell her that I'm in love with a married man. A man who is thirty years older than I am. A man who has grandchildren and a very possessive wife.

The dead bolt clicked and this time she heard it. Lacey stuffed the journal in the desk drawer and shut it. She turned as the door swung open.

Creed glanced at his watch, then his phone. No answering text from Lacey and the last guest from the shower had left five minutes ago. He climbed out of the cruiser once more and walked up the steps to knock on the door.

When it swung open, Miranda stood there looking a bit frazzled. "Hello, Creed. What can I do for you?"

"Everything okay?"

She blinked and tucked a stray strand of hair behind her ear. "Of course. Why?"

"Heard there was some kind of food poisoning issue?"

She laughed, but the sound was forced and Creed's cop senses tingled. "Yes. A small one. We think the salmon cakes were tainted. We thought it best to end the shower early just in case it was more than food poisoning. We certainly don't need to spread any illness that might be going around."

"I understand. I just wanted to check in with Lacey. She's not answering her phone."

"Oh no." Miranda smacked her forehead in a very un-Miranda-like move. "I was supposed to call you and let you know that her phone was doing something strange and not sending texts for some reason. She left a while ago to drive one of the ladies home."

"Which one?"

"I'm not sure, but she said to let you know she'd do that, then call you to pick her up."

That didn't sound right, but knowing Lacey, she would definitely offer to help if someone needed it. However, in light of the current situation, there was no way she'd just take off with him right there. "Are you sure about this? That she left with a woman?"

"I'm sure."

"But you don't know which one?"

"Um, maybe Joanna Rhodes? I'm not sure, but they just left a few minutes ago. If you head toward town, you might catch them. Maybe? I'm sorry, Creed. I really am. It's been chaos in here for the past twenty minutes or so. I haven't kept up with everyone's comings and goings."

She pressed a hand against her head and said, "Now, I've a ferocious migraine coming on. I've got to run."

With that, she shut the door in his face. Two seconds later, Tucker's sedan pulled into the drive. He got out and stopped short when he eyed Creed. "Everything okay?"

"Yeah, I think so. Just trying to track down Lacey."

"Oh."

"Where's the baby?"

"I left him with my mother. She offered to babysit so Miranda and I could have a night out. Only Miranda says she's not feeling well, so I'm just going to check on her."

He backed toward the door and Creed waved, then hurried to his cruiser. He would try to find Joanna and Lacey first on the off chance Miranda's story was true. But something was going on. He didn't know what it was, but he had a feeling he was going to need backup.

NINETEEN

For several moments after the door opened, she and Tucker eyed each other. Then her gaze went to the weapon in his hand, absently noting it was the same one Miranda had threatened her with earlier. The fury returned. This man had cold-bloodedly killed her sister, and not an ounce of remorse was reflected in his eyes.

In fact, Lacey was quite sure he planned to do the same thing to her.

He shot a glance at the room, noting the destruction, and his jaw tightened.

"Where's Miranda?" Lacey asked.

"Doesn't matter. Let's go."

"Where?"

"Just walk until I tell you to stop. We're going out the back of the house, not the front."

Since getting out of the room worked in her favor, she did as he instructed and slipped out into the hallway. He stepped up behind her and pressed the gun against her left kidney. Defense moves played in her head, but now wasn't the time. They were going out of the house. She mentally mapped the area. If she could get to the woods—

"Go. Faster."

Creed was out there. All she had to do was get his attention. She picked up the pace and entered the kitchen. "Through the door to the right and down the steps."

Lacey followed his instructions and made her way down the stairs, her eyes on the door just ahead. As soon as she was out the door, she'd scream her head off and hope Creed came running.

The gun pressed harder against her back as though Tucker could read her thoughts. "You killed Fawn and now you're going to kill me. Are you going to go after Creed and the rest of the sheriff's department? Because they all know you're involved."

He laughed. "Nice try, but no, they don't."

"Fawn said you'd started being nicer to her, that you weren't as bad as you used to be in high school."

"Stop."

She did so.

"When did Fawn say that? Because she never once, in the last three months, mentioned me or Miranda. So, when would she have said that?"

She turned slightly to look back at him. "We talked all the time before those three months she was your prisoner."

"But I didn't really start being nice to her until she was living here. So, how did you know that?" His eyes narrowed and he lifted the gun to press it against her head. "You found the journal, didn't you?"

Lacey froze. She'd messed up.

"Where is it?"

"I don't know."

His hand shot out and he slammed her head against the wall. Stars flashed in front of her eyes and she cried out, fighting a sudden wave of nausea. "Where is it?"

"That's why you burned my house to the ground." She spit at him. "Well, I won't tell you where it is. If you kill me, I'll take great satisfaction in knowing that evidence is out there, detailing what you put my sister through."

For a moment, she thought he might pull the trigger. Instead, he shot a look at the clock on the wall over the washing machine. "Open the door," he said. "And don't think you can run to Creed. He left a few minutes ago."

Dread centered itself in her gut and stayed there. So that was why Tucker was moving her. Creed would want to search the house. She twisted the knob and he shoved her out into the sunshine. "Go."

"Where?"

"To the barn. Hurry up."

The gun slipped from her head and Lacey spun in a smooth move and used her forearm to knock the weapon from him. He yelled and dived for the gun the same time Lacey did. He wrapped his fingers around the grip, and she knew she didn't have the strength to wrestle it away from him. She bolted to her feet and kicked him in the face. His nose crunched, and a raw scream ripped from his throat. One hand went to his face while the other lifted the weapon. She kicked again and caught his wrist. The gun spun out of his grip and she whirled, racing for the barn. If she could get to the road, she could flag someone down.

Something slammed into her back and she went down with a hard grunt. Pain rippled through her right shoulder, but she tried to scramble away from him. His fingers twisted in her hair and another lightning bolt of agony shot through her head. She froze, panting, tears sliding down her temples as she blinked up at the sky.

"Don't move." His order vibrated with a tightly leashed

fury. Lacey stayed still. She couldn't move anyway without him taking a chunk of her hair and skin with him. "Walk to the barn. Now."

Lacey did as ordered, fighting the urge to be sick. She let him get her to the barn. Barns had all kinds of things that could be used as weapons. She'd find one and end this once and for all.

But when they got there, he walked her past a motorcycle, a golf cart and a pitchfork she wanted to grab and couldn't. He shoved her into a room and held the weapon on her while he blocked the door. "You have until I come back to tell me where that journal is. If you don't, I'm going to go after your old boyfriend. Creed won't know what hit him."

"He suspects you're involved in Fawn's death. He'll be on guard."

His eyes blazed, but he didn't shoot her. Instead, he smirked. "Guess we'll find out."

He shut the door and locked it.

Which meant Lacey was trapped once more.

Creed pulled to a stop out of sight of the Glenn home. He let Scarlett out from her spot in the back and fastened the lead to her harness. As he'd feared, he hadn't found Joanna or Lacey. When he felt like he'd been sent on a fool's errand and decided Lacey was still in the house somewhere, he'd done a one-eighty and called Regina to bring him something of Lacey's that would have her scent on it. He didn't know if it would be necessary, but better to be prepared than not. Katherine had let Regina into Lacey's temporary apartment and Regina had grabbed the pillow from Lacey's bed. Then she met him a mile away from the Glenns' house.

"Let me go up to the front door first," he said into his radio, "and ask to search the house. Stay out of sight until I need you."

"Ten-four. Mac just pulled up, too. Ben is almost here."

He clicked to Scarlett. "All right, girl, I hope you can do this without Lacey." At Lacey's name, Scarlett's ears lifted and she looked around. "Yeah, I want to see her, too. Let's go find her."

He knocked on the door and waited. Footsteps sounded, the curtain to his right moved, and the door swung open, revealing Miranda's agitated form. "What do you want now? I told you Lacey's not here."

"Then you won't mind if I search your house?"

Her eyes went wide. "Search my house?" She nearly sputtered the words. "Absolutely not."

"Fine. Then I'm getting a warrant. Lacey wouldn't just leave without telling where she was going."

"And you think she's here?"

"I do. Now, do I get a warrant or do you let me in?"

"Let him in," a voice said from behind Miranda. "She's not here."

Creed pushed past Miranda with Scarlett at his heels. He had the pillowcase in a bag in his left hand. Tucker stepped out of the shadows, holding an ice pack on his face. He had two black eyes. Creed did a double take. "What happened to you, man?"

"I was in the barn and a two-by-four fell out of the loft and smacked me in the face."

"Leave the dog outside," Miranda said. "I don't want that filthy creature in my house."

"Sorry," Creed said, "but the dog goes with me." He held the bag out to her and tried to remember the exact commands Lacey had used with her. "Scent, Scarlett."

"What are you doing?" Miranda fairly screeched.

"Letting Scarlett get Lacey's scent."

"What? No! Get her out!"

Creed knew the others were listening to the entire conversation. His only concern was whether one of them—or both of them—had a weapon. He didn't dare underestimate Tucker. The man was a hunter and had weapons. "Tucker?"

The man waved a hand. "Fine. Search the house. Knock yourself out."

"Thank you." Into the radio, he said, "Regina, can you come in and sit with the Glenns while I check the house?"

Tucker glowered. Miranda twisted her hands and shot looks at her husband that Creed couldn't decipher. Regina stepped inside the house and Creed said, "They've given me verbal permission to search. Just hang out here and I'll be right back."

"Great."

To Scarlett, he said, "Scarlett, find Lacey."

The dog circled the den and then stuck her nose to the floor, then the air, and started for the back of the house. In a lower voice, he said, "Stand by." Scarlett took him through the kitchen and straight to a door. She sat and waited for him to open it. As soon as she could scoot through, she did and scrambled down the stairs. He kept going, giving her the space to work. She wanted out the door at the bottom, and again, he opened it and Scarlett darted out.

"Hey! Stop!"

Regina's shout from the other side of the house pulled him to a halt. Tucker was racing across the yard toward the barn, and just beyond him, he could see Lacey sprinting for the trees.

"Lacey!"

She spun and saw him. Tucker aimed for the barn. "Tucker, stop!" Creed yelled, not expecting the man to listen. And he didn't.

Lacey stopped, spotted Tucker and bolted after him. What was she *doing*?

Tucker disappeared into the barn. Creed reached the door and barely escaped being mowed down when Tucker burst from the barn driving a golf cart. He headed toward the trees that would take him to one of the back roads. Lacey changed direction and raced toward Tucker once more. He realized immediately what she planned. "Lacey, no!"

But she did exactly what he thought she was going to do. She launched herself into the passenger side and kept going, propelling herself into Tucker and sending them both falling from the driver's side to the ground. The golf cart continued at top speed away from the scene while Tucker and Lacey rolled. When they stopped, Tucker pulled back an arm. Scarlett hurled herself at the duo and chomped down on Tucker's forearm before he could land the blow to Lacey's face.

He screamed and Lacey bucked the man off. Scarlett held on, a low growl escaping her. "Get her off me!"

"Scarlett, release!"

Scarlett let go and backed up, her eyes on the man who'd attacked her beloved mistress. Creed hurried forward to grab the man's arms and pull them behind him.

He pressed the cuffs around Tucker's wrists before the guy could get himself together to put up a fight. "Tucker Glenn, you're under arrest." He recited the man's rights and pulled him to his feet.

Regina stepped up beside them, breathing hard from her run across the field. "He got the drop on me."

"It's okay. It's the last drop he'll get. What about Miranda?"

"Ben's got her. She realized Tucker was trying to escape and run out on her and started singing like the proverbial canary."

He nodded and looked at Lacey. "We got them."

"Yeah," she whispered. "We got them. And his brother, James, is involved in everything, too."

"I'll have someone pick him up before he gets wind of everything."

"I've got Tucker," Regina said. "You take care of Lacey."

Creed walked to Scarlett and gave her a belly rub, then pulled the tennis ball from his pocket and threw it. She raced after it and Creed gathered Lacey into his arms. "I love you, Lacey Lee Jefferson."

She stilled and sighed. Then looked up with watery eyes. "I love you, too, Sheriff Creed Payne."

"Good. I've decided to turn in my resignation and move to Charlotte, if that's what it takes to be with you."

She pulled back and gaped at him. "Um, no, I've decided to move back to Timber Creek. I'm going to rebuild the house and plant a big ole tree in honor of Fawn. And—" she blew out a low breath "—and raise her son. Her baby is TJ, Creed."

"How do you know?"

"I found her journal. I'll let you read some of the entries, but she named him Hudson Christopher. Social services has gone to get him. I feel terrible about taking him away from the people who thought they were his grandparents—because they really do love him—but I won't take him out of their lives if they want to see him." She bit her lip and studied him, uncertainty swimming in her gaze. "Is that a deal breaker?"

"Are you kidding me?" Creed could barely speak around the emotion swelling in his throat. "I would love Hudson with all my heart. As if he was my own."

"You've never even met him."

"I don't have to. He's a part of you and Fawn. And he's an innocent child. A gift. I don't take that lightly."

She stood on tiptoe to seal her lips to his. Creed's heart pounded and prayers of thanksgiving whispered heavenward. He pulled her closer, hoping she could feel his love for her in the kiss. He deepened it, sweeping his hands over her hair—and feeling the knot on her head. He pulled back. "You're hurt."

"Kissing you makes me forget about it. Don't stop."

He gave a short laugh but cupped her face. "We need to get you to a doctor. You could have a concussion."

"Then we can call Katherine, but I have a feeling her orders are going to be the same ones the ER doc gave Mac."

"You're stubborn."

"At least you know what you're getting into."

"I do. So, let's make it official." He dropped to one knee and took her hand. Her eyes widened and her cheeks turned pink. "Lacey Lee, will you marry—"

"Yes!" She laid another kiss on him and Creed couldn't contain the bubble of laughter welling up.

He leaned back and she shot him a sheepish look. "Sorry. You can finish asking the question and I promise not to interrupt."

"Aw, Lacey, you can interrupt me anytime."

In fact, she could spend a lifetime interrupting him and it wouldn't be long enough. "I love you, Lacey."

"I love you, Creed."

TWENTY

Four weeks later

Fawn's last journal entry:

> *I suppose I should write down some things in case something weird happens and I die during childbirth. Unlikely, I know, but I'm a doctor and my mind morbidly goes there.*
>
> *Anyway, should I die, the whole process of dispersing my property will be extremely easy. And even though I've forgiven my mother and plan to call her when I can think straight again, everything goes to my sister, Lacey Lee Jefferson. Everything. My will is in my safety-deposit box at High Point Bank in Timber Creek.*
>
> *And, if there's a way, should I no longer be on this earth, I'd want Lacey to raise my son, not Miranda Glenn. Somehow, I have to get out of this deal I've made with them. I just can't figure out how. Telling them "I've changed my mind" just doesn't seem right. They've gone to great lengths to pull off this deception. I'm actually quite stunned at it.*

*And I'm a little scared of Tucker, to be honest.
I'm not sure what his reaction might be should I
tell him I want to back out. I know Miranda would
go completely bonkers. So, for now, I'll continue
thinking and praying about this. Please, God, I
need Your help—an answer in the midst of this
situation I've created. Although I don't wish to
move, I've gone ahead and done the interviews
for the jobs in Charlotte per Miranda and Tucker's wishes, but I doubt I'll take one of them. If,
for some reason, I can't reverse all of this, at least
I can still watch Hudson grow up if I'm living in
the same town.*

*I wish I could talk to Lacey, but I gave my word
to say nothing. And I won't. But I want to. I love
you, Lacey. Maybe one day, I'll be able to tell you
everything.*

Lacey grunted and set the journal aside, tears blur-
ring her vision. "He'll be happy here, Fawn. I promise."

Construction had already started on her childhood
home and it was going to be finished in record time.
Like probably within the next two weeks. Crews made
up of locals and some hired hands had been working
practically around the clock to get it ready, and Lacey
was simply bowled over by the generous people in this
town. And so thankful to them.

Hudson, who'd been sleeping in the bassinet next to
her, let out his "I'm hungry" cry, and Lacey stuffed a
bottle between his lips. She'd learned to be prepared
when he was due to wake up, because he acted like he
was starving from the moment his eyes popped open. He
was a funny little guy and she saw Fawn in him every

time he smiled. He had her eyes and her smile, but he had his father's nose.

She and Hudson had been living in the apartment above the clinic for the past four weeks. Her mother had flown in from California with her husband and come for the funeral. She'd stayed in town for another week, reconnecting with Lacey and spoiling her grandson. Lacey smiled. It had been a good visit. A healing one.

A knock on the door curved her lips even further. Scarlett lifted her head and perked her ears toward the door. "Come on in!" Lacey said.

Creed entered and made a beeline for the bassinet, stopping to plant a kiss on her lips and scratch Scarlett's ears. Then he picked up the baby and held the bottle while Hudson drained it. Creed looked at her. "How are you doing?"

"Aw, you know I have good days and bad." Just speaking the words caused tears to threaten, but she held them back. "Today's not so great. I'm mad at her, Creed," she said, her voice low.

"I know."

"All of this could have been avoided if she'd just been honest."

"Agreed, but sometimes we have to learn things the hard way. Unfortunately, Fawn didn't get a chance to learn from her mistakes."

Lacey fell silent. Being mad at Fawn wouldn't accomplish anything. Her sister was gone. But she'd left a precious piece of herself behind and Lacey knew her anger with her sister would fade in time. "I can't believe Dr. Rhodes really agreed to sign away his rights to Hudson."

Child Protection Services had picked the baby up from Tucker's mother's home and were waiting to hand him over to Lacey as next of kin when she'd come home from the hospital after her encounter with Tucker and the golf cart.

"He doesn't want it known—especially by his wife—that he was unfaithful. Although, I think he'll tell her at some point. He seemed remorseful and repentant." He pulled the empty bottle from the baby's mouth and settled the little guy on his shoulder for a burp. "But for the next eighteen years, Rhodes has agreed not to contact you or Hudson, but said if Hudson wanted to know about him later, he'd consider it."

She nodded. "I want him to know the truth one day. I want him to know everything. But mostly, I want him to know he's loved." As always, the tears hovered near the surface, but she was getting quite proficient at keeping them from falling. "So very loved."

"He's loved," Creed said. "In fact, I almost can't remember life before him." He swallowed and Lacey loved that he wasn't hesitant to show his emotion. "And I'm ready to set the date when you are."

"I'm ready."

"Next week?"

She laughed. "Maybe not quite that ready, but next month should work."

His gaze lingered. "I can't quite believe this is happening," Creed said. "I'm so sorry for the reason you came home, but I think Fawn would be thrilled at the way everything turned out."

Lacey nodded. "She would. She'd wanted me to come home for years." She sighed. "And I wish I had, but..."

He settled on the sofa beside her. "The dogs are all set up at your place in their nice new area and are ready to continue their training. We've got the funds approved to hire one more K-9 handler, Isabelle is all set to watch this little guy while we're at work, and your first day is tomorrow. How are you feeling?"

"Excited." Butterflies swarmed in her belly, but she was ready. "Like it's the beginning of something really, really good."

Creed kissed her with a hint of restrained passion that made her head swim. When he pulled back, he leaned his forehead against hers. "I'm all for new beginnings because I'm *beginning* to be addicted to kissing you."

"I know exactly what you mean."

Joy exploded within her as they shared another lingering kiss. Lacey knew she might have initially followed the trail to find her sister's killer, but that trail had also led her home and back into Creed's arms. And for that, she'd be forever grateful.

Scarlett barked her agreement.

* * * *

Christy Barritt's books have won a Daphne du Maurier Award for Excellence in Suspense and Mystery and have been twice nominated for an RT Reviewers' Choice Best Book Award. She's married to her Prince Charming, a man who thinks she's hilarious—but only when she's not trying to be. Christy is a self-proclaimed klutz, an avid music lover and a road-trip aficionado. For more information, visit her website at christybarritt.com.

Books by Christy Barritt

Love Inspired Suspense

Keeping Guard
The Last Target
Race Against Time
Ricochet
Desperate Measures
Hidden Agenda
Mountain Hideaway
Dark Harbor
Shadow of Suspicion
The Baby Assignment
The Cradle Conspiracy
Trained to Defend
Mountain Survival
Dangerous Mountain Rescue

Visit the Author Profile page at
LoveInspired.com for more titles.

DANGEROUS MOUNTAIN RESCUE

Christy Barritt

Who hath delivered us from the power of darkness,
and hath translated us into the kingdom
of his dear Son: In whom we have redemption
through his blood, even the forgiveness of sins.
—*Colossians* 1:13–14

This book is dedicated to the "coffee lobby" gang at church. I'm so thankful for all the laughs, stories and talks!

ONE

"Bella! Can you hear me?"

Erin Lansing paused at the edge of the trail and surveyed the wintery mountain vista in front of her.

She knew her search efforts were most likely futile. She'd already explored this area twice with no luck.

There were still no signs of her daughter anywhere on this mountain.

As she stood at the overlook and caught her breath, investigators were gathering a team to search for Bella. But Erin couldn't wait for them. Their process was too slow. There was too much time to lose, time she couldn't afford to let slip away.

Would law enforcement drag their feet on purpose? Maybe to get revenge on Erin or to show their loyalty to her ex-husband, Liam?

Ever since Liam had disappeared a year ago, she'd been the number-one suspect in the eyes of his colleagues. Just because she and Liam had had a public fight right before he'd vanished didn't mean Erin was guilty.

Liam had been a cop. But instead of looking at people he'd arrested as potential suspects, investigators had focused all their attention on her.

Had the person responsible for her ex-husband's disappearance decided to come after Bella also?

A rock formed in Erin's gut at the thought. She didn't even want to think about it.

All she wanted was to find Bella.

A sixteen-year-old shouldn't be out in this wilderness alone. The vast Pisgah National Forest of North Carolina, with its deep valleys, steep cliffs and wild animals was no place for an amateur. To make matters worse, Bella hadn't taken her anxiety medication with her.

Erin knew how Bella got when she didn't take her medicine.

She would be beside herself. Close to panic. Jittery.

Tears pressed at Erin's eyes as she glanced at the scenic view in front of her one more time.

But there was nothing to indicate Bella had been there. No clues as to what had happened after her daughter had left for school yesterday morning. All she knew was that Bella had never made it to school and that her car had been found at the parking lot near the trailhead.

Bella had never shown any interest in hiking the mountain before. She wouldn't have come out here on purpose, would she?

Erin heaved her backpack up higher and turned to continue down the trail. She'd keep searching until she found Bella. She was even prepared to sleep in this wilderness if that's what it came down to.

But the one thing she wouldn't do was sit back and wait. Not anymore.

The old Erin had been passive. People had walked all over her. But after adopting Bella six years ago, she'd become a new person. A stronger person.

As her phone buzzed, Erin glanced down, surprised to have any reception out here.

The message on her screen made her blood run cold.

You deserve this.

She sucked in a breath.

Who could have sent this?

Someone evil—that was who. Someone who wanted to put Erin in her place. To let her know she was a villain.

Could this person have taken Bella?

A surge of concern and anger tangled together inside her.

This was becoming even more of a nightmare than she'd thought possible.

Quickly, she typed back.

Where is she? What do you want from me?

She waited a few minutes, but there was no response.

Disappointment clutched her, but she pushed it aside. She needed to keep moving.

Erin continued down the narrow trail that cut along the side of the mountain. She sucked in a deep breath, inhaling the vague scent of pine and old leaves left over from the autumn purge.

The trees around her were fragile from the winter. Branches seemed to reach for her, their sharp edges grabbing her hair and jacket. And the air was so cold out here that every breath hurt her lungs.

Was Bella out here somewhere? Was she cold? What had she worn when she'd left for school yesterday? Erin had already left for work, so she didn't know. What about food? Was her daughter hungry?

The questions made Erin's temples pound, made worry swirl in her gut until she wanted to throw up.

She hadn't passed anyone in the two hours since she'd been out here, even though this trail was normally popular, even in the winter months. But today, clouds threatened freezing rain or snow and kept most of the hikers away. Precipitation, thirty-degree temperatures and slippery slopes didn't make for ideal hiking conditions.

Erin heard a stick crack nearby and paused.

The hair on her neck rose as she turned.

She scanned the wooded landscape around her but saw no one.

So what had caused that sound? Could it have been an animal?

That made the most sense.

She swallowed hard, trying to push down her fear.

But as she continued walking, her fears escalated, fueled by her imagination.

What if Bella had met somebody online and come here to talk face-to-face? Erin had heard stories about things like that happening. Even though she wanted to believe Bella would never take that risk, she couldn't say with one hundred percent certainty that her daughter wouldn't.

Erin rubbed her temples, wishing she could clear the fog from her head. She needed to be sharp if she was going to hike out here. Distraction could get her killed, especially with the craggy rocks, steep trails and slippery passes coming at her from every angle.

She glanced down, watching her steps as rocks rose and jutted out from the soil on the path. A small stream cut down the side of the mountain and trickled in front of her. The moisture and freezing conditions made every step treacherous.

Just last week, someone had died after slipping off a

cliff on one of these trails. The man's death had been all over the news, a grim reminder of how dangerous nature could be.

At the thought, more images of Bella filled Erin's mind and she bit back a cry.

Please, Lord. Watch over her. Please! I'm begging You.

She prayed nothing had happened to her girl. Bella had problems—more than her fair share for someone her age, it seemed. But she didn't deserve this.

Another stick broke in the distance.

Erin's lungs froze as she stopped and turned around. Somebody else was out here. She felt certain of it.

Glancing ahead, she tried to measure how safe the upcoming section of the trail was. When she'd come this way earlier, she'd turned around before continuing through this section. She'd been afraid to go any farther.

A narrow path stretched against the cliff face. If she continued, this part of the hike would be challenging. Maybe even life-threatening.

But if she turned around to head back, she could be confronted by whoever shadowed her.

As she heard another stick crack, closer this time, Erin knew she only had a few seconds to make a choice.

She let out a long breath. For Bella's sake, she had to persist.

Erin rolled her shoulders back before continuing down the trail. She would need to move quickly but carefully.

She hit the first part of the narrow pass without problems—and without hearing any other mysterious sounds behind her.

Just as she reached the end of the stretch, another noise filled the air.

The sound of heavy footsteps rushing toward her.

As she turned to see what was happening, hands rammed into her back.

Then she began falling down the steep rock face into the valley below.

"I'm going to need you to give this everything you've got, boy." Dillon Walker knelt in front of his dog, Scout, and rubbed his head.

The border collie/St. Bernard mix stared back at him, his soulful brown eyes giving every indication that the canine had understood each word Dillon said. The two of them had worked together uncountable hours in order to reach this level of bonding.

Dillon rose and gripped Scout's lead as they prepared to head down the steep mountain trail stretching beside them. As a brisk winter wind swept around them, Dillon pulled his jacket closer. Scout also had on a thick orange vest with "Search and Rescue" on the side.

The temperature had dipped below freezing, which would make the trails both slippery and treacherous. Those conditions also made it more urgent to find Bella Lansing sooner rather than later.

"I appreciate you coming out here to do this." Park Ranger Rick Manning appeared beside him, his breath frosting as soon as it hit the frigid air. "I know it's been a while and that you gave up this line of work."

Dillon held back a frown. "I'm only doing this as a personal favor to you."

Dillon had been a state police officer for nearly a decade before making a career change two years ago. Now, he trained officers on how to be expert K-9 handlers. He taught others so they wouldn't make the mistakes he had. He lived with guilt every day because of those very oversights.

"I wouldn't have called you if it wasn't for the snow-storm headed this way." Rick nodded toward the gray sky above. "We don't have much time, and you are the best K-9 handler I know."

"Some people might argue that point." Dillon frowned as memories tried to pummel him. Accusations. *Truths.*

"You're the only one who's inclined to argue." Rick lowered his voice. "No one but Laura blames you for what happened to Masterson, you know."

Dillon didn't acknowledge his friend's words. Instead, he readjusted the straps of the backpack he'd filled with water, protein bars and dog treats. He wanted to be prepared for anything while they were out here.

A team of rangers would accompany Dillon and Scout in their search efforts.

A teen was missing. She was believed to be out here in the vast wilderness of the Pisgah National Forest in western North Carolina, and they needed to find her.

This was what Dillon and Scout had trained to do. The two made a great team.

But whenever Dillon had to utilize his dog in this way, it was never good news.

Not only was the situation precarious because of the missing teenager, but forecasters were calling for snow tomorrow. If Bella was out there, they needed to find her now.

"We're just waiting for Benjamin to show up," Rick said. "I'd like you to take the lead."

Dillon shook his head. "I'm not law enforcement any-more."

"It doesn't matter. You know what you're doing. You know these trails—far better than the rest of us," Rick said.

Thankfully, Benjamin strode up just then, giving Dillon an easy out in the conversation.

Dillon didn't want to be in charge. However, he'd do whatever it took to find this girl.

He glanced behind him at the parking lot. An ambulance waited there. Paramedics needed to be on call in case the team found Bella in an injured state. Dillon hoped that wasn't the case. He hoped the teen was simply lost but unharmed.

Please Lord, give her a happy ending. I can't handle another replay of Masterson.

Masterson was another hiker Dillon had set out to find. Only there hadn't been a happy ending for that search and rescue mission.

Dillon swallowed hard as he focused on the trail ahead.

The woods surrounding him were part of the Blue Ridge Mountains, and people came from all over the East Coast to experience the rolling peaks of the national forest, which boasted several different waterfalls. The area was simply breathtaking, even now at winter's end when the branches were bare.

As Dillon prepared himself to start, a gloved ranger brought a bag over. He held it toward Scout and opened the seal at the top.

Bella's sweatshirt was inside.

Scout took a deep sniff then lifted his nose to the air, trying to find the girl's scent.

Her beat-up Honda Civic had been found in a lot not far from here. This trail seemed the most logical as to where she would be.

Scout tugged at the lead before pulling Dillon along

the trailhead into the threadbare forest. As he did, Dillon mentally reviewed the case.

Bella Lansing had been missing for twenty-six hours. She'd left home for school yesterday morning but had never returned, nor had she shown up for classes. The rest of the day had been spent calling friends and searching hangouts.

There had been no leads.

Then a ranger had found her car in the lot near these woods this morning. That's when the rescue had been organized.

She wasn't an experienced hiker, nor was she familiar with this terrain. According to the report, Bella had never shown any interest in exploring these mountains. She had no survival training, but her winter coat had been missing from the house. Dillon hoped that meant she was wearing it. She'd need it out here in these elements.

Scout's actions indicated the girl had traveled this trail. What Dillon didn't know was if she'd been alone. As one of the more popular hikes in the area, any footprints would have been concealed at this point.

The rangers working the case would figure out the details. Dillon's only job, along with Scout's, was to find Bella.

"You know who Bella's mom is, don't you?" Rick asked quietly as they started down the trail.

Dillon shook his head. "No idea. Honestly, it doesn't matter if she's a criminal or a philanthropist, either way, her daughter deserves to be found."

"I should have expected that reaction from you." Rick shook his head and let out a light chuckle. "You're a good man, Dillon Walker."

He didn't know about that. He only hoped this search didn't end tragically.

These mountains were no place for the inexperienced. He'd seen too many tragedies happen here. Tragedies that had changed people's lives forever.

Just like they'd changed his.

Pushing those thoughts aside, he continued down the path. Scout was on the scent—and that was a good sign. With every minute that passed, Bella's trail could fade with time and the elements.

If Dillon had known the girl was missing earlier, he would have advised the team to start at sunrise. Instead, they'd already wasted a good three hours of daylight.

What had his friend meant when he'd asked if Dillon knew who Bella's mom was? It truly didn't matter to him, but he was curious. When Dillon had been a state cop, he'd been headquartered an hour and a half from this area. He knew little about the small towns dotting these mountains.

They continued down the trail, the miles passing by.

As he reached an area of the hike known as Traveler's Bend, he tugged Scout to a halt.

What was that sound?

"Dillon?" Rick looked at him.

He raised a finger in the air, indicating for everyone to be quiet.

That's when he heard it again.

"Please, help me!" A soft voice floated from below.

Was it Bella? Had they found the girl?

As if Scout sensed something was wrong, the canine began to bark at the edge of the path.

Dillon hurried toward the slippery, rocky cliff and peered down below.

A woman clung to a branch there, terror on her face. It wasn't Bella. Dillon had seen the girl's picture.

But this woman clearly needed help.

"Stay right there!" he yelled. "We'll get you!"

The woman opened her mouth to speak. But as she did, the rocks beneath her crumbled and she began plummeting to the ground below.

TWO

As Erin felt herself falling, she clung to the branch she'd been hanging on to, praying her grip was tight enough to catch her, praying the branch was solid enough to remain rooted.

Her body jerked to a halt before cascading to the rocky ground below.

Thank you, Jesus.

Her heart pounded in her ears at the realization of how close she'd come to death—again.

She'd heard voices above her. Or had she imagined them?

Was someone really there who could help her? Had the search party caught up with her? Or was it just simply the person who'd pushed her?

She continued to grasp the tree branch, praying her fingers wouldn't slip. Her arm was so tired. She felt so weak.

She tried to look up, but the cliff face jutted out just enough to make it difficult.

"Help me!" she yelled again. Her voice sounded as desperate as she felt.

She tried to take a deep breath in order to yell louder. But her lungs felt frozen.

The position she hung in didn't help. Her body bent, making it hard to get enough air into her system. What air she did pull in was so cold, it nearly took her breath away.

The side of the cliff face was directly in the path of the wind. The icy breeze hit her full-force.

How long would it take for hypothermia to kick in?

Oh, dear Bella... I'm so sorry. It wasn't supposed to turn out this way.

"We're going to help you!" someone yelled above her.

Yes, someone was there!

Someone who sounded like he wanted to help.

Not the person who'd done this to her.

She drew in as deep of a breath as she could. "Help me!" she yelled again. "I'm down here!"

Erin waited, trying to hear a response. But it was no use. The wind muffled the sounds around her.

Had it muffled her voice also?

Despair tried to clutch her, but Erin pushed the emotion away. This was no time for hopelessness. She needed to stay positive.

Just as the thought rushed through her head, a rock crumpled beneath her.

She looked down and saw it tumbling, tumbling, tumbling.

How many feet was it to the bottom?

She couldn't bear to think about it.

She drew in another breath. "I don't know how much longer I can hold on!"

Did the person above her understand the urgency of the situation? What was he doing?

A new sound filled the air.

Was that a...bark?

Erin felt certain that it was.

Maybe help really was here. Maybe this mountain wouldn't be her death.

She'd never meant to draw attention away from Bella and onto herself. And she wouldn't forgive herself for that.

But she needed to be there for Bella once she was found.

She looked up again, straining her neck as she tried to get a glimpse of what was going on.

A man stared down at her. "We're here to help! Are you hurt?"

That was a good question. Was she hurt?

Maybe she'd cut her leg. She might have some bruises. But none of that mattered, not if she was alive.

"I'm fine!" she called. "But please hurry."

"We're going to send a rope down to you. I need you to grab it with both hands."

The thought of releasing her lifeline—a tree branch— caused a shot of terror to rush through her. "I… I can't let go."

"We're going to talk you through it, okay? You can do this."

The man's voice sounded so soothing that Erin wanted to believe him. Plus, he'd said "we." Were there more people up there, more than just the man and his dog?

Another surge of hope swelled in her.

Erin had no *choice* but to trust this man.

From what she'd seen, the man wore a black jacket and a stocking cap. Was he a hiker?

As if to answer her question, someone else also peered over the edge of the cliff. This man wore a National Park Service cap. He was a park ranger, she realized.

Relieved, Erin tried to suck in a few more breaths to calm herself. But the task felt impossible.

"I'm sending down the rope," the first man said. "What's your name?"

She almost didn't want to say. She didn't want the scrutiny in case any of these guys recognized her. But she had little choice right now. "I'm Erin."

"Erin, I'm Dillon. My dog, Scout, is here, too, along with four park rangers. We've already secured the end of this rope to one of our guys up here. It's not going anywhere."

As she waited for the rope to be lowered, her arm continued to lose feeling even as the pain grew. She could feel herself becoming weaker. Feel her grip slipping.

She was so afraid that some kind of natural reflex would kick in and she'd let go.

She couldn't let that happen.

As she tried to find better footing, another rock below her tumbled.

She found herself being pulled downward again.

She scrambled, using her hands and feet to find anything that might stop what was about to happen.

But there was nothing other than air to catch her.

Dillon saw the woman beginning to slip and knew he had to do something.

They hadn't come this far to lose her now.

He swung the rope down, watching as she began to slide along the rock face. Nothing was below to catch her, and that's what concerned him the most.

"Grab the rope!" he yelled.

Her feet continued to skim the surface of the rock. The movement slowed her, at least. But if she kept going like that, she'd end up with crushed bones and a head injury, at the very least. Most likely, she wouldn't survive the impact.

As the rope dangled in front of her, her arm flailed in the air as she tried to reach for it.

"Come on…" Dillon leaned over the ledge, on his chest, and watched. He held his breath, praying she'd grasp it in time.

Just as she began to slide faster, her fingers closed over the rope and she jerked to a stop.

A moan escaped from her, seeming to be partly filled with pain and partly with relief.

But at least she was okay…for now.

"You've got to hold on to that rope," he called. "Use both hands."

"I'm doing my best." Her voice cracked. "But my arm…it hurts."

"You can do this, Erin. I know you can."

Scout barked beside him, almost as if the dog wanted to encourage her also.

She stared up at him, and something seemed to change in her gaze. Finally, she nodded. "I won't let go." She released the branch and transferred her other hand to the rope.

"I have a second rope," Dillon called. "This one has a large loop on the end. I'm going to send it down quickly. As soon as you can, I want you to pull it over your shoulders like a harness. Can you do that?"

"I'll try." Her voice sounded strained, but at least she was trying.

A moment later, the rope reached her. She did as Dillon said and wrapped it over her head and around her shoulders, pulling her arms through one at a time.

"Good girl," Dillon murmured.

If she started to slip again, at least the rope should catch her.

"Help me pull her up," Dillon said to Rick.

"I think that's… Erin Lansing," Rick muttered beside him as he grabbed the rope.

Dillon wanted to glance at his friend, but he didn't dare take his eyes off this woman. "Is that the missing girl's mom?"

"I'm nearly certain that's her."

What was she doing out here? Had she ventured down the trail looking for her daughter herself?

Dillon wanted to shake his head in dismay. But if it had been his daughter out here—if he had a daughter—Dillon would have done the same thing. He couldn't blame the woman for that.

"Now that the rope is secure, we're going to pull you up," he called to her. "If you can, use your feet and help walk up the rock face. Grab hold of the first rope again to help you. Got it?"

"Got it." But her voice trembled as she said the words.

This would be a scary situation for any of them.

Dillon glanced at his team and nodded. They then began working together to pull her from the cliff face. Even Scout used his teeth to help pull the rope. Thankfully, the woman wasn't heavy, so the rescue should be fairly easy.

But Dillon knew this wasn't over until this woman was on solid ground.

Erin felt her body lifting as she was pulled upward. She reminded herself to keep taking deep breaths. To keep trusting these strangers.

She had no other choice at the moment.

Slowly, she rose higher and higher.

She tried to do what the man had said and use her feet to walk up the side of the cliff. She held on tightly to the rope just in case something happened.

She'd never been so terrified in her life.

Then again, that actually wasn't true.

Knowing her daughter had disappeared was entirely scarier.

Still, she was wasting valuable time here, time that the search and rescue team could be using to look for Bella.

Finally, her head rose above the side of the mountain. As it did, two men grabbed her arms and lifted her over the edge of the cliff.

The next instant, she was on her hands and knees on the path she'd been pushed off of.

On cold but solid ground. Her trembling limbs could hardly hold her up. Finally, she collapsed and rolled over.

The air rushed from her lungs as relief filled her.

She was still alive. She couldn't believe it.

The dog who'd peered over the edge of the mountain nuzzled her. She looked up and rubbed his face, thankful for the friendly eyes. The dog was white with brown spots, had intelligent eyes, and almost looked like a small St. Bernard.

The man—Dillon—squatted beside her, concern in his brown eyes. "Are you okay?"

"I think so. Thank you. Thank you so much."

His intense expression remained focused on her. "Can you stand?"

"I think so."

He took her arm and helped her to her feet. Before he

let go, Erin froze, trying to find her balance. Her head still spun from everything that had happened.

Dillon studied her face before matter-of-factly stating, "You're Bella's mom."

Erin felt her cheeks flush. "I am."

"What happened?"

"Someone pushed me."

Alarm straightened his back. "What?"

She nodded. "I was trying to cross the trail. I thought I heard someone behind me. The next thing I knew, someone shoved me and I fell. Thankfully, I was able to catch that branch."

Dillon glanced back at the rangers, making sure they were listening. Rick nodded his affirmation.

"Did you get a glimpse of this person?"

Erin shook her head. "I didn't. I wish I had. I have no idea who would do this."

Dillon glanced at Rick again. "We'll all need to keep our eyes open just in case the person is still nearby. In the meantime, what were you even doing out here?"

"I couldn't wait any longer to search for Bella. I had to come see if I could find her myself. There's a storm coming in…"

Dillon frowned. "We need to get you to the ranger station so you can be checked out. You may have hit your head or—"

She swung her head back and forth. "No. Please. I don't want to go back to the station. I want to keep looking for my daughter."

Dillon's eyes narrowed as he continued to study her, clearly trying to measure her physical well-being and state of mind. "You're in no state to continue hiking the trail."

Her gaze latched on to his. "Please. I can do it. I can. I won't hold you back. I promise."

The man pressed his lips together in a frown before glancing at the men around him.

They all seemed to be waiting for his decision.

Erin wondered who this guy was. He didn't wear a uniform, yet he seemed to be in charge.

"I just need to find my daughter." Her voice trembled as she presented one last plea. "Please. That's all I want."

Finally, he nodded. "You can come. But don't make me regret this."

THREE

To say Dillon had reservations about letting this woman come with them would be an understatement. But if they took her back to the ranger station now, they'd be wasting too much time. Besides, the weather was turning nastier by the moment.

If Bella was out here, they needed to find her. Now.

They walked down the trail, past the narrowest section and on a path that cut through the forest. Dillon took the lead. Actually, Scout did. As Dillon walked behind him, Erin kept up the pace and remained at his side despite her rapid breaths and shaky limbs.

Erin looked younger than he'd assumed she would be, especially considering the fact she had a sixteen-year-old daughter. The woman was trim and petite with wavy dark hair that came to her chin. Her brown eyes were both perceptive and afraid. A splatter of freckles crept across her nose and cheeks.

Since the woman was with them, Dillon decided this might be a good time to get more information about the missing girl. Every detail could help.

"I'm sorry to hear about your daughter," he started, his eyes on the winding trail in front of him.

Scout tugged the lead, his nose on the scent. That was good news. There was nothing worse than a trail going cold, especially when they'd come this far. Especially when the stakes were so high.

"I just can't believe she's missing." Erin's voice sounded dull with grief. "It still seems like a nightmare that I should wake up from. But I haven't."

"Tell me what your daughter is like."

Erin drew in a deep breath. "Bella is… Where do I start? She's funny. Really funny. She makes me laugh a lot. I always think she's one of those people who could make it on a television sketch comedy one day."

"Do you like those late-night shows?" He'd never cared for them himself.

"Not really. They're not for me. But I *do* think you have to be intelligent to be funny."

"So, your daughter is smart? Is she a good student?" He tried to form a better picture in his mind.

"Not always. Bella likes socializing and…"

Dillon heard her hesitation and waited for her to continue. What was she thinking twice about before sharing?

"Bella also has anxiety," Erin finally said. "She takes medication for it every day. That's another reason why we need to find her."

He stored that information away. "What happens if she doesn't take her meds?"

Erin slowed as she climbed over an outcropping of small rocks. "Different things. Sometimes she's so anxious, she's beside herself. She can't focus or even function. Other times, she wants to avoid social situations and just be alone."

"Has she ever wandered away before?"

"No, never. That's why this is so strange to me. Plus, I got a text message."

"What did it say?"

"That I deserved this."

Dillon let that update sink in. "So you think Bella was abducted and the person who took her is mocking you?"

Tension stretched across Erin's face. "I'm not sure what to think at this point."

His mind continued to race. "Does she have a boyfriend?"

Dillon glanced at Erin as he waited for her answer. As he did, he saw her expression darken. There was another story there. He knew it.

"She likes a boy, but I told her she couldn't date yet."

"Did she give you his name?"

"No. She wouldn't tell me. But she's not mature enough to date. It was a bad idea."

"Did you tell the police that?"

"Of course. But I don't think they'll listen to anything I have to say." Her voice cracked.

Her words caught him off guard. "What do you mean?"

Erin glanced behind her at the rangers there. "It's a long story. But my ex-husband used to be a cop."

"Is that right?" Dillon was definitely curious now. Her words alluded to a deep history—a bad history—that she'd rather put behind her.

"It wasn't a good situation," Erin continued. "And it didn't end well…to say the least."

Maybe Dillon would ask around later to find out more information. Or maybe he wouldn't. What he really wanted to concentrate on right now was finding Bella.

Scout still continued to be hot on the trail.

Dillon glanced at the sky in the distance, worried

about being out here if the storm hit them. He knew just how dangerous these mountains could be. They were hard enough to hike on a good day. But add rain, wind and snow? That could be a deadly combination.

He'd give this search another hour. Then they'd need to turn back. They couldn't take the risk.

Dillon knew Erin wouldn't handle that news well.

And he couldn't blame her.

Erin fell into step behind Dillon, incredibly grateful he'd allowed her to come.

The thought of simply waiting to hear if Bella had been located made her feel like her insides were being ripped apart. Bella needed her right now—and Erin needed Bella just as much.

But Dillon's legs were long, and his dog was fast. Erin had to scramble to keep up with him and the team of rangers accompanying him. The last thing she wanted was to hold them back.

She just wanted to find her daughter. To hold her in her arms. To never let her go.

If only she could do that.

As Scout's steps slowed, Erin wedged her way closer to Dillon. He'd pointed out a set of footprints on the ground, ones that seemed to match Bella's shoe size. Based on Scout's body language, the prints followed Bella's scent.

Maybe they were onto something.

Dillon and his dog seemed competent and exuded a sense of confidence that brought her a wave of comfort.

The man seemed like the quiet type. He had broad shoulders and serious eyes. He'd briefly taken his hat off earlier, and Erin had seen light brown hair cut close to his head. But he also seemed experienced and focused, two qualities Erin could be grateful for, especially in this situation.

His casual clothing—cargo pants, hiking boots, and a thick jacket—indicated he was a volunteer. But his command of the situation and confident actions indicated there was more to his story.

Erin needed to connect with the man. She needed him to understand how desperate she felt. She needed a team of people who wouldn't give up on finding Bella—not until she was safe at home.

However, this could all backfire if the man knew who Liam was—and if he turned out to be on Liam's side. Erin would like to think those facts wouldn't change anything, that everyone would still be helpful.

But she knew from experience that wasn't always the case.

"Beautiful dog," she murmured, glancing at the dog again. "Are you a park ranger?"

"I'm a former cop and a current search and rescue volunteer."

A former cop? Erin sucked in a breath.

It was bad enough when she thought he might simply know who Liam was. But what if he had been friends with Liam?

Even worse, what if this man was just like her abusive ex? What if he was dangerous? Or what if he was like all her ex's friends and thought Erin was guilty in Liam's disappearance?

Erin's head swam at the thoughts.

Park rangers, she could handle. Some of them might have known Liam, but that didn't necessarily mean they were on his side.

Cops? Especially local cops?

They *always* took Liam's side—even when she'd had a black eye and a bruised rib.

Erin rubbed her temples, wishing she could clear the fog from her head. She needed to be sharp if she was going to hike out here. Distraction could get her killed.

Bella's image slammed into her mind again.

She didn't want to admit it, but she wouldn't put it past Bella to run. The girl had certainly threatened to do so enough times. She'd had a rough upbringing, and the urge to run seemed to be ingrained in her.

Erin had adopted Bella from out of a bad situation six years ago. Since then, she'd showered the girl with affection, had set clear boundaries, and had even taken her to therapy multiple times a week.

But some issues were hard to fix, no matter how much love and attention someone poured onto the person in need. Still, Erin hadn't given up hope.

And she never would.

"Right here, you can see another set of footprints joins the first set." Dillon paused and pointed to an area in the dirt.

One of the rangers stepped forward to snap pictures and document the prints.

"Where did this second set come from?" Erin asked.

Dillon scanned the area around them until finally pointing to some underbrush. "Based on the direction of the shoe print, I'd say the tracks came from that direction."

Erin followed his hand as it pointed to a rocky out-cropping—the perfect place for somebody to hide out and wait for someone to pass.

Dread filled Erin.

No, it was something worse than dread.

It was terror—terror at the unknown.

"What does all this mean?" Erin couldn't stop herself from asking the question, even though she already knew the answer.

Dillon offered another side-glance at her, his face remaining placid and unemotional. "That's not something I can answer. Maybe one of the rangers can tell you more."

She looked around her, noting how the other rangers seemed distracted with documenting the prints.

More memories pummeled her.

Her ex had been a good cop but a terrible husband.

A man who took his stress and anger out on Erin.

No one had believed her when she'd cried out for help. Liam had been too charming. Too convincing. Too twisted.

Now she had to live with that aftermath.

"What do *you* think it means?" She nodded down at the ground before looking back up at Dillon.

His jaw tightened as he stared at the prints. "I think it means that Bella met someone here."

"Willingly?"

"I can't answer that." He softened his voice, as if he wanted to let her know he understood but had boundaries.

Erin knew he was trying to be professional. But she needed answers, even if those answers terrified her. The truth wasn't something she could be afraid of—otherwise, she'd live her whole life in fear.

She'd done too much of that already.

She stared up at Dillon as they stood there. She wanted to keep moving. But she had to respect the rules of their investigation. She'd promised to do so before she'd headed out with them.

"You think someone abducted her, don't you?" she whispered so just Dillon could hear.

Dillon's gaze said everything even though he didn't say a word. That was *exactly* what he thought, she realized.

She buried her face in her hands—but only for a minute.

Erin couldn't fall apart. Not now.

She'd have time for that later.

Right now, all her energy needed to be focused on finding Bella. Everything else would fall in place when this was over.

Two rangers stayed behind. As they did, the rest of the group continued walking. They veered off the main trail and into the woods.

Danger seemed to hang in the air at every turn.

Just then, Scout stopped walking and sat at attention.

Erin sucked in a breath.

She knew what that meant.

It meant the K-9 had found something.

The park ranger—Rick, if Erin remembered correctly—sprang into action. Using his gloved hands, he moved away some dead leaves.

When he looked up, his expression was grim.

"We have a dead body," he announced.

Dillon pushed Erin back.

She didn't need to see the body.

Instead, he let the ranger take over the scene, and he stayed with her.

She let out a cry and nearly collapsed right there on the trail. Quickly, he reached his arm out and caught her by the elbow.

She practically sank into him as if grief consumed her until she could no longer stand up straight.

"We don't know who it is," he murmured, trying to bring her whatever reasonable comfort he could.

"Looks to me like this person has been dead for a while." Ranger Rick's voice drifted over to them as he talked to the ranger beside him.

Dillon felt Erin straighten ever so slightly. "Is there anything else that you can tell based on what you saw?"

Dillon glanced back, trying to get a better look at the body himself.

"I would say, based on that shoe size, it's a man. Ranger Rick is right, whoever it is has been out here for a while. You can hardly make out any of his features."

"What do you mean by 'a while'?"

"It's hard to say because of the elements. The medical examiner will be better at determining that than me. But if I had to guess, I'd say maybe a year."

She let out a cry. He'd thought that would be good news, that it would bring her comfort.

"Is there something you're not telling me?" Dillon waited, more curious than ever.

She looked up at him, her eyes red-rimmed with unshed tears. "The body…is there any type of jewelry on him?"

There was *definitely* more to this.

Dillon left her for a moment and wandered toward the man for a better look. The rangers had already called backup to help them retrieve the body.

Unfortunately, this was taking time away from their search for Bella. Part of him wanted to continue on with Scout. But it was too soon to do that.

As he studied the man, Dillon's eyes narrowed. It was hard to tell much about the body as a lot of decomposition had already started. But a piece of gold glimmered near the man's neck. He *was* wearing a piece of jewelry.

He squinted. It almost appeared to be a necklace with an eagle and a rose on it.

The jewelry was definitely unique.

"Dillon?"

He turned back toward Erin and saw the questions in her eyes.

After a moment of hesitation, he nodded. "There's a necklace."

"Does it have an eagle and a rose on it?"

His back muscles tightened at her exacting description. "It does. How did you know to ask that question?"

She ran a hand over her face, the despair on her expression making her appear years older. "Because that's the necklace my ex-husband always wore. He disappeared a year ago."

A bad feeling swelled in Dillon.

What in the world was going on here?

FOUR

Erin's thoughts continued to reel.

Could that really be Liam? Could he have been dead all this time?

Her hand went to her throat as she thought through the implications. Before, people had only *suspected* her of doing something. But now, if they had a dead body, Erin could only imagine the accusations would grow even greater.

How much more could she handle? It was a marvel that people in town hadn't yet run her off. They would have if it hadn't been for Bella.

Bella wanted to stay in Boone's Hollow to finish out high school. After that, Erin planned on finding a new place to settle down—a place away from people's watchful and accusing gazes. Somewhere where people didn't know her history and she could begin again.

"What was your ex-husband's name?"

Dillon's voice snapped Erin out of her dazed state and she turned toward him, trying to ignore the way he studied her face.

She swallowed hard before announcing, "His name was Liam. Liam Lansing."

Recognition flooded his gaze.

At that moment, Erin knew he'd no longer be on her side. At first, the former cop had seemed oblivious to her identity. It was part of the reason she'd felt drawn to him. Maybe he hadn't already formed a judgment about her.

But now all of that would be different. He'd probably look at her with the same disdain that everyone else did.

Dillon stepped closer and lowered his voice. "We don't know for sure that's him. Authorities will have to do an autopsy and get a better identification on him."

Maybe that was true, but the necklace seemed like it sealed the deal.

"What about Bella?" Erin's throat constricted as she said the words.

Liam had already taken so much away from her. But even from the grave—if that was his body—Erin wouldn't let him take away the opportunity to search for her daughter.

Dillon glanced at his phone and then up at the sky. "The storm is coming fast. We really need to head back."

"Now?" Grief—and a touch of panic—clutched her heart.

Giving up was the last thing that Erin wanted. She wanted to stay on these trails until she found her daughter.

It was only fair.

If her daughter was suffering, then Erin deserved to suffer, too. It had been her job to take care of Bella, and she'd clearly failed. Otherwise, her daughter would be safe and sound at home right now.

"What we don't want is another casualty while we're out here searching." Dillon's voice remained low and calm as he said the words, and his expression matched.

Erin tried to hold back her tears but hot moisture pooled in her eyes. They were so close. She could feel it.

"But Scout is on the trail," she said. "We can't lose Bella's scent, and after the storm…"

Dillon pressed his lips together and Erin knew she'd made a valid point.

"We'll go a little farther," he finally said. "But it's probably going to be you, me and Scout. The rest of the team will probably want to stay here to investigate this body."

Erin nodded. She would take whatever she could get.

Dillon went and talked to Ranger Rick for several minutes before returning. A moment later, the ranger pulled out a plastic bag, opened it, and Scout sniffed the sweatshirt inside.

Bella's sweatshirt.

Scout barked before starting through the woods again.

As a brisk wind swept over the landscape, Erin shivered and was again reminded that she wasn't cut out to do this type of search and rescue mission.

But she'd do anything for her daughter.

Even if it meant getting hurt herself.

Dillon had to give Erin credit for keeping up with him. Even though she didn't look totally steady on her feet, she was making a valiant effort as they continued to traverse the rocky terrain.

But his thoughts continued to race as they moved forward.

Liam Lansing had been her husband? The fact still surprised him.

Dillon had run into the man a few times while working as a state police officer, and he'd never been impressed. Anger seemed to simmer beneath the man's gaze.

But Liam Lansing had also been the type who could be charming and attract people to him. He was the type of guy who could get people on his side.

Whether or not that body they'd found was Liam's, Dillon could only assume at this point that the man was dead. He'd been missing for at least a year. He would guess that someone Liam had put in jail had found him and exacted revenge.

Dillon paused as they came to an especially rocky section of the trail. He reached back and helped Erin down. The last thing they needed right now was for anyone to get hurt on this trail. Planning and preparation meant they could use their time wisely.

Yet they'd already had so many setbacks.

"Thank you," Erin muttered before quickly releasing his hand.

He nodded and continued moving, not wanting to waste any more time.

Dillon knew a lot of people had blamed Liam's ex-wife for his disappearance. Looking at the woman now, seeing the fear in her eyes, he found it hard to believe that someone like Erin would be capable of something like that.

He generally had good instincts about people, and those instincts told him that Erin didn't have it inside her to hurt someone.

Still, he needed to be on guard.

A sharp wind cut through the mountain path, invading the layers of his clothing to hit his skin.

The winter storm was getting closer. Too close for comfort.

He didn't want to turn around now. Not with Bella still missing out here and Scout still on the trail. But he was going to have to make some calls soon, calls that may not be popular with Erin.

Several minutes later, Scout reached an area where water had trickled over the trail and had now frozen.

Dillon paused.

"What's going on?" Erin asked. "What does this mean?"

"That means Scout is losing the scent," Dillon said.

"Wouldn't it make sense that the trail would continue following this path?"

"As you can see, the path goes two ways from here, one down into the valley and the other up this mountain to an overlook."

She frowned. "Which way are we going to go?"

Dillon swallowed hard before launching into his decision. "Here's the thing. We're running out of time."

Erin's eyes widened with something close to desperation. "But we're right here. We can't turn back now."

Just as she said the words, a smattering of snowflakes floated down around them. The icy precipitation brought with it the promise that more was coming.

"The weather's going to turn bad quickly," Dillon explained. "We don't want to be stuck out here when it does."

"But Bella…" Erin's voice cracked.

Dillon frowned, understanding the dilemma all too well. Understanding why she wouldn't want to leave. Understanding how heartbreaking this must feel to her.

"Erin, the truth is, we're going to be no good to Bella if we're killed out here ourselves. How would we search for her then?"

"But…" She stared at the trail in the distance, agony flashing in her gaze.

More snow began falling, snow that was mixed with freezing rain.

"Scout's lost the trail," he reminded her. "I know it seems logical that Bella went either to the left or to the right. But there are a lot of possibilities here. When the storm lets up, we'll have the helicopters out. We can put search parties out. We can narrow it down to this area. But right now, we need to get back to where it's dry and warm."

Erin said nothing.

Dillon lightly touched her arm. "I'm sorry, Erin. I know this isn't what you want to hear. But it's my job to ensure the safety of my team. Right now, you and Scout are my team."

Her hand went over her lips, almost as if she wanted to let out a cry. She didn't. Instead, she nodded resolutely. "Okay then."

Dillon studied her a moment. She seemed submissive now. But he wouldn't put it past Erin to head back out into this wilderness by herself. He needed to make sure that didn't happen.

These mountains were no place for inexperienced hikers, especially with the weather like this.

He nodded in the direction they'd just come from. "Let's get going before this turns worse. There are a few passes that will be nearly impossible if they freeze over. There's another path we can take as a shortcut to the parking lot. I think we should take that."

Erin's eyes widened as if she hadn't thought of that yet. She nodded. "Let's go. I just pray that Bella is somewhere warm and dry right now."

Erin couldn't stop thinking about everything that happened. It felt like Dillon and his team were so close to answers. With every step Scout took, his nose on the trail, she'd felt like finding Bella was within their grasp.

And then it wasn't. Just like that.

What happened to Bella's scent? How had it suddenly disappeared like that?

The whole thing didn't make any sense. Bella's scent couldn't have just disappeared out of the blue, right?

Erin's heart pounded harder, louder, into her ears as anxiety squeezed her again.

All she wanted was her daughter safe and in her arms. Out of the unknown. Out of these harsh elements.

The wind was so, so cold, and turning cooler by the moment. What if Bella didn't have shelter?

At that thought, Erin decided she'd come back here herself if she had to—at the first chance she had.

Erin started forward when Dillon pointed to another trail cutting through the forest.

"This is going to be a shortcut back to the parking lot," he said. "I think we need to go this way."

Disappointment filled her. She'd hoped to again go past the scene where they'd found that body, before taking the shortcut. She'd hoped to hear if the rangers had any updates for her.

But it didn't look like that was an option right now.

Instead, she nodded and continued walking.

Several minutes later, Dillon nodded toward a rocky ledge they would have to cross ahead. "We're going to need to be very careful at this section."

Even from where Erin stood, she could already see that the trail was slick. There was no handrail. Just a sheer drop—one similar to the area where Erin had been pushed.

Her heart raced as she remembered her earlier fall. As she remembered the person who had done that to her.

"Can you tell me more about what happened before you felt someone push you off that cliff?" Dillon asked.

Erin shrugged, wishing she didn't have to replay the scene. But she knew it was necessary if they were going to find answers. "I thought I heard somebody in the woods behind me a couple of times. Then I thought maybe I was imagining things. I wasn't really sure. But the next thing I knew, I felt two hands on my back and I began falling."

"Who would have done that?" He glanced back at her. "The person who grabbed Bella?"

"Why would the person who took her follow you and try to kill you?" Dillon's eyes looked just as intelligent as Scout's as the man observed her, his thoughts clearly racing as he tried to put the pieces together.

She shook her head. "I wish I knew."

Erin sucked in a breath as she began to walk along the rocky ledge. Panic wanted to seize her.

She'd wanted to argue with the decision to turn back, but Dillon had been right to make the call. If they had been trapped out in a snowstorm, all three of them would also be in danger. As much as she hated to leave, staying out here wasn't an option.

"Keep your steps steady and slow. You can do this."

Dillon's words sounded surprisingly comforting, and Erin was grateful he was there with her.

She did as he said and moved carefully. As she started to look down, she paused. She glimpsed the vast expanse below her and quickly averted her gaze.

She couldn't put herself in that mindset. She just needed to focus on where she was going, not where she *could* go if she slipped up.

That was what she always used to tell Bella also. *You have to focus on the road ahead while remembering the lessons behind you.*

Erin's heart panged with grief as she thought about her daughter again.

Often, she'd wished she could go back to the sweet times when Bella had only been ten or eleven. Times when they'd had fun going on road trips. When they'd cooked together. When Erin had braided Bella's hair and they'd painted each other's fingernails.

But something had happened as soon as the girl turned fifteen. It was almost like her daughter had transformed into a different person. Certainly, hormones had played a role in that. But so had Liam. That had been when Liam's anger problems had worsened. When he'd stopped trying to hide from Bella that he took his frustrations out on Erin.

That's when Erin had known she'd had to get out. Not only had the relationship become unhealthy for her, it had also become unhealthy for Bella.

Finally, Erin stepped onto solid ground again. She breathed a sigh of relief once she was finished with the crossing.

As she did, she glanced back and saw Dillon and Scout carefully walking past the area. They did it with much more grace and ease than she had.

They continued walking. Erin wished she could carry on a conversation as they did so, but the air had turned colder and hurt her lungs. She pulled her coat higher and tried to breathe into the collar.

But as the snow came down harder, her discomfort grew. She had to watch every step. Concentrate every thought on getting out of this forest in one piece and without any broken bones.

Finally, they reached the clearing where the parking lot was.

When she walked over to her car, she pulled in a deep breath.

Her tires had been slashed.

Tears pressed her eyes as she soaked in the deep gashes in the rubber.

Who would have done this?

As Dillon stared at the slashed tires on Erin's car, a bad feeling began to grow inside him. Somebody was bent on making Erin suffer.

Why was that? And who would want to do something like this?

"I'm going to send a crew out to look at your tires," he told her. "But right now, we need to get out of the elements."

"Of course." Erin continued to stare at her vehicle as she said the words, but her eyes looked duller now than they had earlier.

"I'm parked over here." Dillon nodded to his Jeep. "How about I give you a ride? Would you be okay with that?"

She stared at him a moment as if contemplating her answer before finally nodding. "I would appreciate that. Thank you."

"It's no problem."

They walked across the parking lot to his Jeep. He helped Erin into the front seat before lifting Scout into the back. Then Dillon climbed in and cranked the engine. As he waited for the vehicle to heat, he gave Scout some water. Then he reached into the back and grabbed a blanket.

He'd just washed it, and the scent of fabric softener still smelled fresh between the folds. He handed it to Erin. "This will help take the edge off until the heat kicks in."

"Thank you." Her teeth practically chattered as she said the words.

As the air slowly warmed and heat poured from the vents, it offered a welcome relief from the otherwise frigid temperatures outside.

"I'm going to go ahead and call about your tires now before we take off," Dillon explained. "I'd also like to see if there are any updates on our search mission, as well as the dead body."

"Of course." She pulled the blanket higher around her shoulders.

He dialed Rick's number and his friend answered on the first ring. Dillon explained that they'd come back from the hike and told Rick about Erin's tires being slashed.

"How about you?" Dillon asked. "Any updates?"

"We were able to retrieve the body before the snowstorm came. I'll take it back to the medical examiner's office to get some more answers. We also recorded the scene and tried to find any evidence that had been left behind there."

"Hopefully, you'll get some answers to that soon."

"I'm glad you called," Rick said. "Chief Blackstone called and wants to know if you can bring Erin in for some additional questions."

Chief Blackstone? Dillon didn't know the man well, but he'd worked with the Boone's Hollow police chief on a couple of operations. He'd found the man to be overbearing and quick-tempered. In other words, he wasn't Dillon's favorite person.

Dillon glanced at Erin, aware that she had no idea what they were talking about. Instead, she reached back and rubbed Scout's head.

Dillon looked away, turning his attention back to the situation. "I'm sure I can do that. Do you know what it's pertaining to?"

"I think he has more questions for her concerning Bella's disappearance. That's all that they told me."

"Very well." Dillon ended the call and glanced at Erin again, wondering how she was going to take this update.

He cleared his throat before saying, "The chief would like to speak with you."

Her face seemed to go a little paler. "Why?"

"I'm sure it's just routine."

She squeezed her lips together before saying, "Nothing is routine when it comes to Chief Blackstone. The man hates me."

Dillon wanted to refute her statement. But he couldn't.

He didn't know what exactly she'd been through after Liam, and it wouldn't be fair to state an opinion based only on a guess.

"I can stay with you and give you a ride home afterward," he offered.

The breath seemed to leave her lungs for a moment and she stared at him as if trying to read his intention. "You would do that? I'm sure you need to get home and tend to your dog."

"I don't mind."

Maybe it was curiosity or maybe it was concern. But Dillon wanted to stay with Erin and find out exactly what was going on here. Plus, he sensed that this woman didn't really have anyone else to help her.

Giving her a ride was the least that he could do.

He put his Jeep into Reverse and backed out. "Let's get going. The storm isn't going to be letting up anytime soon, and these roads can get bad."

Erin nodded and crossed her arms over her chest.
She had to be living a nightmare right now.
Dillon just prayed that she would have a happy ending.

FIVE

Erin knew Dillon was trying to paint this visit to the police station in a positive light for her sake. But she knew the truth.

She knew how this would play out.

Just as when Liam had disappeared, Erin was most likely going to be the main suspect in Bella's disappearance as well.

Didn't Blackstone and his crew know that she would never hurt her daughter? These guys just needed a suspect and, for some reason, Erin seemed to fit the bill.

A sickly feeling began to grow in her stomach. She didn't want to go to the police station. But if she ran, she'd only look guilty. On the other hand, if she were arrested, how could she help find her daughter?

The questions collided inside her until Erin felt off-balance.

What was she going to do? What if Blackstone *did* try to arrest her?

And was Dillon just playing nice? Was he playing good cop trying to get information from her?

Erin wished she could trust men in uniform. Most of them were probably good guys. But the ones she knew weren't. Their loyalties were misplaced and their justice biased.

She stared at the road in front of her. To say the weather had become blustery would be an understatement. It was downright nasty out here.

In fact, it was nearly impossible to even see the road as the snow created whiteout conditions.

She uncrossed her arms and grabbed the armrest, trying to remain calm.

She remembered the time in her life back before she'd met Liam. She'd been so carefree and happy. As an only child whose parents had been divorced, she'd been determined to make a different future for herself.

But everything had changed and she could hardly remember that idealistic person anymore. Her parents had both remarried and started new lives. She hardly ever spoke to them anymore.

"This could get slippery," Dillon muttered.

As far as she was concerned, slippery roads and mountains didn't mix. "Are you good at driving in snow?"

"I'd like to think so. This girl hasn't let me down yet." He patted the dash of his Jeep.

Erin glanced into the back seat and saw that Scout looked pretty laidback as well. Couldn't dogs sense danger? Maybe the fact that Scout looked relaxed was a good sign. Maybe the dog knew things Erin didn't.

The road turned with the bends in the mountain. Erin had come up this way a few times before, and she knew that at one point the road traveled alongside the path of a stream. Then it climbed back up the mountain. Eventually, it even became a gravel road.

The truth was that, even on a good day, the road was

hard to manage. Throw in this kind of weather and the trip was even scarier.

Erin pressed her eyes shut.

Dear Lord, I know You haven't let me down yet. Please, be with me now. Everything is falling apart, and I feel helpless. But I know I have You. I know You have a plan. I just need You now more than ever.

She'd prayed prayers like that before, especially when she'd been with Liam. It was so easy to think that things couldn't get worse.

But life had proven to her that they could, indeed, get worse.

Would that be the case now also?

Erin glanced outside again, trying to get a glimpse of where they were. Dillon was traveling slowly, which made her feel better, more secure.

But she sensed something shift in the air. It was Dillon's body language, she realized. He seemed more tense. More alert. Had something happened?

She glanced behind her, desperate for answers. "Dillon?"

He gripped the steering wheel and glanced into the rearview mirror again. "I think we're being followed."

"You mean somebody is just behind us?" Even as she said the words, she knew they didn't sound correct.

His jaw tightened. "I can't be sure. Most people in their right mind aren't out on the road right now."

The breath left her lungs.

Erin knew what he was getting at. There hadn't been anybody behind them in the parking lot when they'd left. The rescue crew and the remaining rangers had already left. Only Erin's car had remained behind. Not only that, but there were no other roads between that lot and where they were on the road now.

That meant somebody had parked on the side of the street.

Had that person waited for Dillon and Erin to go past and then pulled out behind them?

She remembered the person who'd pushed her down the cliff. What if that person was following them now? What if that person wanted to fix the mistake they'd made earlier when Erin hadn't died?

Dillon hadn't wanted to alarm Erin. But the woman was observant and had noticed the tension threading through him. It was only fair of him to tell her the truth.

Right now, the car behind him maintained a steady distance. Dillon could barely see the vehicle. Occasionally, he got a glimpse between the drifts of snow coming down.

The drive was already treacherous. The last thing he needed was somebody tailing them. Dillon just hoped that the person behind them would maintain a steady pace and not try to do anything foolish.

He quickly glanced at Erin and saw that she seemed to be getting paler and paler. If somebody was following them, was this person connected to Bella's disappearance? Could it be the same person who'd pushed Erin off the cliff?

If Erin were guilty in her daughter's disappearance, why would somebody be going through all this trouble?

Dillon knew the answer to that question.

They wouldn't.

So many questions collided in his head, but this wasn't

the time to think about them. Right now, he needed to focus all his attention on the road.

He gently pressed on the brake as the road in front of him disappeared into a blur of white. He looked for any type of markers to show him where he needed to be.

There were too many unknowns in this area. Even though Dillon had driven this path many times, he hadn't memorized every inch of it. He hadn't remembered every turn and every drop-off. The lane was already narrow.

In different circumstances, he might pull off and try to wait the storm out. But the snow showers weren't supposed to be over until tomorrow. Forecasters hadn't even known that this system was going to come on this quickly, either.

Pulling off right now could be deadly. Especially if somebody else heading down the road wasn't expecting him to be there. Visibility was nearly down to zero.

Dillon glanced in his rearview mirror again and saw a brief glimpse of the car.

His heart rate quickened.

The vehicle was closer, probably only six feet behind them.

Was that on purpose? Dillon didn't know. But his gut told him he needed to remain on guard.

"Dillon?" Erin's voice sounded shaky beside him.

"Yes?"

"What's going on?" She still gripped the armrest.

"I'm just taking this moment by moment." He didn't bother to hide the truth.

"I don't even know how you're driving in this. It's completely white all around us."

"That's why I'm going slow. My Jeep has excellent

traction." Those things were the truth. But there were many other hazards he didn't mention.

Just as the words left his mouth, he felt something nudge the car.

It was the vehicle behind them.

The driver was trying to run them off the road, wasn't he?

Dillon had to think quick if he wanted to walk away from this drive with his life—and the lives of those in his vehicle—intact.

As Erin felt the Jeep lurch forward, a muffled scream escaped.

Somebody *had* been following them.

And now somebody wanted to run them off the road.

Her thoughts swirled.

This couldn't really be happening...but it was.

She glanced behind her and could barely make out headlights there. From what she could tell, this guy was gearing up to ram them again.

Next time, she and Dillon may not be so lucky. That driver might succeed and push them right off one of these cliffs.

It was nearly impossible to see what was about to happen. Erin had no idea if the Jeep was at the center of the road, if anybody was coming toward them, or how close they were to the cliff on one side of them or the river on the other.

She squeezed her eyes shut and began to pray even more fervently.

Dillon could be as experienced a driver as there was out there, but his skills would only get them so far in these circumstances.

Please, protect us. Guide us. I can't die. Not with Bella still out there. Please.

Scout let out a whine in the back seat. Erin reached back and rubbed his head, feeling his soft fur beneath her hand. "It's going to be okay, boy."

Comforting the dog helped distract her from her own fear.

The reprieve didn't last long.

The vehicle behind them rammed them again. This time, the Jeep careened out of control.

Erin gasped as they slid down the mountain road. The tires hit rocks and began to bump, bump, bump over them.

She squeezed her eyes shut as the bottom dropped from her stomach.

Where would they stop?

She didn't know. But she prepared herself to hit water. To hit a rock wall. To soar from a cliff.

To die.

SIX

"Hold on!" Dillon yelled.

Dillon fought to maintain control of the vehicle. But it was no use.

The icy road was winning.

Now he just had to work with the situation.

As he jerked the wheel, trying to avoid going off an unseen cliff, Erin gasped beside him.

The other vehicle revved its engine as it sped past them.

He strained to get a glimpse of who might be behind the wheel or what the vehicle looked like.

It was no use. All he'd seen was a flash of gray.

Finally, the Jeep slid to a stop.

Dillon let out a breath, halfway still expecting the worst. A sudden fall from the cliff or for the ground to disappear from beneath them.

But nothing happened.

His heart pounded in his ears as they sat there for a moment.

Then he glanced at Erin. "Are you okay?"

She let out a long, shaky breath. "I think so. You?"

He nodded. "That was close, to say the least. Did you get a glimpse of the vehicle when it went past?"

She shook her head, appearing disappointed she didn't have more to share. "All I saw was that it seemed to be gray. But everything…the snow was so thick that it was almost impossible and—"

"I know. You don't have to explain." He reached into the back seat and rubbed Scout.

The dog appeared to be okay still. They were *all* okay. That was good news.

But what waited for them next?

Dillon let out a long breath.

The three of them couldn't stay here. It was dangerous for any oncoming traffic, for starters. Plus, Dillon had no idea exactly where they were.

Had they skidded onto a pull-off on the side of the road? Had they hit a rocky patch of the road itself? He wasn't sure.

Based on the fact that he'd seen the car zoom past them on the right side, he could assume the roadway was there.

What would happen when Dillon started traveling down the road again? Was the other driver going to wait for them to pass and try these shenanigans again?

He wanted to say no. But he really had no idea.

"Should we call for backup?" Erin's voice cracked with fear.

He grabbed his phone and looked at the screen. It was just as he thought. There was no signal out here. Most places in these mountains didn't have a signal.

He frowned. "We're going to have to see if we can make it out of here ourselves. It's the best option of what we've got."

Erin rubbed her throat as if she were having trouble swallowing, but she nodded. "Whatever you think is best."

Dillon wished he knew what was best. There had been a time when he'd trusted his instincts. When his life had depended on doing so.

But after what had happened with Masterson, that was no longer the case.

He let out a long breath before slowly pulling onto what he hoped was the road. He waited for a moment, hoping for a break in the snow or the wind—something just enough to allow him to see where he was.

A moment later, he got his wish. The snow seemed to hold its breath and offered him a glimpse of the winter wonderland around them.

Dillon could barely make out a street sign in the distance—but it was something. That was where he needed to head.

At this rate, it would take him at least an hour to get to the Boone's Hollow police station, if not more.

He didn't care about how long it took, only that they arrived safe.

He began inching back down the road, ignoring the ache that had formed between his shoulder blades.

This wasn't the kind of weather people needed to be out driving in. Back when he'd been a cop, he'd seen way too many accidents happen in conditions like these. He didn't want to be one of those statistics.

Still, he pressed forward.

The good news was that the other car hadn't appeared again.

Maybe the driver had assumed they'd crashed. That would be the best-case scenario for them now.

Once they managed to get through this crisis, Dillon

knew there would be another one waiting for them at the police station.

He never thought his day would turn into this.

He glanced over at Erin.

He was certain that she hadn't thought that, either.

Erin's relief was short-lived.

They'd finally managed to get off the mountain back-road and onto a highway. But now they'd pulled up to the police station. Now she was going to be facing another type of struggle.

You could run, a quiet voice said inside her.

She reminded herself again that, if she ran, she'd only look guilty. Besides, she had nothing to hide, nothing to be ashamed of.

As soon as Dillon parked the Jeep, she glanced over at him.

Something shifted in him also, almost as if arriving at the station had caused him to shift personas. Or was that only what Liam did?

Her emotions tangled with her logic until nothing made sense.

Was he getting ready to treat her like she was a criminal? Had he secretly needed to bring her in for questioning?

Erin didn't know the man well enough to say so. She only knew he was handsome and kind and brave. Not that any of those things mattered right now. There were so many more important things to worry about.

"Thanks for getting us off that mountain," she finally said instead.

Dillon nodded, his gaze still assessing hers. "It's no

problem. I'm glad we're all okay right now. It was a close call back there."

That was an understatement. Erin's life had flashed before her eyes again—for the second time in one day.

He nodded toward the modest, one-story building in the distance. "Are you ready to head inside?"

She stared at the police building. It was still snowing, but at this very moment, it wasn't coming down hard. Memories flooded back to her.

Memories of bringing Liam lunch while he was on his break. Of the hope she'd felt when he'd first gotten the job.

Then she remembered how hostile it had all become when things went south. The uneasy feeling she'd felt whenever she'd stepped inside.

Was she ready to relive those moments? Not really.

That's why she'd gone to the park rangers when Bella went missing, instead of the local police. But she'd known they would eventually get involved.

She didn't need to tell Dillon all that. He'd already carried enough of her burdens today.

She'd never answered his question. *Are you ready to go inside?*

"I suppose I'm ready," she finally said, wishing her heart wasn't beating so hard and fast.

Dillon stared at her another moment, something unspoken in his gaze. Erin wished she knew what he was thinking, but she didn't know him well enough to ask. Besides, he didn't owe her anything—definitely not an explanation.

"Let's go." He opened his door and a brisk wind swept inside.

Moving quickly, he retrieved Scout from the back seat.

As he did, Erin climbed out and pulled her jacket closer as she ambled to the front doors of the station. The lot was slippery and snow still seemed to stockpile on the ground. The sudden darkness wasn't helping, either.

This place had so many bad memories. At one time, the building had seemed like a place of hope. When Liam first got his job here, it was like a dream come true for him. They'd even gone out to his favorite restaurant to celebrate afterward.

But Erin had never envisioned the ways that Liam would change. Not only had his personality shifted, so had the way he'd treated her. She wasn't sure what exactly had caused that change in him, but Erin had borne the brunt of his frustrations.

She continued to carefully plod over the icy surface, headed toward the front door of the building with Dillon by her side.

It certainly hadn't helped that Liam was a likable guy. He was the type of person who could make friends wherever he went. In fact, he would have made a great salesman.

Erin couldn't be certain about everything Liam must have said about her at work. But it was clear he hadn't painted her in a positive light around his colleagues.

That was why, when he disappeared, Erin was one of the first people they'd looked at.

The betrayal still hurt. At one time, these people had been her friends. In the blink of an eye, they'd turned against her. Sometimes, it felt like everyone in town had turned against her.

As she hurried toward the front door, Dillon lightly placed his hand on her back. His concern—or was it his touch?—caused her breath to catch.

His concern. It was definitely his concern that had caused that reaction.

It had been a long time since anyone had wanted to be associated with her. For someone like Dillon to go out of his way to offer a small measure of comfort and assistance touched her in surprising ways.

They reached the front door and Dillon opened it for her. Erin slipped into the warmth of the police building.

But the welcome of warmth was short-lived. As soon as she saw Chief Blackstone head toward her, a deep chill wracked her body.

The look in his eyes indicated that her troubles were just starting.

And, unfortunately, she already felt like she was at her breaking point.

Dillon watched as Chief Blackstone's eyes instantly darkened as soon as he saw Erin.

The man was in his early forties, with only a fringe of dark hair around the sides of his rectangular head. His burly frame and stiff movements made him an intimidating figure—for some people, at least.

The man obviously had a chip on his shoulder for the woman. Dillon's curiosity spiked. Just what had transpired after Liam disappeared?

"Erin, I'd like to see you in my office." Blackstone's voice didn't contain even an ounce of warmth.

She nodded, looking resigned to that fact and like a lamb going in for the slaughter.

"Dillon, I'd like to talk with you also," Blackstone called. "Can you wait around?"

Dillon glanced at Erin, wishing he could go with her and shield her from some of what was about to happen.

Because, based on the look in Blackstone's eyes, he was about to give her the third degree. Most likely, he'd show no mercy.

Why did he feel such a protective instinct toward the woman? It didn't make sense.

But he could feel the heartache she was going through right now. Plus, based on what had happened today and what he'd experienced with her, Dillon didn't believe she'd had any part in her daughter's disappearance. It just didn't make sense. She had no motive for harming her daughter.

Dillon planted himself near the door, still gripping Scout's lead. "I'll stick around."

Blackstone nodded to him.

Erin gave him one last glance before following the chief into his office.

Chief Blackstone cast a glance at Dillon before closing his door. Dillon clutched Scout's lead as he wondered exactly what was about to go down.

He hesitated a moment, unsure what to do with himself.

As he thought about everything Erin had already been through—about the grief in her gaze—something stirred inside him.

The woman had no one to stand up for her. No one to lean on.

That just wasn't right.

If Dillon's instincts were correct, she was about to experience another nightmare in the chief's office.

He couldn't let that happen.

As instinct took over, he started toward the chief's door. He knocked but pushed it open before Blackstone could answer.

"Yes?" A shadow crossed the chief's gaze.

"I'm wondering if I could stay in here and assist you with anything that you need to talk about."

Chief Blackstone narrowed his eyes. "Why would you want to do that?"

"I've been with Erin all day, so I can offer my perspective on today's events also. Including the fact that we were almost run off the road and her tires were slashed."

The chief stared at him a moment until finally nodding. "I suppose that's fine. As long as it's also fine with Erin."

Erin glanced at him and something that looked like relief flooded her face. "Yes, that's fine."

He stepped inside and closed the door. He and Scout stood in the corner, out of the way.

"Where were you when Bella disappeared?" The chief didn't waste any time before jumping right in and focusing his accusation on Erin.

Erin quickly shook her head as if the question had startled her. "Where was I? I was at work. I have a whole classroom full of kids who can verify that."

He glowered. "But what about before that?"

"Before I went to school?" She blinked several times as if his question didn't make sense. "I was getting ready to go to school, just like I do every day."

"And nobody was with you?"

She shook her head, and Dillon sensed her rising frustration.

"As I'm sure you know, the elementary school starts before the high school," Erin said. "So I left the house by seven that morning to head into school. Bella was in the bathroom getting ready when I left and that was the last time I saw her. I went through this with the park rangers."

The chief's expression showed no reaction—except maybe a tinge of skepticism. "You haven't talked to Bella since then?"

"That's correct. I've tried her cell, but she hasn't answered. I've texted her. Nothing."

"And your car was found parked beside the trailhead also…"

Erin's lips parted as if the chief's questions continued to shock her. "My car was only there because I drove to the area to search for her myself."

"Somebody said your car was there yesterday right after school hours."

Erin sucked in a breath, her eyes widening with outrage. "That's a lie. I didn't go there yesterday. I didn't even know that Bella's car had been found there until this morning. Who told you that?"

"It doesn't matter. I'm just telling you what a witness has come forward to say."

She swung her head back and forth in adamant denial. "Then somebody is trying to set me up. Are there security cameras there at the lot?"

Chief Blackstone shook his head. "I'm afraid there aren't."

"Well, you can talk to my neighbors. They'll tell you that I came home after school. That's when I realized that Bella wasn't there and I started making phone calls."

"I'd say that's a problem. We talked to your neighbors and none of them said they saw you."

"What?" Her voice trailed off.

Dillon felt a stab of outrage burst through him. "Are you accusing Erin of her daughter's disappearance?"

Blackstone's raised eyebrows showed annoyance at the question. "We're trying to cover all our bases here."

"Well, I can personally attest to the fact that her tires were slashed and someone tried to run us off the road. That's not to mention the fact that Erin was pushed off a cliff. If she was truly guilty, why did all those things happen?"

"That's a good question." The chief practically smirked. "One we need to look into."

Dillon's back muscles tightened. The chief obviously had a target on Erin's back.

If Blackstone was already convinced he knew what had happened, he wouldn't look at anyone else except Erin.

That didn't make things look promising as far as finding Bella.

SEVEN

Erin looked up and tried to offer Dillon a grateful smile.

She was glad he was there, even though she still wasn't sure why he'd barged into the chief's office. Still, his presence brought with it a strange comfort.

At first, she'd feared Dillon was one of the chief's minions. But the protective set of his jaw made her believe otherwise.

She hoped she wasn't wrong; that Dillon wasn't some kind of spy for the law enforcement head. Blackstone had so many people in his pocket that it made it hard for Erin to know whom to trust.

"Is there any other reason why you want to keep Ms. Lansing here?" Dillon's gaze locked with the chief's.

Chief Blackstone's eyes hardened. "We just wanted to hear her version of events again."

"I told you. So now, you tell me. Do you have any leads on Bella?" Erin rushed to ask, trying to keep the exasperation from her voice. But it was hard to do that when she felt like they were wasting valuable time. "Have you heard anything else? I'm so worried about her."

"No. Nothing yet." Chief Blackstone's expression—and tone—showed no emotion or regret.

Disappointment cut deep inside her. Erin had hoped for something more, even though she'd fully expected him to say those words. Once a person was guilty of something in this man's eyes, then they were always guilty. Always a suspect. Never to be trusted.

"Unless there's something else you need, I need to get her home." Dillon gripped her arm, nearly pulling Erin from her seat. "The weather is turning bad."

Erin's breath caught. Would this work? Would Dillon actually be able to get her out of here?

Chief Blackstone raised his eyebrows, a shadow darkening his glare. "*You* do? Is that right?"

Dillon shrugged. "Like I said, her tires were slashed."

Scout barked as if adding his agreement.

The chief nodded slowly, unspoken judgment lingering in his gaze. "I can get one of my guys to give her a ride home."

"That won't be necessary," Dillon said. "I don't mind."

Erin held her breath as she waited for the chief's response. Scout sat at attention as if he was also waiting.

Chief Blackstone's eyebrows flickered before he tilted his head in a nod. "Very well then. We'll be in touch if we have any more questions."

Erin wished the chief had said they'd be in touch if they had any more updates. But the way he'd worded the statement made it clear he still thought Erin could be guilty.

How could the chief think that? Did he hate her that much?

Right now, Erin just wanted to get out of there.

She stood and headed toward the door before the chief could ask anything else.

Without another word, Dillon directed her outside.

As she stepped into the lot, she noted that snow was still coming down but not as heavily as earlier. Still, the ground was covered with the icy, white flakes. The ride home would be slippery.

"Hello, Erin," someone said behind her.

She turned and saw Officer Brad Hollins standing there.

A friendly face.

He'd been a rookie who'd trained under Liam. The man had eaten at their house and come to cookouts. He was one of the few people who hadn't turned his back on Erin when everything went down.

"Hi, Officer Hollins." She paused. "You're looking good."

He grinned, but it quickly faded. "I'm sorry to hear about Bella. I'm keeping my eyes and ears open for any leads. I just wanted to let you know that."

"I appreciate it. Thank you."

She said goodbye before continuing to the Jeep. They all climbed inside. Only when the engine started did Dillon speak.

"Old friend?" he asked.

"He's one of the good guys. He's always been kind to me."

"Good. I'm glad to hear that. Listen, I'm sorry about that back there." Compassion wound through the strands of Dillon's voice.

Erin swallowed hard and glanced at her hands as they rested in her lap. What did she even say? If she overshared, would that make Dillon suspicious of her?

She finally settled on the obvious. "In case you can't tell, the chief doesn't really like me."

"Because of Liam?"

She nodded as she remembered the comradery the two men had shared. "Blackstone thought of Liam as a son."

"I see. So, Blackstone took it hard when Liam disappeared?"

"He did. He had tunnel vision and thought I was responsible for it. He was so convinced it was me, he hardly looked at any other possibility."

Dillon frowned. "I can see him doing that…"

She turned toward him and studied his face, his expression, for any sign that he was on Blackstone's side. "You mean you didn't fall under the chief's spell? Under Liam's spell?"

"I try, to the best of my ability, not to fall under spells." He offered a small grin.

Erin wanted to smile in return but she didn't. This was no time to find any kind of enjoyment out of her circumstances.

"Now, where do I need to take you?" Dillon asked.

She rattled off her address, which was located about ten minutes from the police station, just on the outskirts of town.

Using the same caution on the slippery streets as earlier, Dillon started down the road toward her place.

As the station disappeared from sight, at once she felt every ounce of her exhaustion.

What a day.

She needed to get a good night's rest so she could start again tomorrow. If it wasn't for the weather, she would keep searching tonight. But it would do no good, and she knew that.

"How long have you lived here?" Dillon's voice cut through the silence.

"I moved to Boone's Hollow when Liam and I got married, and he got a job on the force."

"Is that right? But Liam was a local, wasn't he?"

She nodded, surprised that he knew as much about Liam as he did. Then again, maybe she shouldn't be surprised. "He was. Born and raised in Boone's Hollow."

"I see. Where did you meet him? If you don't mind me asking…"

Her mind drifted back in time. "In college. Liam was studying criminal justice and I was working on my teaching degree."

"Do you teach at a local school?"

Erin shook her head. "I work two towns over. I switched after Liam went missing. It's a forty-minute drive both ways, but I figure it's worth it just for the peace of mind."

His jaw tightened. "I can't even imagine what that must be like. I'm surprised you haven't moved."

"I thought about it many times. And it's tempting. But Bella wants to graduate from high school here. Thankfully, she hasn't gotten as bad of a rap as I did. People still seem to like her because she's Liam's daughter." She frowned as she said the words.

It was a wonder they'd accepted Bella as much as they had, especially considering that Liam wasn't her biological dad.

The thoughts continued to turn over in Erin's head.

Finally, they turned onto the street she lived off of. It wasn't in a neighborhood but instead her home was a smaller cabin located on a back road. The woods surrounding the property offered her some privacy, which had been welcome the week that everything had happened.

But as Dillon pulled up to her house and his headlights

shone on the front of it, she saw a message that had been spray-painted there.

It was the word "Killer."

The blood drained from her face.

Somebody had wanted to send a message, and it had worked.

As Dillon stared at the word painted on the front of Erin's house, the severity of the situation hit him once again.

Not only was this woman's daughter missing, but people in this town were bent on making it seem like Erin was responsible. He could only imagine the pressure Erin felt right now.

As Dillon glanced at her, he saw the tears well in her eyes as she stared at the painted letters on her porch. What a shock it must be for her to see this.

"Let me make sure you get inside okay," he said.

She quickly wiped her eyes before waving her hands in the air. "You don't have to do that. You've already gone above and beyond."

"I'd feel better if I was able to check it out for you. I can't leave you here now when danger could be lurking just out of sight. I wouldn't be able to live with myself if something happened to you."

After another quick moment of hesitation, she finally nodded. "Okay then."

He took his key out of the ignition before climbing out and grabbing Scout from the back seat. Cautiously, he walked toward the front of the house, scanning everything around them as he did so.

He didn't see anybody waiting out of sight. But they still needed to be cautious.

"Stay behind me," he muttered as Erin trailed close to him.

He looked again at the letters across the front of her house. They'd been scrawled in red spray paint—of course. The color only added to the threatening effect.

How could someone do this? How could they think Erin was guilty without even knowing any details?

His stomach clenched at the thought of it.

The keys rattled in Erin's hand until finally she managed to open the door.

"Let me. Wait here." Dillon pushed himself in front of her and motioned for her to stay in the living room near the door while he checked out the rest of the place. He handed her Scout's leash, and Erin grasped it as if it were a lifeline.

Dillon checked out the house, but everything appeared clear. No threatening messages. Lurking intruders. Unsightly surprises.

As he met Erin in the living room, a fresh round of hesitancy filled him. He didn't want to leave her. She looked terrified with her wide eyes, shallow breaths and death grip on Scout's leash.

He wished he knew her better. Wished he was pushier.

But that wasn't his place. Not right now. Not when considering he'd only known her for less than twenty-four hours.

"Should I call the police?" Erin remained plastered against the wall, almost as if she were frozen in place.

Dillon let out a long breath as he considered her question. In ordinary circumstances, he would definitely say yes. But he'd seen the way the chief had spoken to Erin. Most likely, if she called for help, they wouldn't take her request seriously. Not only that, but no evidence as to who had done this had been left behind.

"How about this?" Dillon started. "I'll take a picture of the message that was left so we can record it as evidence. Then I'm going to clean it off."

"You don't have to do—"

"I want to." His voice remained firm, leaving no room for questions. "If you want to do something, how about you fix some coffee and maybe light a fire? After I finish cleaning this up, I'm going to need to warm up."

Erin stared at him another moment, hesitation in her gaze. Finally, she nodded. "Okay. If you don't mind, that would be a huge help."

She gathered the supplies he needed. Then Dillon went outside and did exactly as he'd promised. Scout stayed inside with Erin. She'd put some water in a bowl for him, and Dillon had pulled the canine's food from his backpack.

He knew Erin was in good hands with Scout. Not only was the dog an expert in search and rescue operations, Scout was also protective.

As Dillon scrubbed the spray paint, his mind went back to his own guilt. The accusations others had flung at him.

He knew what it was like to be guilty in the eyes of those around you. He knew what the weight of those accusations felt like. Maybe that's why he felt so compassionate toward Erin now. In some ways, he felt like he could understand.

As soon as Dillon finished washing the paint off, he stepped inside. The scent of fresh-brewed coffee filled his senses.

Erin waited for him to take his coat off before handing him a steaming mug.

"Smell's great. Thank you."

"I made a few sandwiches, too, just in case you're hungry." She nodded toward a tray she'd put together on the kitchen counter.

"That was thoughtful. Thank you." Now that she'd mentioned it, he was hungry. He hadn't eaten much all day.

He'd drink his coffee, eat a sandwich, and warm up a few minutes before heading back to his place.

But he doubted he'd get any sleep tonight as he wondered how Erin was doing…and if she was safe.

Erin was so grateful for Dillon. He'd truly been a godsend. If he hadn't been there for her today, she might not be alive right now.

Her throat tightened at the thought.

As she sat in a chair near the fireplace, her hands trembled. She attempted to take another sip of her coffee, but everything was tasteless. Enjoying herself was a luxury she didn't deserve right now, especially not when she thought about Bella.

Bella…

Erin continued to pray that God would protect the girl right now, whatever she was going through—whether Bella had been abducted or if she were wandering lost in the woods. Whatever the case, Erin only wanted her daughter to be safe.

However, she remembered that second set of footprints.

It looked like someone had abducted her daughter, just as she'd feared.

The hollow pit in her stomach filled with nausea at the thought of it.

"Tell me about Bella." Dillon leaned forward in his chair, his eyes fixated on Erin.

Scout lay between them, in front of the fire, his eyes closed as if he could finally relax for a little while. The dog's belly should be full, and the warmth of the fire seemed a welcome companion for all of them.

Erin set her coffee mug on the end table beside her. "I told you some basics earlier. But I guess what I didn't tell you is that Bella is adopted."

His eyebrows shot up. "Is she? I had no idea."

Erin nodded as memories flooded her. "She was ten when she came to live with me and Liam. An old friend from high school had a rough go at life and ended up in jail for quite a while. She personally asked me if I would adopt Bella, and, of course, I said yes."

"How did Liam feel about that?"

The day the adoption was finalized flashed back into her mind, replaying like an old film reel. "He was all in favor of it. At least, at first. But later, I couldn't help but wonder if he felt jealous."

Dillon narrowed his gaze. "Jealous because you were giving her more attention?"

Erin offered a half shrug. "Maybe. It never really made sense to me. I felt like I gave Liam plenty of attention. They both deserved all my attention, and I did the best that I could."

"It sounds like you're a good mom."

She shrugged, feeling another round of guilt wash through her. "Sometimes I don't know. If I was such a good mom, then why is Bella not here with me now?" Her voice broke.

Dillon leaned toward her. "Sometimes in life, there are things out of our control. You can try to be a helicopter parent all you want, but there comes a point when you have to realize that some things are out of our hands."

"That's hard to stomach when you try to play by the rules and do everything right. And sometimes you try to play by the rules and do everything right, and everything still goes desperately wrong." She swallowed hard, feeling a knot form in her throat.

"Do you believe in God, Erin?"

Dillon's question nearly startled her. But Erin quickly nodded. "I do. I more than believe in Him. I try to follow Him."

"Good. Because that faith will sustain you now. Hold tight to it. Know that we have hope, not only in the way things turn out in this life, but also in the eternal."

His words caused a burst of comfort to wash through her. It meant a lot to have someone here who understood, who could remind her of those important things in life.

"I've been trying to cling to my faith. But it's definitely being tested right now, to say the least."

"I'll continue to pray for you. I know that prayer has helped sustain me through some of my toughest and darkest moments also."

She wondered exactly what Dillon meant by that. It sounded like there was more to the story.

Before she could respond, her phone buzzed. She started, wondering if it was a text either from Bella or about Bella.

Quickly, she looked at the screen.

But the same unknown number from earlier popped up. Along with another cryptic message.

You bring destruction wherever you go.

A cry caught in her throat. Why was someone so determined to make a bad situation even worse? Why did they want to try and be her jury and judge?

"Erin..." Dillon looked at her with a questioning look in his eyes.

Before she could say anything, a creak sounded on her porch.

Scout suddenly stood, his body tense as he looked at the door and began to growl.

Was someone outside?

Could it be Bella?

Or was it someone who wanted to make Erin suffer for sins they only assumed she'd committed?

EIGHT

Dillon felt his muscles bristle.

"Stay here," he told Erin.

From the look on her face, she wasn't expecting anybody. Hope and grief seemed to clash in her gaze as she stared at the front of her house.

If somebody was here for a friendly visit, they would have knocked.

Dillon instructed Scout to stay beside Erin before pulling out his gun and creeping toward the door. He stood at the edge of it and flipped the curtain out of the way.

A shadowy figure paced outside.

What was someone doing out there? Coming to leave another message? To finish what he'd started when his attempt to push Erin off the cliff hadn't been successful?

Moving quietly so his presence wouldn't be noticed, Dillon gripped his gun with one hand and the door handle with the other. He then threw the door open and stepped outside with his gun drawn.

"Freeze!" he ordered.

The man on the porch held up his hands. But there wasn't an apology in the intruder's gaze—only vengeance.

"Who are you?" the man demanded as he sneered at Dillon.

Dillon stared at the man. He didn't have the impression this guy was Erin's boyfriend or even a relative. Yet he seemed familiar with the house.

"I'm the one with the gun," Dillon said. "I suggest you answer that first."

The man narrowed his gaze. "I'm Arnold Lansing."

Realization hit Dillon. "You must be Liam's brother."

The man's scowl deepened. "That's right. Who are you?"

"I'm with the search and rescue crew. What are you doing here?"

"I came to see Erin. Do you have a problem with that?" Anger edged into the man's voice as if he silently dared Dillon to defy him.

Before he could respond, Dillon heard a shuffle behind him, and Erin appeared. Based on her body language, she wasn't happy to see Arnold. Instead, she crossed her arms and glared at the man.

"You're not welcome here." Her voice hardened with every syllable.

Arnold bristled as he stared at her. "This was my brother's house. I'll always be welcome here."

"Your brother's not here right now," Dillon said. "So I would rethink those words. If the lady says you're not welcome, then you're not welcome."

"My brother bought this property with his own money." Arnold's voice rose as he jammed his foot onto the ground.

"He bought it while we were married. As soon as I'm able to sell it and move somewhere else so I can get away from these bad memories, I plan on doing just that."

"Now, what are you doing here?" Dillon asked as he stared at Arnold.

Arnold's gaze remained on Erin, still cold and calculated. "I heard about what you did to Bella."

Erin adamantly swung her head back and forth. "I didn't do anything to Bella. I'm desperate to find her. If you were any kind of uncle to her, you'd be out there with me helping with the search efforts."

"Just like you did with my brother?"

"You know good and well I did not do anything to your brother." Erin's voice sounded at just above a hiss. "Liam outweighed me by a hundred pounds at least. What exactly do you think I could have done to him?"

"You're smart. I'm sure you could figure out something."

Dillon had heard enough of this exchange. He stepped forward, placing himself between Arnold and Erin. "I think it's time for you to leave."

"What are you going to do?" Arnold let out a sardonic chuckle. "Call the police?"

Dillon felt himself revolt. Guys like this were the kind who gave cops a bad name. And when one cop had a bad name, it damaged all cops.

"You need to go," Dillon repeated.

Arnold stared at Erin a moment longer before taking a step back. "Very well then. All the best. With everything. You're going to need it."

Dillon waited at the door until he saw the man drive away. Then he turned back to Erin.

What exactly was going on here?

There was clearly more to her story.

And the more he learned, the more he realized just how much danger she was in right now.

* * *

Erin pulled a blanket over herself but that didn't help her chill. The icy feeling came from down deep inside her.

As she rubbed her hands over her arms, she felt the scrapes on her palms from her fall down the cliff earlier today.

She was going to make it through this, just like Dillon had said. She just had to remember that her hope went beyond all these circumstances.

Dillon pulled his chair closer and sat in front of her, his studious gaze on her, worry rimming his eyes. "Are you okay, Erin?"

She nodded even though she felt anything but okay. Every part of her life had been shaken up, and she wasn't sure if she'd ever recover.

"Arnold's never really liked me that much, if you can't tell."

Dillon's regard darkened. "He has no right to treat you that way. How long has he been giving you a hard time?"

"Basically, from the moment we met. Who knows what Liam told him about me, for that matter."

"It doesn't sound like Liam treated you very well, either."

Erin shrugged, unable to fight the memories any longer. "He did at first. He was charming and sweet. But after we were married, that started to change. Then when we adopted Bella, it really changed. I was afraid he might lash out at her one day. As soon as I realized that was a possibility, I left him."

"I didn't realize that you were separated before he went missing."

"We were more than separated. We were divorced. And I got the house in the divorce, for the record."

Dillon leaned back, the thoughtful expression remaining on his face. "So why do people think that you're responsible for his disappearance?"

Erin rubbed her arms again and stared into the fire as more memories flooded her. "We were seen fighting the morning Liam disappeared. We got into a huge argument, and several people were around to hear it."

"How does that prove anything?"

"Apparently, in some people's minds, that means I did something to Liam. But I wouldn't have done that. Even though I don't always trust the legal system, I tried to go through the proper means of ending my relationship with him. Instead of enacting my own form of justice, I did everything the legal way instead."

"It doesn't sound like Liam was able to accept the terms of your divorce."

She stared into the fire, watching the flames dance. "He didn't want a divorce. But eventually he conceded, and it was finalized."

"How often does Arnold confront you like he did tonight?"

"It's random," Erin said. "I won't hear from him for months, and I'll think he's gone from my life. Then suddenly he'll show up, and I'll see him several times in a row."

Dillon frowned. "That's got to be hard."

"It is. I especially don't want Bella to have to see it or have any part of it. But Arnold even harassed her one time while she was at school."

Dillon seemed to stiffen. "What did he do?"

"He called to her through the fence at the school and told her that her mom was a killer. She was so upset… as you can probably imagine."

"That's terrible. Did you report it?"

Erin shrugged, no longer feeling disappointed in the local police. She'd simply accepted that they'd never be on her side. "No, it's like I said, the police believe I did something to Liam. They don't care about anything that I have to say."

"That's a shame. I'm sorry that you're having to go through all of this."

The sincerity of his words made Erin flush. "I appreciate that. But I suppose that I made my bed and now I have to sleep in it, as the saying goes. My friends never really liked Liam. Told me that I shouldn't marry him. I thought I knew better. And now look at me."

She wanted to laugh, but she couldn't. It wasn't a laughing matter.

Liam had slowly separated her from all those friends who hadn't wanted her to be with Liam. He'd told her lies about them. Told her they were just jealous. Eventually, in order to preserve her marriage, she'd pulled away from them.

Which was exactly what Liam had wanted.

She'd become isolated, with no one to talk to and no one to support her.

In other words, she'd been trapped and hopeless.

But adopting Bella had changed that.

"We all make mistakes," Dillon said. "What about that text you got right before we heard someone outside? What was that about?"

Erin found the message on her phone and showed it to him. His eyes widened as he read the words *You bring destruction wherever you go.*

"What an odd message for someone to send you," he muttered.

"What am I going to do, Dillon?" She heard the desperation in her voice, but she couldn't take it back. The emotion was raw—but it was true.

"First thing in the morning, we're going to get the search parties together again and we're going to look for Bella. We're not going to give up until we find her."

She let his words sink in and slowly nodded. "Okay then. But I doubt I'm going to get any rest tonight."

Dillon frowned before saying, "How would you feel if I slept on your couch? I just don't want to see any trouble come back here. Besides, the roads are bad, and it's late."

"I'm sure you have a life outside of this." His offer was kind, but he'd already done so much for her. Gone above and beyond. Done so much more than anyone could reasonably expect.

"I'm not married," Dillon explained. "And I have somebody who can help me with the dogs back at my place. My nephew lives there. I'll give him a call."

She nibbled on the inside of her lip for a moment as she contemplated his offer. "Are you sure this won't be too much trouble?"

"I'm sure. In fact, I'd feel a lot better if you'd let me stay."

Erin stared at him another moment before nodding. This was no time to let her pride get in the way. Dillon staying here answered a lot of prayers.

"Okay," she finally said. "Thank you. I owe you big-time for this."

His gaze locked with hers. "You don't owe me anything."

Erin had brought Dillon a pillow and blanket so he could sleep on the couch. But he knew he wouldn't be getting much rest tonight. He had too much on his mind.

He paced toward the front window again and glanced outside at Erin's front yard. He had a strange feeling they were being watched right now.

Had the person who'd taken Bella come back to see what Erin was doing? Was this all out of some sort of twisted revenge against the schoolteacher?

What about Arnold? Could he be behind this? If Liam had resented Erin for adopting Bella, maybe Arnold wanted to give Erin some payback by taking Bella away from her now. Dillon wasn't sure if his theory had any validity, but he kept it in the back of his mind.

Scout stood from near the fireplace and paced over to him. The dog appeared more triggered than usual as he panted and seemed like he couldn't settle down.

Scout knew something was going on, didn't he?

Dillon thought about going outside to check things himself. But he knew that wouldn't be wise.

He didn't know what he was up against nor did he know this landscape. He was better off staying inside and being prepared for whatever might come. If anyone got too close to the house, Scout would alert him.

Instead, he decided to make a few phone calls about tomorrow's search and rescue mission. But first, he checked the weather. The snow was supposed to let up and pass by then.

Still, that didn't change the fact that everything was going to be covered in a layer of the icy precipitation. After what had happened today, they were going to need to be very careful. Not only would the trails be dangerous, so would the drive to get there.

Dillon glanced at the time and saw it wasn't quite midnight. Still, he knew Rick was a night owl. He called him to get a quick update on what happened today. Besides, Dillon could use someone to talk to, to bounce ideas off of.

"It took you longer to call than I thought it would," Rick answered.

"It's been a busy day. Any updates since we last talked?"

"I wish there were. But no, not yet. If the weather allows, we'll go back out tomorrow and keep searching the trails for Bella," Rick said. "We don't want too many volunteers in the forest right now because of the icy conditions. It could be dangerous."

That didn't surprise Dillon. They didn't want to add another tragedy to an already tense situation. "What about a helicopter?"

"We have one lined up to use tomorrow. How did it go with Scout? Did he stay on the trail?"

Dillon's mind drifted back to the moment they'd had to turn around. "I felt like we were so close to finding Bella today when we had to go back."

"It was a good thing you did because conditions got even worse. It was bad out there with the temperatures dropping so quickly." Rick paused. "I guess you know who she is now."

Erin's face flashed through his mind. "I do. But that doesn't change anything."

"I just want you to be careful."

"You actually think she did something to Liam Lansing?" Dillon honestly wanted to know his friend's opinion.

"I never cared for the man much myself," Rick said. "But a lot of people suspected her. You know the spouse or the ex is always one of the first people considered in an investigation like that one."

"It sounds to me like people in town didn't like her and wanted a reason to find her guilty."

"The community bonds are strong in Boone's Hollow," Rick said. "Everyone loved Liam, but Erin was still an outsider. I also know that Liam had a way of getting people on his side. Who knows what the truth is? It's usually somewhere in the middle."

"Usually. But sometimes that's not the case. Sometimes the truth squarely rests on one person's shoulders and not the other's."

"I can't argue with that."

"What about Blackstone?" Dillon continued. "Do you trust him?"

"I try not to deal with the man unless I absolutely have to."

That said it all as far as Dillon was concerned.

"Listen, I'm still filling out all this paperwork, but we're going to meet at 8:00 a.m. so we can start our search efforts again," Rick said. "Send me the quadrants where Scout last picked up on Bella's scent, and we'll start there. I'll send you more information first thing in the morning. Sound like a plan?"

"That sounds great. I have a feeling Erin will be coming along, too."

Rick didn't say anything for a moment. "Are you sure that's a good idea?"

"I'm sure I won't be able to keep her away. She's determined to find Bella—either with us or on her own. On her own, she might get herself killed."

"Okay then. As long as you know what you're getting into."

Did Dillon know what he was getting into? He wasn't sure.

But he wasn't going to change his mind now.

NINE

As Erin rode in the Jeep with Dillon and Scout the next morning, she prayed that today would be successful.

She'd hardly gotten any sleep last night as she'd prayed those words over and over. Prayer was the only thing she could rely on right now. Not only that, prayer was also the best thing she could do right now.

She needed to trust in God because He was the only one who could get her through this situation.

She'd heard Dillon on the phone last night. Heard him pacing. Heard Scout bark a couple of times.

When she'd asked Dillon about it this morning, he'd shrugged her question off. But she had a feeling that someone else had been outside her place last night.

Had Arnold come back? Had another member of Liam's family come by to make their presence known?

She had no idea.

She only knew that today was probably going to be just as treacherous as yesterday had been. Erin had tried to mentally prepare herself for that fact, but she wasn't sure she'd succeeded.

"The search and rescue team is hoping to get the copter out today." Dillon's calm voice cut through the silence.

A helicopter? Maybe that would find something. "That would be good."

"Even though it seems like winter is a bad time to get lost—and it is—the good news is that without all the leaves on the trees, it's much easier to see things from the sky."

She supposed that could be a good thing.

She crossed her arms as she glanced at him again. "Is law enforcement still treating this as if Bella has run away?"

"My understanding is that they're exploring both options—that she could have run or that she could have been abducted. Until they have confirmation, that's what they'll continue to do."

"What about that second set of footprints?"

"It indicates she could have met someone. But that still doesn't mean she was abducted."

Erin rubbed her throat, knowing she couldn't argue with him. He was absolutely correct.

"Besides, if someone snatched her, you would have probably received a ransom call by now." Dillon glanced at her before turning his gaze back onto the road.

"I don't have money. I thought cases like that usually involved wealthy people."

"Sometimes, but not always."

"I just worry that someone abducted her, and that person has her in a car right now and is taking her as far away from this area as possible." Erin's voice cracked as emotions tried to bubble to the surface.

"That's a call that Rick and Blackstone will need to make. I know it's hard to trust Blackstone. We can go above him, if necessary."

Erin did a double take at him. "If you go above him,

there's no way they're going to hire you to work search and rescue anymore. You'll be blacklisted in this town."

He shrugged. "Sometimes that's the cost of doing what's right."

"I don't want to cost you your career."

Dillon glanced at her. "I appreciate your concern, but I assure you that I can handle myself."

She nodded and stared out the window, feeling like every minute that passed, the mess around her grew. It was bad enough that Liam's disappearance had upended Erin's life. But now Dillon was willing to risk his career for this.

She admired the man for his stance, but she hated to think of more innocent people getting caught in the cross fire.

Finally, they reached the parking area near the trailhead. This time, no one had followed them, nor had Erin received any more threatening text messages. She took that as a good sign.

A brush of nerves swept through her as she climbed from the Jeep and merged with the rest of the search and rescue operation. Several new people had joined the team, people Erin assumed were volunteers, based on their clothing. A few people sent her strange glances.

Did they think she was guilty?

Erin knew there was a good chance the answer to that question was yes.

But she had to push past those opinions and keep her focus on finding Bella. That was the only thing that mattered.

She prayed that today would be successful. That today would be the day they found Bella. Her daughter had been missing for almost forty-eight hours now.

That was enough time for someone to have taken her far away from here.

Bile rose in Erin's stomach at the thought.

What if Bella was never found?

Dillon and Scout led the way down the icy trail. This was going to be trickier than he would have liked. But he knew time was of the essence right now.

More people had shown up to help search—but only experienced SAR volunteers.

They'd been divided into six different groups so they could cover more of the area. Dillon, Scout and Erin were on one team. Right now, they walked with Rick and two other rangers—Dan and William.

Later on, further down the trail, they would split up, but for now they all headed in the same direction.

It had been good to see the volunteers who wanted to help. The more of this wilderness they could cover, the better.

The teams threaded their way through the woods back toward the area where they'd been last night, the spot where the trailhead split and where Scout had lost Bella's scent.

Dillon had already decided that he would head down into the valley—that was unless Scout somehow picked up Bella's scent again.

He knew there were a few old hunting cabins out here and had to wonder if maybe the girl had somehow gotten inside one of those.

But this wilderness was so vast. Someone had gotten lost here one time and a search party had come out looking for him for two weeks, to no avail. People didn't realize how dangerous these mountains could be until they were in the middle of them. By then, it was usually too late.

Of course, Dillon didn't tell Erin that. She was dealing with enough harsh realities without him adding to her burdens.

As he glanced behind him, he noted that Erin was being a real trooper as she kept up with them. She wasn't complaining, though she was breathing heavy.

"How long have you had Scout?" she asked after she seemed to notice him glance back at her.

"Four years," he said. "Someone left him at the pound. As soon as I saw him, I knew he had to come home with me."

"Is it normal for dogs from the pound to become search and rescue dogs?"

He climbed over a downed tree before reaching back to also help Erin across. "They make the best search and rescue dogs, I'd say. Those dogs know they've been rescued and they just want to give back."

"That's really beautiful."

"It's true."

It was cold out here and slippery. Nothing about it was enjoyable. But it was necessary.

When they got to the area of the path where it split, Dillon nodded toward the trail leading into the valley. "This is where we part ways."

Rick nodded. "We need to stay in touch and make sure that everybody stays safe. Clearly, these conditions are treacherous, to say the least."

"We'll be careful," Dillon said. "And we'll be in touch if we need you."

With one final nod to each other, he, Scout and Erin began their descent into the valley.

He paused near a particularly rocky portion of the trail

and held out his hand to help Erin down. As her hand slipped into his, a shock of electricity coursed through him.

Electricity? That made no sense.

He wasn't interested in dating or anything romantic. After his engagement had ended last year, he'd written off love for good. His fiancée had decided she couldn't handle a rough patch, and she'd left him.

He quickly released Erin's hand and they continued along the trail.

Just as they reached a relatively flat area, a new sound cracked the air.

Gunfire.

"Get down!" Dillon shouted.

He turned toward Erin, hoping he wasn't too late.

Erin ducked behind a boulder as another bullet flew through the air.

Why in the world was someone shooting at them? Was it a mistake? Had they been caught in a hunter's cross fire?

No, those bullets had been purposeful, Erin realized. Someone *wanted* to hurt them.

Was it the same person who'd abducted Bella? If so, why would this person come after Erin and Dillon now?

So much didn't make sense.

"Stay down." Dillon crouched with Scout across the trail behind another boulder.

As he said the words, another bullet split the bark on the tree in front of the boulder.

Erin pressed her lips together, determined not to scream and give the shooter any satisfaction. But her pulse pounded in her ears and she could hardly breathe.

When would this nightmare end?

She glanced at Dillon again and saw he'd withdrawn his gun.

Her pulse pounded even faster.

As he held the weapon in one hand, he pulled out a radio with his other hand and called in what was happening. Erin assumed Rick and his team were a considerable distance away at this point. She was just thankful the radio was working. Her cell phone had no service out here.

She had no idea how this situation was going to end up playing out.

"He's getting closer." Dillon slipped his radio back onto his belt and peered around the boulder. "We're going to need to move."

Erin froze. The last thing she wanted to do was to move. She felt safe behind the rock—at least, she felt safer here than she did running.

But she needed to trust Dillon's advice right now.

As another bullet rang through the air, she realized she had no other choice.

She glanced over at Dillon again and he nodded at the trail in the distance. "That path will be our best bet. It's going to be slippery, and you'll need to watch your step."

Erin nodded, trying to process everything that was happening and keep her head in the game.

"I'm going to stay behind you," Dillon continued. "Whatever you need to do, remember that we need to keep moving."

She nodded, but her brain felt numb, almost as if she even attempted to process all this, it would shut down.

Was this what Bella had gone through also?

She held back another cry, unable to think about that.

"Let's move," Dillon said. "We don't have any more time to waste."

As he said the words, another bullet pierced the air and Erin gasped. This guy wasn't letting up.

She wanted to peer over the rock, to see who it was and where the bullets were coming from. But she didn't dare.

As Dillon ran toward her, she rose from her hiding spot and darted down the slippery trail. Her breath came out in short, wispy gasps that immediately iced in the frigid air.

The first part of the trail was manageable. But as the path turned rocky *and* icy, her shoes practically skated on the slippery surface beneath her.

She hesitated, trying to keep her footing.

As she did, she felt another bullet whiz by. She sucked in a breath.

The bullet had practically skimmed her hair. It was that close.

This guy was following them, wasn't he? Hunting them?

He wouldn't stop until they were dead.

Erin held back a cry at the thought of it.

"You can do this, Erin," Dillon said behind her. "You just need to keep moving."

She didn't have the energy to respond. Instead, she kept walking, just as Dillon told her.

The ground in this area wasn't only icy, but the rocks were uneven. The terrain would be hard to navigate on a nice day when they weren't running for their lives. Today, it almost felt impossible.

You can do it, she told herself.

Erin kept moving…and moving…and moving.

As another bullet cracked the air, she sprang into action and darted forward. As she did, her foot caught on a rock. Her ankle twisted.

She gasped as she fell to the ground.

"Erin!" Dillon muttered as he rushed toward her.

She'd sprained her ankle, hadn't she? The pain coursing through her seemed to confirm her fears.

Despair built deep inside her.

No...not now.

Dear Lord...

How was she going to get out of this one?

TEN

Dillon leaned over Erin, trying to shield her from any oncoming bullets.

But this didn't look good. The way she grasped her ankle made it clear she was in pain.

He'd known it wasn't safe to run around in these elements. But the gunman had left them little choice.

Another bullet split the air behind them before hitting the ground several feet away.

Erin gasped as her eyes lit with fear.

Dillon leaned closer. "Can you put any pressure on your ankle?"

"Let me see." With Dillon's help, Erin tried to stand, but she nearly crumpled back onto the ground as soon as any weight hit her ankle.

Dillon was going to need to think of a way to get them out of the situation—and quickly.

Footsteps sounded—closer this time.

He gripped his gun and peered around the boulder.

He didn't want to use his weapon—but he would if he had to.

When he saw a figure dressed in black raise his gun, Dillon had no choice but to raise his own weapon. He quickly lined up his target and fired.

The bullet hit the man's shoulder and he let out a groan.

Dillon had just bought them some time—he didn't know how much.

That wound would slow the man down, but wouldn't necessarily stop him.

Dillon turned back to Erin. "I'm going to put my arm around you and help you down the rest of this trail. Then we're going to find shelter. We're going to get through this, okay?"

She glanced up at him, fear welling in her gaze. She nodded anyway.

Dillon slipped his arm around her waist. He let go of Scout's leash and let the dog walk in front of them. Then he helped Erin along the treacherous path.

He still held his gun in his other hand, and he craned his neck behind him, looking for any signs of danger.

There was nothing.

Not at the moment.

He needed to find one of those old cabins he'd been thinking about earlier. A cabin would offer them shelter from the elements and protection from this gunman—for a little while, at least.

The only thing that protected them right now were the bends and curves of the trail. Plus, the gunman seemed to have slowed down.

Erin drew in deep, labored breaths as they continued down the path. Dillon had to give her props, however. She was doing her best to keep moving.

"You're doing just fine," he assured her.

She nodded, but still looked unconvinced.

Dillon stole a quick glance behind him and thought he saw a flash of movement. Was that the gunman?

It was his best guess.

He knew that Rick and Benjamin were on their way right now. But he had little hope they'd get there in time.

As Dillon glanced ahead, he thought he saw a structure in the distance.

Was that one of the cabins he vaguely remembered being out here?

Going inside might buy them a little time. Plus, the structure would give them a place to hunker down until backup arrived. Erin needed to take some weight off her ankle.

"Do you see what I see?" Hope lilted in Erin's voice.

"That's where we're headed. Do you think you can make it?"

"I'll do my best," she said. "I'm sorry that I'm slowing you down."

"It's not your fault. You were only doing what I told you."

He kept his arm around her and helped her navigate the terrain. She let out little gasps, obviously in pain. But she kept going, kept moving. Her determination was admirable.

They continued over the rocky, uneven trail. At least it was flatter here, with no cliffs now that they were closer to the valley.

As the cabin neared, Dillon observed the small structure. It was probably less than five hundred square feet. Trees grew all around it, and junk had been left around the foundation—wood and cinderblocks and buckets, even a ladder.

Scout ran ahead and climbed onto the porch, almost as if he knew exactly what Dillon wanted him to do.

Moving as quickly as possible, Dillon climbed to the front door and pulled on it.

But it was locked.

He let out a breath.

Now they had to figure out plan B.

As Scout growled at something in the distance, Dillon realized they had no time to waste.

The gunman was getting closer and they were running out of time.

"Dillon?" Erin's voice trembled despite her wishes to stay strong.

"Give me a second," he muttered as he glanced around.

She couldn't believe they'd made it this far only to find the door was locked. What were they going to do now?

Certainly the gunman was getting closer and closer. What would the man do once he was near enough to shoot them point-blank?

A chill washed through her.

She couldn't bear to think about it.

And her ankle…she wished it didn't throb like it did. She wished she could put weight on it. But every time she tried, she nearly collapsed.

"I hate to do this but…" Dillon reached down and picked up an old board from the ground.

In one motion, he thrust it into the window and broke the glass. Using the same board, he cleared the shards from around the edges. Then he turned to her.

"You're going to have to climb through this."

Erin nodded, trying to imagine how that was going to happen. But this was no time to overthink things. She just needed to move.

Using his hands, Dillon boosted her through the window. She slid inside and landed on the couch below the window. A moment later, Dillon lifted Scout inside before climbing through himself.

Once he was inside, he didn't miss a beat. He paced to the center of the room and surveyed the area. "I need to get you away from these windows."

Moving quickly, he went to the kitchen table and turned it over. He then helped Erin behind it.

She nestled between the cabinets and table with her knees pulled to her chest. Scout lay beside her, almost as if the canine sensed she needed comfort. She reached over and rubbed his fur, grateful that the dog was here now.

She heard Dillon moving in the other part of the room and something scraped across the floor. Was he moving furniture?

A moment later, Dillon sat beside her, his gun drawn and his posture showing he was on guard.

Her heart pounded in her chest.

Would they have a shootout? She hoped that wasn't the case. But certainly Dillon was preparing for what could be the worst-case scenario.

She continued to rub Scout's head as she waited for whatever was going to unfold.

As she did, her thoughts wandered. She remembered what Dillon had said to her when they'd reached the cabin. When he'd assured her that this wasn't her fault and that she had done her best.

The words had brought such an unusual comfort—an unusual comfort that surprised even her.

Liam…he would have lashed out at her. Told her everything was her fault. Blamed the situation on her and put it all on her shoulders.

It was what Erin was used to and what she'd been prepared to hear. But hearing the compassionate and rational words from Dillon reminded her that there were still good people in this world.

Not every man was like Liam—thank goodness.

"Are you still doing okay?" Dillon glanced over at her.

Erin nodded, probably a little too quickly. "I think so. What can I do?"

"Stay low and stay by Scout. I'll do the rest."

"But what if the gunman comes…?"

He locked gazes with her. "I'm just taking each moment as it comes."

Just as he said the words, a creak sounded outside.

Was the gunman on the porch?

Fear shot through her.

What was going to happen next?

Dillon's muscles tensed as he waited.

The gunman was clearly here. Even Scout sensed someone's presence. The dog's fur rose.

Dillon grasped his gun as he aimed it over the table, waiting to strike.

This wasn't the way he'd wanted things to play out. All he'd wanted was to find Bella. To make sure that the girl was okay. Now, somehow, it had turned into a confrontation.

He'd been in situations like this before. He'd trained to handle himself during standoffs.

As much as he'd like to believe there would always be a positive outcome, he knew that wasn't the case. One of his colleagues had been killed in a bank robbery a few years ago. That event had reminded him of the fragility of life.

Dillon didn't intend to share his thoughts with Erin. Not now.

She was already scared and on the verge of breaking, and he didn't want to add to that.

He waited, holding his breath as he prepared himself for whatever would happen. A shadow moved across one of the windows.

He'd moved a bookshelf in front of the broken window in the hope of slowing whoever was outside. If it were Rick or another ranger, they would have most likely announced themselves already.

That only left the gunman.

Dillon glanced around the small cabin. A loft stretched above them. There were four windows total. One by the bookshelf. One the shadow had crossed. And two other smaller windows on either side of the cabin.

Those two would be difficult to get to because the deck didn't span the sides of the cabin, which would make them harder to access.

So what kind of play would this guy make next?

"Dillon?" Erin sounded breathless as she said his name.

He put a finger over his lips, motioning for her to be quiet. Instead, she began to rub Scout's fur again.

The footsteps stopped.

What exactly was the man planning now? Did he have other tricks up his sleeve?

Dillon's heart thrummed in his ear.

He thought he'd put these high-octane days behind him. But part of him would always be a cop. It almost seemed ingrained in him.

Quiet continued to stretch outside.

Dillon wished he knew what the man was doing. What he was planning. Why he was after them.

Was this person who'd abducted Bella now determined to kill Erin? Why? Why abduct Bella first?

The details just didn't make any sense to him. But he'd need to figure that out later.

A new sound filled the air.

A creak.

This time, it came from the direction of the bookcase.

Did this guy know that they had come inside?

The gunman had been close enough that it wouldn't surprise Dillon if the man had seen them, if he'd spotted the broken window. Plus, he, Erin and Scout had no doubt left tracks in the snow, which would make it easier to follow them.

Dillon gripped his gun, still pointing it in the direction of the front door and the window beside it. Still bracing himself for the worst.

He heard another noise. It almost sounded like wood scraping against the floor.

The next instant, the bookcase crashed to the ground and a bullet fired inside.

ELEVEN

Erin swallowed back a scream.

The man was here.

And he was going to kill them.

She ducked and buried her face again, pulling Scout closer.

As she did, she heard Dillon fire. The smell of ammo filled the room and more fear clutched her heart.

How were they ever going to get out of this alive?

She began to pray furiously. *Dear Lord, help us! Protect us! All I want is to find Bella. She's the only thing that's important. But I need to stay alive in order to do that.*

More bullets flew and she heard wood splintering behind her.

Dillon fired back again.

How much ammo had he brought with him? How long could he hold this guy off?

Erin had no idea. There was nowhere else to hide.

The gunfire paused for another moment.

She held her breath, anticipating the man's next move. Waiting for more gunfire.

But there was nothing.

Her heart thumped so loudly that she was certain Dillon and Scout could hear the *thump, thump, thumps*.

Scout raised his head, almost as if he were also curious about what was going on.

Had the gunman regrouped? Was he headed to another part of the cabin to fire on them from a different angle or take them by surprise?

Dillon's thoughts seemed to mirror hers. "Stay low," he murmured.

He still grasped the gun, and his shoulders looked tight. At least if Erin was stuck out here, she was with Dillon and not alone. If she'd been on her own, she'd most certainly be dead right now.

No more gunfire sounded…not yet.

But another sound filled the air.

What was that?

The noise was faint but getting louder by the moment.

Had the man planned something else? Was more danger headed their way as they sat there unassuming?

"Dillon?" Erin's voice cracked with fear.

"I hear it, too," he muttered.

A moment later, the sound became more clear.

Whomp, whomp, whomp.

Erin released her breath.

If she wasn't mistaken, that was a helicopter.

Was it from the search and rescue mission?

Even more so, had the sound scared the gunman away?

She hoped and prayed that was the case.

Just as the thought crossed her mind, she glanced at the floor and her breath caught.

She reached forward and picked up a pink scrunchie—one that had images of a laughing cat on it.

"Erin?"

"This is Bella's."

* * *

The rescue crew had found a clearing to land in. Another ranger met them there and had taken Dillon, Scout and Erin to a local hospital to have Erin's ankle checked while the rest of the team searched the cabin for evidence and the woods for the gunman.

Had someone snatched Bella and taken her to that cabin? Or had she wandered there by herself? It was still a possibility that she hadn't been abducted; that she'd just run.

They had too many questions and not enough answers at this point.

Dillon waited outside Erin's room, Scout beside him, until the doctor okayed her to leave. Surprise stretched across her face when she stepped out and spotted him in the hallway.

"Dillon...you didn't have to wait." She leaned down and patted Scout's head. "You, either, boy."

"How did you plan on getting home then?" Dillon raised an eyebrow, trying to add some levity to the situation.

Erin let out a sheepish laugh. "Good point. But really, I feel like I've turned your life upside down, and you don't even know me."

He shrugged, trying not to make a big deal of his decision. "You didn't ask me to do any of this, so you have no reason to feel guilty. How about if I give you a ride?"

"Is your Jeep even here?" More confusion rolled over her features.

"I had one of the rangers bring it by for me while the doctor was treating you." He paused. "I hope I didn't overstep, but I also had someone tow your car from the lot. My friend Darrel is going to take it into his shop and replace the tires for you."

"That was so thoughtful of you. Thank you." She offered a grateful smile.

Dillon glanced at her foot, which was now in a walking cast. "How are you?"

"The doctor said it's just a sprain. He wrapped it, and I can put a little weight on it for now. Nothing too strenuous."

"That's good news at least." They could both use some good news considering the events of the past twenty-four hours.

"It is." Erin paused and shoved her hands into her pockets as she turned to address him. "Thank you so much for everything that you did today."

He stared at her a moment. Stared at the lovely lines of her face. Her expressive eyes. The grief that seemed to tug at her lips.

He hadn't expected to be impressed. He'd expected a grieving, panic-stricken mother.

She was those things—of course. It would be strange if she wasn't.

But she also had a quiet strength, an unwavering determination, and a fragile vulnerability. She'd been given an unfair hand. She didn't deserve the scrutiny people had put her under. She needed the community's support right now.

She might not get that support from her neighbors now, but she would get it from him.

He rubbed his throat before saying, "I'm sorry we haven't been able to find Bella yet."

Erin's lips tugged into a frown. "Me, too. The more time that passes, the less the chances are that we're going to find her. I've watched enough TV shows to know that."

She sniffled, as if holding back a sob.

He wanted to reach out to her. To offer her some comfort. To tell her everything would be okay.

Instead, he settled on saying, "Don't give up hope."

"I'm trying not to." She ran a hand across her brow. "I really am."

Dillon nodded to the elevator in the distance. "Are you ready to go?"

"I am. More than ready to go, for that matter."

They silently started toward the elevator. There wasn't much to say. Dillon was still processing exactly what had happened. It would take a while to comprehend the scope of the danger they were in.

He helped Erin and Scout into his Jeep and then cranked the engine. He felt like there were things that he wanted to say, he just wasn't exactly sure what those things were.

Part of him wanted to apologize, even though he knew none of this was his fault. But the situation had to be frustrating for her. Now it was already later in the afternoon. They'd have to wait until tomorrow to search again.

"Are there any updates in the search for Bella?" Erin looked up at him, her eyes glimmering with hope.

He somberly shook his head. "I wish there were. But there's no new news."

She frowned again. "I checked my phone just in case there were any messages. I didn't have service in the mountains, but part of me hoped someone had left a message. Maybe Bella. Or, if she was abducted, then from the person who took her. The silence is maddening."

Against his better judgment, he reached over and squeezed her hand. "I know this has to be really hard on you. I'm sorry."

Erin glanced at his hand as it covered hers before offering a quick smile. "Thank you."

Scout barked in the back of the Jeep.

"I think Scout agrees with me."

Her smile widened. "He's a good dog."

Dillon pulled his hand back and gripped the gearshift. Immediately, he missed the soft feel of her skin.

He cleared his throat and turned his attention to Scout instead.

"You're getting hungry, aren't you, boy?" Dillon murmured.

Erin glanced back at the dog and rubbed his head. "Do we need to stop and get him something?"

"I packed some food for him, but I *am* out now."

"Do what you need to do. Scout is a hero as far as I'm concerned."

He stole another glance at her. "Are you sure you don't mind if we swing by my place?"

"Not at all," Erin said. "I'm in no hurry to get back home. Who knows what's waiting for me there?"

Dillon let her words sink in before nodding. "Okay then. I'll make sure that this doesn't take long."

Erin's eyes lit up as she stared at Dillon's home.

The mountain farm was complete with an old homestead and several outbuildings. With snow covering the property, it looked like a winter wonderland. No neighbors were visible for miles, just trees and gentle slopes.

The property looked like a slice of heaven.

"This is amazing," Erin said as she stepped from his Jeep.

Dillon climbed out and paused beside her. "I like it. It's my place where I can get away."

"Everybody needs a place like that, don't they?"

Scout barked in reply, and Dillon and Erin shared a smile.

Dillon nodded at a building in the distance. "How about I give you a quick tour?"

"I'd love one."

As they walked, Dillon held out his arm to offer some additional support. Normally, Erin might have refused, but not this time. This time, the last thing she needed was to sprain her other ankle or hurt herself in some other way.

Plus, she liked his touch.

When he'd touched her hand in the Jeep, she'd felt her insides go still. She'd liked it a little too much.

And that realization terrified her.

She wasn't interested in dating again, and she certainly wasn't interested in dating a cop again—or a former cop.

But she had to remind herself that not every cop was like Liam, despite what her emotions told her.

They walked toward a barnlike building. She wasn't sure what to expect inside. But when Dillon opened the door, various dog kennels and barking canines greeted her in the finished, heated space.

As soon as he closed the door behind them, warmth surrounded Erin—a welcome relief from the brittle cold outside. Dillon released Scout from his lead and let him run free. He stopped and greeted each of the dogs in their luxury-sized runs.

"These are the dogs I train," he explained.

Erin walked down the center aisle, peering at each dog as she did. They appeared to be remarkably cared for and happy.

"They all look amazing." She paused beside a husky and rubbed the soft fur.

"They are. They're working dogs. But they enjoy what they do, and they're good at it."

Erin straightened and turned toward Dillon. "It's good to do something that you love."

"Yes, it is," he said. "Do you enjoy your job as a teacher?"

Dillon's question surprised her. He hadn't gotten personal with her. Yet, in some ways, she felt like she'd known this man much longer than she actually had.

She thought about his question a moment before answering. "I do. I love working with kids. I feel like it's my calling in life." She glanced up at him. "How about you?"

"Same here. As soon as I started training canines, I knew that this is what I should be doing."

"Do you like doing this more than you liked being a cop?"

His face instantly sobered. "Maybe. It's different. I get to help people through this job. That's what I like most about it."

She smiled. "That makes sense. Now, let me meet these guys."

For the next half hour, Dillon took her kennel by kennel and introduced her to the various dogs inside. She rubbed each of their heads and talked to them for a few minutes.

This place seemed like a fantasy getaway to her. She couldn't even imagine what it would be like to live here. Bella would love this.

Her daughter loved animals even more than Erin did. In fact, she'd been asking lately if they could get a dog, but Erin had told her not now. With Erin teaching eight hours a day and having to drive forty-minutes to and from work, it just wouldn't be possible to give a dog the attention it would need.

Dillon paused once they reached the other side of the building and pointed to the outside door behind him. "Listen, do you mind if I run inside a moment?"

"Not at all."

As they stepped toward the door, it suddenly opened and a shadowy figure stood there.

Erin gasped and stepped back.

Was it the gunman? Had he returned to finish what he'd started earlier?

TWELVE

"Carson," Dillon said.

He instinctively felt Erin's fear and pushed her behind him.

But it was just his nephew.

As Carson stepped into the light, his features came into view. The boy was seventeen, with thick, dark hair and an easy smile.

"Erin, this is my nephew, Carson. Carson, this is Erin Lansing. Carson helps me take care of the dogs, especially when I'm gone like I have been."

Erin's hand went over her heart as if it still pounded faster than necessary after Carson's surprise appearance. "Of course. It's great to meet you."

Carson nodded at her. "Same here. Any success today looking for that girl?"

"Unfortunately, no," Dillon said. "But it's Erin's daughter who's missing."

Dillon knew he needed to put that information out there before Carson asked any questions that might come across as insensitive.

Carson's face instantly stilled with reverence. "I'm really sorry to hear about your daughter, ma'am."

"Thank you," Erin said. "I appreciate that."

"Wait…your last name is Lansing?" Carson asked. "Is your daughter Bella?"

A knot formed between Erin's eyes. "She is. You know her?"

"Not well, but we've met a few times. Have you talked to Grayson yet?" Carson stared at her, looking genuinely curious.

"Who's Grayson?" The knot on Erin's brow became more defined.

Carson's eyes widened as if he realized he'd said something he shouldn't have. He stepped back, almost as if he wanted to snatch his words back. He opened his mouth but quickly shut it again.

"Carson, who is Grayson?" Dillon repeated.

"I'm sorry, I thought you knew." Carson swallowed hard, his Adam's apple bobbing up and down.

"Knew what?" Erin's voice cracked with emotion, as if she were on the brink of tears.

"I've seen Bella around a few times at some football games between my school and hers. She's been hanging out with Grayson Davis."

Dillon sucked in a breath. He knew who Grayson Davis was. The whole family was trouble.

"What aren't you telling me?" Erin stared at Dillon, questions haunting her eyes.

"It's probably nothing." Dillon didn't want to alarm Erin for no reason. "I just know that Grayson's dad and grandfather—and even a couple of uncles—have been in prison before."

Erin's face seemed to fall with disappointment, and she squeezed the skin between her eyes. "What?"

He resisted the urge to reach out and try to comfort her again. That might be too much, too fast. "That doesn't mean he has anything to do with this. But you had no idea?"

She swung her head back and forth. "No, I even asked Bella if she liked anyone. She rolled her eyes and stared and told me there was no one."

"It's not unusual for teens to want to keep information like this from their parents," Dillon said before looking back at Carson. "Is there anything else that you know?"

"No, just that she was hanging out with Grayson." Carson shrugged. "I'm sorry I can't be more help."

"You're doing just fine, Carson," Dillon said. "But if you hear anything else, please let us know."

"Of course. Whatever I can do." The boy nodded, his gaze unwavering and assuring them he'd keep his promise.

"Let's get you inside." Dillon put his hand on Erin's back to guide her toward the door. "Then we'll figure out our next plan of action."

Erin followed Dillon into his home, yet he couldn't help but note that her eyes looked determined. He knew exactly what she was thinking. She wanted to go talk to Grayson Davis herself.

That could turn into an ugly situation.

They desperately needed answers before Erin did something she might regret.

How could Bella have been seeing someone and not told her? When had this happened? When had Erin's relationship with her daughter turned from easygoing and conversational to a bond riddled with secrets?

The questions wouldn't stop pounding inside her head until finally an ache formed at her temples.

She wanted her daughter back. She wanted her *old*

daughter back. She wanted to turn back time and some-how erase this mess, this heartache.

"I know what you're thinking." Dillon's voice pulled her from her thoughts.

She jerked her head up as he stepped into the kitchen from the back hallway.

She leaned her hip against the counter there and waited.

Normally, she'd be curious about his house or pictures on the fridge or the slight scent of evergreen permeating the air. But right now she could only think about Bella.

Erin stared up at Dillon. He'd claimed to know what she was thinking. "What's that?"

His gaze locked with hers. "That you want to talk to Grayson."

She crossed her arms, feeling a wave of defensiveness. "Can you blame me?"

Dillon shook his head, his perceptive eyes warm with compassion—and absent of the judgment she'd come to expect.

"Not at all," he murmured. "I'd say we should leave it to the police, but I'm beginning to think that's not such a great idea."

Erin released a breath she hadn't even realized she'd been holding. It felt so good to have someone who actually sounded like he was on her side.

"I'm going to leave Scout here with Carson, so he can rest. But if you'd like to go speak to Grayson, I'd like to go with you."

"You would do that for me?" Surprise lilted her voice.

"Of course. I'd want someone to do this for me if I were in your shoes."

Gratitude rushed through her, so warm and all-en-compassing, it nearly turned her muscles into jelly. "I know I've said this before, but you've been a godsend, Dillon. Thank you so much for everything that you've been doing."

A compassionate smile pulled at his lips and his gaze softened. "It's no problem."

A few minutes later, they were back in his Jeep and heading down the road. Part of Erin felt like they'd been doing this together forever.

But it had only been a day since Dillon had rescued her from the cliff. Since then, so much had happened. Enough to fill a lifetime it seemed.

She just wanted this to be over with. She wanted to find Bella and try to sleep at night.

Being a single parent wasn't an easy task, but it was worth it. She would make whatever sacrifices necessary for Bella. But the past couple of years hadn't been a cake-walk, especially with Liam's disappearance and the cloud of doubt that had been hanging over Erin since then.

A few minutes later, they pulled up to Grayson Davis's house.

The place was an old two-story house with broken blue siding, a busted window, and piles of junk lining the porch and yard. It wasn't the nicest-looking place, not that it mattered to Erin. But she was glad Dillon was with her in case things turned ugly. She didn't know much about this family, but from the brief snippets she'd heard, the Davises could get rowdy.

Dillon glanced at her before offering an affirmative nod. "Let's do this."

They climbed out and Erin hobbled toward the door.

Before they even climbed the porch steps, the front door opened and a man stepped out, holding a shotgun.

"What do you think you're doing here?" he sneered as he stared them down.

Erin sucked in a breath as she observed the man. Probably in his sixties. Salt-and-pepper beard. Dirty button-up shirt. Old jeans. Hair that could use a good wash.

Then her gaze went back to his gun.

Was he planning to pull the trigger on them?

"Burt Davis," Dillon said. "Do you remember me?"

The man remained silent for several seconds until finally his eyes lit. "You were that cop who helped me find my Emmaline when she wandered off."

Burt's wife had dementia and was known to wander. Dillon and Scout had helped track her down when she'd once gone missing. They'd found her on the edge of a nearby lake. She'd been about to take a swim, despite the winter weather. If they hadn't found her when they had, she would have perished in that water.

"That's me."

Erin listened to every word Burt said, surprised at this side of Dillon. Not that he hadn't seemed heroic already. But hearing about him from someone else offered a different perspective—an affirmation.

Her respect for the man continued to grow.

Burt's shoulders softened. "What brings you by now?"

"We were actually hoping that we could talk to your grandson, Grayson," Dillon said.

Burt's eyes narrowed, not with anger but with what appeared to be resignation. "What's my boy done now?"

"Probably nothing," Dillon said. "Did you hear about the girl who went missing?"

He stared at Dillon, wariness in his gaze. "I did hear something about her while I was in town. What about her?"

"We heard Bella and Grayson were friends, and we're hoping he might have some information that will help us find her." Dillon kept his voice level and even.

"Is that right?" Burt stared at Dillon a moment, that skeptical look still in his gaze.

The man remained silent, chewing on something. Maybe bubble gum. Maybe tobacco. She wasn't sure.

But enough time passed that Erin was certain Burt was going to refuse to let them talk to his grandson.

Despair tried to well inside her again. Had all this been for nothing?

Finally, the man nodded and twisted his head behind him. "Grayson! Get down here. You have someone here who wants to talk to you."

Erin's lungs nearly froze. He was going to let them talk to Grayson!

Thank you, Jesus!

She couldn't wait to hear if Grayson had additional information to offer about Bella. She prayed that was what would happen, and that this lead might be the one that cracked the case in Bella's disappearance wide open.

Dillon sat at the dining room table. Erin sat beside him and Grayson hunched in his seat across from them. Grayson's granddad stood behind him with his arms crossed and his eyes narrowed, almost as if he dared Grayson to say something he didn't approve of.

Mountains of leftover meals and trash littered the table between them. With it was the scent of rot mixed with old socks and recently cooked collard greens.

Dillon stared at the boy.

Grayson Davis was sixteen with blond hair that he kept cut short. His build was stocky enough that he could play football. He had a thin stubble on his chin, and his gaze focused on the table instead of making eye contact with anyone in the room.

"Thanks for meeting with us," Dillon started, keeping his voice pleasant.

There was no need to start this conversation as if they were enemies. As they sat there, Dillon felt Erin's nerves in her quick movements and shallow breaths.

Thankfully, she was letting him take the lead right now. They didn't want to spook the boy and make him go silent.

"What's going on?" Grayson swallowed hard, his eyes shifting from Dillon to Erin then back to Dillon again.

"We understand that you are friends with Bella Lansing," Dillon said.

Grayson rubbed his hands on his jeans and nodded. "Yeah, we talk."

"When was the last time you talked to her?"

Grayson ran a hand through his hair. "I'm not sure. Maybe two days ago."

Dillon watched the boy carefully, looking for any signs of deceit. "You are aware that she's missing, right?"

Grayson nodded. "I know. I heard. I keep hoping to hear that she has been found."

"Why haven't you come forward to the police yet if the two of you were friends?"

Grayson sighed. "I don't know. I guess because I didn't have anything to tell them. I didn't have anything to offer. Plus, with my family's reputation, I was afraid that they would look at me as a suspect."

"You care about Bella, don't you?" Erin's voice sounded calm and soothing.

Grayson stared at her for a moment before nodding. "Yeah, I do. But she knew you wouldn't approve."

Erin sucked in a breath, his words seeming to shock her. "Is that what she told you?"

"She said that she's not allowed to date. But the two of us really like each other."

"Did she tell you anything that might have indicated that she was in danger?" Dillon asked.

Grayson shifted again, rubbing his hands across his jeans as if he were nervous.

He definitely knew something. The trick would be getting him to share.

"I don't know."

Dillon leaned toward him, clearly about to drive home a point. "Grayson, if there's anything you know, it's important you tell us. We need to find her, and you may know something that will help us do that. You're not in trouble. We are just looking for information."

Grayson remained quiet but sweat had beaded across his forehead.

"You can trust him," Burt said. "Dillon is one of the good guys."

Grayson looked at his granddad and nodded, his eyes still darting all over the place as if he were nervous.

Finally, he looked back at Dillon and Erin. "The day before she went missing, Bella told me she felt like she was being watched."

Erin sucked in a breath beside him. "What else did she say?"

Grayson shrugged. "Not much. She tried to laugh it off and say she was being paranoid. She talked about how much people in this town hated you guys. I think she assumed it was probably just somebody from Liam's side of the family."

Dillon made a note of the fact that Grayson had said

Liam instead of her dad. How exactly did Bella view Liam Lansing? He'd ask Erin later.

"No one approached her or did anything?" Dillon continued to press. "Was it just a feeling or was there any action to justify it?"

Grayson rubbed his throat again. "She said she felt someone watching her a couple of times, but she never saw anyone nearby. If anything else happened, Bella didn't tell me."

"Do the two of you text or email each other?" Erin asked.

Grayson nodded, his eyes misting. "I've been trying to talk to her since she left for school two days ago. But I haven't heard back. That's when I knew something was wrong."

Grayson's voice cracked and he wiped beneath his eyes.

He was fighting tears, wasn't he? He really cared about Bella. That was obvious.

Dillon nodded and glanced at Erin. "Anything else?"

Erin shook her head, her eyes lined with grief. "No, but thank you for sharing what you did, Grayson. I'm glad that my daughter has a friend like you."

Relief seemed to fill his gaze at Erin's approval. "I'll let you know if I hear anything else."

As they started toward the door, Burt joined them.

He leaned close to Erin and whispered, "If I were you, I would have killed Liam, too."

Erin froze and glanced at the man, alarm racing through her gaze. "I didn't kill him."

His expression remained unapologetic. "I wouldn't blame you if you did. I had a couple of encounters with him. That man thought he was above the law."

"Yes, he did." Erin's words sounded stiff, as if she were hesitant to agree.

"But if you didn't kill him, then my bets are on the Bradshaws." Burt nodded as if confident of his statement.

Dillon's mind raced. The Bradshaws were a deeply networked family in this area who had drug connections. Dillon suspected they grew pot and sold it, but police were still trying to prove it. Basically, they were trouble, and everyone in these parts knew it.

Dillon put his hand on Erin's arm. He had to get her out of here. Not only did they need to process everything they'd just learned, he could tell she was uncomfortable with where this conversation was going.

"Thank you again for your help," he told Burt and Grayson.

But just as they stepped out the door, a truck drove past. The passenger leaned out the window, his baseball cap pulled down low.

As they watched, the man tossed something from the window.

The next instant, the front yard exploded in flames.

THIRTEEN

"Get down!" Dillon yelled.

The next thing Erin knew, he threw her on the ground and his body covered hers.

An explosion sounded in the front yard before flames filled the air along with the scent of smoke.

Erin's mind could hardly keep up. What had just happened?

She lifted her head and saw fire spreading across the grass in the front yard. She heard a truck squealing away.

The flames appeared to be contained to a small patch of grass. Leftover snow had prevented the fire from spreading.

That was good news.

But it could have turned out a lot differently if she and Dillon had taken just a few steps into the yard.

Dillon rolled off her and also glanced back. "Is everyone okay?"

Burt and Grayson nodded, still looking like they were in shock as they stood inside the doorway.

"What just happened?" Erin muttered.

Dillon rose to his feet before reaching down and helping Erin stand. She brushed imaginary dust from her jeans, mostly so she could forget the tingling feeling she'd felt when her hand touched Dillon's.

She especially didn't trust any tingly feelings or mini firework explosions.

But something about Dillon felt different. Still, she'd be wise to remind herself to keep her distance right now.

"My guess is that it was a bottle bomb." As Dillon scowled at the scene outside, he pulled his phone out and called the police.

"Do you really feel like they'll do anything?" she asked after he ended his call.

"It's hard to say. But we do need to report it." He knew what she was thinking: that the police here weren't reliable anyway.

"Did anybody recognize that truck?" Erin glanced around the room, but everybody shook their head.

"At least I got a partial of the plates," Dillon said. "But everything happened so fast that I wasn't able to memorize the whole thing."

She shook her head and shivered as the explosion replayed in her mind.

Who would be behind this? The same person who took Bella?

Again, nothing made sense. This whole thing was a nightmare she couldn't seem to wake up from.

She glanced at the front yard again and saw that the flames were gone, leaving smoke, a wide black circle in the lawn, and a few scraps from the bomb itself.

If Erin had to guess, the person who'd done this probably hadn't wanted to kill them. They'd simply wanted to send a message.

What was that message? Was it that Erin wasn't welcome here in Boone's Hollow? That they still thought she'd had something to do with one of these crimes?

It was hard to say. A bad feeling lingered in her gut.

The feeling only worsened when she saw Chief Blackstone pull up several minutes later.

Would he still give her a hard time? Would he ever be on her side, be someone she felt as if she could trust?

She had no idea.

But it was going to take all of her energy and mental strength to get through this next conversation.

"I'll run the plates and see if we get any hits." Chief Blackstone glanced in the distance at Burt before looking back at Dillon.

They all stood in the driveway outside. Three police cars had arrived on scene, and the other officers were collecting evidence and questioning people.

"What are you guys doing here anyway?" Chief Blackstone asked.

"Can't we just pay a friendly visit to some of the town folk?" Dillon didn't want to give this man any more details than he had to.

For some reason, he'd never really liked Blackstone, but his respect had been decreasing steadily ever since this investigation into Bella's disappearance started.

"It's just that you all don't seem like the type who'd hang out with each other." The chief spoke slowly, as if he were purposefully choosing each word. "Unless maybe you're conspiring together."

Dillon felt irritation prickle his skin. "Chief, respectfully, you know that Erin had nothing to do with Bella's disappearance. When you look at all the pieces of the puzzle, it doesn't make sense that she'd do something like this. Besides, how would you explain all the threats that have been made toward her if that was the case?"

Blackstone shrugged. "I like to look at every angle. Maybe she set this up so she wouldn't look guilty."

"What possible reason could she have for wanting to make her daughter disappear?" He didn't bother to keep the exasperation from his voice.

"That's an excellent question. But I heard her girl was giving her a hard time lately. Someone who killed her own husband might be willing and able to do the same to her daughter, too."

Dillon felt Erin tense beside him. Her uptight body language and quick breathing clearly indicated she could pounce at any minute. He didn't want to put her in a position that would only make her look more guilty.

He gently touched her arm, silently encouraging her to remain quiet.

He understood her anger. He was angry also.

"You know that doesn't make sense." Dillon kept his voice even and diplomatic—for the time being, at least. "I know Liam was your friend and that you need to figure out what happened to him. But you need to expand your pool of suspects outside of Erin."

Blackstone narrowed his eyes and pressed his lips together, not bothering to hide his aggravation. "It sounds like she's got you under her thumb."

"I'm just looking at the evidence. Objectively. That's what you should be doing, too."

Chief Blackstone scowled and took a step back. "You best watch your tone if you want to get any more jobs around here."

Dillon heard the underlying threat in the man's voice, but Dillon wasn't one to be deterred. His sense of right and wrong was stronger than any threats that could be made against him.

Dillon crossed his arms, unfazed by the chief—and determined to let the man know that. "By the way, any updates on that body that we found in the woods?"

"Not yet," the chief said. "It's still with the medical examiner. In the meantime, we'll look into what happened here tonight. But, based on the lack of evidence, I doubt we're going to figure out who threw this bomb. It was probably just some kids trying to play an innocent prank."

"Bombs are never an innocent prank." Dillon's voice hardened.

"Then maybe this isn't about you guys. Maybe this is about those two." Blackstone nodded toward Burt and Grayson as they stood near the garage and listened. "They like to hang out with unsavory types."

"You don't know what you're talking about," Burt called, his gaze daring the chief to defy him.

Dillon turned back to the chief, not liking how this conversation had gone. "Chief Blackstone, I'd appreciate you looking into this matter and taking it seriously."

The man's eyes narrowed. "Need I remind you that I don't take orders from you?"

"Don't be that guy, Chief Blackstone."

The chief stared at Dillon a moment before frowning and walking back to his car.

Dillon hoped that he had laid enough pressure on him that the chief might think twice about how he proceeded. But given the chief's nature, that wasn't a sure thing.

Erin stared out the window, replaying everything that had happened, starting with that conversation with Chief Blackstone.

How could the man be so rude? Such a jerk? And how had he gotten away with it for so long?

She believed in cops. Believed that they did good work. She hated the fact that a couple of bad ones could make all cops look bad, even when that wasn't the case.

But once certain people got into positions of power, like Blackstone had, it felt nearly impossible to change that. To oust them from their positions. And because that was the case, the power trips just seem to keep growing.

Chief Blackstone's was the biggest one of all right now.

"Listen, I know you don't know me that well," Dillon started beside her. "I don't want this to sound weird. But I don't think you should stay at your place by yourself tonight."

Erin froze at Dillon's words. She knew exactly what he was getting at.

Her place wasn't safe.

She wasn't safe.

Erin didn't want to stay by herself, either. But short of leaving town to go stay with family, she didn't have many options. There was no way she would leave this area with Bella still missing.

Dillon had stayed on her couch last night, but she couldn't ask him to do that again. It was too much.

"I'm sure I'll be fine." She didn't sound convincing, even to her own ears.

"How would you feel about sleeping in the spare bedroom at my place? Carson and I will be there, along with all the dogs, of course. You'd have your own space and most people wouldn't even know that you're staying out there."

He raised a good point. Everybody would assume she

was staying at her place. Maybe that would allow her to get some rest so she could start fresh the next morning.

"Are you sure you really don't mind? You're going deeper and deeper with me, and I'm afraid that it's going to ruin things for you here in this town."

He ducked his head until they were eye to eye. "Erin, I know it probably feels like everybody here hates you, but I have a hard time believing that's true. Anybody who knows you can clearly see you have a good heart. That you're a good person. Just because a few people— a few loud people—bad-mouth you, don't think they speak for everyone."

Something about his words caused her cheeks to warm. He sounded so sincere, so much like he was speaking the truth. She hadn't expected to crave hearing an affirmation like that. His words brought a strange sense of comfort to her.

"Thank you." Her throat burned as the words left her lips. "I really appreciate that. If you don't mind, I think I will take you up on your offer. I'd feel better if I wasn't at that house by myself tonight."

"Let me just run you past your place so you can pick up a couple of things then."

A few minutes later, she'd packed a small overnight bag and was back in the Jeep with Dillon and Scout. They headed back to his place, another day coming to an end.

Another day without Bella.

Erin continued to pray that her daughter was safe and unharmed. But every day, her prayers felt more and more frail, like she was losing hope that her requests would actually be answered in the way she wanted.

She didn't want to lose faith.

But it was becoming more and more of a struggle.

FOURTEEN

Dillon got Erin settled in the spare bedroom at his house before returning to the living area and starting on some dinner.

He was famished. He'd grabbed a quick sandwich while at the hospital earlier. But certainly Erin was hungry also. Today's events had made him build up an appetite.

He didn't have much to eat, but he could throw together some chicken-and-potato stew. It was one of his go-to staples, and it sounded especially good on such a cold day.

Erin emerged from her room a few minutes later with her hair wet and wearing fresh clothes.

He had to drag his gaze away from her.

He hadn't expected that reaction.

He'd known from the moment he'd met Erin that she was an attractive woman. A very attractive woman. The more he'd gotten to know her, the more he'd been impressed with her character as well.

He'd meant what he had told her earlier. Anybody who had the privilege of actually getting to know Erin had to know she couldn't be responsible for the events that had happened. It was a shame she'd been painted in such a negative light.

He continued to stir his stew as she sat across from him at the breakfast bar. "Dinner?"

"I figured that we both needed to eat," Dillon said. "Carson, too."

She pushed a wet strand of hair behind her ear.

"Thank you for everything you've done." Her voice sounded raw—but sincere—as she said the words.

"I'm just sorry I haven't been able to do more. I want to find Bella also." He bit down, meaning what he'd said. He wasn't going to feel any peace until they had some answers.

"Where do you even think she is right now?" Erin asked. "Do you think she's in the woods? Or did she simply start in the woods? Did she go there to meet somebody who ended up snatching her? If that's the case, where did this person take her?"

"I wish I had those answers for you. But I do know that people have cabins out in those woods where they can live off the land and never be seen. When I was a cop, we assisted park rangers with a search and rescue mission when this woman thought her husband had disappeared. Turned out that instead of divorcing her, he'd run away. He'd lived off-grid for three years before anyone ever found him."

"Wow," Erin muttered. "What did you think when Burt said that the Bradshaws could be responsible? Are you familiar with them?"

"I've heard of them. A lot of people suspect they have a drug enterprise going on in their home. But without any evidence, the police haven't been able to act."

"I see."

Dillon cast another glance at her. "Did you ever suspect that your husband got himself too deeply into a case and disappeared because somebody wanted to silence him or exact revenge?"

"I've tried to think of every angle. But the circumstances of it all were just strange—as was the timing. Especially considering it happened right after a huge fight we had out in public."

"Who initiated the fight?"

"He did. He thought I was seeing someone else, and he told me I shouldn't do that."

"He was the jealous type, huh?"

She frowned and nodded. "To the extreme. We had Officer Hollins over once, and he accused me of flirting with him when I laughed at one of his jokes."

"That doesn't sound healthy."

"It wasn't. All of our fights seemed to go back to him wanting to control me. When things got physical… that's when I knew I had to get out. I couldn't put Bella through that. I couldn't let her see the way he treated me and think that it was okay."

"Leaving him sounds like it was the right thing. I'm sure it also took a certain amount of bravery."

She shrugged. "I don't know about that. But I felt like a burden had been lifted after I'd made the choice. He didn't make it easy on me, unfortunately."

"I can imagine."

Dillon tried to store away every detail just in case it became important later.

He stirred the stew one more time and realized it was close to being done. He was about to grab some bowls when suddenly Scout stood and growled at the front door.

Dillon abandoned his food and pulled his gun out instead.

After everything that had happened, he couldn't take any chances.

"Stay back," Dillon said. "Let me make sure that trouble hasn't found us again."

Erin backed deeper into the kitchen.

Not again.

It just didn't make any sense. Why couldn't this person leave her alone?

She watched as Dillon crept to the window and peered out. Scout stood at his side, on guard and ready to act at the first command.

"Do you see anything?" Her voice trembled as the words left her lips.

"There's a flashlight in the woods," he said.

She sucked in a breath. Somebody really was out there.

Of course.

Scout didn't seem like the type of dog who would react otherwise.

Why would someone be back there? What was this person's plan?

Dillon turned to her, his muscles tight and drawn, as if he were ready to act. The hardness in his eyes surprised her. This whole situation was beginning to get to him as well, wasn't it?

"I'm going to go check it out," he announced.

Alarm raced through her at the thought of him being out there with this person. "Dillon…you could be hurt."

"This needs to end," he said. "Somebody is stalking and threatening you. The situation is bad enough without adding those elements to it."

She couldn't argue with that statement. But… "I don't want you getting hurt. Too many people have already been hurt."

His determined—and undeterred—gaze met hers. "I'll be careful. I'm going to go out the back door and sneak around the other side of the woods to see if I can take this guy by surprise."

"Do you really think that will work?"

"I don't know, but it's worth giving it a shot." He paused. "Carson!"

A few minutes later, his nephew appeared from upstairs. "Yes?"

"I need you to stay here with Erin and keep an eye on her. You know where the guns are, right?"

Carson stood beside Erin and nodded. "I do. What's going on?"

"Somebody is outside, and I need to figure out who."

Carson stiffened. "Understood. Be safe."

"Always." Dillon nodded at Erin, giving her some type of silent reassurance that everything would be okay.

She wished she felt as confident. But she didn't. Not with so much on the line right now.

Carson went to the closet and opened a safe inside. He pulled out a gun and paced toward the window. He remained there, watching everything outside.

"Do you still see somebody out there?" Erin asked.

He didn't answer for a moment as he stared outside. "Yes, somebody with a flashlight is out there. I can see them moving."

She rubbed her throat, fighting worst-case scenarios.

"My uncle knows these woods better than anybody." Carson seemed to sense her anxiety, to read her mind. "He was a good cop. Competent. He won't put himself in unnecessary danger."

Erin closed her eyes and began lifting prayers. She hoped that Carson was right.

Because her feelings for the man had apparently grown much more quickly than she had ever imagined possible.

* * *

Dillon moved carefully through the woods. He couldn't risk giving away his presence. Not if he wanted to take this person by surprise.

And that was exactly what he wanted to do.

He'd meant what he'd said inside. It was time to put an end to this. This trauma had gone on for far too long.

Besides, if the person in the woods was the same person who'd taken Bella, then Dillon needed to sit him down and demand answers.

None of this made sense to him. None of these games. Now it was time to find some answers.

He slipped between the trees, watching his every step. If he stepped on one twig wrong, it could mess up everything.

He quietly walked through the woods at the back of the property, skirting the edge of those woods and carefully remaining out of sight.

The person he'd spotted had been lurking near the front of his property. The flashlight Dillon had seen had indicated movement.

Was this person looking for a good vantage point to spy on Erin? Or was the reason someone was out here even more deadly? Perhaps the intruder was searching for the best position to pull the trigger.

Anger burned through Dillon's blood at the thought.

Erin didn't deserve to go through this. If Dillon could do anything to stop it, he would. It was the same reason that he was determined to leave in the morning and to begin search efforts for Bella again. If the girl was out in the Pisgah National Forest, Dillon wanted to find her.

He gripped his gun, his muscles tense as he wondered exactly how this would play out. Though he'd given up being a cop, another part of him would always be a cop. Would always want to look out for people who needed help. To be a voice for the voiceless.

He continued forward, snow crunching beneath his boots. As the temperature dropped, everything was becoming icy again. The threadbare trees didn't allow much cover. But he was deep enough in the forest that he could maintain his distance.

He rounded the curve of the trees, headed toward the front of the house where he had seen the light.

As he did, he paused.

Where had the trespasser gone? Enough time had passed that the person could have walked deeper into the woods or closer to the driveway. Dillon couldn't afford to walk into a situation not knowing what was happening around him.

He held his breath as he waited, watching for that flashlight he'd spotted earlier. Listening for any telltale footsteps.

If he'd wanted to risk it, he could have turned on his own flashlight and shone it on the ground to search for any footprints. But that was a risk he couldn't afford to take. He couldn't give away his presence.

He continued to wait and listen.

Still nothing.

As he waited, he wondered how the person had even gotten here without his noticing a vehicle.

If he had to guess, the intruder had probably parked on the side of the road and then cut through the woods.

Dillon would check that out later, if necessary.

For now, maybe the man had moved farther away.

Dillon crept forward a few more steps, trying to find a different vantage point.

But as he did, a stick cracked behind him.

The next thing he knew, something hard came down over his head and everything began to spin.

FIFTEEN

Erin stood at the window and stared out the crack between the curtain and the wall. She knew that Dillon wouldn't want her standing that close. Especially if bullets were to start to fly again.

Whoever was behind these threats was certainly persistent. In fact, he was relentless.

Could it be Liam? If so, where had he been hiding out the past year?

But when she remembered the body they'd found with his necklace on it, she knew that wasn't the case. That had to be Liam, right? Who else would it be?

Could Liam's family be behind everything that was happening? Or had Liam made someone mad and now this person was trying to get revenge on Liam's family as some type of ultimate payback?

Erin had no idea, but she didn't like any of this.

"Are you doing okay?" Carson stood on the other side of the window, gun in hand.

She shrugged. "I guess as well as can be expected."

"It sounds like you've gone through a lot."

"It feels like I've gone through a lot."

Carson glanced outside again before saying, "Dillon used to be one of the best cops out there, you know?"

"Is that right?" Erin really wanted to ask what happened, but she figured it wasn't her business. Maybe, if she were lucky, Dillon would tell her later.

"It seems like every cop has that one case that gets to him," Carson said, still keeping an eye on the window. "My uncle went to find a missing hiker. His team searched everywhere but didn't find him. A day after they called off the search, the man's body was discovered within a half-mile radius of where my uncle searched. He's beat himself up over it ever since."

Erin soaked in each new detail, a better picture of Dillon forming in her head. "Certainly it wasn't his fault. He seems very thorough."

"He would have probably realized that eventually," Carson said. "But the family of the hiker who died began to attack my uncle. They sued the police department, and Dillon became the poster child of botched rescue operations. He was the face that they put with their grievances."

She let out a small gasp. "That couldn't have been easy."

"It wasn't. He was engaged at the time, but his fiancée couldn't handle the pressure. She broke things off with him. Talk about a hard time."

Erin shook her head, unable to understand how somebody could leave someone they loved in the midst of turmoil. "I can only imagine how difficult that had to be for him."

Carson kept one eye on the front yard as he talked. "It definitely changed him. But I truly believe he's doing what he loves right now. He's really good with dogs and training them. Plus, I think that in some way it helps him to feel like he can make amends for the mistakes that he blames himself for."

The new insight into Dillon painted him in a different light.

In some ways, Erin could understand exactly where he was coming from. She had lived under the weight of accusation. It wasn't a fun place to be, and people rarely came out the same on the other side.

"If you don't mind me asking, how long have you lived with your uncle?"

"Two years," he said. "He's not really my uncle, but he's my father's best friend. My mom left us when I was thirteen and my dad started drinking pretty heavily. He needed help. Uncle Dillon paid to send him to rehab. He's still trying to get his life back together, to be honest. Uncle Dillon said I could stay here for as long as necessary."

"I'm sorry to hear about all that, but I'm glad you have someone like Dillon in your life." Again, her perspective on Dillon changed—in a good way.

He was a good man. It wasn't just a mask he wore around her.

Her admiration for the man grew.

Erin's gaze went back to the window, and she wondered what was happening outside. She was going to give Dillon five more minutes. Then she would push past Carson and go check on Dillon herself.

What if something was wrong? What if he needed them?

He had done so much for her. There was no way Erin was going to leave him in his time of need, especially since she was the source of all this trouble.

She crossed her arms over her chest and waited.

Five minutes.

That was all.

Then she was going to have to take action.

Just as Dillon felt everything spinning around him, a shock of adrenaline burst through him and he sprang into action.

He swirled around and saw a man in a black mask standing in front of him with a shovel in his hands.

He braced himself for a fight before muttering, "I don't think so."

As the man swung the shovel at him again, Dillon ducked. His shoulder caught the masked man in the gut, and they crashed to the ground.

As another wave of nausea rushed over Dillon, the man flipped him over. The guy's fist collided with Dillon's jaw, and pain rippled through him.

But Dillon still had more fight in him left. This was far from over.

He grabbed the guy and shoved him backward. Dillon's hand went to the man's throat as he pinned the intruder to the ground.

The man grunted and thrashed beneath him. Whoever he was, he was strong, and Dillon had to use all in his energy to keep the man pinned.

If only Dillon could see who was on the other side of that mask. But if he shifted his weight to pull it off, he feared the guy would take advantage of his disheveled state and get the upper hand.

"Where is Bella?" Dillon demanded.

The trespasser grunted.

In one motion, the man shoved Dillon off and burst to his feet.

Dillon stood just in time.

With his hands in front of him, the man rammed Dillon into the tree.

His head spun.

Dillon straightened to go after the man again, but before he could, the man took off in a run.

Dillon staggered forward, still not ready to give up. But as everything swirled around him, he realized he wasn't going to make it if he chased this guy.

That blow to his head was making him light-headed and nauseous.

He started to take one more step forward just out of stubborn determination.

As he did, he crumpled to the ground.

He'd been so close to finding answers. So close.

But he'd let the man get away.

"I'm going out there." Erin stepped toward the door.

Carson moved in front of her, blocking her path. "I can't let you do that. I promised my uncle that I wouldn't."

"He might need our help."

"He can handle himself." Carson's voice contained full confidence in his words.

"He's been out there too long. What if he's hurt?" Her voice trembled with emotion. She was honestly worried about Dillon.

Something flashed in Carson's gaze. Was that fear? The realization that she might be right?

"You stay in here." Carson's voice hardened with surprising maturity. "I'll check."

"I'm going with you," Erin insisted. "There's no way I'm letting a teenager go out there and get hurt on my account."

He stared at her a moment before marching to the closet. He pulled out another gun and handed it to her. "Do you know how to handle one of these?"

She stared at the small handgun and nodded, her throat suddenly feeling dry. "I do."

"Good. Bring it with you. It's fully loaded. Use it if you need to."

A shiver of apprehension raced down her spine. Erin really prayed that she didn't have to use this. But if it came down to Dillon's life or someone else's?

She knew that she had to protect these people who had protected her. She would aim for a shoulder or a knee or something nonlethal. She could do this.

As she walked with Carson toward the back door, another surge of apprehension rippled up her spine. She really had no idea what she was doing right now. She only knew she had to help Dillon.

"We're going to skirt around the backside of the property, just like my uncle did," Carson said. "We don't want to make ourselves easy targets for this guy if he's still out there."

Erin nodded and gripped the gun in both hands.

With one more nod from Carson, they both stepped outside into the dark, tranquil night. She scanned everything around her, looking for a sign of anything that might have happened. Dark woods stared back at her, looking deceitfully peaceful with the white snow covering the branches and ground.

Everything seemed still and quiet.

Carson motioned for her to follow, and they took off in a run toward the trees. Once they reached the cover of the woods, they followed a small path around the edge of the property.

The temperature had dipped close to zero, and it felt every bit like it. Snow crunched beneath her feet no matter how hard she tried to stay quiet. Her nose already felt numb, as did her fingers.

But those were the least of her concerns. Dillon was her main focus right now.

As they neared the area where they'd seen the flashlight, Carson put a finger over his lips, motioning for her to be quiet. They slowed their steps as they crept forward.

Erin kept her gaze on everything around her, looking for any signs of trouble.

She saw nothing. No one. No lights. Nor did she hear anything.

Exactly what had gone on out here?

What if that man had grabbed Dillon just like someone had grabbed Bella?

A sick feeling gurgled in Erin's gut at the thought of it.

She continued forward and, with every step, the tension in her back muscles only increased.

Erin had hoped they would have found Dillon by now. That he would have offered an explanation for what was taking so long and then ushered them back into the warmth and safety of the house, giving them a good lecture in the process.

But that wasn't the case.

Her thoughts on Dillon, Erin nearly collided into Carson's back. He let out a breath in front of her, and that's when she knew that something was wrong.

She peered around him and spotted Dillon on the ground.

Not moving.

Alarm raced through her. Was he dead?

Oh, God. Please...no!

* * *

Dillon startled when he heard a noise above him. But as he tried to sit up, pain shot through his skull.

At once, everything rushed back to him.

The intruder in the woods. The one who'd hit him with a shovel. Who'd pushed him into the tree. Had ultimately gotten away.

Or had he?

Dillon felt the shadow over him and raised his fists, ready to fight.

"Wait! It's just us, Dillon."

Slowly, Carson's face came into view. Erin stood beside him, worry in her gaze as she looked down at him.

Dillon scowled as he rubbed the back of his head. "What are you guys doing out here? I told you to stay inside."

"We came to check on you," Carson said. "It looks like it's a good thing we did."

He rubbed the back of his head again, wishing that it didn't hurt as badly as it did. There was no way he could pretend that he wasn't in pain. No way that he could pretend nothing had happened out here.

Carson took one of his arms and Erin the other as they helped him to his feet.

"Where's the person who did this to you?" Carson demanded, his gaze hardening with anger.

"He got away. I tried to catch him, but we ended up in a fistfight."

"You obviously hurt your head." Erin stared at him, worry still lingering in her gaze.

"I'm fine." He brushed her concern off with the shake of his head.

"You don't look fine." Erin wrapped her hand around

his arm so she wouldn't lose her grip. "We need to get you inside and check your head for injuries."

Dillon knew better than to argue at this point. Besides, his head pounded with every new line of conversation. The sooner he could get this over with, the better.

He dropped an arm over both of their shoulders, and they helped him through the woods and back into the house. Scout greeted him with a wet nose as soon as he stepped inside, letting out a little whine to let him know he'd been worried also.

He rubbed the dog's head before sitting on the couch. Erin hurried across the room and grabbed a glass of water, handing it to him and insisting he take a drink.

He complied.

Even as he did, all he could think about was that man. Dillon had been so close to catching him, to finding answers.

Just like he had been so close to finding Michael Masterson.

Guilt seemed to dogpile on top of his regret and he squeezed his eyes shut.

"Let me see the back of your head," Erin said. "Carson, can you get him some ice for his face?"

Carson hurried into the kitchen.

As he did, Erin moved to the back of the couch and leaned over him. "I don't see any cuts. But you might have a concussion. We should take you to the hospital."

He started to shake his head when everything wobbled around him again. "I'll be fine."

"I think she's right." Carson returned and handed an ice pack wrapped in a dishtowel to his uncle. "It couldn't hurt to be checked out."

"I'm telling you, I'm fine. I'm going to have a headache, and I need to watch myself when I go to sleep tonight but, otherwise, I'm going to be okay." He pressed the compress against his cheek.

He didn't miss the look that Erin and Carson exchanged with each other. They were both worried about him. He supposed he should be grateful he had people in his life to worry over him. Some people didn't have that privilege.

"How about some coffee?" Erin asked. "Would that make anything better?"

"That sounds great." The caffeine would help him stay awake, which he knew was important right now. Plus, he needed some space.

A few minutes later, she brought him a cup before lowering herself beside him on the couch. Her wide-eyed gaze searched his. "What happened out there?"

As tonight's events filled his thoughts, he closed his eyes, wishing he could have a replay. But that wasn't always possible in life.

Instead, he sighed before starting. "The guy must have heard me coming. He hit me in the back of the head with a shovel. I thought I was coming out ahead until he pushed me into a tree. Everything went black around me. The last thing I remember is him running away."

"Did you get a good look at him?" Erin asked.

Dillon frowned. "Unfortunately, I didn't. He was wearing a black mask, and it was dark outside. I couldn't even tell you his eye color."

"What about his voice?" Carson asked. "Was there anything distinct about it?"

"I already thought about that. I wish I had something to report to you guys. I really do. But there's nothing. I even tried to ask him where Bella was, but he just grunted in response."

"If he wasn't involved in this, then he would have denied it, right?" Erin's voice contained a touch of fear that mingled with hope.

"I definitely think he has something to do with what's going on. I don't know if he's the person who grabbed Bella or not. But this is all connected. We just need to figure out how."

Erin's hand went over her mouth as she squeezed her eyes shut. "I shouldn't be here. I'm putting you in danger."

The thought of her leaving and being on her own right now caused a strange grief to grip his heart.

"I don't want you to leave." The surprisingly raw and honest words surprised even him. And Erin, too. Clearly, because her eyes widened. "I'd just feel better if you were here where we can keep an eye on you."

"But if these attacks continue and you're constantly in the line of fire…"

His gaze locked with hers. "I'm in the line of fire because I put myself there. You leaving won't take me out of that position now. Do you understand?"

She stared at him another moment, and Dillon wasn't sure what she was going to say. Part of him thought that she might just up and leave.

He held his breath as he waited to see what her response would be.

SIXTEEN

If Erin were smart, she'd leave. If she really cared about Dillon, Carson and Scout as much as she thought she did, she'd get out of here before any more damage could be done.

But as she stared at Dillon now and saw the sincerity in his eyes, everything in her wanted to stay.

She knew it was selfish. She didn't want to do anything that she would regret. But she felt certain that if she went back to her house tonight, things wouldn't end well. The person who was pursuing her wasn't letting up. The only way this would end would be with her dead.

She licked her lips before nodding at Dillon as he sat on the couch, compress still against his face. "If you don't mind, I will stay. But the moment you want me gone, you let me know, and I'm out of here. I'm serious."

Something that looked close to relief flooded Dillon's gaze. "Good. I think you're making a smart decision."

Erin reminded herself that Dillon's reasons for wanting her to stay were purely professional. Nothing about this case was personal. She needed to remember to keep her walls up as well. Just because she felt safe with Dillon didn't mean anything.

Quickly, she stood and went into the kitchen to check on the stew. "Would you like some? I think it's done."

"Maybe some food is just what the doctor ordered."

"You stay there. I'll get it ready." She found some bowls and spoons. A few minutes later, she had the table set for three.

Erin wanted to pretend like this was just a normal dinner with new friends, but she knew it was anything but. They were together right now simply because they wanted to survive.

After praying, they all dug into the warm meal.

Erin took her first bite of the stew and the flavors of nutmeg and garlic washed over her taste buds. "This is delicious."

She hadn't known what to expect.

"It's my mom's recipe," Dillon said. "She's quite the cook—and comfort food is her specialty."

"Where are you parents now?" she asked.

"They retired down in Florida. I still get to see them several times a year, though."

"That's nice."

"How about you, Erin?" Dillon asked. "Where are you from?"

"I grew up closer to Raleigh, but Liam and I met in college. He was from this area, so we moved here."

"This is God's country," Carson said. "At least, in my eyes that's what it is."

Erin smiled. "No one can deny it's beautiful out here."

They chatted about the area as they finished their meal, and then Erin cleaned up while Dillon moved to the couch, still looking worse for the wear after the confrontation in the woods.

As the dogs began barking outside, Dillon glanced at Carson. "Would you mind checking on the dogs?"

"No, sir. I'll do that now." Carson grabbed his coat and started toward the back door.

"Be careful out there," Dillon called.

His words were a reminder of the danger they were all currently in.

As he left the room, Erin sat beside Dillon on the couch and felt the tension stretch between them.

Now that her emotions over what happened were settling down, she had to wonder what they were going to talk about. She sucked in a deep breath, deciding to address the unspoken issues they were both certainly thinking about.

She cleared her throat. "Are you sure you don't want to call the police and tell them what happened tonight?"

Dillon's expression tightened. "No, they're not going to do anything. First thing in the morning, I'll go out and investigate for myself."

He really didn't like Blackstone, either. Why did Erin find so much comfort in that thought?

She pulled her legs beneath her and leaned against the couch as she turned to Dillon. "Have you heard anything about the search and rescue operations for Bella tomorrow?"

"Rick told me they're going to take the helicopter out again and that there will be more search and rescue teams. I'll take Scout out and see if he can pick up her scent again. At least we have a basic idea of what direction Bella traveled in."

Erin nodded, trying not to show her anxiety.

Dillon shifted closer to her before lowering his voice.

"Erin, I haven't been in your exact shoes. But I feel like another part of me knows what you're going through."

She stared at him, curious about what he might share. Was this concerning what Carson had told her? About his ex-fiancée who'd left him?

"How so?" she finally asked.

He lowered his compress and put it on the table as a far-off look flooded his eyes. "A lot of people turned against me when one of my search and rescue missions went south. Even my fiancée ended up leaving me because she couldn't take the pressure of it."

"I'm sorry to hear that."

"I deal all the time with people who have missing loved ones. I feel like I live their experiences with them sometimes."

Spontaneously, she reached forward and grabbed his hand. "I can only imagine."

As they looked at each other, their gazes caught.

Their grief had bonded them, hadn't it? They'd both been through ordeals that only the other could understand.

Erin still marveled at the fact that Dillon was so unlike Liam. He was a breath of fresh air—and he brought her a renewed hope.

"Erin?" His voice sounded scratchy as he said the word.

"Yes?" Was she imagining things or was he leaning closer?

The next moment, he reached forward and pushed a lock of hair behind her ear. His gaze almost looked smoky with emotion—and the look in his eyes took her breath away.

It wasn't just attraction there. It was genuine care and concern.

His thumb brushed across her cheek as he moved in closer.

She closed her eyes, anticipating what might happen next.

Until a new sound cut into the moment.

Dillon's phone.

He pulled back, seeming to snap out of the impulsive moment.

Instead, Dillon excused himself and grabbed the device from the table.

Erin tried not to feel disappointed.

It was best that kiss hadn't happened. The interruption was probably a godsend, a reminder that she was better off going solo rather than getting tangled in a bad situation again.

So why did it feel like Dillon would never create a bad scenario in her life?

Dillon saw Rick's number on the screen and his breath caught.

His heart still pounded out of control from the near kiss. It only accelerated more when he realized his friend might have an update.

He answered and put the call on the speaker. "Rick, I'm here with Erin. She's listening."

"Perfect," Rick said. "I just wanted to let you know that a hiker on a different trail found a shoe that I believe belongs to Bella."

Dillon's breath caught. "What trail?"

"Gulch Valley," Rick said.

Dillon frowned as he pictured the layout of trails in the park. "That's on the other side of the park."

"I know." Rick's voice sounded somber. "It doesn't make any sense."

Dillon shook his head as he tried to think through this newest update. "Scout couldn't have been that wrong. Bella was definitely in the part of the forest that we searched."

"I agree. But how did her shoe end up nearly twenty miles away?"

Dillon bit down as he imagined various scenarios. None of his theories rose to the surface, however. "That's a good question."

"It's a possibility that someone took her shoe and left it as a means of misdirection," Rick said.

"Do you think somebody would do that?" Erin's voice sounded wispy with surprise.

"It's hard to say for sure," Rick said. "We've involved several other local police departments in our search, including the guys from Boone's Hollow. Chief Blackstone said his guys were going to search that area tomorrow as well and see if they could pick up on anything."

"I'm glad he's doing something," Dillon muttered.

They ended the call with a promise to keep each other updated.

Then silence stretched between them.

As the back door opened, Carson wandered inside. "The dogs are fine. I'm not sure why they started barking."

"That's good news, at least." Erin stood and rubbed her hands down the sides of her pants as if she were nervous. "Now that Carson is back, I think I should probably be getting some rest."

Dillon nodded, wondering if something had spooked her. Had he said something? Or was it just this situation?

"I'm going to get Carson to stay awake with me for

a little while," Dillon finally said. "I probably shouldn't go to sleep right now after my head injury."

"That's probably a good idea. Do you need me to—"

Dillon shook his head before Erin could finish the sentence. "I'll be fine."

Erin stared at him a moment, questions lingering in her gaze.

Maybe the two of them needed a little time apart. Their emotions had grown quickly, fueled by the danger around them. The last thing he wanted was to do something in the heat of the moment that they would both later regret.

"Carson and I have got this," Dillon insisted. "You get your sleep."

Erin stared at him a moment longer before nodding. "Okay then. I'll talk to you in the morning."

"I'll see you then."

But as she disappeared down the hallway, he couldn't help but wonder what kind of trouble tomorrow would hold.

As Erin laid in bed, she couldn't stop thinking about the kiss she'd almost shared with Dillon.

What would it be like to open herself up to somebody again? Part of her felt thrilled at the possibility and another part of her only felt fear.

Liam had been the only guy she'd ever dated, and she hadn't dated anyone since he'd disappeared. She'd had no desire to.

But something about Dillon was different. He was gentle. Respectful.

Then again, Liam had been those things at first also. People said you never really knew a person until you went through the hard times with them. That was when their true colors seemed to appear.

Erin had to agree with those words.

She frowned at the memories.

It was a good thing that the kiss had been interrupted. Erin needed to slow down. They both did. Their emotions were clearly out of control.

But another part of her felt like there could be something special there between her and Dillon.

As she punched her pillow, trying to get comfortable, she tried to put any thoughts of Dillon out of her mind. The only person she needed to think about right now was Bella. To engage in any type of romance while her daughter was missing would be uncouth.

That was right.

Until Bella was found, romance was totally off the table, even with someone like Dillon.

Besides, who knew what was going to happen once this was all over. What if Bella wasn't found? Just like Liam hadn't been found.

Or Bella might need help after she was rescued. Erin's life might be devoted to counseling sessions as she tried to help Bella deal with the aftermath of this ordeal. That *had* to be Erin's first priority.

As she turned over in bed again, a noise in the corner of the room caught her ear.

She froze.

What was that?

Sometimes, new houses had different sounds, she reminded herself. Had the heat kicked on? Had a branch scraped the window?

Erin listened, desperate to hear the sound again so

she could confirm the noise was mundane and nothing to be worried about.

All was quiet.

She waited a few more seconds, trying to write off the sound. Maybe sleep would find her. Maybe her brain would turn off. Maybe she could stop worrying so much over something so trivial.

Liam had always said Erin liked to make big deals out of nothing.

He'd used the word *trivial* quite a bit. Now, even the thought of that word made Erin's insides tighten as bad memories began to pummel her.

She turned over, determined to get some rest.

But just as she did that, the noise filled the room again.

The next instant, somebody pounced on top of her and a hand covered her mouth.

SEVENTEEN

Erin felt tension pulsing through her as the intruder pinned her down.

She froze, unable to move, unable to defend herself. All she wanted to do was panic.

Who was in her room? How did he get in here?

Even worse: what was he planning?

"You're not going to get away with this," a deep voice muttered in her ear. "Do you understand me?"

Erin remained frozen, unable to react or respond. Her heart thudded in her ears at a rapid pace.

"I said, do you understand me?" he repeated, his voice a growl.

Erin forced herself to nod. The man's hand clutching her mouth made it impossible to speak.

"You deserve to suffer," he continued. "You deserve everything you've got coming for you."

Her blood went cold. Why was this man doing this?

He didn't seem interested in hurting her—only in making her suffer.

But why?

Did this go back to Liam?

"Don't make me tell you again. And yes, I have more in store for you. Ending it like this would be too easy."

What was this guy talking about?

Maybe Erin didn't want to know.

"I'm going to slip out of your room," the man continued. "If you make a sound, I will kill Bella. Do you understand me?"

Kill Bella? *This* was the man who'd taken her? Why had he broken into Dillon's house? Just to threaten her like this?

Her chill deepened.

"I said, do you understand?" His rancid breath hit her ear.

Erin nodded again, more quickly this time.

"Good, because I'm going to be watching. One wrong move and she's dead."

A cry caught in Erin's throat at the thought.

The next instant, the weight of the man's body lifted from her.

Erin pulled in a deep breath, relishing the gulp of air as it filled her lungs.

In a flash, the man opened a window and rushed out.

A cool wind swept through the room.

Otherwise, everything was quiet.

Erin waited, her pounding heart the only sound she heard.

Had that really just happened? It still seemed like a nightmare.

She waited several minutes and tried to compose herself. She knew she needed to move. But she couldn't seem to force her body into action.

Get up, Erin. You're wasting time. Push through the fear!

Finally, she threw her legs out of bed. Her limbs trembled as adrenaline claimed her muscles.

She rose to her feet and peered out the window.

But the man was gone.

Erin had to get Dillon. Had to tell him what had just happened.

She only hoped she could make it out of this room in time.

Dillon straightened from his position on the couch as he heard footsteps rushing down the hallway. Carson sat in the chair across from him, so that had to be Erin.

Was she having trouble sleeping?

When he saw the expression on her face, he knew something was wrong.

He rose, worry pulling taut across his back muscles. "Erin?"

"A man…was in…my room." She clung to the wall as her red-rimmed eyes stared at him.

Even from across the room, Dillon could see her shaking.

He darted toward her and slipped an arm around her waist. He led her to the couch and lowered her onto the cushions before she collapsed.

"A man was in your room? Here at my house?" Had Dillon heard her correctly?

"He went out the window. He's gone now." Her voice broke as if she fought a moan.

Dillon looked at Carson, who'd also risen to his feet. "Did you see or hear anything?"

"No." He shook his head, his stiff shoulders indicating he was on guard. "Not a single thing."

Dillon turned back to Erin, desperate for more information. "What did he say?"

She drew in a shaky breath. "He said I wasn't going

to get away with this, that I deserved to suffer, and that I deserved everything I had coming to me."

Concern pulsed through him. He couldn't believe Scout hadn't picked up on the stranger's scent. But the evening had been hectic. He had noticed the canine whine once, but he'd assumed it was from the chaos around them.

"Anything else?" Dillon asked.

"He said he had more in store for me, and that ending it like this would be too easy. Before he left, he said he would be watching, and if I made one wrong move, Bella would die." Her voice broke as a sob wracked her body.

Dillon put an arm around her shoulders before pulling her to him in a hug.

He didn't say anything for a moment. He just held her, comforted her. Carson set a box of tissues beside them, and Erin grabbed one to wipe her face.

She drew in another breath and seemed to compose herself for a moment. "What am I going to do?"

"That's what we need to figure out," Dillon muttered. "Why would someone go through the trouble of breaking in just to tell you that?" Dillon asked.

"It's like he said—he wants to make me suffer. To let me know that I have no control, yet all of this is my fault." Erin's voice broke as if she held back a cry.

Her words settled on him. They made sense—in a twisted kind of way at least.

"That was why that man was outside the house earlier," Dillon mumbled.

Erin sucked in a quick breath as she stared up at him. "Do you mean that he drew us outside just so somebody else could sneak inside?"

"That's my best guess. That's the only thing that makes sense."

"But *none* of this makes sense. Why would the person who abducted Bella go through all this trouble?" She pressed the tissue into her eyes again.

The truth slammed into Dillon's mind. How had he not seen this before?

"That's because this isn't about Bella," Dillon muttered. "This is about you, Erin."

Realization spread through Erin's gaze and she nodded. "You're right. This *is* about me. I'm the actual target here, aren't I?"

Dillon almost didn't want to agree with her, but he had no choice. Erin had to know what she was up against.

"What am I going to do, Dillon?" Her wide eyes met his, questions filling their depths.

His heart ached for the woman.

He reached forward and squeezed her hand. "I don't know. But I'll be here with you to help you figure it out."

Erin startled awake.

Where was she? What was going on?

All she felt was a cold fear that pierced her heart.

Danger seemed to hang in the air around her.

"It's okay," a deep voice murmured beside her.

Erin jumped back even farther.

Who was that?

She glanced up and her eyes slowly adjusted to the darkness.

Dillon's face stared back at her.

Erin let out a breath. She must have fallen asleep on the couch. Had her head been on his shoulder?

Her cheeks heated at the thought of it.

The events of last night flooded back to her and she

shivered. Especially when she remembered the man who'd been in her room—the person who wanted to strike fear into her heart.

He had succeeded. He'd taken away everything that was precious to her. Erin's sense of security. Her peace of mind. Her faith in humanity.

Most of all—he'd taken away Bella.

She held back a cry.

The only thing the man hadn't taken was her faith in God, but even that felt like it was on shaky ground lately. This situation was definitely a test of her faith.

Dillon shifted beside her before softly murmuring, "I didn't want to wake you."

Erin raked her hand through her hair and nodded. She vaguely remembered Dillon holding her as they'd sat on the couch. She remembered resting her head on his shoulder.

She must have fallen asleep.

She rubbed her throat as she felt another wave of self-consciousness. "I'm sorry... I didn't mean to..."

"No need for apologies." Dillon glanced at her, his eyes warm and almost soft. "I'm glad you were able to get some rest."

She studied his face for a moment, wondering how his concussion was—not to mention his swollen cheek. She wasn't the only one suffering here.

"How about you?" She studied his face. "Do you feel okay?"

"I'm fine."

He shrugged, but Erin knew that meant he hadn't gotten any rest. He was simply trying to play it off, and maybe he was even worried that Erin might feel guilty over all that had happened.

He was always so considerate of her feelings, a fact she deeply appreciated.

"What time is it?" Erin rubbed her eyes again, wishing she didn't feel so groggy.

"Almost 6:00 a.m."

She let out a breath. She must have been out. On a subconscious level, she had realized she was safe with Dillon so close.

Her cheeks heated at the thought.

"I can't believe I slept that long," she murmured.

"You must have needed it."

She couldn't argue with that point. "Have you heard any updates?"

Dillon shook his head. "Unfortunately, no."

Erin pushed herself to her feet, needing a moment to compose herself. "Would it be okay if I hopped in the shower real quick?"

Dillon's perceptive eyes met hers. "Go right ahead. Maybe that will make you feel better."

She wished something as simple as a shower had that power. But all she wanted right now was Bella.

She needed her daughter.

With every day that passed, her worry only grew.

And there didn't seem to be an end in sight.

She only hoped today might provide some answers.

EIGHTEEN

Dillon instructed Carson to stay inside the house to keep an eye out for trouble. While Carson was on guard, Dillon put his boots and coat on before going outside to search for any evidence of what happened last night.

Just as Erin had told him, footprints came from the window near her bedroom.

Anger zipped through his blood at the thought of what had happened. The person behind this was brazen—a little too brazen for his comfort.

Yet the man hadn't wanted to hurt Erin. He'd only wanted to scare her. To draw out her suffering.

He pulled out his phone and took some pictures of the footprints, using a dollar bill for size. Then he continued following the footprints.

The steps led into the woods. As Dillon crossed into the tree line, memories of being whacked in the head with that shovel filled him. Each thought made his muscles tense.

His head still throbbed, but he felt better today than he had yesterday. He was grateful to be alive. He'd known people who'd lost their lives after taking blows like that.

He continued into the woods, but the footsteps became

harder to follow under the brittle canopy of branches above. They'd protected the ground below, preventing snow from reaching it. Without as much snow here, the tracks weren't as obvious.

As Dillon crossed through the small patch of woods to the street on the other side, he spotted tire prints on the edge of the road. Just as he'd expected, someone had pulled of the street, parked there, and then done their dirty deed.

This whole thing didn't make sense to Dillon.

Why go through so much trouble just to teach Erin a lesson? What kind of logic was this person following?

Unless there was something he was missing.

Dillon frowned.

He had to get to the bottom of this and soon.

Dillon headed back to the house. He'd need to change and get ready also so he could meet the rest of the search party. He hoped that maybe they could find some answers today.

Not only for Bella's sake, but for Erin's well-being also.

How many more hits could she take?

He didn't know, but she'd had more than her fill.

Erin glanced up as Dillon stepped back into the room. She quickly flipped a piece of bacon on the griddle.

"I hope you don't mind," she said. "But I figured we could both use our energy today."

"No, not at all. It smells great." He stomped his boots to get the snow off as he closed the door behind him. After hanging his coat on a rack, he strode toward her.

Erin hadn't been sure if she should cook or not. She hadn't wanted to overstep.

She'd taken a quick shower and hadn't bothered to

dry her hair. At least she had clean clothes on, and she'd brushed her teeth. Despite her doubts, Erin felt a little more alert than she had earlier.

"Anything new outside?"

When Carson had told her that Dillon had stepped out, Erin had figured he was looking for clues. But as she'd prepared breakfast, she hadn't been able to stop thinking about what Dillon might have discovered.

"I found footprints and tire prints." Dillon paused near her. "I took pictures of them, just in case."

"At least it's something." Erin wasn't sure what else to say. It wasn't exactly like she'd been expecting Dillon to catch the person responsible.

Dillon pulled out a barstool across from the kitchen island cooktop and sat down. "Can I help?"

She shook her head as she flipped another piece of bacon. "I'm fine. You can just take it easy. In fact, if you want to go get ready, our food should be done by the time you change."

He nodded and stood—almost seeming reluctant do so.

As Erin watched him walk away, her throat tightened.

Something about this arrangement felt a little too cozy. Why was Erin letting her emotions get the best of her like this? The rush of attraction she felt for Dillon threw her off balance, especially given everything else that was going on.

"Life can be pretty confusing sometimes, can't it, Scout?" She glanced down at the canine who sat at her feet, probably hoping she'd drop some food on the floor.

He raised his nose in the air and sniffed in response.

Just as she'd predicted, Dillon had finished getting ready just as Erin pulled the eggs off the burner. A few minutes later, they sat across from each other at the small dining room table, Carson joining them. After Dillon prayed, they all dug in.

Erin was especially touched by the prayer he had lifted for Bella.

Be with Bella. Keep her safe as only You can do, Lord. Wrap Your loving arms around her and give her comfort. Most of all, help us find her.

But as soon as she took her first bite, Dillon turned toward her. The serious look in his gaze indicated that something was wrong.

"Rick called just as I got out of the shower," he started.

She wiped her mouth before leaving her napkin on her lap. "And?"

Dillon's face tightened as if he were having trouble forming his words.

That couldn't be good.

"Bella's other shoe was found," he finally said. "It was located about five hundred feet from the first one."

Erin stared at him, trying to read between the lines. Trying not to jump to worst-case scenarios. Trying to stay positive.

But she had to ask… "Is that a bad sign?"

He pressed his lips together, the ends pulling down in a frown, before he finally said, "There was a small amount of blood on it."

Dillon practically inhaled his breakfast.

There was no time to waste.

As soon as he took his last bite, he stood and turned to his nephew. "Carson, I'm going to need you to utilize all that training we've been working on. You need to take Scout out there in the search for Bella."

Erin's breath caught beside him. "Why wouldn't you go? I hear you're the best."

"You're not going to be able to walk those trails." He nodded at her twisted ankle.

"Then you can go without me," she insisted.

He shook his head, knowing that wasn't going to work out for multiple reasons. "I don't want to leave you alone. Not after everything that has happened. It wouldn't be safe."

"But finding Bella is more important than my safety!" Her voice rose with each word, a haunting desperation floating through the tone.

Dillon leaned forward and squeezed her hand. "I know what you're saying. But I have another idea for us. I'd like to go talk to the Bradshaws."

Her face went still as she seemed to process that thought. "Why do you want to do that?"

"Because Burt mentioned them, and he's right. Liam worked a case against that family that could have left them with a lot of resentment toward Liam. Maybe they're the ones who did something to Liam. And maybe that wasn't enough. Maybe they want to do something to Bella also. I think we should talk to them. I'd like to do it myself and not leave it to Chief Blackstone."

Erin stared at him a moment, her eyes glimmering with uncertainty, until finally she nodded. "Okay then."

He turned his gaze back Carson who stood in the doorway. "Do you think you can handle this?"

Carson nodded quickly. "I can do it. I know I can. Thank you for trusting me with this."

"We've been through all these drills before. I have total confidence that you'll be able to handle the situation. There are going to be a lot of teams out there searching today. I heard the park service put out a call for volunteers."

"Is anyone from Boone's Hollow coming out to help?" Erin rubbed her throat as if anticipating the worst.

"I'm not sure. But I know that people from the surrounding counties are coming. There should be a good group there to scour the woods."

"I am grateful for that at least." But her voice still sounded tight.

"While they handle the search and rescue operation side, we're going to talk to the Bradshaws and see if we can get any answers from them. I know we don't need to waste any more time here. I think this is our best option."

She stared at him a moment before nodding. "Then let's do it."

NINETEEN

Erin stepped from the hallway, still gripping her phone and reeling from the conversation she'd just had. When her phone had rung, she'd stepped away for privacy.

"Erin?" Dillon glanced at her as he stood at the front door waiting.

"Bella's best friend, Gina, just called." Erin rubbed her temples as the conversation replayed in her mind. Each time made her feel like she'd been punched in the gut.

"Is everything okay?" Dillon's forehead wrinkled as he stepped closer to her.

"Gina told me the police brought her in this morning for questioning. And she…" Erin drew in a shaky breath.

Dillon squeezed her arm. "It's okay. Take your time."

Erin gulped in a deep breath, trying to keep her composure even as panic raced through her. "She told them Bella and I had been fighting lately and that I'd threatened to kick Bella out of the house."

Dillon continued to wait for her to finish, no judgment on his face. "Okay…"

She squeezed the skin between her eyes. "Bella and I have been fussing with each other recently, but it's just been the normal type of parent-teenager argument that happens. I did tell Bella that she needed to straighten up, but I had no intention of kicking her out or putting her on the street."

"So why did Gina tell the police that?"

"She said they kept pushing her. She said that she knows I'm a good mom, but the police kept pushing her to say something. Finally, she cracked." Erin closed her eyes, willing herself not to cry. There had already been too many tears.

And tears wouldn't help her find Bella. This was no time to feel sorry for herself. That would only waste time.

Concern filled Dillon's gaze. "Is that all she said?"

"She said she had the impression the police were going to bring me in for questioning again." Her voice trembled as unimaginable scenarios raced through her head. "They're going to arrest me, aren't they?"

"A verbal argument between you and Bella doesn't give them probable cause for arresting you."

Her gaze met his. "But I already have a target on my back. Who says these guys are going to play by the rules?"

"I know what you're getting at. You think they're looking for an excuse to put you behind bars."

"They've wanted to for over a year."

"We are not going to let them arrest you," Dillon finally said.

She shook her head. "I don't see how we can stop them."

"Right now, we're just going to keep doing what we'd planned on doing."

"Are you sure?" Tension threaded through her voice.

Dillon nodded. "I'm sure. Now, let's keep going. We don't have any time to waste."

Erin nodded, but her thoughts still raced.

How could Gina have said that? How could the police have kept pushing her until she did? Now she was just going to look even more guilty than she already did. People in this town were going to have another reason to hate her.

Just once Erin had thought things couldn't get worse, that's exactly what they seemed to do.

Dillon typed the Bradshaws' address into his GPS. The family consisted of three brothers—Bill, David and Samson. Each was a powerhouse in his own way, and people in town knew it was best not to mess with them. Mysterious incidents would happen if they did—slashed tires, smashed car windows, unexpected fires.

But nothing could ever be traced back to the family, though everyone knew they were guilty.

Their place was a good thirty-minute drive from here.

As he headed down the road, his thoughts continued to race.

He wondered how Carson and Scout were doing. He wanted to call to get an update, but he didn't want to interrupt the operation, either. They would contact him if they needed to.

Meanwhile, he hoped that he wasn't leading Erin right into the line of fire. He knew this family wasn't safe, but he also knew he couldn't leave Erin alone.

In an ideal situation, he would have brought backup. But since Dillon wasn't officially a cop anymore, there was no one to ask to come with him. Plus, with the suspicion that had been cast on Erin, he wasn't sure how many of his friends would be willing to help. Especially if it meant risking their career.

"Tell me about when you adopted Bella," he started.

Erin glanced up, her gaze still looking strained. "I was friends with Bella's mom in high school. Her name was Stephanie. She didn't have a good home life and had gotten involved with drugs and more of the party crowd. But I used to always help tutor her in math, so we became friends, I suppose."

"Okay…"

"We lost touch for a long time," Erin continued. "Then Bella ended up in my first-grade class. I knew her mom was having a hard time. I could see it in her eyes, and I'd heard through the grapevine that social services was on the verge of taking Bella away from her."

"What happened next?" Dillon glanced in his rearview mirror, feeling like they were being followed again. He didn't tell Erin. Not yet.

"One day, out of the blue, I got a phone call from Stephanie. She was hysterical, and I could tell that she was on something. She asked me if I would take care of Bella for her. She said she needed to go get help."

"And you said yes?"

"I did. I love Bella. Even when she was just my student, I thought she was a great kid. So I told Stephanie that her daughter could come live with me and Liam."

"What happened next?"

"Stephanie tried to get help, but it was too late. She called me again and said she wanted me to adopt Bella, that she couldn't handle being a mom anymore. I tried to convince her to keep getting help, tried to encourage her that she could change. But Stephanie wouldn't listen and insisted that Bella needed to be with me, that I was a good person. I didn't know what to say."

"What did Liam think?" Dillon asked.

"At first, he was supportive. I think it made him look good that we'd taken in a little girl and helped her out. He liked the accolades he got because of that. In fact, when I mentioned to him that we could adopt her, he was all in favor at first. I don't think he really realized what he was saying yes to."

"Was Bella troubled?"

Erin sucked in a deep breath. "She'd had a rough past, and of course that affected her. It would affect anybody. But we were working through it. Bella isn't a bad girl by any means. Like I told you earlier, it's mostly her anxiety that gets to her."

"And eventually Liam realized that and held it against you?"

Erin nodded. "His fuse just kept getting shorter and shorter. I thought he might change if we had a child in the house. That it would awaken a gentler side of him. I was wrong. He only escalated and things got worse and worse."

"But Liam never hurt Bella?"

"No, I made sure of that," Erin said. "Bella was the reason I ultimately decided I couldn't stay with Liam. I couldn't risk him ever hurting her."

"What about Bella's birth mom? Did she totally disappear after that?" Dillon glanced in his rearview mirror again. Somebody was definitely following them. The vehicle maintained a steady distance behind them.

Erin rubbed her throat as she stared out the window. "Once the adoption was finalized, I never saw her again. I still wonder what happened to her. Where she ended up. If she is still alive."

"How about Bella? Does she ask about her?"

"She did when she first came to live with me. But over

the years, the questions faded. I'm sure she still thinks about her mom, though. Who wouldn't? But perhaps she got tired of hearing the same answers."

"I'm sorry to hear that. I can only imagine that must have been really hard on her."

"It was. I hate to see a child go through that. I did what I could—I'm *doing* what I can—to give her a good life. But in so many ways, I feel like I failed her also."

He shot a quick glance at her, curious about her words. "What do you mean?"

"Maybe I should have said no to the adoption. Part of me feels like I took her from one bad situation and I put her in another." Her voice caught.

"But you did everything that you could to protect her." He understood the guilt—even if he thought the guilt wasn't justified. It just added more pain to an already difficult situation.

"Bella is gone now. Whether she ran away or if she was abducted, either way, it kind of feels like I fell down on the job, doesn't it?"

Dillon squeezed Erin's hand, wishing he could offer her some more comfort. "I know it might feel like that now, but you have to know that's not the truth."

Before she could respond, Dillon looked into the rearview mirror again and saw that the car was still there.

Somebody was definitely following them.

And it was time to end this.

Now.

Erin sucked in a breath as the Jeep suddenly skidded to a halt. The back of the vehicle fishtailed until the Jeep blocked the road.

Her eyes widened. What was happening?

She knew by the stiff set of Dillon's jaw that something was wrong.

When she glanced back, she saw a red pickup behind them.

They were being followed again, weren't they?

Not only that…but that truck looked familiar. Where had she seen it before?

"Stay here," Dillon growled.

He grabbed his gun before stepping from the Jeep and storming toward the person following them.

"Get out of the car with your hands up."

Erin held her breath as she waited to see what would play out.

After several minutes, there was still no movement.

This wasn't good. What if the driver opened fire? Or what if that person decided to ram them?

There were so many unknowns.

A moment later, the truck door opened.

Her heart throbbed in her chest.

Then a familiar face came into sight.

That's why Erin had recognized that truck.

It was Arnold, Liam's brother.

She lowered her window so she could hear what happened next.

Arnold raised his hands in the air as he scowled at Dillon. "Let's talk this through."

"You didn't seem interested in talking when you were following us just now."

Erin climbed from the Jeep and stood behind Dillon. "What are you doing, Arnold? Do you have Bella?"

He pulled his head back in shock. "Why would I have Bella?"

She started to lunge toward him when Dillon stuck his arm out to stop her from going any closer.

"Why would you do this to me? Why would you take her?"

"I didn't take Bella," Arnold said. "Why would I do that?"

"Why are you following us right now?"

He sneered. "Isn't that obvious?"

"Clearly, it isn't obvious," Dillon said. "Now, why don't you give us some answers before I take you in?"

"Last I heard, you weren't a cop anymore."

"That doesn't mean I can't march you down to the police station so they can question you there. Don't think that I won't do it."

Arnold stared at him another moment, as if trying to ascertain if he was bluffing.

He must have decided that he wasn't because he finally spoke. "I didn't take Bella. I may not like you, but that doesn't mean I want to hurt the girl. Besides, everybody knows *you're* the one who did something to her."

Fury sprang up inside her, and she fisted her hands at her sides. "Arnold, you have to know me good enough to know I'd never do something like that."

His gaze locked with hers. "You did something to my brother."

Erin's throat burned as emotions warred within her. "You know that I didn't do anything to your brother. He was the one who hurt me."

Arnold's gaze darkened. "Then you just had to exact revenge on him, didn't you?"

"If you knew he was hurting me, why didn't you try to stop him?"

Arnold's shoulders bristled. "It wasn't my place. He said you got what was coming to you."

The burning in her throat became even greater. More tears welled in her eyes, but Erin held them back. She wouldn't give Arnold the satisfaction of seeing her cry.

"You're saying that you're not the one who took Bella?" Dillon's voice sounded hard and unyielding.

Arnold crossed his burly arms over his chest. "I didn't take Bella. That's ridiculous."

"And why are you following us now?" Dillon continued.

"Because I need to let Erin know she's not going to get away with this."

Realization dawned on her. "You're the one who's been sending me those text messages, aren't you?"

Arnold said nothing.

"You probably left that message painted on the front of my house also. And you're the one who threw that bottle bomb at us."

His nostrils flared. "I just want to see justice for my brother."

Dillon bristled beside her. "Threatening Erin isn't the way to do it."

She heard the anger—and protectiveness—simmering in Dillon's voice.

"I can't let her get away with it," Arnold growled as he glowered at them.

"I think you know, if you look deep inside yourself, that Erin isn't guilty of this," Dillon said. "Now, you're just hindering our search for Bella. You're hindering our search for an innocent sixteen-year-old girl who's probably been abducted. I hope you can live with yourself knowing that."

Arnold's gaze darkened again, but he said nothing for a few minutes. "I didn't do it. I have chronic obstructive pulmonary disease. You know I do. There's no way I could have carried out a plan like this. Besides, I was at a doctor's appointment in Asheville the day she disappeared."

Erin let his words sink in. That seemed provable enough.

But she still didn't like this man and didn't want him around. He was dangerous in his own way.

"If I see you around one more time, I'll be calling in all the favors I'm owed by the local law enforcement community." Dillon's voice sounded hard, like he wasn't someone to be questioned. "Don't think I won't do it. Do you understand?"

Arnold stared at him a moment before nodding. "Understood."

TWENTY

As they continued down the road, Dillon's pulse raced.

That man had a lot of nerve.

He wished he had the power to arrest him now. But they had more important matters to attend to. At least they now knew where those texts had come from along with the message on Erin's house.

Was Arnold the person who'd tried to run them off the road? Dillon's gut told him no. He'd thought that vehicle had been gray, and this man's truck was clearly a bright red.

Was he the one who had been in the woods? Who'd thrown the bomb?

"Are you doing okay?" He glanced at Erin.

Certainly, that whole conversation had shaken her up. It would shake anybody up.

She crossed her arms over her chest and shrugged. "Hate can do horrible things to people, can't it?"

"Yes, it can. I'm sorry you have to be on the receiving end of that."

Before they could say any more, Dillon's phone rang and he saw that it was Rick.

He hit the talk button, and the man's voice came out through his Jeep's speakers.

"Hey, Rick," Dillon started. "I'm here with Erin."

"Good. I can talk to both of you at once. There are a couple of updates I want to give you."

"What's going on?" Dillon waited, hoping for good news. But by the sound of his friend's voice, he wasn't sure that's what they were going to get.

"First, I just heard through the grapevine that Blackstone got a warrant to search Erin's house. He's probably going to take her computer and look for any evidence that she may have done something to Bella."

A muffled cry escape from Erin beside him.

Dillon frowned.

Another hit. How many more could she take?

"I also wanted to let you know that we got our official report from the medical examiner," Rick said. "The body that we found in the forest that day wasn't Liam's."

Erin gasped. "What? But the necklace…"

"It appears that somebody placed the necklace on the body. Maybe they did that just to throw us off."

"Then whose body was it?" Dillon asked.

"It belonged to a drifter named Mark Pearson. He went missing about fifteen months ago, not long before Liam went missing."

"How did he die?"

"It looks like he had a head injury. He was known for his involvement in drugs. That probably played a role also."

"Thanks for letting us know."

"Where are you now?" Rick asked.

"We're headed to see the Bradshaws and give them a visit."

"The Bradshaws? Be careful. They're not a family that you want to mess with."

Dillon's spine tightened at his friend's reminder. "I know. We'll watch our backs."

"If you need anything, let me know."

Dillon rubbed his jaw. "We will."

Erin's heart continued to race.

That body wasn't Liam's.

She still didn't have confirmation about whether he was dead or alive.

Sometimes, she just wanted an answer. Living with the unknown was too hard. At least if that had been Liam's dead body, she could put that part of her life to rest.

Now the possibility still remained that he was alive and out there somewhere.

Otherwise, things didn't make sense. Why would Liam have run away and hidden? For this long, too?

He was the type of person who loved people. He loved being the center of attention, and he wasn't the type who wanted to hide in a cave for an indefinite period of time. If he was doing that, he was desperate.

"What are you thinking?" Dillon's voice snapped Erin from her thoughts.

"I'm just trying to process all this."

"I understand."

"I can't believe the police are searching my house. Then again, I shouldn't be surprised." She rubbed the sides of her arms, suddenly feeling chilled.

"That's pretty standard in investigations like this," he said. "They always look at family first."

She shook her head, feeling half numb inside. "They're not going to find anything—unless somebody has planted something."

A sick feeling filled her gut. What if that were the

case? Given everything else that had gone wrong, it did seem like a possibility. Somebody wanted to make her look guilty. This could just be another way of making her suffer.

"Let's not think about that. Let's wait and see what happens next."

She nodded, knowing she had no choice but to do exactly that.

Dillon pulled up to a house that was set off the road on a long lane. The log cabin, which looked almost like a lodge, had probably cost a pretty penny. Yet despite its massive appearance, the place wasn't well cared for. Too much trash was outside. Too many cars in the driveway. The lawn was too unmanicured.

As Dillon parked the Jeep, he turned to Erin. "Stay here while I talk to them. Whatever you do, don't get out."

Erin heard the warning in his voice and knew that he wasn't messing around.

But before Dillon could even open the door, gunfire rang through the air.

"Get down!" Dillon shouted.

They ducked below the dash as more bullets filled the air.

The Bradshaws were shooting at them.

Dillon could feel the adrenaline pumping through him.

He drew his own gun as he tried to figure out his next move.

He hadn't come this far to leave now. But he didn't want to put Erin in danger, either.

At a pause in the rounds of ammunition, Dillon raised his head. "I'm just here to talk!"

"Who are you?" one of the men yelled back.

"My name is Dillon Walker."

"What do you want?"

"I want to talk to you about Liam Lansing."

Silence stretched as he waited for the man's response. Finally, the man said, "What do you want to know?"

"We want to know if you know what happened to him," Dillon said.

"Why would I know that?"

Dillon raised his head again. "Look, can we just talk? Without any guns?"

The man was silent another moment until he finally said, "Come up to the porch. But don't try anything or there will be consequences."

Dillon glanced at Erin again. He didn't like this and knew things could go south fast. "Listen, if anything happens, I want you to get behind the wheel and drive away as fast as you can. Do you understand?"

"Dillon…" Her voice cracked with worry.

His gaze met hers. "I mean it. I don't want you getting hurt. Bella is going to need you when she's found. Do you understand?"

Erin stared at him, emotions filling her gaze until she finally nodded. "Okay."

He climbed out and started toward the house.

As he did, he felt the tension thrumming inside him. Would this guy do what he had said? Criminals in general couldn't be trusted. Dillon hoped he wasn't walking into an ambush.

Bill Bradshaw stepped onto the porch, a shotgun in his hands. The man was in his fifties, with short silver-threaded hair and a hooded gaze.

He was well seasoned in his life of crime. He had whole networks of people working for him. Even though his home wasn't well maintained, it probably had cost more than a million dollars. Money wasn't an object for him. His drug business clearly paid well.

"What do you want to know about Liam?" Bill asked, a cold, hardened look in his gaze.

"His daughter is missing," Dillon said.

"I heard that. But I still don't know what this has to do with me."

"We're wondering if there's a connection between their disappearances."

Bill raised a shoulder and scowled. "Why would I know?"

"I heard that you have some bad history."

"He tried to arrest us, if that's what you're talking about." Bill's eyes narrowed. "Do you think I killed him?"

"We have no idea what's happened. But we wonder if Liam's disappearance is somehow connected with the disappearance of his daughter Bella. Bella's mom is worried sick, and I'm just trying to find some answers."

The man stared at him, his eyes narrowing even more. "You were one of those state cops, weren't you?"

The fact that this man knew that fact didn't surprise Dillon. Bill probably studied all the local police departments so he would know what he was up against in case something tried to come between him and his drug operations.

"Is there anything you know that might help us to find him?" Dillon asked.

"I don't want that guy found. I don't help cops."

"So you don't know anything?"

He continued to stare at Dillon.

He *did* know something, Dillon realized. But what?

"Now I need you to get off my property," Bill growled.

"Just a few more questions—"

"I need you to get off my property now."

Dillon stared at him and heard the warning in his voice.

But as he took a step back, more gunfire rang out.

He spotted one of the Bradshaw sons in the window— holding a gun.

Dillon needed to get out of there. Now.

TWENTY-ONE

Erin heard more bullets being shot and gasped.

She'd promised Dillon she'd leave at the first sign of trouble.

A promise was a promise.

But she couldn't leave him here. He'd be a sitting duck.

Quickly, she climbed into the driver's seat, trying to remember everything she could about driving a stick shift. She'd learned in high school, but that seemed like a long time ago now.

With her hand on the gearshift and foot on the clutch, she managed to get the Jeep into first gear.

She nibbled on her bottom lip and had to make a quick split-second decision.

Leave or help Dillon?

It was a no-brainer.

Releasing the clutch and pressing the accelerator, she charged toward the house in front of her.

She wasn't leaving Dillon behind.

As she got closer to Dillon, she slowed and opened the door. "Get in!"

Dillon's eyes widened, but he dove inside.

Before he closed the door, she did a quick U-turn and charged back down the lane.

As she did, a bullet pierced the back glass, shattering it.

But as long as she and Dillon were okay, that was all that mattered.

Keeping her foot on the accelerator, Erin shifted the gears again and drove as fast as she could to get away from the house.

She had to keep Dillon safe and she had to stay alive in order to help Bella. Those were her only two goals right now.

She turned back onto the street just as Dillon sat up and jerked on his seat belt.

"I told you to leave," he muttered.

"I did leave. I just picked you up first."

He shook his head before a laugh escaped.

A laugh? That wasn't what she had been expecting.

"You have a lot of guts, Erin. Don't let anybody ever tell you that you don't."

"I'm glad you made it out okay. But did you find out anything in the process?"

His eyes softened with concern. "Not really. They definitely know something, but the Bradshaws aren't going to share what it is."

"I remember overhearing a few things and thinking that Liam and this family were mortal enemies. Maybe *they* did do something to Liam."

Dillon leaned back. "Did the police ever look into them?"

"It's hard to say." Erin let out a sigh. "What now?"

"Let's head back into town, and maybe stop to grab a quick bite to eat in the process."

"But first, we're going to switch seats. No way am I going to try to drive this up the mountain."

He grinned. "I think you're doing a pretty good job."

"Then I need to stop while I'm ahead."

What Erin had done was risky. But it may have saved his life. If she hadn't had the nerve to drive by and pick him up, he could be dead right now.

What she had done had also meant that she could have been hurt. And that wasn't okay.

As she pulled off onto the side of the road, Dillon climbed out to switch seats with her. As their paths crossed behind the Jeep, he paused and grasped her elbow.

"Thank you." His voice came out throatier than he had intended.

Her cheeks turned a shade of red. "It's no problem. You would have done it for me."

"You're right. I would have."

Their gazes caught and, for a moment, all he wanted to do was lean down and press his lips into hers.

The urge surprised him. It was so unexpected.

All of this was.

A search and rescue case had turned his life upside down once. Now it appeared that another case might turn his life upside down again. Maybe it wouldn't be in a bad way this time.

Right now, he needed to concentrate on finding Bella.

Dillon cleared his throat, wishing it was that easy to also clear his thoughts.

"It's cold out here," he finally said. "We should probably get back in the car."

Erin stared up at him, something swirling in the depths of her eyes. She felt it, too, didn't she? Dillon had a feeling she was in the same boat that he was.

She wasn't looking for a relationship. It sounded like

the one relationship she'd had in her life had put her through the ringer.

He swallowed hard again before stepping back. "Let's get inside. You've got to be hungry. Maybe we'll grab a quick bite to eat and then we can keep looking."

Erin seemed to startle out of her daze as she nodded at him. "Sounds like a plan."

They both climbed back into the Jeep, and he took off down the road.

As he did, his thoughts raced.

It seemed as if they could rule out Arnold as being involved. But Dillon would guess that whoever was behind this wasn't a stranger. This seemed too personal for that. It wasn't about money; when a stranger was involved in a crime like this, it was usually for financial reasons. Erin clearly did not have much cash.

So if they ruled out Arnold, who did that leave? Could the Bradshaws be involved? It seemed like there was a good chance, but what would their motive be?

There was still a lot they needed to figure out.

He stared at the road in front of him. There was another town near, one adjacent to Boone's Hollow. Dillon knew of a diner where he and Erin could grab a quick meal before they continued looking for more answers.

Part of him was looking forward to spending more time with Erin and getting to know her even more.

What would the future hold when this was over?

Dillon didn't know. But he did know that the most important thing was that when this was all over, Bella was safe.

Erin glanced at the restaurant in front of her. Surprisingly, she'd never been here. She wasn't much for going out to eat, not when she could cook things on her own.

Besides, that was the way Liam liked it, and she'd tried to respect his wishes.

"They have great BLTs if you're interested," Dillon said.

"That sounds great." As if in response, Erin's stomach rumbled. She was clearly hungrier than she'd thought. Maybe all this danger had worked up an appetite.

It had certainly worked up questions within her.

As soon as they stepped inside, the scent of comfort foods filled her senses. Was that roast beef? Gravy? Maybe even chocolate?

She couldn't be sure, but whatever the scents were, they were alluring.

"What do you think?" Dillon glanced at her. "Do you want to sit down for a few minutes and regroup? Or should we get this to go?"

Erin glanced at her watch. "I suppose that if we can eat something quickly, we can stay."

It was always good to recalculate and figure out the next step. Plus, this wasn't Boone's Hollow. Maybe she could grab a bite to eat without everyone scrutinizing her like they did back in her hometown.

The waitress led them to a seat in the corner and handed them laminated menus. But Erin didn't even need to look at it. She would get a BLT just as Dillon had suggested. That selection sounded good.

She glanced around the outdated but friendly-looking restaurant before turning back to Dillon. "Do you eat here a lot?"

"Not really. But on occasion I want a meal that reminds me of Grandma's. When I do, this is where I come."

Erin wanted to engage in simple chitchat, but her heart wasn't in it. Not when so much was on the line.

Instead, she said, "Can we review everything we know?"

"Of course." Dillon shifted across from her.

Erin's mind raced through everything as she tried to sort through her thoughts. "So this is what we have so far. Bella disappeared when she went to school three days ago. Her car was found in a parking lot near a trailhead. A body was found on the trail, but it belongs to a drifter and doesn't appear to be connected to the case other than the necklace found on the corpse."

"Correct," Dillon said.

"Meanwhile, Arnold sent me threatening texts as well as left a message painted on the front of my house," she continued. "He also threw that bomb."

"Also correct."

"One of Bella's shoes was found twenty miles away, at a different section of the park. Five hundred feet from that, her other shoe was found. In the meantime, there's been no real contact."

"That sounds accurate."

She frowned and nibbled on her bottom lip for a moment. "Somebody's also been trying to run us off the road, watching us from the woods, they've shot at us, and that man was in my room last night."

Dillon reached across the table and squeezed her hand. "Unfortunately, all of those things are correct. Someone certainly is weaving a tangled web."

"Yes, they are. And when you put it all together, what do you have?"

"That's the million-dollar question. Who could possibly be behind this?"

His question hung in the air.

Erin heard the door jangle open behind her and glanced over her shoulder.

The person who stepped inside made her eyes widen.

She pulled away from Dillon's grasp and stared at the woman.

"Erin?" Dillon said from across the table. "Do you know that person?"

Erin nodded, her thoughts still reeling. "That's Stephanie. Bella's birth mom."

TWENTY-TWO

Dillon felt himself bristle as Erin stared at the woman who'd stepped into the restaurant.

He had a feeling he knew who this woman was.

Stephanie—Bella's birth mother. The two looked like each other and this woman was in the right age range.

As if to confirm his gut feeling, Erin muttered, "Stephanie?"

He was right. So what was Stephanie doing there?

He tensed as he waited to see what would happen next.

The woman's gaze latched on to Erin. Stephanie had obviously known Erin was there and had come to find her. But how had she known that? Had she been following them?

His muscles tightened even more at the thought.

The woman ambled toward their table now.

She had straight blonde hair that was pulled into a sloppy ponytail, and wore faded jeans and an oversized sweatshirt. The gaunt expression on her face, combined with her thinning hair and dull eyes, seemed to indicate a history with drug abuse—in Dillon's experience, at least. Her red-rimmed eyes showed grief…and maybe more.

"Erin…" She paused at the edge of their table, her hands fluttering nervously in the air.

"Stephanie." Erin's eyes widened with surprise. "What are you doing here?"

"I… I needed to talk to you. I heard what happened and…"

"Of course." Erin scooted over in the booth and patted the space beside her. "Have a seat. Let's talk."

Stephanie carefully perched herself there, but her body language seemed to indicate she could run at any minute. Her muscles were stiff. Her gaze continually drifted back to the window. Her fingers flexed and unflexed.

Dillon leaned forward to introduce himself. "I'm Dillon, a friend of Erin's. I'm trying to help her find Bella."

Stephanie frowned and nodded. "I know. I've been keeping an eye on things ever since I heard the news about Bella. I know that probably sounds strange, and I don't want to come across as creepy. I just didn't know what to do or if I should approach the two of you or not."

Erin reached over and squeezed the woman's arm. "We're doing our best to find Bella. I promise we are."

Stephanie used the sleeve of her sweatshirt and rubbed beneath her eyes as if wiping away unshed tears. "I know you are. I know that the scuttlebutt around town is that you may have done something to Bella. But I know that's not the truth."

"I would never hurt her." Erin's voice caught.

"I can't believe people would say that you would. I know you love her."

Erin placed a hand over her heart as relief filled her gaze. "I can't even tell you how relieved I am to hear you say that. I know you trusted me with your daughter, and I'd never want to let you down."

Stephanie sniffled and stared out the window before

drawing in a shaky breath. "Giving Bella up was a hard decision. But I know that it was the right one, even with everything that's happened."

"So why did you come find me now?"

Stephanie ran a hand over the top of her head. "I want to do whatever I can to help. I don't just want to sit back and pretend like this doesn't affect me."

"You haven't heard anything, have you?" Dillon asked. "Or seen anything?"

"No. I wish I had something to offer you. But I don't."

Disappointment filled his chest cavity, even though he'd expected that response. "I understand."

"We need to find her." Stephanie's voice cracked as her gaze connected with Dillon's. "What if she's hurt? What if someone took her?"

"That's what we're trying to figure out," Dillon assured her.

"Or what if she's just like me? What if she ran, trying to escape all her problems?" Her expression pinched with pain.

Her words hung in the air.

Her questions were valid. There were a lot of variables in place here.

And time was quickly running out.

As Erin and Dillon headed back down the road, Erin's thoughts wandered.

On one hand, it was a relief to know that Stephanie didn't blame her for what had happened. That Stephanie thought she was a good mother. That she didn't regret her decision to let Erin adopt Bella.

On the other hand, the fact that Stephanie had shown up now of all times made Erin cautious. She hadn't seen the woman in years. Stephanie had smelled slightly of alcohol and cigarettes. And she'd looked so nervous.

Was that because Bella was missing? Or was there more to the story?

"That was surprising," Dillon said beside her, almost as if he could read her thoughts.

"You can say that again."

"I hate to ask this, but I feel like I need to. Do you think Stephanie could have anything to do with Bella's disappearance?"

Erin blinked as she processed his question. "I don't think Stephanie's the violent type, if that's what you're asking."

"No, but do you think there could be more to this?"

The implications of his question hit her. "Wait...you think that maybe this is all a scheme? That Stephanie wants Bella back, so she snatched her?"

Dillon shrugged. "It makes sense, and it wouldn't be the first time that something like that has happened."

Erin swung her head back and forth. "I just can't see her doing that."

"The timing is uncanny."

"I can't argue with that. But I just don't know... I don't want to think she's capable of doing something like that."

"I just want you to be careful," Dillon said. "It's hard to know who to trust with everything that's happened."

"I know. And I appreciate your concern."

Silence stretched between them for a moment.

Finally, Erin glanced back over at him. "Where are we going?"

"I need to swing by the house and check on the dogs since Carson isn't there. It will only take a few minutes."

She nodded. "Of course. Have you heard any updates?"

"Unfortunately, no. But everyone is still searching. That's good news."

Erin stared out the window, trying not to be bothered by the conversation. But she knew Dillon had to ask about Stephanie's sudden appearance. He wasn't the type to skirt around the fact that Stephanie could have ulterior motives.

A few minutes later, they pulled up to his house. Erin scanned the buildings and woods around them to make sure there were no signs of danger. Everything looked clear.

For now.

After all that had happened, they had to be careful. Danger could be hiding around any corner.

Dillon parked his Jeep and turned to her. "Let's do this. And then we'll figure out our next steps."

Erin nodded, but tension still coursed through her.

She was growing more and more anxious by the moment.

Dillon escorted Erin inside so she could freshen up. Once he'd secured the doors and made sure everything was safe, he headed outside to the kennel to check on the dogs.

As he did, Erin slipped into the bathroom and stared at herself in the mirror. This experience seemed to have aged her. She didn't remember dark circles beneath their eyes before. Didn't remember looking so tired or her hair looking so dull.

She leaned against the sink and closed her eyes. *Dear Lord, please help Bella right now. Help us to find her. Lead us to her. Please. I'm desperate, and I'm sorry for those times that I've doubted You. Because right now, I know I'm not going to get through this without You.*

After muttering, "Amen," Erin opened her eyes and splashed some water in her face before wiping it dry with a towel. She'd promised Dillon she would wait inside until he came back just as a precaution.

As she wandered toward the living room, her phone buzzed.

She looked down at the screen and the words that she saw there made her blood go cold.

If you want to see Bella alive, meet me at the Buckhead Trailhead. Come alone. Or else.

Her heart pounded in her ears. Was this for real?

Erin knew that it was. The number wasn't the same one Arnold had used to send her those other threats.

This had most likely been sent by the person who'd abducted Bella.

Erin nibbled on her bottom lip as she thought through her options. Clearly, she didn't have a vehicle here. Her own car was in the shop, the tires being replaced.

Maybe she should just tell Dillon. Maybe he could help her figure something out.

The instructions were explicit. The sender had said Erin had to come alone.

And the penalty if she didn't?

Bella would be hurt—or worse.

It was a risk she couldn't take.

But how was Erin going to meet anyone without a vehicle?

As the question fluttered through her mind, her gaze fell on the keys Dillon had left on the kitchen counter.

The keys to his Jeep.

She swallowed hard before glancing out the window to where the dog kennel was located.

Dillon was still inside. Still out of sight. Still occupied.

Erin thought about her decision only a moment before grabbing the keys.

She could slip outside and borrow his Jeep.

Dillon would be angry with her. Erin knew he would be. Really angry.

But she had to do this for Bella.

She had no other option.

Before she could second-guess herself, Erin started for the door.

She prayed this was the right choice.

TWENTY-THREE

As an unexpected noise sounded in the distance, Dillon rushed from the kennel.

As he did, he saw his Jeep pulling from the driveway. His Jeep?

He darted toward his house, praying that Erin was safe.

After searching inside, he knew she was gone.

Realization spread through him.

Erin had taken his Jeep, hadn't she? Why would she do that?

Was she setting out to find Bella on her own?

The thought of her doing that sent concern ricocheting through him.

There had to be more to this story.

But Dillon didn't have time to ponder that. Right now, he needed to catch her and find out what was going on.

He darted to his desk and pulled the drawer open. After riffling through paperclips and notepads, he finally found what he was looking for.

The keys to a truck he kept inside his barn.

He grabbed them before sprinting outside, yanking the barn doors wide, and climbing into the old truck.

After a few tries, the old truck engine finally rumbled to life. He eased through the open doors and made his way to the end of his driveway, he headed to the right, the same direction Erin had traveled.

But a few minutes later, when he reached a T in the road, Dillon realized he had no idea which direction she'd gone.

He contemplated his choices for a minute.

If he went to the left, it would lead him to the national forest where Bella was last seen.

If he had to guess, that was the direction Erin had headed.

Dillon jerked the wheel that way. As he did, he prayed—prayed that Erin was safe. That she would use wisdom. That God would protect her.

What could have happened to lead her to do something like this? Whatever it was, certainly Erin didn't realize what kind of situation she might be getting herself into right now.

Most likely, she was headed directly into danger. Whoever had taken Bella wouldn't stop until they got what they wanted. Dillon feared that what this person wanted was to make Erin suffer more and more.

It looked like Erin might be giving them that opportunity.

Now the challenge would be figuring out exactly what part of the national forest she might have headed toward. The place was large—500,000 acres—with uncountable trailheads. There was no way Dillon would be able to cover them all.

He had to figure out what he was going to do…and fast.

Erin felt the sweat across her brow as she headed down the road.

She prayed she was making the right choice. Prayed she wasn't making a bad situation worse.

What if she was playing right into the hands of the person who'd taken Bella? She knew there was a good chance she was.

But she'd sacrifice whatever necessary if it meant Bella would be safe.

She wiped her forehead with the sleeve of her sweatshirt before shifting gears as the Jeep climbed higher up the mountain.

It had been a rough ride. But she was doing okay.

Now she just needed to make it up this mountain.

And find the Buckhead Trail.

She should have looked up an address before she'd left, but she hadn't thought about it. She'd had to leave right then before Dillon stopped her. She'd had no time to waste.

Dillon...she frowned. She hadn't realized until now just how much she truly cared about that man.

But she did.

Even though it was crazy that her feelings had grown so quickly in such a short period of time, that's exactly what had happened.

Dillon had been a rock for her. He'd cared about her when no one else had. And he hadn't doubted her story.

She wiped beneath her eyes.

Please, Lord, keep him safe. Don't let my decision hurt him. Help him forgive me.

She muttered an amen and then pulled herself together. Right now, Erin had to concentrate on Bella. Everything else she would deal with later.

What would the person who'd sent her the text do when Erin arrived? Take her to Bella? Kill her on the spot?

She had so many questions, so much that didn't make sense.

There were too many possible players in this scheme, and Erin didn't know which one might be behind this.

Whoever it was wanted to make Erin pay. She just didn't know what mistakes this penance was for.

Her hands gripped the wheel, white-knuckled.

The mountain road was steep, and as she traveled to a higher elevation, the air became cooler. The road became icier.

You can do this, Erin!

She gave herself a mental pep talk. But the higher she climbed, the more her anxiety grew.

She should have told Dillon. Coming alone had been a bad idea. With every turn of the wheel, that seemed more and more clear. But there was no going back now. Erin doubted she even had any phone reception at this point.

More sweat beaded across her skin.

Finally, she spotted a sign on the side of the road.

Buckhead Trail.

It was only a mile away. She was getting closer.

She continued up the mountain, shifting gears and praying she could figure this out.

Finally, she reached the parking area for the trail.

She was here.

Erin let out a breath, even though she knew her trouble was probably just beginning.

The person who'd texted her had said for her to come alone. It was too late to change her mind now.

She'd followed the instructions and played by the rules.

Now maybe she could get Bella back.

She parked the Jeep and sat there a moment, her heart racing.

What next?

She glanced at her phone, but it was as she'd expected. She didn't have any reception.

How would she get her next set of instructions?

She leaned back and waited, her heart pounding in her ears.

Waiting would be the hardest part, especially if she started to second-guess herself.

As another car pulled into the parking lot, she sucked in a breath. Who else was here?

Her eyes widened as the vehicle came into focus.

It was a police car.

The cops were here?

Had they tracked her down so they could arrest her?

She pressed her eyes closed.

No.

Not now.

Not when she was so close.

Dear Lord...what am I going to do?

As she saw the door open and someone step out, she braced herself and tried to figure out how to handle this situation.

With every mile that went past, Dillon's worry grew.

Where had Erin gone? What had happened to make her do this?

Dillon only prayed he found her in time.

So far, he'd checked out every road that pulled off from this main one. But the task was tedious and taking too much time.

If only he knew where Erin was.

If he had more time, he could search his Jeep's GPS to see where the vehicle was located. But to do that he would need to go back to his house. For now, he would keep searching in his truck.

There were entirely too many pull-offs in this area. Working this way would take forever. But he had little choice right now.

He studied each of the various trailhead signs as he passed, wondering if Erin may have decided to go search by herself. With her ankle being sprained and conditions being what they were, it sounded like a terrible idea.

Plus, he'd just heard while checking on his dogs that another snowstorm was headed this way. The last thing Erin needed to do was to be stuck on this mountain during a storm in her present condition.

He had to admire her determination as a mom. He knew that mothers were protective of their kids, and Erin had proven that to be true.

Dillon hoped there was a good solution for the situation, one where Bella would be rescued and Erin would be okay.

He shook his head as he pulled onto another lane branching from the main road that wound through the mountains.

Erin should have told him what was going on. She should have never left on her own.

Just as those thoughts raced through his head, he spotted a vehicle in the distance.

His breath caught.

Was that his Jeep?

He pressed the accelerator harder as he headed toward it. Quickly, he pulled up behind it and then rushed to the front doors. He already knew what he would most likely find inside.

He was right.

Nothing. No one.

Erin wasn't here.

He bit back a frown.

He glanced around at the trees surrounding him.

Where had Erin gone?

As he stepped back, he spotted another set of tire tracks in the space beside the Jeep.

Erin had met somebody here.

But who?

Could Arnold really be guilty? Was he working with someone to teach Erin a lesson?

Or what about Stephanie? What if she really was involved?

Or there was always the Bradshaws. They had a long history of crime and violence.

He wouldn't put anything past that family.

It almost seemed like there were too many possible suspects.

There was no way Dillon would be able to track down all these people on his own.

He was going to need to call in backup.

As soon as he got phone reception, he would talk to Rick and find out what his friend could do to help.

Because something was majorly wrong here.

And if Dillon didn't get to the bottom of it soon, he feared Erin may not make it out of this situation alive.

Erin felt her throat tighten as she sat in the back seat of the police cruiser. She'd tried to explain that she couldn't leave. Tried to convince the officer that this was a mistake, that she was innocent.

But Officer Hollins hadn't listened.

Instead, she'd been placed in the back of the police car like a criminal.

Panic fluttered up inside her as the officer backed out and started down the road.

"How did you find me?" Her voice squeaked as the words left her lips.

"We've been watching you." Hollins glanced back at her. "Be glad I'm the one who finally tracked you down and not Blackstone. He's furious, and he has a major chip on his shoulder."

"He's had a chip on his shoulder for a long time." Erin shifted and glanced out the window.

As she did, more panic rose in her. How was she ever going to find Bella now? Her one opportunity had slipped away. She hated the helpless feeling swirling inside her.

"Hollins, you've got to listen to me." She leaned forward so he could hear the desperation in her voice. Her argument hadn't worked the first time, but maybe it would now. "If you don't let me meet the person I was supposed to meet, they're going to do something to Bella."

"What do you mean?" Officer Hollins glanced back at her in the rearview mirror.

"I got a text saying I had to meet whoever had taken Bella at that location. If I'm not there, I don't know what's going to happen to her."

He continued to stare at the road ahead. "I can send an officer out."

"You can't do that. It had to be me." Her voice came out higher pitched and louder with each word.

"I told the chief that I would bring you in. He'll figure something out."

"You know that's not true. You know he thinks I'm part of this." Despair bit deep into her.

"You're just going to have to trust us."

But that was part of the problem. Erin *didn't* trust them. It was why she'd had to take matters into her own hands.

Erin squeezed her eyes shut. She desperately wished that Dillon was there right now. He would know what to do.

But she'd made the decision to go without him, and now she had to live with it.

She hoped this wasn't the biggest mistake of her life.

She slowly opened her eyes again, trying to regain her focus. "What are you going to do with me?"

"I'm going to take you into the station for questioning. The chief said he found something on your computer."

Alarm raced through her as questions collided in her mind. "On my computer? There was nothing on my computer."

Had Erin been set up again? When would the hits stop coming?

"I'm just telling you what I heard," Hollins said. "I'll do everything I can to make sure Blackstone handles this in the right way."

At least Officer Hollins had picked her up. At least he was one of the good guys.

But there was so little positive Erin could see in this situation.

As Hollins turned off the street onto another road, Erin's spine straightened. "This isn't the way to the police station."

"I just need to make a quick stop first."

"A quick stop? Where?"

"You'll see."

But as Hollins said the words, a bad feeling grew in Erin's gut.

There was more to the story, wasn't there?

The truth nagged at her, but she didn't want to face it. Didn't want to think she could be right.

Instead, she braced herself for whatever would happen next.

TWENTY-FOUR

As soon as Dillon got reception, he called Rick and gave him the update. Rick promised to keep his eyes open and to alert the other park rangers that Erin might be missing. He also told Dillon there were no updates out on the trail and that the teams were going to head back soon.

It was a double set of bad news.

Before he ended the call, Dillon asked one more question. "Is Blackstone with you?"

"No, he's not out here today," Rick said. "He said he's manning the station. Why?"

"I'll explain later."

Dillon knew exactly where he needed to head next. He had to talk to Blackstone and let him know what was going on. Even if the man didn't take him seriously, there was no way Dillon could find Erin on his own. He needed help.

As he continued down the road, Dillon made a few more phone calls. He let his colleagues with the state police also know what was going on so that everybody could have their eyes open for Erin.

A bad feeling brewed in Dillon's gut as he thought about the possibilities of what had happened.

What if the person Erin had met in the parking lot was the same person who had taken Bella?

It was clear this person wanted to make Erin suffer. If Bella's abductor had been able to finally snatch Erin, maybe this would fulfill the last step of his plan.

Yet there were other things that didn't make sense. The person behind this had the opportunity to grab Erin after breaking into Dillon's house. Why hadn't he? Maybe he had some kind of weird timing he wanted to follow.

It was hard to always predict how criminals thought. But in this case, this guy obviously had some type of agenda.

And Erin was at the center of it.

Dillon's gut clenched as he thought about it.

Finally, Dillon arrived at the police station. He quickly threw the truck into Park before hurrying inside. He bypassed the reception area and barged right into Chief Blackstone's office.

The man looked up at him and narrowed his eyes when he saw Dillon standing there.

"Can I help you?" Blackstone's voice sounded tense with irritation.

"Erin is missing."

His eyebrows flickered up. "Is she missing? Or did she sneak away to go check on Bella?"

Anger surged through Dillon. "You know Erin's not responsible for this. You just want to make her pay because Liam disappeared."

"You don't know what you're talking about."

"It's as plain as day that that's the case. I think somebody may have taken Erin. Most likely the person who took Bella."

Blackstone tapped his finger on his desk. "Why would they want both of them?"

"Clearly, it's because someone has some type of agenda. I need your help."

Blackstone shrugged. "I'm not sure what I can do. Most of my guys are out on the trails right now, looking for Bella. If Erin had just told us where she had taken her…"

Dillon slammed his hand onto the chief's desk. "You need to listen to me. Somebody took Erin and Bella, and we've got to find them before it's too late. Do you understand that?"

The chief stared at him for another moment. "I hear what you're saying."

"And what are you going to do about it?" Dillon hated to speak to the chief like that, but being nice wasn't cutting it with this man. He had to let him know he meant business.

Blackstone rose from his seat. "I'll let my other guys know what's going on, and they can be on the lookout."

At least that was something. But Dillon needed more. "Can you try to trace her cell phone signal?"

He stared at Dillon a moment, and Dillon braced himself for whatever he was going to say.

But finally, Blackstone nodded. "Let me see what I can do."

As Hollins pulled off onto a side road, Erin's heart went into her throat.

"Where are you taking me?" she demanded. Her fingers dug into the seat beneath her as tension curled her muscles.

"It's like I told you. I just need to make a quick stop."

"Hollins…"

"Stop asking questions." His voice hardened.

As soon as she heard his words, Erin realized her worst fears were true.

Hollins was part of this somehow, wasn't he?

She leaned toward the plastic divide separating them. "You don't have to do this."

He didn't bother to look at her. "I don't know what you're talking about."

"I thought that you were my friend."

One of his shoulders tensed, rising slightly as he sat there. "You did wrong by Liam."

Wait… Hollins was doing this to honor his friend? Was that what this was all about? "Hollins…you don't know this whole story. You only know what Liam told you."

"You adopted Bella and then you kicked Liam out of the house. You took everything he'd worked so hard for. Liam tried everything to get you back."

"There's more to that story," Erin rushed to insist.

She glanced at the door handle, wanting to grab it and yank it open. But she knew the door was locked, and she couldn't open it from the inside.

There was no way out of this car.

She tried to push down the panic that wanted to bubble up inside her.

"I'm sure you're going to say he treated you badly," Hollins said. "That's what people always say."

"But Liam *did* treat me badly. I'm not even just talking about yelling at me. He hurt me, Hollins."

His jaw tightened. "He would never do that. He's a good man."

"Whatever you think you need to do right now, you

don't have to do it," Erin told him, praying she might be able to convince him to change his mind.

"Yes, I do."

Erin swallowed hard, trying to think through ways she might convince him to change his mind. No good ideas hit her. Maybe she needed more information first.

"Are you the one who broke into Dillon's house and threatened me?"

He finally glanced over his shoulder and shrugged. "I wanted to send you a message."

"Why not just kill me there and get all of this over with?"

"Kill you?" His eyes widened. "You think that's our goal?"

Erin didn't miss the fact that he'd used the word *our*. Who else was a part of this? "What else would you want to do?"

"Plenty. You'll see. You're asking too many questions."

"Hollins…"

"Enough!" He sliced his hand through the air. "Enough talking. Anything else you want to know, you're just going to have to wait. Understand?"

Erin leaned back in her seat and stared at the forest as they traveled deeper and deeper into the woods.

How could Hollins be involved in this? Did he really want to make Erin pay this badly for what he perceived as a slight against his friend?

How was she going to get herself out of the situation? Especially considering the fact that she wouldn't be able to run, not with her hurt foot.

Hollins pulled to a stop at the end of the lane.

There was nothing in front of them.

They were miles and miles into the heart of the Pisgah National Forest, she realized. Clearly out of cell phone range. Where nobody else would be around for miles and miles.

Nausea gurgled in her stomach.

There was no one out here to help her, she realized.

Erin was going to have to rely on her own skills if she wanted to get out of the situation alive.

As promised, Blackstone had pinged Erin's cell phone, but it was out of range. Instead, Dillon had tried to follow the tire tracks away from that parking area. But in the lower elevations, the snow had faded and so had any tire tracks.

He'd only been probably ten minutes behind Erin, however. So if someone had picked her up, Dillon would have passed them—and he hadn't passed anyone on his way up the mountain.

The questions only made his temples pound harder.

There was only one way he could think to find her. It was a long shot. But it might work.

Dillon called Carson and told his nephew to meet him at the parking area where his Jeep had been found.

Normally, in situations like this, search and rescue dogs could follow a scent on foot. But considering the treacherous mountain road, the fading daylight and approaching storm, that wouldn't be safe.

Instead, Dillon had grabbed a piece of clothing Erin had left at his place and then met Carson and Scout near the Buckhead Trailhead.

As soon as he saw Scout, he squatted on the ground and rubbed his dog's head. "You ready to work?"

Scout leaned into his hand.

"I need you to find Erin," Dillon continued. "Can you do that?"

Scout raised his nose as if he understood the question.

Without wasting any more time, Dillon let Scout sniff Erin's sweatshirt.

A few minutes later, the dog raised his nose into the air and sniffed. Scout began pulling Dillon back toward the entrance of the parking area.

Dillon knew the chances were slim, but he was going to give it a try.

With Carson driving, Dillon would sit in the front seat with Scout. He'd put the window down and let Scout reach his nose out.

They slowly took off down the road.

Dillon hoped the dog would remain on the scent.

They crept back down the mountain. Dillon knew the next turnoff wouldn't be for another mile, but as they passed a section of woods, Scout began to bark.

Carson tapped the brake. "What do you want me to do?"

Dillon peered between the trees. "It looks like there's a service road right here that's just barely big enough for a vehicle to go through. The way the tree branches fall in front of it, it's nearly impossible to see from the road."

"I didn't notice it," Carson said.

"Let's see what happens. Turn here."

Carson did as he'd said, and they pulled down the narrow lane.

Just as Dillon had thought, the space was barely wide enough for them to fit through, and some of the overhead branches scratched the roof of his Jeep. Dillon would worry about that later.

Slowly, they continued along the gravel lane.

It was possible that Erin and whoever had taken her had gone down this lane before Dillon arrived. It was probably the right distance away that Dillon wouldn't have seen them.

His heart pounded harder. Maybe he was onto something.

Because he desperately wanted to find Erin.

In the short amount of time they'd known each other, he'd realized there was something special about her. He needed to find her and tell her that. He needed to stop holding on to the hurts of his past relationships and open himself up to more possibilities for the future. Possibilities with Erin.

There was a lot that needed to happen first.

Starting with finding Erin and Bella.

The task nearly felt insurmountable. But for Dillon, failure wasn't an option.

At the end of the lane, Carson pulled a stop.

Right behind a police cruiser.

Carson nodded to the vehicle. "Do you know who that belongs to?"

Blackstone's face flashed in Dillon's mind.

But Dillon didn't think the police chief could have gotten here in the time since they'd spoken. Was the chief working with somebody? Had he sent one of his guys here to take care of business?

It was a possibility.

In other circumstances, Dillon would call in the car

to see who it belonged to. But out here, he had no phone reception.

Scout barked out the window at the car.

He was still on the scent.

That meant Erin had been here recently.

"We're going to have to go the rest of the way on foot," Dillon said.

Carson nodded beside him. "I want to help. Just let me know what I need to do."

Erin nearly stumbled down the trail as Hollins gripped her arm. He wanted her to move faster than she possibly could.

The trails were too steep. Too slippery. Her ankle was too weak.

He didn't care about that. All he cared about was that she kept moving forward.

So that's what Erin tried to do.

But every time she breathed a gulp of air, her lungs hurt. It was so cold out here and the wind was only getting stronger and cooler by the moment.

If her gut instinct was right, a storm was headed this way. It was the only way to explain the sudden drop in temperature and why such a sharp breeze had stirred.

"Where are you taking me?" Her words came out between her gasps for air.

"I told you to stop asking questions."

"You're not like this," she told him. "You like doing the right thing. I can see it in your eyes."

His eyes narrowed. "Sometimes the right thing isn't black or white. Sometimes you have to go off course in order to do the right thing."

What did that mean? Could she break through to him? She was going to keep trying.

"I don't know what you think the right thing is, but I assure you that this isn't it," Erin said. "I'm innocent in all of this. I don't care what anyone has told you."

Blackstone's face flashed in her mind. He'd put his officer up to this, hadn't he? As vengeance for Liam's disappearance. It was the only thing that made sense.

"Just keep moving," Hollins muttered. "You're not going to change my mind on this."

"Do you have Bella?" Erin's voice cracked as the question left her lips.

"I said, no more questions."

"Please, I have to know. Is my daughter okay?"

He didn't say anything for a moment until finally blurting, "She's fine. Now, keep moving."

As Hollins shoved her forward, Erin nearly stumbled. Her knee hit the boulder in front of her and pain shot through her. She winced but didn't have any time to recover.

Hollins kept his grip on her arm and urged her down the path. "We don't have much time. The weather's going to turn bad."

"It's not too late to turn around now." Erin knew he wouldn't listen to her, but she felt like she had to try anyway.

"Keep moving," he grumbled.

With her shoulders tight, Erin did just that. She kept moving forward.

Finally, a cabin came into view. Yellow lights glowed from the windows.

The whole place looked like it was less than a thousand square feet, and there was no smoke coming from the chimney. It was probably cold inside.

But this was clearly where Erin was heading.

Hollins dragged her up the steps and opened the door.

The figure waiting for her there took Erin's breath away.

TWENTY-FIVE

"Liam?" Erin blinked as she stared at his oversized form.

He still looked basically the same, except now his blond hair had grown longer and a beard and a mustache covered part of his face.

But his eyes…they were still cold and calculating enough to send a shiver through Erin.

"Are you surprised to see me?" His words sounded full of malice as a mix of satisfaction and dark amusement mingled in his tone.

She tried to back up but Hollins caught her and pushed her forward. "I thought you were dead."

"That's the point. Everybody is *supposed* to think that I'm dead."

Hollins shut the door behind her, and the brisk wind disappeared for a moment.

They couldn't use the fireplace. From a distance, the smoke would have drawn too much attention. Instead, piles of blankets were on the couch and there was an electric heater. If she had to guess, this place was solar-powered.

"Why do you want people to think you're dead?" Erin

stared at Liam, still unable to believe he was standing in front of her.

"It's a long story," he muttered.

Her gaze wandered around the room, looking for any signs of Bella. Looking for any signs of what was going on here.

Nothing caught her eye.

"Why did you bring me here?" Erin drew her gaze back up to meet Liam's. She needed answers. Would he offer her any? "Why have you done all of this?"

He stepped closer and ran his finger down her arm. "You're here because you're mine. If you thought that you were just going to divorce me and walk away and I was going to pretend like none of this happened, then you were sadly mistaken."

She cringed and tried to back up. But Hollins was still there, holding her in place. "So you're just going to live out the rest of your days here? Pretending that you're dead?"

"Maybe. But for now, I'm safe here."

Her breath caught as more realizations raced through her mind. "You got yourself in some type of trouble, didn't you?"

His gaze darkened. "That's not important. What's important is that you're here now. Our little family is back together."

"Where's Bella?" Erin demanded.

He nodded at Hollins. Hollins took his cue, walked over to a door off to the side and opened it. A moment later, Bella nearly tumbled to the floor.

As soon as Bella spotted Erin, tears flooded her eyes. She drew herself to her feet and darted toward Erin. "Mom!"

"Bella!" Erin threw her arms around her daughter as tears flooded her eyes. "I was so worried about you."

"I'm so sorry, Mom," Bella breathed. "I should have never gone without you."

Erin had so many questions for her daughter, but now wasn't the time to ask them.

Now was the time to figure out how she and Bella were going to get out of this seemingly no-win situation.

With an arm still around Bella, Erin turned back to Liam. "Now that you have us both here, what are you going to do with us?"

His eyes sparkled with some kind of unspoken plan. "I thought we could just settle down and live like the perfect little happy family for a while."

Was he serious?

There was no amusement in his gaze. That realization terrified her.

"There's nothing happy about the situation," Erin reminded him.

He nodded at the window. "There's a snowstorm coming, so you might as well get comfortable. We have a lot of catching up to do."

A sickly feeling trickled in Erin's gut.

Liam really had lost his mind, hadn't he? Who exactly had he gotten himself into trouble with—enough trouble that he'd had to hide away from the rest of the world?

Liam had been perfectly content to let people think that Erin had done something. It was one way of making her pay for divorcing him.

Erin had to figure out how she was going to get out of the situation.

She had no time to waste.

* * *

Dillon and Carson followed the trail as Scout pulled them along.

Erin had definitely come this way. Dillon had no doubt about it.

As they walked, a smattering of freezing rain fell between the branches above them. Conditions were only going to get worse and worse.

They had to find her and soon.

Dillon looked at his phone. He still had no reception. Thankfully, he'd told his state police officer friends as well as Rick where they were heading. Maybe they would know to follow this trail just in case they needed some backup here.

Dillon paused Scout on the path and sucked in a breath.

Carson nearly collided into them. "What's going on?"

Dillon put a finger over his lips. Then he pointed to the ground. "Look at all the footsteps here. If Erin came this way, she either had an army with her or people were following her."

Carson's eyes widened. "But there were no other cars in the parking lot."

His nephew raised a good point. "There's probably more than one way to get to this trail. Either way, we need to be on guard. We don't know exactly who we're up against here."

Carson nodded and they continued, quietly making their way down the trail. They had to watch their steps to make sure they had no more injuries. That was the last thing they needed to slow them down.

Dear Lord, please be with Erin now. Keep her safe. Protect her. Bella also. Guide our steps and help us to find them.

The deeper they headed into the valley, the rockier the trail became. They weren't moving as quickly as Dillon would have liked, but he reminded himself that slow in actuality meant fast. Being careless would only make them trip up, and he couldn't afford to do that.

As something in the distance caught his eye, he paused.

"It's a cabin," he muttered.

Carson stopped beside him. "Do you think that is where Erin is?"

"It's my best guess."

Scout would get a nice reward later for leading them here.

Dillon kept his hand raised in the air, motioning for Carson to remain still. Then he scanned everything around him.

He spotted three men hiding in the brush in the distance. If he wasn't mistaken, they had guns in their hands—guns that were aimed at the cabin.

Best he could tell, they hadn't spotted him, Carson or Scout yet.

Dillon would have to be careful as he planned his next move.

Erin still held Bella as they stood facing Liam.

"I still don't understand why you're doing this," Erin said.

"You don't have to understand." He sneered at her. "You just need to be pretty."

Erin narrowed her eyes. "You're the one who called and told the police chief that my car was on the trailhead on the day Bella disappeared, weren't you?"

His grin was answer enough for her. "I wanted them to scrutinize you. I wanted you to feel the heat."

"I'm guessing you sent Hollins into the woods near Dillon's place? He was the one who broke into Dillon's home." She glanced at Hollins as he stood guarding the door, his face expressionless.

"I just wanted to send you a message. I understand you and Dillon were getting pretty cozy."

She shook her head. No doubt, that had only upset him more. But Dillon was the last thing she wanted to talk to Liam about.

"Everything still doesn't make sense," Erin continued. "You had opportunities to snatch me, if that's what you needed to do. Why go through all the trouble of taking Bella and then sending me those threats?"

"I've always liked playing games with you."

She sucked in a breath. His words were true. He'd tested her, left dishes in the sink just to see if she'd wash them, rearranged drawers to see if Erin would straighten them.

And if she hadn't met his expectations…then she'd paid for it.

So Liam had taken Bella, knowing that would make her suffer the most. Then he'd sent Hollins to keep an eye on her. To threaten her. To let her know there was more to come.

Enjoying her mental anguish was just a small gratification for him.

The thought made disgust roil in her stomach.

Erin turned her thoughts back to the present. She surveyed the cabin, trying to find any means of escape.

But even if she and Bella managed to get away, there was no way the two of them could navigate these mountains. It would be dark soon. Freezing rain hit the roof. And Erin's ankle and leg throbbed.

She looked at Liam again. "What are you going to do with us now?"

"Right now, I want you to sit down and be quiet for a few minutes. There's been way too much talking for my comfort."

Erin took Bella's hand and led her to the couch.

"Hollins, keep an eye on them," Liam ordered.

"Yes, sir."

Liam disappeared into a different room while Hollins stood guard with his arms crossed over his chest. As he did, Erin turned to Bella.

"How are you?" she asked, looking Bella over. "Did he hurt you?"

With tears rimming her eyes, Bella shook her head. "No, he just scared me."

"How did he even lure you away?"

"Someone left me a message on a piece of paper saying that I needed to meet at the trailhead, that your life was in danger. But when I got there, I saw Officer Hollins. He told me he was going to take me to you."

Erin's eyes flickered to Hollins, and she scowled.

"Instead, he led me down the trail. Liam was waiting for us. Hollins left me with him, and Liam insisted I had to come with him. He had a gun. He made me walk down these trails and over cliffs until we got to this cabin."

Erin's heart lurched into her throat as she imagined what Bella had been through. "I'm so sorry that happened to you. We've been looking hard for you."

"I know you have. I knew you wouldn't give up."

Erin wrapped her arms around Bella and held her. "You have no idea how worried I was."

"I love you, Mom. I'm sorry you're here with me now, but I'm glad to see you at the same time." She sniffled.

Erin didn't let go. "I know, sweetie. I know."

"What are we going to do?"

Erin glanced around the cabin again. "I wish I knew. But we'll figure out something. We just need to be brave."

"I wouldn't do that if I were you," Hollins muttered. He'd clearly been listening to their conversation.

"How did you get involved with this?" Erin asked. "I always thought you were a good cop."

"Liam trained me," Hollins said. "He told me what you were like. He told me about the conspiracies against him. Told me I couldn't believe anything."

"Conspiracies about what?"

"About—"

Before he could finish, the window shattered.

A bullet had flown through that window.

Someone was outside, and they were shooting at them.

It couldn't be Dillon. He wouldn't be that careless.

If Liam and Hollins were inside, then who could possibly be behind the gunfire now?

TWENTY-SIX

When Dillon heard the gunfire, he knew he had to spring into action. There was no time to waste.

He pushed Carson back and handed him Scout's lead. "Stay here."

Carson nodded and ducked behind a boulder.

Crouching low, Dillon moved closer to the cabin. He gripped his gun, prepared to use it if necessary.

Aiming carefully, he took his first shot. He hit one of the men in the shoulder.

The man let out a yelp before falling to the ground.

One down. Two more to go.

But he knew those two remaining guys could do a lot of damage.

Especially now that they knew Dillon was there.

Just as the thought raced through his mind, a bullet split the bark on the tree beside him.

Dillon was going to have to get closer. Those guys were going to breech that cabin, and there was no telling what would happen then.

As he crept closer, another bullet flew through the air.

Before he could duck out of the way, pain sliced his arm.

Dillon let out a gasp.

He'd been hit.

* * *

"Get behind the couch!" Liam yelled. "Now!"

Erin heard the anger in his voice and rose. Wasting no time, she shoved the couch from the wall and pulled Bella back there with her.

More bullets continued to fly.

As they did, Liam pulled out his gun and crouched beneath the window.

Things began to click in Erin's mind.

Liam was hiding because he'd made someone mad, wasn't he? Likely, it was the Bradshaws.

Now he had no choice but to hide out or they were going to kill him.

It made sense.

"Mom…" Bella's wide eyes stared at her.

Erin squeezed her hand and held her close. "Just stay low."

More bullets flew.

What was going to happen if the gunmen outside got inside? Would they all be goners?

It was a good possibility. At least Liam appeared to want her alive for a little while.

As more bullets flew, Erin heard someone gasp. She raised her head enough to see Hollins drop to the floor.

He'd been hit in the chest. Blood filled his shirt.

She swallowed back a scream.

Just as Erin thought things couldn't get worse, someone burst through the door. When she heard Liam mutter something beneath his breath, she knew they were in trouble.

The gunman was inside.

Dillon glanced at his biceps.

The bullet had grazed his skin.

He might need a few stitches, but otherwise he was going to be okay—other than the pain from where the bullet had sliced into his arm.

As he saw the gunmen moving toward the cabin, Dillon crept closer. One man approached the door while the other stood back.

Dillon got in place behind the tree and then aimed his gun. When he pulled the trigger, the bullet hit the one man in the shoulder and he fell to the ground.

Now it was just the gunman at the door.

And whoever else was inside.

As Dillon heard another bullet fire, a scream sounded from inside.

His heart pounded harder. Was that Erin? Was she okay?

He had to get closer.

He darted toward the back of the cabin. There was a window there, and he should be able to see inside.

Remaining low, he crouched beneath it and peered inside.

Liam stood there, his back to the window.

He was alive.

Dillon sucked in a breath.

And the man was probably behind most of this chaos.

Dillon would deal with it later.

He continued to scan the interior of the cabin. He spotted two people huddling behind the couch.

Erin and Bella...

They were okay!

Relief filled him at that realization.

Thank you, Jesus!

But he had other issues to address first...starting with the fact that Bill Bradshaw stood in front of Liam with his gun raised.

The Bradshaws were also involved in this. They'd probably been hunting Liam this whole time. Somehow, when Erin came here, she must have led them right to Liam.

While Dillon didn't care what happened to Liam, he couldn't risk something happening to Erin and Bella.

"You thought you were going to get away with this," Bill muttered.

"How did you find me?"

"I've been following that state cop and your ex-wife ever since they came to my house," Bill said. "I figured they might lead me to you, and I was right. Now, I need you to put your gun down."

Liam's nostrils flared. "That's not going to happen."

He turned his gun toward Erin. "Then I'll shoot them first."

"I don't care if you shoot them," Liam said. "But you're not walking away from here alive."

"You've been trying to find evidence to take my family down, haven't you?" Bill said. "But you got in with the wrong people. You're not going to get away with what you've done."

Dillon continued to listen. What exactly had Liam done?

"I didn't do anything," Liam insisted.

"You stole money from us! Money you found during a police operation. Then you tried to bribe us."

Liam said nothing.

But suddenly everything made sense.

Liam had tried to blackmail a crime family. They'd probably put a bounty on his head, and he'd been forced into hiding.

Except, Liam was too much of a narcissist to simply disappear. He'd wanted his old life back—one way or another. That's why he'd come after Erin and Bella.

In the blink of an eye, Bill shifted his gun toward Liam and pulled the trigger.

Erin screamed.

Liam collapsed on the cabin floor.

Bill had shot him, Dillon realized.

"Now it's your turn," Bill grumbled, his gaze on Erin.

Wasting no time, Dillon rose, aimed, and pulled the trigger.

But not before Bill also fired his gun.

Erin huddled with Bella behind the couch, praying they'd stay safe.

When she glanced up, she spotted someone peering in the window.

Was that… Dillon?

Her breath caught.

It was! He was here!

He was okay.

Thank you, Jesus.

But what about everybody else? What was happening inside this cabin?

Erin dared lift her head even more.

When she did, she saw both Liam and Bill Bradshaw on the floor. They'd both been shot.

"Stay here," she whispered to Bella.

Quickly, Erin darted from her hiding space. Both men were still alive, their chests rising as they breathed. If they were alive, that meant they were still dangerous.

She kicked the gun away from Liam before he could grab it from the floor. Instead, she darted across the room and snatched the weapon herself. She needed to have it on hand, just in case.

At the thought, Bill raised his head and moaned.

Her eyes rushed to the ground.

His gun was still at his fingertips. One move and…

She knew she didn't have time to grab the gun.

Before she could figure out what to do, men in SWAT uniforms invaded the cabin.

"Police! Put your hands up!"

The state police. They were here.

The gun fell from her hands, clattering on the floor as relief filled her.

Erin nearly collapsed to the floor herself.

But before she could, arms caught her.

She looked up and saw Dillon there.

As the police took over the scene and a paramedic checked Bella, Dillon folded her into his embrace.

This was finally all over.

She melted in his arms.

"Are you okay?" Dillon muttered.

"I am now that you're here."

He pulled her closer. "I was so worried. You shouldn't have left without me."

"I know. It's a long story. I'll explain later."

Dillon's gaze was full of warmth as he pulled away just enough to lock gazes with her. He gently placed a kiss on her cheek, one that assured her everything would be okay.

"We'll have time to talk later," he said. "I hope we'll have a lot more time for talking together."

A grin spread across her face.

Erin liked the sound of that.

She glanced over at Bella again. Right now, she had to concentrate on her daughter.

But she and Dillon would definitely finish this conversation later.

TWENTY-SEVEN

"This is like my dream come true!" Bella hurried from dog kennel to dog kennel so she could meet all the canines at Dillon's place.

As she did, Erin and Dillon stood back and smiled as they watched her.

Seeing her bounce back after such a horrific ordeal was wonderful. Erin had been anxious that what had happened would set Bella back—and in ways, it had. The healing process would take time.

But overall, Bella was doing so well.

A month had passed since Bella had been rescued. Liam and Bill Bradshaw were now behind bars, as were their henchmen. In the midst of the media blitz about everything that had happened, Blackstone had been in the hot seat over his handling of the case. That had eventually led to the mayor firing him and offering Dillon the job. Dillon had turned the position down.

He liked what he was doing here apparently. As he should.

He was a great dog trainer, and the work he did was valuable.

Dillon wrapped his arm around Erin's waist and pulled her closer.

"I think Bella likes it here," Erin murmured, still watching her daughter. They'd purposely waited a while before bringing Bella here. They hadn't wanted to rush things.

But, so far, Bella and Dillon had really hit it off. Seeing Dillon come to their rescue had only helped their quick bond.

"I think she does, too," Dillon muttered.

Scout deserted the bowl where he'd been lapping up water and wandered toward them. As he did, Erin knelt on the ground in front of the canine. "And how are you doing today, boy?"

She rubbed his head as the dog leaned into her.

Thankfully, Scout hadn't been hurt in the middle of the shootout. Carson had kept him safe.

"I think he likes you," Dillon said.

"You led Dillon to me, didn't you?" Erin murmured. "You helped save my life. Thank you, boy."

She'd already thanked the dog numerous times, showered him with attention, and even brought him some bones.

Erin gave Scout one more head pat before rising again.

As she did, Dillon caught her in his arms. He stole a glance over his shoulder as if checking to see if Bella was still occupied.

When he saw that she was, he planted a kiss on Erin's lips. "In case I haven't told you this yet, I'm so sorry about everything that happened. But I'm so glad this path led me to you."

Erin's heart warmed as she stared into his warm eyes. "Me, too. You've been a real godsend, Dillon Walker."

He leaned forward and kissed her again.

"I love you, Erin Lansing," he told her.

Erin grinned. "I love you, too."

"Am I going to have to tell you two to knock it off again?" Bella called from the other side of the building.

They laughed before turning to her, arms still around each other.

Bella strode toward them, her eyes on Erin. "It's actually nice to see you happy. You never looked like this when Liam was in your life."

Erin's smile faded. "You're right. I didn't."

Until she'd met Dillon, Erin didn't know what a good relationship could look like. She was so grateful God had brought him into her life.

She looked forward to their future together...a future complete with Bella and Scout.

* * * * *

Get 4 FREE REWARDS!

We'll send you 2 FREE Books plus 2 FREE Mystery Gifts.

FREE
Value Over
$20

Both the **Harlequin® Special Edition** and **Harlequin® Heartwarming™** series feature compelling novels filled with stories of love and strength where the bonds of friendship, family and community unite.

YES! Please send me 2 FREE novels from the Harlequin Special Edition or Harlequin Heartwarming series and my 2 FREE gifts (gifts are worth about $10 retail). After receiving them, if I don't wish to receive any more books, I can return the shipping statement marked "cancel." If I don't cancel, I will receive 6 brand-new Harlequin Special Edition books every month and be billed just $5.49 each in the U.S. or $6.24 each in Canada, a savings of at least 12% off the cover price, or 4 brand-new Harlequin Heartwarming Larger-Print books every month and be billed just $6.24 each in the U.S. or $6.74 each in Canada, a savings of at least 19% off the cover price. It's quite a bargain! Shipping and handling is just 50¢ per book in the U.S. and $1.25 per book in Canada.* I understand that accepting the 2 free books and gifts places me under no obligation to buy anything. I can always return a shipment and cancel at any time by calling the number below. The free books and gifts are mine to keep no matter what I decide.

Choose one: ☐ **Harlequin Special Edition**
(235/335 HDN GRJV)
☐ **Harlequin Heartwarming Larger-Print**
(161/361 HDN GRJV)

Name (please print)

Address   Apt. #

City   State/Province   Zip/Postal Code

Email: Please check this box ☐ if you would like to receive newsletters and promotional emails from Harlequin Enterprises ULC and its affiliates. You can unsubscribe anytime.

Mail to the **Harlequin Reader Service:**
IN U.S.A.: P.O. Box 1341, Buffalo, NY 14240-8531
IN CANADA: P.O. Box 603, Fort Erie, Ontario L2A 5X3

Want to try 2 free books from another series? Call 1-800-873-8635 or visit www.ReaderService.com.

*Terms and prices subject to change without notice. Prices do not include sales taxes, which will be charged (if applicable) based on your state or country of residence. Canadian residents will be charged applicable taxes. Offer not valid in Quebec. This offer is limited to one order per household. Books received may not be as shown. Not valid for current subscribers to the Harlequin Special Edition or Harlequin Heartwarming series. All orders subject to approval. Credit or debit balances in a customer's account(s) may be offset by any other outstanding balance owed by or to the customer. Please allow 4 to 6 weeks for delivery. Offer available while quantities last.

Your Privacy—Your information is being collected by Harlequin Enterprises ULC, operating as Harlequin Reader Service. For a complete summary of the information we collect, how we use this information and to whom it is disclosed, please visit our privacy notice located at corporate.harlequin.com/privacy-notice. From time to time we may also exchange your personal information with reputable third parties. If you wish to opt out of this sharing of your personal information, please visit readerservice.com/consumerschoice or call 1-800-873-8635. **Notice to California Residents**—Under California law, you have specific rights to control and access your data. For more information on these rights and how to exercise them, visit corporate.harlequin.com/california-privacy.

HSEHW22R3

HARLEQUIN
PLUS

Try the best multimedia subscription service for romance readers like you!

Read, Watch and Play.

Experience the easiest way to get the romance content you crave.

Start your **FREE TRIAL** at
www.harlequinplus.com/freetrial.